ENDGAME

MALORIE BLACKMAN

PENGUIN BOOKS

PENGUIN BOOKS

UK | USA | Canada | Ireland | Australia
India | New Zealand | South Africa

Penguin Books is part of the Penguin Random House group of companies
whose addresses can be found at global.penguinrandomhouse.com.

www.penguin.co.uk
www.puffin.co.uk
www.ladybird.co.uk

The authorized representative in the EEA is Penguin Random House Ireland,
Morrison Chambers, 32 Nassau Street, Dublin D02 YH68

A CIP catalogue record for this book is available from the British Library

HARDBACK ISBN: 978–0–241–44398–9
PAPERBACK ISBN: 978–0–241–44399–6

All correspondence to:
Penguin Books
Penguin Random House Children's
One Embassy Gardens, 8 Viaduct Gardens, London SW11 7BW

Penguin Random House is committed to a sustainable future for our business, our readers and our planet. This book is made from Forest Stewardship Council® certified paper.

Praise for Malorie Blackman's books

'The Noughts & Crosses series are still my favourite books of all time and they showed me just how amazing storytelling could be'
Stormzy

'Flawlessly paced'
The Times

'Unforgettable'
Independent

'A work of art'
Benjamin Zephaniah

'A book which will linger in the mind long after it has been read'
Observer

'A gritty read'
The Bookseller

For Neil and Liz,
with love as always

And a huge thank you to all those who have come with me on this journey into the lives of the Hadleys and the McGregors

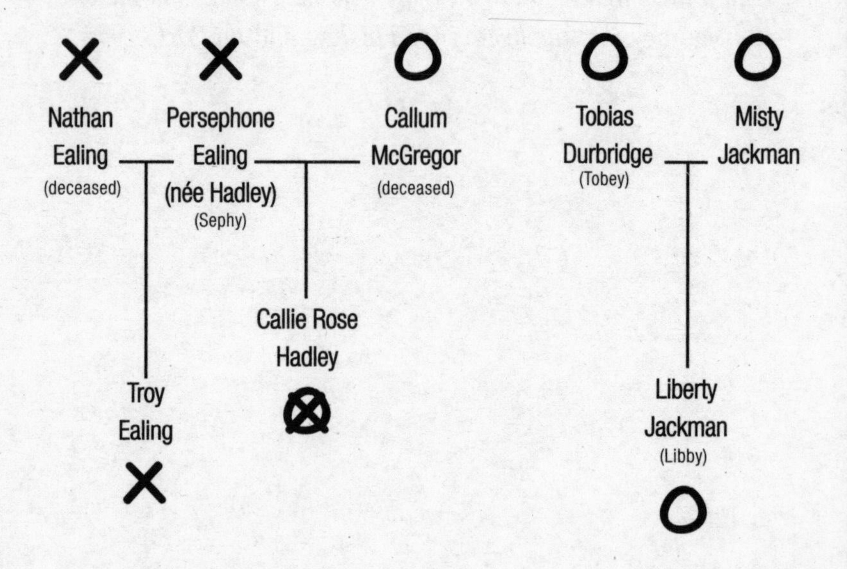
Nathan
Ealing
(deceased)
Persephone
Ealing
(née Hadley)
(Sephy)
Callum
McGregor
(deceased)
Tobias
Durbridge
(Tobey)
Misty
Jackman
Troy
Ealing
Callie Rose
Hadley
Liberty
Jackman
(Libby)

Give sorrow words: the grief that does not speak
Whispers the o'er-fraught heart and bids it break.

MACBETH 4.3

NOW

one. Tobey

29 October 02:29

To Sephy Ealing:

From the video provided, you'll see that we have Troy Ealing and Liberty Jackman. This is not a joke or a hoax. You will ensure the instructions below are followed to the letter or you will never see your loved ones again. If you involve the police, or any other security detail, we will know and you'll never see your loved ones again. This has been sent to you so that you can keep your daughter Callie in line. Make sure she doesn't get any unfortunate ideas – like going straight to the police.

This will be our only communication.

Send the following messages to Callie Rose Hadley and Tobias Durbridge.

TOBIAS DURBRIDGE, you will do the following within the next twenty-four hours:
– Plead guilty in court to the murder of Dan Jeavons.
– Go public with the admission of your guilt.
If you fail to do either of the above, you will never see your daughter Liberty again. This is NOT a bluff.

CALLIE ROSE HADLEY, you will do the following within the next twenty-four hours:
– Remove the super-injunction forbidding the press from reporting on Tobias Durbridge and his forthcoming court case.
– Remove yourself as Tobias's lawyer.
If you fail to do either of the above, you will receive your brother Troy back in pieces. This is NOT a bluff.

So many unanswered questions. I reread the text message forwarded to me by Callie, who had received it from Sephy, her mother. A man – who claimed to be working on behalf of Dan Jeavons – had called Sephy, using her son Troy's mobile phone, to state his list of demands. He had followed this up in writing.

Working on behalf of Dan Jeavons . . . There was just one problem with that – Dan was dead. He'd been murdered and I was on the hook for it. Someone out there was desperate to see me spend the rest of my natural existence rotting in prison.

On behalf of Dan Jeavons . . .

What did that even mean? Had someone from within 'the Outfit' decided to branch out for themselves and this was a way of proving their worth? Or were they doing it to avenge Dan's death? Maybe this whole thing had been orchestrated by Owen Dowd, head of a rival set-up, in an attempt to cause real problems for the opposition.

Whoever it was who'd spoken to Sephy had backed up his verbal threat with this text message spelling out all the kidnappers' demands. And now Troy's phone was untraceable. On my instructions, my personal executive assistant, Jade Habari, had already tried to find out the location of Libby's and Troy's phones, but they'd been switched off – or smashed. The last recorded location of both was Heathcroft High School, the last place they were seen. No help there then.

Where was my daughter?

Had her kidnappers tied her up? Were they looking after her as the goose that was about to lay them a golden egg, or were they . . . abusing her? Perhaps they'd already got rid of her? Dark thoughts were knitting my insides together. I read the text message for the umpteenth time.

Plead guilty in court to the murder of Dan Jeavons.

None of the kidnappers' demands had been met. In court yesterday, I had entered a plea of not guilty. Callie hadn't recused herself as my lawyer, nor had she removed the super-injunction. In their text, they referred to themselves as 'we', so I had to work on the assumption that there was more than one.

Now I stood at my bedroom window in the dark. A black hole was opening in my gut and trying to suck me into it. I was officially, if covertly due to the press injunction my blackmailers clearly knew about, on trial for Dan's murder. I confess, a large part of me had thought the case would be thrown out by Judge Okafor on the grounds of insufficient evidence – or because I am now PM – ha! No such luck. I was in the fight of my life. Not just for my political career, but my freedom. My Liberty. There was a very real chance that after this trial I'd never look up at the sky from outside prison walls again.

I'd pleaded not guilty, rationalizing that it was the best way to try and keep my daughter alive. If I immediately gave in to the kidnappers' demands, what reason would they have to keep her in good health, knowing that if she was freed she could identify them? Pleading my innocence in court meant that her abductors had to keep her around to try to coerce me into doing what they wanted – at least that had been my frenetic thinking. I was doing this for my daughter. But was I really?

Liberty . . . If anything happened to her because of me . . .

I hated this. Patience was not one of my virtues.

Having refused to submit to the kidnappers' demands, Callie and I now had to wait for them to make the next move. But I was no good at waiting for the ball to be batted back to me. It was time to set wheels in motion. As Dan used to say, 'Some people have a plan A and possibly a plan B as backup. You, Tobey, use at least half the alphabet to work out your alternatives.'

I wasn't about to apologize for that. There was nothing

wrong in believing in the seven Ps – Prior Proper Preparation Prevents Piss-Poor Performance. That way Callie and I stood half a chance of making it through this and getting our loved ones back home safe and sound. And, once I had my daughter back, I intended to send a very clear message.

By the time I'd finished, no one, and I mean *no one*, would dare come after me and mine again.

Ever.

two. Libby

The silence in the basement after the last nail had been hammered home was deafening. I stared at the now boarded-up door, unable to look away. Troy and I had escaped; we'd even made it all the way to the harbour wall, but then I'd spoiled everything by not jumping into the river when we had the chance. And Troy had refused to jump in and escape without me. So stupid. If he'd left me behind and swum for the opposite bank, he could've escaped. He could've been miles away by now and getting help. But I can't swim and was too terrified to leap into the murky, dark water. Thanks to me, we'd both been recaptured and brought back to this hellhole basement.

And we were going to turn into dust down here.

Troy launched himself at the door, bouncing off it like a tennis ball to ricochet off the banister handrail behind him at the top of the stairs.

'Oof!' He rubbed his shoulder, then his back, before he tried again.

Surprise, surprise! The same thing happened, except this time it looked like it hurt much more.

'Troy, you're wasting your time,' I said.

For heaven's sake, if we couldn't open the door before it

was boarded up, what on earth made him think he could burst through it now? He glared at the door and leaned forward, slightly side-on, head down like some kind of demented charging bull. He flung himself at the door yet again, shoulder first. This time the rebound threw him backwards onto the handrail behind him again, except the rail cracked and snapped, and, with a startled cry, Troy fell through it, his arms flailing like a fledgling's wings.

I rushed forward, thinking I could catch him and break his fall or something. But I was too late. Troy hit the ground with a sickening thud, crumpling up like a concertina.

'TROY!' I rushed to his side, kneeling beside his motionless body. He lay half on his side, half on his back. I took his hand in mine and fumbled around on his wrist for a pulse, but I couldn't feel one.

I couldn't find one.

TROY—

Serves me right.

This is not what I had planned. Not even close. It is, however, what I get for relying on other people. People always – and I mean **always** *– mess up. I have yet to meet one who hasn't let me down sooner or later. Usually sooner. This was supposed to be an easy job, a means to an end – nothing more. A way to pay off some serious debts owed to some ruthless people and to make a very healthy profit on the side too. I should've guessed that Misty, Liberty's mother, and Pete, her equally worthless boyfriend, would muck things up. For God's sake, all they had to do was hold on to her daughter for a couple of days until Tobias Durbridge proved to the world, but mostly to himself, how much he loved his secret daughter by paying the ransom. It should've been a piece of Makeda sponge cake. But no. Misty and her shit-for-brains boyfriend decide to bring in his brother, Oliver, who had even larger quantities of shit for brains.*

I first met Pete drinking alone in a pub while he was waiting for Misty to turn up. We got to talking and Pete lowered his voice to inform me that Misty claimed her daughter, Liberty, was also the daughter of Tobias Durbridge, the politician. Pete had laughed it off, not believing a word of it. Me? I wasn't so sure that it was all a fantasy. I mean, why claim something that would be so easy to disprove? DNA tests were now cheaper than a restaurant meal for two. So maybe there was something in it after all.

I hung around until Misty arrived and insinuated myself into their night out, laughing and joking and making sure I kept the drinks flowing. We all went for a meal, which I insisted on paying for. By the end of the night, I was their new best friend. I checked with the General Records Office, and Tobias Durbridge was indeed listed as the father of Liberty Alba Jackman. That's when I began to plant the idea of tapping him for money. After all, it was what Misty and Pete deserved. If Tobey had money and they didn't, surely it was only fair that they did what was necessary to balance those scales. Pete was all for it. Misty took a little more persuading – but not much. After a few weeks, I shared with them the plan that I'd taken great care to work out. It was foolproof. Or so I thought. I didn't count on the three biggest cretins on the planet ruining it.

Instead of grabbing Liberty off the street to keep it real, like we'd agreed, and just securing her for a couple of days, what did they do instead? They grabbed Libby's friend Troy Ealing as well. Troy Ealing, for God's sake. Just my damned luck. What was Misty thinking? Company for Libby? There was no other earthly reason to bring him along. For Shaka's sake, he's just a teenage boy. One punch and they could've knocked him on his arse and out cold, left him on the pavement and fled with Libby. Sweet as a honey-roasted peanut. But no – they just had to take Troy along for the ride as well. And who is Troy's sister? Callie Rose Hadley. I mean, you couldn't make it up!

Just my damned luck.

Oliver must've persuaded the other two that, though greed was good, to cut me out of the deal and go it alone would be even better. Well, look where that got them. Weighed down and feeding the fishes in the River Thames. The word is out that they breathe no more. Where does that leave me? Precisely nowhere – for now.

Liberty Jackman, or rather her father's money, was supposed to be my all-expenses-paid ticket out of here to a stress-free, very comfortable existence. Damn it, it's my due. Now all my plans have been shot to hell. So I have no choice but to play a waiting game.

What I need to do now is keep my mouth shut, my eyes open, and watch and learn. Then maybe, just maybe, there can still be a pay day at the end of all this for me. Perhaps there's even a way to turn this fiasco to my advantage. After all, who knows of my involvement? Damn few and they're all dead – or they soon will be. The first thing I need to do is get to Liberty and Troy before they can be interrogated by anyone else.

Lord knows what Misty might've revealed about me before she was killed. Did she tell Liberty that I was the one who masterminded the whole plan in the first place? If Liberty and Troy know enough about me to spill the tea before I get to them, then I'll be up to my bottom lip in churning-crap creek with my mouth wide open. The bullets in my gun have their names on them and the choice is simple – it's them or me. And it sure as hell isn't going to be me.

I wish it hadn't turned out like this, but it is what it is. I've come too far now to turn back. I can't and won't let anyone get in my way.

There's an unexpected vampire bite to the chill late October night air. Car horns blare. The laughter and chatter *of late-nighters competes with the cacophony of too much traffic, even at this late hour. The residual smell of burgers, diesel and urine wafts round me. City smells – I love them. That's why I'm driving with my car window halfway down. When I depart for pastures new, I shall miss this. The constant noise, the city aromas and, the cherry on top, all the people intent on minding their own business.*

There it is, Ava's – what used to be Dan Jeavons' old nightclub. Now it belongs to Eva Foxton, Dan's successor.

Hedda, my eyes within Eva's organization, is inside. Almost three years ago, when I'd been trying to track down a missing bouncer who worked at the nightclub, I'd spotted Hedda entering the place. She was going to work in the kitchen as a sous-chef. I'd recognized her at once. Her husband, an ex-cop, had been banged up on corruption charges – not the sort of news Hedda had wanted to become common knowledge. It'd been a fraught negotiation, but I'd persuaded Hedda to provide me with info on Eva and her exploits as and when required – plus there would be a generous fee for services rendered. Although reluctant, she'd finally agreed. Even way back then, I knew Eva was one to watch.

Within the last hour, Hedda had sent me an urgent message to come and get her out. She's afraid her cover has been blown, which – if true – is a damned shame. Over the years, the intel Hedda provided has proved priceless. What had she done to give herself away? It sure as hell can't be my fault.

It might be a ploy to bleed me for more money. If, however, her fears are justified, we have a problem. On any other day of the week, extracting Hedda would be a straight in-and-out job – but not this evening.

This evening, I know for a fact that Eva is in there too. And, where Eva goes, at least two – usually more – of her armed, muscle-headed minions go as well. With her neatly bobbed silver hair, her cyanotic shade of lipstick and her round-framed, rimless glasses, she looks like a soap-opera regular just waiting to dish out praise and punishment in equal measure. Those who underestimate her because of her appearance or the quiet way she speaks don't live to repeat the same mistake.

I used to work for Dan on a mutual backscratching basis. I'd provide him with info as and when requested or required and he'd do the same for me. It'd been a symbiotic relationship based on need and greed – and it worked. But then Dan was inconvenient enough to get himself killed. And Eva had firmly closed the door on my services. Bitch!

The traffic is so bad that it takes me a ridiculous ten minutes to drive round the block as I search for a parking space, but it does give me a chance to get my head together. Earlier today, Callie Hadley proclaimed in court that she was Tobias Durbridge's defence counsel. That decision is going to bite her on the arse and then keep chomping.

I resign myself to yet another circuit in the hunt for a parking space when luckily someone pulls out of a spot almost in front of the nightclub where I imagine Eva sits like a queen spider in her web filled with silk-wrapped victims. Dinner for days. Before me, some stationary driver in an SUV has their reversing lights on, waiting for the car that's about to vacate the parking spot I've got my eye on. The moment the car pulls away from the kerb, I nip into the space before the SUV driver has a chance to reverse. They beep their horn. Ignoring it, I get out of my car.

'Didn't you see that I was waiting for that parking space?' A beautiful Cross woman with locs and hooped earrings winds down her window to shout at me.

Ignoring her, I head towards the nightclub.

'You! I'm talking to you. Didn't you see that I wanted that space?'

I call back. 'Like my mother repeatedly told me – I want doesn't always get.'

'Arse. Hole!' the woman screams at me to a backdrop of other drivers beeping at her to move and stop blocking the road.

I've been called worse. Besides, if you snooze, you lose. The woman driver should have learned that life lesson by now.

Looking at the nightclub, I decide that a more discreet approach might serve me better. I could just try walking in the front door, but if I did that the chances of being carried out in a rubbish bag were fair to middling. I don't fancy those odds. The alley at the side of the club it is then. It's lined with industrial bins, filled to overflowing with black bags. The smell alone is enough to knock anyone of a weak disposition off their feet. As I approach the back door of Ava's, I hear an unmistakable sound which pins my feet to the ground.

Pop! Pop!

Pause.

Pop! Pop! Pop!

The sound is like hands being clapped with cupped palms. I'd know it anywhere. The pitch of the second set of pops was slightly lower than the first, indicating at least two different guns had been fired. Guns with suppressors to silence the blasts.

I stumble backwards into a bin that scrapes along the wall thanks to the weight of my body. The noise isn't a lot, but it's enough. And enough might as well have been a trumpet blasting. I turn and sprint back down the alleyway, hugging the bins as I run. Behind me, I hear the back door that leads straight to Ava's kitchen being opened, its prolonged creak an indication of years of neglect.

I duck down behind the closest bin. Some bags of rubbish have spilled out beside me and onto the ground. I don't hesitate. Squatting down on my haunches, I pull the filthy bags over myself. My hand bursts right through one of them, entering a slimy, stinking mass that's a mess, but the least of my worries at the moment. Running footsteps are fast approaching. I duck down further, pulling another reeking bag over my head. The smell alone makes me want to gag. I clench my lips together and hold my breath to try and control my upchuck reflex. Two sets of footsteps run right past.

'Shit! Where did he go?' A woman's voice begins to curse up a blue streak.

'He can't have got far.' The accompanying man's voice answers her.

Their footsteps start again, fading away like a sinister Doppler effect. I throw off the bin bags and immediately strip off my jacket to give it a good shake. Bits of food and worse fly off my now-ruined woollen jacket. My olive-green jeans are in only marginally better shape. Wiping my hands on my jacket and using it to brush down my trousers, I fold it over my arm and stroll out of the alley like I haven't a care in the world, heading in the opposite direction to the footsteps.

I force myself to saunter. Running into a crowd of ambling pedestrians will immediately give the game away. I head back to my car. Those around me who get too close take one whiff and immediately widen the distance between us, giving me a whole colour palette of dirty looks. Like I set out to pong like this on purpose. Anyway, let them gawp. That's fine by me. I turn my head with a deliberate frown, hoping it seems like I'm looking for someone.

Ah . . . A few metres behind me, among the pedestrians, stands a Nought man with collar-length blond hair and matching blond eyebrows. He's wearing a mac and dark trousers. Beside him is a taller brunette woman in jeans, a dark jumper and a brown leather jacket. I might not have noticed them if they hadn't been standing and scanning the people around them who are all on the move. The man and woman each have one hand tucked beneath their coats. They still have their guns.

Heading towards my car, I dig into my trouser pocket and press the car-key fob. Thankfully, there's no need to take it out. I open the door with slow, steady movements – nothing rushed, nothing suspicious. Immediately locking the doors from the inside, I wait for a gap in the traffic to pull out. A sudden rap on my window makes me start. The tall brunette woman, with doll's eyebrows and a vivid red-lipstick smile, is peering in at me. She indicates that I should lower the window.

'Can I help you?' I take a surreptitious glance in the driver's mirror. There's a bus behind me indicating that it's about to pull into the kerb.

'Could you wind down your window, please?' the brunette says, one hand still inside her jacket. 'You've got a lettuce leaf stuck to your arse.'

'And you think it's yours?'

A tap on the passenger window. The blond guy has joined her in flanking my car. He taps again on the window and points downwards. The bus pulls in, momentarily blocking the traffic. I floor it, wrenching the steering wheel round to dart out into the street. The woman beside my car leaps out of the way, only just in time. I see the two of them racing after me, arms outstretched, guns pointing in my direction.

A single shot shatters my back window and whizzes past my ear out of the front windscreen, leaving a hole with a spiderweb of cracks around it. Rude! The traffic light up ahead turns amber, then red. I'm practically standing on the accelerator now. My car roars over the junction just as the oncoming traffic starts moving. I hear the squeal of brakes and a colossal bang as one car rear-ends another, but I don't look back. What the hell just happened? That was clumsy. I can't believe I was amateur enough to let Eva's minions almost get the drop on me. And, worse, they'd seen my face.

I must be losing my touch. Another reason to get the ransom money quickly and run. Proof positive that I'm getting too old for this shit. I'll need to ditch the car and report it stolen. Damn shame. I like it. Time to regroup and do some fast thinking. First and foremost, I need to find out who it was in Ava's nightclub who'd just gone to meet their maker. If it was Hedda, then I only have a couple of days to voluntarily vamoose. My to-do list for the next twenty-four hours has to be strictly priorities only.

- *Job number one – find Troy Ealing and Liberty Jackman.*
- *Onerous but necessary: next job – keep them alive just long enough to ensure I get money from Tobias Durbridge.*
- *No mercy. Dispose of Troy and Liberty and get rid of any and all evidence that I had anything to do with them reaching their expiry dates.*
- *No slip-ups. Disappear to somewhere lush where no one will find me.*
- *Yay for me! Live in comfort and harmony with my conscience and, more importantly, my bank account for the rest of my days.*

Now that was a plan I could definitely live with. First things first. Find Troy and Liberty.

Daily Shouter Online

Home. News. Politics. Celebs. Entertainment. Sport. Tech. Health. Science. Money. More.

Prop use skyrocketing among Crosses. Juma Diniti, Health Secretary, calls for a 'whole-health approach' to solving drugs crisis

Figures released by the National Public Health Authority (NPHA) revealed a significant rise in the number of Crosses addicted to Prop. The synthetic drug has long been a scourge within Nought communities, but there has been a sharp rise in its use among the rest of the population of Albion.

Juma Diniti, Health Secretary, stated that the government had to employ a 'whole-health approach' to tackling the drugs crisis. 'This government is committed to rolling out more drugs prevention programmes across our schools nationwide and the building of many more rehabilitation centres. We will also be working tirelessly to hunt down and bring to justice those involved in the manufacture and distribution of this evil drug. Prop ruins lives and families. We in the government need to fight fire with fire.'

Sean Laverty, director of Abbey Rehab Centres, said that the government have been slow beyond belief in tackling the serious problem of Prop addiction in this country. 'Funny how, when Prop was seen as a mainly Nought problem, the government's rhetoric was all about punishment and prison. Nought kids on Prop – lock them away. Nought men and women on Prop – send them to prison. Nought families and communities devastated – don't do drugs then.

But, when the Prop problem begins to spill over into Cross communities, then it's a different story altogether. Cross kids on Prop? Send them to hospital and juvenile rehabilitation centres. Cross men and women on Prop? Send them to rehab and spend money to help them get their lives back on track. Cross families and communities devastated? Track down and crack down on Prop drug manufacturers and dealers. We have been begging the government for years to take this problem seriously. If they had listened, Prop use and abuse wouldn't be sweeping through the country at the rate it is now.'

THEN

Dan's Dinner Party

three. Place Names

As I circled slowly round the dinner table, checking the place name cards, my frown deepened. No, no, no. This wouldn't do at all. Irritation rose, entirely focused on George, my absent butler, and the proposed dinner-guest placement, even though I'd given no specific instructions as to where my guests were supposed to sit. Gathering up the cards, I buzzed round the table, rearranging them.

Each card was thoughtfully placed with malicious intent and a satisfied smile. That was better! I was at the head of the table where I should be, and directly opposite Tobey. I wanted to look my so-called friend in the eyes when I rained down vengeance on him.

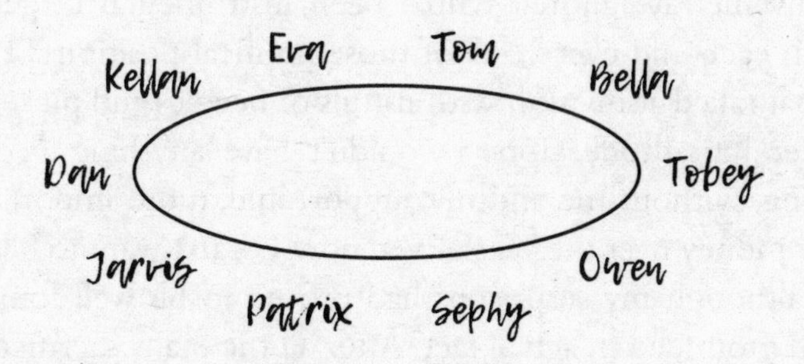

My forthcoming *sinner* party was going to be a winner. There wasn't a single guest attending who didn't have a dodgy past or something to hide. Not one.

That's what made each of them so perfect.

They had all accepted my invitation to dinner after it was made clear that *no* was not an acceptable answer. I didn't particularly care what made them turn up so long as they came. Because, as much as they loathed me, each of them despised Tobey Durbridge that much more – and that's precisely what I was relying on.

Tobias Durbridge, set to be elected Prime Minister of the entire nation within days, was about to choke on his just deserts. And I was going to be front and centre to do the serving. Tonight was all about payback.

Tobey had moved onwards and upwards from Mayor of Meadowview to Junior Minister for the Environment to Shadow Minister for Education to actual Prime Minister. Quite a trajectory for someone still in his thirties, and until now unheard of for a Nought. And, on his journey, Tobey had lost sight of the first rule of getting ahead: don't forget your friends. Certainly don't abandon them. He'd conveniently ignored who'd been instrumental in getting him each and every one of those political positions. That's what raked at my skin with fistfuls of needles and pins – the utter ingratitude. Tobey wouldn't have anything, *be* anything, without me and my support and, more importantly, my money over the years. Even now, I didn't want to believe it, although my suspicions had proved to be well founded and grounded in actual fact. After all the many sacrifices I'd made, Tobey was going to kick me in the teeth by kicking me to the kerb. He thought he could toss me out like yesterday's garbage. Well, I had a gift bag in mind for each of my dinner guests, something none of them would ever forget.

Including Tobey.

Especially Tobey – the unappreciative son of a bitch. Tonight he was going to get exactly what he deserved. The anticipation was delicious.

'Mr Jeavons?' There came a discreet knock on the dining-room door before George the butler appeared. 'Mr Jeavons, I thought I should let you know that Ms Monroe has found her present and its accompanying note.'

Shit. 'And her mood?'

'I think it's fair to say she's not happy, sir.' George was, as ever, the master of understatement.

'Where is she?'

'Looking for you, sir.'

'I'll see her in my study.'

'Very good, sir.' George left the room as discreetly as he'd arrived.

I wasn't far behind him. I headed through the kitchen and straight along the hall to get to the study, circumventing the rest of my apartment. I'd barely sat down and warmed the leather chair behind my desk when Bella flung open the door and burst into the room like a tornado. An extremely pissed-off tornado. I braced myself.

Incoming.

four. Isabella Monroe

'Dan, what is this?' Bella strode up to my desk and jiggled the necklace in her hand in front of my face. I leaned back. She was too close. I didn't appreciate people getting all up in my personal space like that, not without an invitation.

'A sapphire necklace. What does it look like?' I asked. 'Chopped liver?' It was a gift, and a bloody expensive one at that. 'Don't you like it?'

'It's ridiculously garish.'

More ingratitude. 'Give it back then.' I held out my hand.

Bella ignored the gesture. 'Never mind the necklace – I'm talking about the note attached to it.' She was furious. She lowered her gaze and started to read out my handwritten note. '"Bella, thanks for the fun times and memories. George will take you to wherever you want to go. Good luck." What the hell is this?'

'I'm letting you go,' I said evenly. 'It is what it is.'

'You're doing *what*?'

'Did I slip into some obscure Martian dialect or something?' I frowned. 'OK, here it is in as few syllables as possible. You're out of here. You don't live here any more. It was fun while it lasted, but we both knew it wouldn't be forever.'

The range of emotions twisting on Bella's face was fascinating to watch. She was trying to figure out precisely how to play her next card.

'But, Dan babe, we're good together. You said so yourself.' Her voice took on a wheedling, needy, baby-girl tone.

The wrong play. I shook my head.

'We *were* good together. For a while, you served your purpose,' I said honestly. And yes, I admit I was being brutal, but it would take nothing less to shake off Bella. Any hesitancy on my part and she'd cling like a limpet mine – with the same destructive results. 'We've had some fun these last few weeks, Bella. Let's just leave it at that, shall we?'

'But I love you, Dan—'

I burst out laughing, a genuine, raucous chortle. I couldn't help it. 'Oh, please don't insult my intelligence, Bella. You chased after me for one reason and one reason only: to get back at Tobey. And, as you're not a Neapolitan Mastiff to look at, I let you. But it's over.'

'What about you? Why did you ask me to move in with you? Why let me live here all these weeks? Because it suited your inferiority complex to have someone who was once with Tobey warming your sheets? That's it, isn't it? You are so jealous of Tobey that you can hardly see straight. He's smart, ambitious, good-looking, charismatic and a great lover – all the things you will never be and can never buy, in spite of all your blood money.'

This bitch!

'And what does that make you?' I asked, forcing myself to stay calm. 'I'm so deficient, yet it didn't stop you accepting my invitation to live here for a while, did it? And no doubt it'll take you less than a week to find some other poor rich schlub to take my place. Bella, it's over. Tomorrow morning I want you gone. Be a good girl and accept that.'

'You bastard!' The change in Bella's tone was not unexpected, but chilling nonetheless. 'You're throwing me out? Well, this *woman* is going to make you regret treating me like shit on your shoe. You just see if I don't.'

'I hope you're not going to make a scene in front of my guests tonight,' I said with a sigh. 'You know how I hate unnecessary drama. I had hoped to give you the necklace tomorrow morning – that's why I hid it in my desk drawer – but I guess you had to go and snoop.' I couldn't resist adding, 'You're good at that.'

'What's that supposed to mean?'

Really?

'Oh, we both know exactly what it means – *babe*. You're a sensei at minding everyone else's business but your own. Now leave. I have some phone calls to make.'

'You are a scum-weasel and I'll make you pay for this,' said Bella stormily.

'Oh, have some class and get lost,' I said, my patience finally at an end.

A moment later and the study door was slammed with such ferocity that my ears popped. What were the chances of Bella leaving my apartment before the dinner party? Slim to microscopic. Not while she still thought she stood a chance of changing my mind. My guess was she'd be the perfect dinner-party guest, alluring and entertaining, to try to make her last night in my apartment the perfect one. No doubt she was hoping that I'd be stupid enough to think twice about kicking her out. It wasn't going to happen, but it'd be fun to watch her work. What were the chances of Bella accepting that it was over? Slim to non-existent. And the chances of her finally leaving my residence within the next twenty-four hours with no drama whatsoever? Minuscule.

We were all in for an evening of fireworks – to say the least.

five. Kellan Bruemann

Kellan Bruemann was the first external guest to arrive. Of course he was. Free booze. He wasn't so much a man as an odious little dagger tick, latching onto my skin every chance he got, to try to suck the lifeblood from me. George came into the study to announce his arrival, but, as it was only Kellan, I didn't bother to get up. He and Bella could entertain each other for a while. Kellan was a bore and a tedious one at that. No doubt he'd already found his way to the drinks cabinet and was making friends with some of my finest cognac. There'd be time enough to deal with him later.

However, the desire to finish some paperwork didn't save me from interruption. Less than five minutes after George announced his arrival, Kellan strode into my study uninvited and unwelcome. His cornrowed hair was not as neat as it might've been, and he wore khaki trousers with a nondescript grey shirt under a mud-brown jacket. Had he got dressed in the dark? Kellan had barely taken a couple of steps into the room when he stumbled and had to grab the back of a chair to steady himself. Tipsy already? Typical of that clown.

'What d'you want, Bruemann?'

'I want to buy back all the shares in my company that you currently own,' said Kellan as he straightened up.

What?

Well now . . .

'You're broke. How d'you propose to buy them back? With your leg hairs?'

'I have a sponsor,' Kellan announced with a degree of arrogance I hadn't seen from him in quite some time – a number of years, in fact. 'A backer who is prepared to lend me money on very favourable terms to help me get back my company from you.'

And the joker honestly thought that was all there was to it. He really was a fool. His sponsor though . . . Now that was troubling. Who'd be crazy enough to lend this drunken sot that kind of money?

'I want to buy back my business and buy out the mortgage you hold on my home. Everything you own of mine, I want to buy back,' Kellan continued.

'Just who is this benefactor of yours?'

Kellan clamped his lips together like a petulant child.

'When did this angel first get in touch with you?' I asked.

'Last week.'

'By phone? In person? By intermediary? How?'

'What difference does it make?' Kellan said with hostility. 'The point is, I can reclaim everything that was once mine. Everything you took from me.'

'Not without my agreement you can't. Just because it was once yours doesn't mean it stays that way for ever and ever, amen. You sold your shit to me, Kellan. That makes it legally mine, and I have the paperwork and the lawyers to prove it.'

'I will pay you the market price for my company's shares

and repay you more than my home is worth. I just want to wind the clock back and turn my life around,' said Kellan.

'Wouldn't it be lovely if life had an undo-redo button like that?' I smiled.

Kellan shook his head. 'Dan, please. I'm making you a more than fair offer. Please.'

'Tell me who your sponsor is and I might consider it.'

'I can't do that.'

I shrugged. 'Then I can't help you. The answer is no.'

'Please, Dan. This is my last chance to get my wife and children back.'

'Which part of "no" is confusing you? The *N* or the *O*? I'm not selling you one share, one brick, one molecule of air that you previously sold to me. Everything you once owned belongs to me now and that's the way it'll stay.'

Kellan stood before me, pure, undisguised hatred freezing on his face. He was not so much shaking as actually vibrating with rage. I couldn't suppress the smile that played on my lips as I watched. This man truly hated my guts. I had better buckle my breastplate.

'Serves me right for thinking I could do business with a man like you in the first place,' said Kellan, bitterness deepening his voice.

'A man like me?' I enquired.

Kellan's eyes narrowed. 'A money-grubbing, no-class thug who's read a few books and throws around the odd fancy word or two to try and convince everyone that he's not the scum-sucking turd he really is.'

My smile broadened. 'That's quite accurate actually. No lies detected.'

How fascinating that, in his summation of my many deficient qualities, being a blanker was not mentioned as one of them.

'But, Kellan, don't forget: you came to me because no bank would lend your failing business any more money. You were running your construction company into the ground by not moving with the times, and you wanted money and muscle, and didn't care where either came from. Don't come bleating to me because you couldn't be arsed to read the small print.'

'I had some cash-flow problems and some union-activity snags. You took advantage—'

'I took advantage?' OK, now I was triggered. I stood up. 'You had some . . . stains in your life and I took care of them as requested. You're the one who reneged on our contract to pay back what you owed and you want the whole world to feel sorry for you. Why don't you try owning your shit instead of dumping it at my front door?'

'Dan, I'm warning you. Give me back what's mine while you still have the chance,' said Kellan.

'Or what?'

'Or suffer the consequences.'

'Oh, do be brief! Is that all you've got, Bruemann? What will you do? Give me a sideways look? Stick pins in a straw effigy? Damn, but you're pathetic. Listen closely because I'm only going to say this once more. I have no intention of selling my shares or anything else back to you. It's called business, Kellan. Just business. Close the door on your way out.'

'You don't want to test me, Dan,' said Kellan quietly. 'You don't want me to get drastic.'

I burst out laughing. 'You? Get drastic? Oops, did I blink and miss it? Go away, you pitiful parasite. Go drown yourself in a drink or five.'

I sat back down and bent my head to peruse the paperwork on my desk. I didn't look up again until I heard the study door click shut.

Loser!

NOW

six. Libby

My hand went to Troy's chest over his heart and then I felt for a pulse in his neck. Still nothing. I closed my eyes and inhaled slowly before trying his wrist again. When at last I detected a pulse throbbing against my fingers, I could've cried with relief. Troy's eyes were still closed. He must've knocked himself out.

What should I do?

Turn him onto his back? No. If he'd injured his spine or his neck, that could make things worse. Plus turning him over might result in him swallowing his tongue and not being able to breathe.

Think. Think.

Medical textbooks and books on human biology had been my favourite reading material for years. It was time to call on some of that information. Troy needed to be put into the recovery position, if I remembered correctly. I bent his right leg and folded his right arm over his chest to turn him onto his side, before placing his right leg in front of his body to stop him rolling over onto his stomach. He was now on his left side, facing me, his eyes still closed.

'Troy, wake up.' His forehead was clammy, as were his cheeks. I felt for a pulse again. It was much easier to find this time, now that I'd remembered what I was doing, but it was so fast. Too fast?

'Troy, come on. Please. Wake up.'

He was out cold.

And I didn't have a clue what to do.

'Troy, please. Wake up. Please.' I knelt beside his motionless body, my fingers still pressing against his wrist to monitor his pulse. I bent so that my cheek was almost touching his nose. His breath was warm against my skin.

'Troy, wake up.'

His eyes fluttered open. I could've hugged him for that alone.

'Thank God. Don't do that again! You scared the hell out of me. Are you OK? I thought . . . for a moment there, I thought—'

'Ow!' Troy groaned. 'What happened?'

'The banister rail gave way and you fell,' I told him. 'Later, when you're feeling better, I'm going to rant at you about the stupidity of charging at a boarded-up door. Can you sit up?'

Rubbing the back of his head, Troy struggled to pull himself upright.

With my assistance, apart from the odd grunt or groan, he managed it, but he didn't look good. He was looking more ashen by the second.

'Can you stand?' I asked. 'I'll help.'

Getting to my feet, I took Troy's hands in mine to pull him up. Manoeuvring his legs beneath him, he started to stand, only to let out a howl like I'd never heard before. He let go of my hands and collapsed back onto the ground, sweat beads erupting across his forehead.

'What? What is it?'

'My foot . . .' Troy's entire face had a sheen to it as he tentatively pulled up his right trouser leg.

He wasn't kidding either. His ankle had swollen up like a balloon.

'What the—?' Troy exclaimed when he saw it. 'Great. Just great.'

'Stay still.' I took a look at his ankle. 'Can you wiggle your toes?'

Troy did so, though he winced. Hmm . . . Actually, being able to wiggle his toes wasn't necessarily proof that his ankle wasn't broken. It could just mean that the muscles and nerves that allowed his ankle to move hadn't been affected by the fracture – if that's what it was. Cautiously I touched his ankle. Immediately he flinched.

'D'you have any numbness at all?' I asked.

Slowly Troy shook his head. 'I don't think so. Is it broken?'

'I can't tell,' I admitted. 'If there's no numbness or tingling, then I don't think so, but I don't know for sure. It could be a bad sprain or it could be a fracture. Until we get out of here, the only thing I can do is strap it up and you'll have to stay off it as much as possible.'

'That's all we need,' said Troy.

'It's not like you were scheduled to run a marathon any time soon. Come on.' I stood up and reached for his hand. 'Let me help you stand and get to a crate.'

It took a while to get Troy to his feet, or onto his one good foot rather, and then a couple of minutes of him leaning his full weight on me to hop to the nearest crate. Every time he hopped, he jarred his bad ankle, which was agony for him, and his instinct most times was to put his right foot down, which made it worse. By the time he collapsed onto the crate, sweat was pouring off both of us.

'Could you turn your head, please?' I asked.

'Why?' asked Troy.

'I need to take off my trousers,' I said.

'Er, why?'

'Just do it. OK?'

Even though Troy turned his head, I was still full-frontal blushing as I pulled my school trousers down. Kicking off my shoes, I peeled off my black tights, then quickly put on my trousers and shoes again before some verminous creature could run over my bare feet.

'Finished,' I announced.

'What're you doing?' asked Troy as I squatted down in front of him.

'Sorting out your ankle,' I snapped to cover up my embarrassment.

Troy's eyebrows shot up, but thankfully he didn't say anything. How to do this with no scissors . . . ? I carefully wrapped one leg of my tights round Troy's ankle. I had to be careful not to strap it too tightly or I'd stop his circulation, but it had to be tight enough to provide some relief.

Troy grimaced, flinched and even yelled out once while I carefully knotted my makeshift bandage. With each wince, I kept saying sorry until he barked at me to stop apologizing. It took all my self-control not to snap back. By the time I'd finished, his skin was almost grey with agony.

'I'm sor— I mean, I hope that helps,' I said, wrapping the other leg of the tights lightly round the first and tucking it in at the top of the makeshift bandage. Troy tried to tug down his trouser leg, but the tights made a bulky lump and the trouser leg had to stay bunched up at his knee.

'Thanks,' he whispered.

'Are you OK?'

'No. I feel sick.'

'Are you dizzy? Have you got a headache?'

'No. Why?'

'You rubbed your head when you sat up. Did you bang it? Is it hurting?'

'Libby, stop panicking. Apart from a trashed ankle, I'm fine. I'll survive,' Troy insisted.

'You fainted—'

'I momentarily passed out because of the pain in my ankle when I hit the ground,' Troy corrected pointedly.

If I didn't know any better, I'd say he was embarrassed.

'Tell me if you start to feel dizzy.'

'And what will you do?' asked Troy. 'Worry about me?'

OK, he didn't need to make it quite so plain that he thought I was useless. I sat down on the crate beside him, but turned my head so he wouldn't see the tears glistening. Troy sighed.

'Libby, I'm sorry, OK? What happened was my own stupid fault and I'm angry, but not with you. I shouldn't take it out on you.'

I turned back to him and did my best to smile, but it felt like my face was wet clay being moulded into a caricature of a smile.

Troy's ankle was swollen, he couldn't stand unaided, his face was still grey, and we were in deep, deep trouble.

'Libby, listen to me. I'll survive.'

'If I take your hand and stand beside you, d'you mind if I survive with you?' I asked.

Troy looked me in the eyes and said, 'I wouldn't have it any other way.'

Daily Shouter Online

Home. News. Politics. Celebs. Entertainment. Sport. Tech. Health. Science. Money. More.

BREAKING NEWS. Government announces 'review' of Human Rights Bill

The government announced today that there will be a formal 'review' of the Albion Human Rights Bill as it currently stands. Review proposals include the right to ban any demonstration, protest or march attended by more than ten people deemed to be 'disruptive'. This includes any demonstration described as 'too noisy'.

A government spokesperson stated, 'The pendulum has swung too far in one direction. Organizations and government departments cannot be held to ransom by individuals with an axe to grind bringing frivolous cases to trial. A revision of the Albion Human Rights Bill now that we may be leaving the Zafrikan Trading Alliance is long overdue.'

Shadow Home Secretary Helena Hayden, however, stated, 'We must ensure that the laws and processes that allow us to hold the powerful to account are protected for the good of democracy in this country. It's called the Human Rights Bill, not the Big Organizations Rights Bill, for a reason. The right to march, protest and hold big businesses accountable for their actions is a fundamental tenet of any true democracy. This government is seeking to undermine the protections that have been the right of every Albion citizen for decades. We must not allow them to water down the bill or we will all suffer.'

THEN

Dan's Sinner Party

seven. Patrix Ellerman

'Ah! Here you are. Heya, Dan, my favourite man!'

Patrix was all smiles as he entered the study uninvited. More bad manners. What was it with people barging into my room without even knocking first? I needed a better class of dinner guest. Keeping my expression neutral, I sat back, ready to deflect whatever bullshit Patrix thought he might fling in my direction. This evening was already getting on my nerves and the first course hadn't even been served yet. Still, there was a point and a purpose to all this, and the end result would be worth it. I forced myself to be civil.

'Hello, Patrix. How's life treating you?'

As if I didn't already know. I took in his denim jeans and his spotless, long-sleeved white polo shirt at a glance. All three buttons of the shirt were undone. How long had he stood in front of the mirror, deciding how much chest to put on show?

Patrix's gaze swept over my desk. His head tilted as he noted the framed photo just beside my laptop. He started round my desk for a closer look, but immediately I slammed the picture face down and waved him back.

'D'you mind?' I snapped. Rhetorical question. What the hell did he think he was doing? If I wanted to show the photo to anyone who came into the room, it would be facing towards the door rather than me. Patrix took a step back, placating hands palms out, his fixed smile unwavering.

'What can I do for you, Patrix?' I said, still peeved.

'Well, since you asked, I was wondering if I might borrow another cheeky little one hundred thousand,' said Patrix in a rush, though his faux-bonhomie smile never wavered. 'Just until the end of the year.'

One hundred thousand was *cheeky* now, was it? Maybe in the cloud cuckoo land where Patrix obviously resided. Meanwhile, down here on earth, that was a shit-ton of money.

'What happened to the cheeky little fifty thousand you borrowed from me three months ago?'

Patrix shrugged, unable to quite look me in the eye. 'I've had a run of bad luck, but I know that's about to change.'

'You already owe me a great deal of money, Pat. Why on earth would I throw good money after bad by lending you more?'

His smile faded. 'Look, my friend, I know I owe you some money—'

Close to seven digits was not just *some* money.

'But you know I'm good for it, right? I've just had some bad luck at the roulette wheels recently—'

And the card tables and the horse-racing fixtures and with online gambling. Particularly with online gambling. Did he really think I wouldn't find out?

'Dan, don't look at me like that. We're mates. Like I said, my luck is about to change – I can feel it,' said Patrix.

'How's your law practice?' I asked.

Stunned, Patrix's eyes widened, only for the shutters to come down fast – but not fast enough.

'My partners and I are regrouping and merging with another firm under a new banner,' he said carefully.

'And what part will you play in this new company?'

'More of an advisory, behind-the-scenes role,' came the reply.

More like a permanently-left-the building role. He'd been bounced out for helping himself to company funds. Oh, they'd kept it very hush-hush, but not hush-hush enough.

'Patrix, you've got seven days to pay me back every penny you owe me plus fifty per cent interest or I will do what must be done to recover my money. And, what's more, I'll do it as publicly as possible.'

'What?' If Patrix was shocked before, it was nothing to the panic now scrambling over his face. 'You can't do that. Where am I supposed to come up with that kind of money in seven days?'

'Not my problem. You have seven days or I will show the whole world exactly what a crooked lawyer looks like.'

'You don't want to do that,' said Patrix slowly. 'I was your lawyer for quite a few years. I know all about your business dealings—'

'And I know where your wife and sons live,' I countered.

Patrix stared at me. Was he finally beginning to get the message regarding exactly who he was dealing with? If so, it had taken long enough.

'Patrix, you have seven days.' The phone on my desk began to ring. I checked the caller ID. 'I need to take this. See yourself out.'

'Dan, please. J-just give me six weeks. Can we talk about this some more after dinner?' Patrix pleaded.

'Yeah, yeah.' Whatever. The message wouldn't be any different, but I wanted him gone. I waved him away with one hand as I picked up my phone with the other. 'Just a moment, Jarvis,' I said.

Eyebrows raised, I waited for Patrix to get the unsubtle hint and leave. It took a few seconds, but he finally caught on. I shook my head as he closed the door behind him.

'It took you long enough to get back to me.'

'I was driving. What d'you want?' Jarvis's tone was surly, to say the least.

'Kellan Bruemann has someone ready to stump up enough money to buy back his company and his home from me. I want to know who that is and I want to know tonight.'

'On it.'

The call was disconnected. I replaced the phone on my desk. I didn't know who it was – yet – but the person funding Kellan had just made a very powerful enemy. When I brought down Kellan once and for all, I was going to make sure I included his new friend. No one worked against me and got away with it.

No one.

eight. Tobey Durbridge

After another ten minutes or so, it was time to join my guests. Most but not all had arrived. I circled round the lounge, a tall glass of sparkling water, ice and lemon in my hand, making my apologies for my delayed appearance.

Jarvis arrived, followed by Tobey only a few minutes afterwards. I acknowledged them both with a brief nod. After making the obligatory circuit of the room, I had to discipline Kellan for bad-mouthing me to Tobey. That somewhat soured the atmosphere, which I then had to work hard to repair. Once the air had been cleared, and most people were chatting again, I sought out Tobey who was still talking to Kellan.

'Tobey, may I see you in my study?' I said rather formally.

He frowned. 'Of course.'

As we walked side by side along the east hall, Tobey kept throwing curious looks my way.

'What's Sephy Hadley doing here?' he asked.

'Sephy Ealing.'

'Whatever. What's she doing here?'

'I invited her.'

Tobey's impatient intake of breath had me smiling inwardly.

'I gathered that. I'm asking why?'

'She's my insurance.'

'Insurance? I don't understand.'

'You will before the night is out. Sephy and I have unfinished business, as do you and I,' I said pointedly.

'I didn't know Sephy was on your radar,' said Tobey.

'Maybe you don't know me as well as you think you do,' I said silkily. 'By the way, a while ago, when we were both drunk at my birthday party, you told me that if you ever became PM you'd use all your power to win back Callie Rose Hadley. Is that still your endgame?'

'Why?'

'Just curious.'

Tobey shrugged. 'You shouldn't believe a word anyone says when they've had a skinful.'

People inevitably spoke a lot of shit when they were drunk and their guard was down, but they also sometimes spoke a lot of truth too. '*In vino veritas*,' I pointed out.

'In wine maybe. In the forty-five-per-cent-proof fire-water you were serving at that birthday party, not so much,' said Tobey.

'If you say so.' I wasn't about to argue.

Another speculative look from Tobey. We entered the study. I indicated he should sit down before I did the same behind my desk.

'Strange mix of guests you've brought here tonight,' Tobey pointed out.

I shrugged.

'You're not a fan of Bruemann,' Tobey said. 'And yet you invited him here and, even more bizarrely, he showed up.'

'Of course he did,' I replied with a curl of my top lip. 'That scrounger would turn up to the opening of a fridge door if he thought he'd get a free drink out of it. The world is full of parasites.'

Silence.

'Dan, are you all right?'

'Why wouldn't I be?' I asked.

'My brother, I know you. You seem a bit . . . off,' said Tobey. 'What's wrong?'

What's wrong—? Oh, Tobey, I have killed for you. There was a time I was ready to die for you. I thought we were true friends in a world of false promises. Proper brothers . . .

'Tobey, a little bird tells me that you intend to cut me loose once you're Prime Minister.' I had neither the time nor the inclination to beat about the bush. 'Is that true?'

Tobey straightened up, as did I. We regarded each other and all the years between us fell away to gather lifeless at our feet. We were back in McAuley's office, standing over him as he lay dying; we were back at the Wasteland, arguing about a dodgy tackle during our regular game of Monday-evening football; we were back to being boys together in primary school, sharing chocolate buttons and swapping comics. Tobey and I and our whole history together had now been condensed into these fraught moments in my study.

'Well? What the little bird told me, is it true?'

'A little Bella bird by any chance?' asked Tobey.

'She lives with me so you have to expect at least some pillow talk,' I said deliberately.

Tobey didn't wince, didn't flinch; he didn't even blink.

I persisted. 'Is that what this is about? You're looking to cut me loose in retaliation for Bella moving in with me?'

'*Pfft!* No skin off my nose. I guess it's true what they say about cats always landing on their feet. Or on their back, whichever is more comfortable,' said Tobey, sounding remarkably unconcerned.

'Is it true?' I asked again. 'Will you be making changes once the election is in the bag?'

'Well, I didn't want to do this today, but, since you asked, now that you've branched out into . . . let's call them less savoury, more public pursuits, I can no longer afford to be linked too closely with you, so I'll be putting my interests under new public-relations management,' said Tobey. 'We are and always will be friends, Dan. I owe you a lot, but I don't owe you my career.'

'The less savoury pursuits, as you so very quaintly called them, were pursued without my knowledge,' I protested.

'But the point is they're linked to your name and, what's more, the powers that be know all about them and are gunning for you. I've been assured that it's only a matter of weeks – if that – before they take you down.'

'Wait just a minute, Tobey—'

'No, you wait, you idiot! How could you be stupid enough to get involved in people trafficking? I told you there were certain things I wouldn't tolerate – and that was in my top three, along with the production and distribution of drugs – and you've been busy with all of them. You know my family history; you know about my sister, Jessica. What were you thinking? "What he doesn't see, he can't complain about"?'

Tobey's eyes flashed with something sharp and reproachful – or was it my imagination that he was hurt?

'Tobey, it wasn't like that—' I began.

'I don't want to hear it,' Tobey interrupted. 'Either you deliberately started making drugs and to hell with me and my views, or someone in the Outfit decided to go behind your back and do it for you. Neither is a good look.'

'Like I said, someone in my operation took it upon themselves to branch out.'

'No one who works for you should have the balls to try something like that without your say-so. You're losing your grip, Dan, and the Serious Crime Agency is standing below you with a huge butterfly net and handcuffs, just waiting for you to fall.'

'Your faith in me is touching.'

'I'm a realist. You of all people should know that,' said Tobey. 'So, as of now, you and I are friends, but no longer business associates.'

Just like that. He hadn't even attempted to listen properly to my side of the story.

Decades of friendship counted for absolutely nothing.

'You haven't won the election yet,' I reminded him.

'But we both know I will.' Tobey was all confidence.

'Oh, Tobey, you really believe what you're saying, don't you?' I contrived to make my tone amused and pitying at the same time. 'You seriously think you can treat me like one of your discarded whores? You actually believe that all you have to say is, "Dan, we're done," like it was some magic spell and that's it, with no hard feelings?'

'I'm hoping we can both be grown up about this, yes,' said Tobey.

'Tobey, I can't believe I have to say this out loud, but here goes – our working relationship is over when I say it is and not before.'

Tobey stood up, his mahogany-brown eyes almost black as he considered me. 'Dan, I think you're forgetting who you're talking to. I want to keep this amicable, but that's entirely up to you. Either way, we won't be working together any more. I'm washing my hands of the entire business. Deal with it.'

I got to my feet. 'And you forget I know where the bodies are buried and there's always space for more.'

'Oh, my friend, I wouldn't go there if I were you. You know I don't respond well to threats.' Tobey's voice had taken on a scalpel-sharp edge. He hadn't raised his voice once, but then he didn't have to.

'You know I deal in promises, not idle threats,' I replied. 'By the way, how is Callie Rose Hadley?'

Pause.

The air in the room was being slowly sucked out. Tobey and I faced each other like enemies in a boxing ring, sizing each other up before we went in for the kill.

'She's fine, last I heard – thanks for asking,' said Tobey, his tone calm and even. 'And God help us all if she isn't, because I will scorch this earth and beyond if any harm comes to her.'

So it was like that. Sephy's daughter still ruled his heart and his head, both of them. Even though my gaze never left Tobey's face, I was very aware of his fists slowly clenching and I doubt he even knew he was doing it. Time for a tactical retreat.

'Look, this is neither the time nor the place,' I said with a smile. 'We've been mates for too long to end a mutually beneficial partnership in five minutes. Let's have a proper discussion later, OK? I have a couple of phone calls to make, so I'll see you at the dinner table.'

'I won't change my mind, Dan.' Tobey turned on his heel and headed for the door.

'Well, Tobey, if you insist that our working partnership is over and you don't change your mind, I'll have no choice but to inform tonight's dinner guests about all the ways I've helped you over the years, including how you double-crossed Alex McAuley and your involvement in his death, and how you really became Mayor of Meadowview. More than a few people got caught in the crossfire during that campaign, to their cost. I'll also be more than happy to tell tonight's guests all about your links to the Outfit. Once that's out in the public domain, let's see how long your political career lasts.'

'You do what you have to do, and I'll do the same,' said Tobey, reaching for the door handle.

'You want to know the main reason for the eclectic guest list tonight?' I called after him. 'Because each one despises you. Once I've spilled my guts about all the nasty little shenanigans you've used to rise to the top, you may be able to bully, bribe or barter with some of them to keep them quiet, maybe even most of them. But not Sephy. Not if there's the slightest chance of you and her daughter getting together again. Sephy will move heaven and earth to keep the two of you apart – and all she has to do is tell Callie the truth about you. So, whichever way you look at it, you lose.'

'Ah, but the game is not over yet, Dan,' said Tobey softly.

'It is for you,' I said, smiling.

Tobey and I regarded each other as the temperature in the study dropped by several degrees. Without saying another word, he left the room, closing the door quietly but firmly on our past and our future.

I stared at the door long after it was shut. I deserved better from Tobey. I'd thought he and I were solid. How wrong I was. Even though I'd planned for this outcome, I still didn't want to believe that it was not only our business partnership but our friendship that was permanently out for the count. Only now did I finally admit to myself how much Tobey cutting me loose had burned. To hear from Bella, of all people, that Tobey considered our friendship a liability, and was looking to distance himself from me after the election, had cut bone-deep. And then the knowledge that I was definitely about to be set adrift had been confirmed by a third party, one of Tobey's close-protection officers who was also on my payroll. That I hadn't even heard it from Tobey first made it that much more brutal. After all these years, I expected better. Maybe we both had, but this is what it had come to. I'd meant what I said. Every word. If Tobey didn't change his mind about dropping me, I would set fire to his career and all his political ambitions. He wasn't the only one who would scorch this earth in pursuit of revenge.

I was about to make a powerful enemy, but so be it. Tobey was a man of Meadowview like me. We didn't do love, hatred, friendship or retribution easily, but, when we did, it was with our whole chest. And, when we made enemies, we made them for life. It struck me that Bella and I maybe weren't so different after all. Neither of us handled rejection well.

Tobey and I were heading for a showdown and the only thing certain was that neither of us would emerge unscathed.

nine. Circulating

I was back in the lounge and circulating. All my guests had arrived and I was waiting for the right moment to make my declaration about Tobey so that I could bring this godawful evening to a close. They may have been Tobey's enemies, but they certainly weren't my friends. I felt low, sort of heartsick and deflated, but there was a sharper edge to it than that. Now that I'd heard it from Tobey himself, I couldn't shake off the sense of betrayal riding my back, lashing at me. After everything we'd been through, Tobey was supposed to have my back. Always. What a sad, sorry joke.

After a brief platitudinous conversation with Eva and Patrix, I spotted Owen seated at the piano across the room, deep in conversation with Sephy. There was an earnest back and forth between them that was growing in not just intensity but animosity. From their body language, it was safe to assume they weren't discussing the pros and cons of the proposed football ultra league. Whatever they were debating, it looked like a conversation I should be a part of, so I headed in their direction. They were so intent on each other, they didn't even register my arrival.

'If you're thinking of selling Specimens to Jeavons instead

of me, I would strongly advise against it,' said Owen. 'I will match and surpass any offer he makes.'

'How many more times? Neither of you are offering what Specimens is really worth, but it makes no difference. I'm not selling my restaurant to either of you,' Sephy insisted. 'It was my husband's enterprise and I'm keeping it. It's what he would've wanted.'

'Oh, spare me the false sentiment, Persephone. You're great at the holier-than-thou act, aren't you? Yet I have it on good authority that you and your restaurant are about to be investigated by the ARCS for under-reporting your profits. You've been skimming money off the top, probably for years. And d'you really think it's not known that you killed your husband Nathan for the insurance? Everyone knows Specimens was in trouble, so what better way for you to get money in a hurry—'

Sephy drew her hand back and walloped Owen so hard and fast that I got sympathetic whiplash.

'Say that again. I dare you,' Sephy challenged.

Dowd looked like he was going to return Sephy's slap with interest. In my apartment. At my dinner party. Hell, no! Out of the corner of my eye, I saw Tobey start forward to get between them, but I beat him to it.

'Don't even think about it,' I told him quietly. Then louder: 'Owen and Sephy, I think you've forgotten where you are and that you both have an audience.'

By now Jarvis was standing next to me, just in case Dowd was feeling particularly frisky. When Sephy threatened to leave, I had to persuade her that that would be a really bad idea, but even so she was practically out the door until I got

Dowd to apologize. Sephy stayed, but didn't even try to disguise the contempt she had for me as she looked me up and down. I'll say one thing for Persephone Ealing – she had guts. Not a lot of people would dare to look at me like that quite so openly. I admired her for it, even if it did piss me off. One way or another, I'd make sure she paid for that. And the fact that she was about to be investigated by the Albion Revenue and Customs Service was just another hollow-point bullet I could add to my arsenal to use against her.

After Owen and Sephy's difference of opinion, the atmosphere among my guests was severely strained. Bella and Tobey studiously avoided each other, though she made a point of walking past and round him as often as possible – no doubt to show him what he was missing. She'd changed into a gold sequined dress that hugged every toned contour of her body and she looked delectable. Patrix wouldn't stop making snide remarks to my brother, his every other word dripping with the venom he didn't dare trickle on me. Someone else who was going to pay for their lack of manners. And as for Eva and Owen, well, that was strange. The strenuous efforts they were making to completely ignore each other just drew more of my attention to both of them. Hmm . . .

It was a relief to everyone when we finally sat down for our first course of crab and lobster terrine with a cucumber and dill foam. George had surpassed himself. Having a butler who was also a master chef was just one of the many reasons I was happy to pay over the odds for his services. George really was a jewel. The food was exceptional, like nothing I could've dreamed of growing up. The champagne flowed.

The conversation, which ran like ice cubes up a grassy hill, did not.

I wasn't oblivious to the considered looks Tobey kept throwing my way either.

It was a dinner of knives, with each of my guests seated next to at least one person they would happily stab in the vitals. The antagonism between them would ensure there would be no collective attempts to buy them off or persuade them to keep my announcement a secret.

Which was just the way I wanted it.

NOW

ten. Troy

How could I have been so stupid? In spite of what I'd said to Libby, my ankle was hurting like a son of a bitch, and just hopping from the stairs to the crate had been excruciating. I had almost passed out again from the pain that clawed at me with each rabbit hop across the room. Libby's tights were providing some relief, but the pain was making me feel like I was about to puke. If, by some miracle, the basement door were to open, I wouldn't be making a sudden mad dash for freedom any time soon.

Into the stillness of the room, I asked, 'What d'you think this new lot of kidnappers are demanding in exchange for us?'

Libby shrugged. 'Money probably.'

'From your dad or my mum?'

'Is your mum rich?'

'Comfortable, I think, but not rich, not like sit-on-your-purse-all-day-doing-nothing-while-your-money-works-for-you rich. Mum works hard at Specimens. Some days she doesn't get home until midnight. What about you? Is your dad rich?'

'He's Prime Minister of the Democratic Alliance party. Can you be Prime Minister and still be scratching for cash at the same time? I doubt it. The ones who took over from Mum know who we both are so they're probably asking for something from both our families.'

Which made sense. That's what I would do. 'D'you think they'll get what they're asking for?'

Libby looked at me and sighed. 'Yeah, I do, but that doesn't mean they'll let us go. We've seen too much.'

Which was the same conclusion I'd already reached. Libby and I both stared up in silence at the locked, bolted and boarded-up door at the top of the stairs. The basement left us with nowhere to hide from the truth. We'd been sealed in because our kidnappers had no intention of letting us out. Ever. Even if they got whatever ransom they were demanding, Libby and I were going nowhere.

I took Libby's hand in mine. She squeezed it so tightly my eyes began to water. Or maybe they began to water for a different reason. I risked a glance at her. Her face was pale, bloodless. Her breath kept hitching audibly at irregular intervals. She was too terrified to even cry. What little hope she had of getting out of our prison was dancing away from her, losing itself in the shadows of the basement. How did I know? Because she was me and I was her – and all without a word being said.

We'd been locked in and boarded up and left to die. How long before we starved to death? Or more likely died of thirst?

Libby started scraping her right arm against the metal edge of the crate we were both seated on. Again.

'Libby, stop it.'

'How long before we asphyxiate down here – or is it

suffocate?' Libby whispered, adding, with a humourless laugh, 'What's the difference? We'll be just as dead.'

'Whoa! Slow down there. We're not in a bank vault. This room isn't airtight.' I frowned. 'There must be airbricks in the walls otherwise it'd stink of damp and mould – well, a lot worse than it already does.'

'Airbricks? Really?' Hope lit her eyes and lightened her voice.

'Yeah. Of course. I felt a draught on my foot coming from one of them when we first explored the room.'

Not exactly a lie. But not exactly the truth either. There had to be some kind of ventilation down here and, on the plus side, that meant we'd die of thirst or hunger long before we ran out of air. Silver linings.

'If we don't suffocate, we'll just starve to death,' Libby said, reflecting my thinking.

Scrape . . . scrape . . . Libby went back to rubbing her forearm against the crate.

'Liberty, stop it. Seriously. How does getting sepsis in your arm help our situation?'

'God, you're Mr Sensitivity, aren't you?' she replied.

'At this precise moment, I'm Mr We've-got-enough-on-our-plates-without-you-adding-to-it. So give it a rest.'

'Like I said, Mr Sensitivity.' Libby scowled at me – and I deserved it. I was being a dick. Yes, I was terrified and my ankle felt like it was on fire, but that was no reason to take it out on her. Time for a subject change.

'I spy, with my little eye, something beginning with—'

Libby's eyes rounded like dinner plates. 'Seriously? *Seriously?* We've literally been left to rot and you wanna play I spy?'

'Not in the mood for that?' I queried. 'OK, how about Animal, Vegetable or Mineral? You can ask me up to twenty questions, then you have to guess the object I'm thinking of.'

'How about I slap you back to factory settings?' Libby glared.

I wagged a finger at her, imitating my Nana Meggie. 'Violence is never the answer. Embrace love, peace and cheesecake.'

'Oh. My. God. You're so annoying,' Libby said, exasperated.

'But adorable with it.'

'A legend in your own head,' said Libby.

'And beyond.' I winked.

Libby shook her head, but at least she'd stopped rasping her arm against the crate. Mission accomplished. 'How about you channel that anger you're currently feeling and help me figure out a way to get us out of here?'

'We've already tried that. There isn't one.'

'Yes, there is. We just haven't found it yet,' I argued. 'Besides, I refuse to die before I've met Beyoncé.'

Libby and I regarded each other. I raised an eyebrow, deadly serious. She reluctantly smiled. 'Troy, you're an idiot. You know that, right?'

'Yeah. You've told me that at least once before,' I reminded her – and myself.

'But this time I'm saying it with appreciation.'

OK . . . wasn't quite sure how that worked as a thing, but never mind. I took stock of what we had going for us. The light was still on, sickly as it was. We had one-third of a bottle of water left. We were still alive. And the things we had going against us? We were locked in this basement with no obvious means of escape. We had no more food and were running out of water. The temperature in the basement was dropping from fridge to freezer. As if to reinforce my thoughts, Libby shivered beside me. I immediately put my arm round her only to pull it away again.

'Sorry. I should've asked first. You OK with me putting my arm round you to warm us both up?'

Libby took my arm and placed it back round her shoulders. I guess she was. Not that sitting closer and hugging was going to do much, but it had to be better than nothing. I'd only just begun to clock the strange look Libby was giving me. Her smile faded before she did something totally inexplicable. She leaned forward and kissed me. On the lips. Mouth to mouth. What the actual hell? Shock froze me in the moment. Then I drew back rapidly like she'd slapped me instead. Actually, a slap I would've expected and been prepared for. This? Not so much.

'What was that about?' I frowned.

'Just because.'

'Because of what?'

'Because we used to be good friends. Because you kept my secret all those years. Because you didn't desert me back at the harbour wall when you could've and should've. Because my mum is . . . was a liar who didn't give a damn about me. Because, like I said before, you've been a better friend than I deserved. Plus I don't want to die without ever having been kissed.'

'And a kiss from me, a Cross and someone you consider lower than pond scum, is better than no kiss at all?'

'I didn't say that.'

Yeah, right. Two days ago, Libby would've happily cut my heart out with a rusty chainsaw. What a difference a day made.

'Liberty, we're not about to kick the bucket, so stop this.' I frowned. 'You're freaking me out.'

Given a choice between having Libby be civil because she reckoned our minutes were numbered, or having Libby be her normal salty, obnoxious self for the rest of a long life, I knew which one I preferred. But, when you got right down to it, there should've been a sign put up outside the now boarded-up door at the top of the basement stairs:

HERE LIE LIBERTY JACKMAN AND TROY EALING.
FINALLY ABLE TO DO IN DEATH WHAT THEY
COULDN'T DO IN LIFE:
BE IN THE SAME ROOM FOR LONGER THAN FIVE
MINUTES WITHOUT KILLING EACH OTHER. UNABLE
TO LIVE TOGETHER, THEY DIED TOGETHER INSTEAD.

'Cause that's what this basement felt like – our final resting place. We could sit in it, stand up in it, walk and talk in it. The walls were brick. The floor was soft dirt strewn with rotten and broken floorboards. As coffins go, it was spacious, but a roomy coffin was still a coffin. Libby made a strange choking sound and turned her face into the crook of my arm. Then the dam broke. Her arms clamped round my waist as she gave in to her misery. My arms round her shoulders tightened. Neither of us said a word. What was there to say?

A sick question lodged itself in my head and refused to budge.

How many days or weeks or months would pass before they found our bodies?

Or maybe we'd never be found and Libby and I were destined to live out our last seconds in this basement, never to be seen again. Maybe we'd be ghosts, doomed to haunt this room until our bodies were discovered and properly buried. Maybe we'd be ghosts for as long as our loved ones remembered us. Or perhaps we'd unknowingly died and were already ghosts.

Now wouldn't that be a bitch?

THEN

Dan's Winner Party

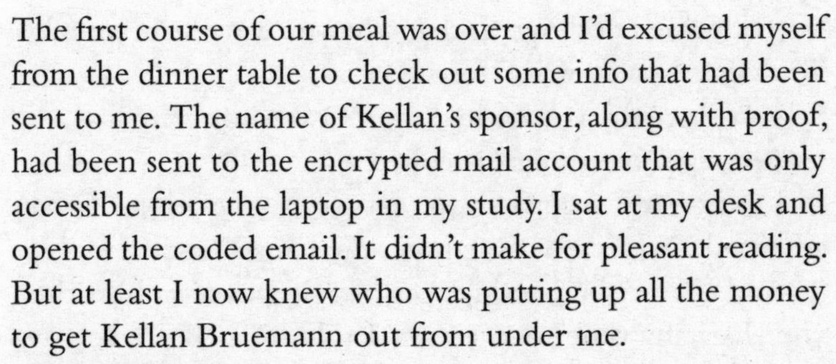

eleven. Owen Dowd

The first course of our meal was over and I'd excused myself from the dinner table to check out some info that had been sent to me. The name of Kellan's sponsor, along with proof, had been sent to the encrypted mail account that was only accessible from the laptop in my study. I sat at my desk and opened the coded email. It didn't make for pleasant reading. But at least I now knew who was putting up all the money to get Kellan Bruemann out from under me.

Owen Dowd.

I shook my head, seriously annoyed. What game was Dowd playing? What purpose would bailing out Kellan serve apart from garnering his appreciation, which, let's face it, wasn't worth a damn?

A brief knock at the door, then Owen Dowd strode in like he owned me. This dagger was too reckless. That's why he didn't have long for this world. But, with his minions seated in the reception area on the ground floor and as a guest in my home, for tonight, at least, he was untouchable. He wore a black suit with a dark blue shirt, no tie, and even I had to admit that he looked the business. Everything about him was carefully groomed, right down to his trimmed moustache and goatee. What did he use on that thing? Manicure scissors?

'Dan, I believe we're due a private conversation,' said Owen.

'Oh yes?'

'Eve tells me you've been making noises about a possible partnership, a merger between us to serve both our interests.'

Had she now? 'Oh yes?'

Owen's eyes narrowed shrewdly. 'Was she lying or mistaken?'

I confirmed nothing. 'Is that why you came here tonight? To discuss a merger?'

'Isn't that why you invited me?' Owen countered.

'Among other things,' I replied.

'I was very surprised to get your invitation,' Owen admitted. 'You're not exactly on my Crossmas-card list.'

'And I won't be inviting you to a sleepover and braiding your hair any time soon either,' I told him. 'But I do have an announcement to make once our meal is over. Something I know you'll want to hear. Can our proposed merger discussion wait until after that?'

'What kind of announcement?' Owen asked, his eyes narrowing.

'If I told you that, it'd spoil the surprise.'

'I don't like surprises,' said Owen. 'Never have.'

'You'll love this one. I guarantee it,' I told him. 'In the meantime, why don't you go and enjoy yourself at the dinner table with the rest of the guests?'

'You sat me next to Sephy Ealing,' said Owen sourly. 'I fully expect to end the evening with a steak knife in my thigh.'

'Sephy wouldn't do any such thing.'

'Don't you believe it. The way she's been scowling at me, I expect nothing less. Besides, anyone is capable of anything given the right circumstances and motivation,' said Owen.

'You think so?'

'I know so. And, if you haven't learned that by now, you've been sleepwalking through this existence and are due for a rude awakening.'

'You misunderstood me. If you threaten Sephy, she wouldn't stab you in the thigh with a steak knife, she'd go for the jugular.'

'Thanks for the heads-up,' said Owen. He got to his feet. 'We'll talk later, no doubt.'

'No doubt,' I replied.

I didn't take my eyes off Owen till he left the room, closing the door behind him. Dowd was the one who'd offered Kellan a way out from under. Why? To stick it to me? Or to buy Kellan and all his business connections? Whatever the reason, Dowd was a serious liability. It was time to step up my plans to get rid of him.

Permanently.

twelve. Eva Foxton

After a heavy knock, Eva entered the study, pushing the door shut behind her. We regarded each other for a few moments before she sat down in the chair closest to my desk. Eva wore black floaty trousers over stiletto-heeled black boots and a silver top to match her silver, swept-back hair. The last time I saw her, which had been a couple of days ago, her hair was past her shoulders. Now it was cut in a more androgynous style, longer on top and at the front than at the back and sides, with a semi-fringe over half her forehead. It suited her. Her lipstick was her usual purple, which strangely suited her too. She told me once that she always wore that colour because it had been her daughter Ava's favourite as a child. After her daughter died, Eva never wore any other colour. She looked exactly what she was: a formidable woman.

'You've invited an interesting range of guests tonight,' said Eva dryly.

'It's been said. I had my reasons.'

'Care to share them?'

'Not right now, no,' I replied. 'I've also had an interesting conversation with Dowd.'

'Oh?'

'Yes. All about the merger you've been trying to set up between his organization and mine.'

'Dan, let me explain—'

'How dare you?' Though my voice was calm, Eva knew better than to think I wasn't incensed. After all, she'd known me long enough. She sat up straighter, her whole stance now more wary.

'Calm down,' she had the gall to say. 'I was acting in our best interests—'

'How. Dare. You?'

'Dan, you're too angry to see it right now, but I was doing you a favour. If we're not careful, Dowd will run all the major Prop routes up and down the country, not to mention people trafficking. We're falling into irrelevancy, but you're too busy playing kingmaker to Tobey bloody Durbridge to see that.'

That was a slap in the face and no mistake. This woman had once saved my life. She was more of a mother to me than my real mother had ever been. Didn't she realize what she meant to me? Maybe she did. Maybe that's why she now thought she owned me. Big mistake.

'Eva, what makes you think I'm interested in Prop routes or people smuggling? If I were interested in those activities, I'd be all over them.'

'Dan, don't you get it? Owen Dowd and his crew are laughing at you. You're passing up a chance to make vast amounts of easy money. Prop production has put us where we should be, on top – and that's thanks to me. There's nothing and no one able to stop us or even touch us now.'

'Eva, your daughter died of a drugs overdose. You're the last person to push for more Prop on the streets.'

Eva sat up ramrod-straight, her eyes steely. 'Ava is dead. The rest of this world is just . . . noise, so why shouldn't I get all I deserve?'

'After all these years, is that what our relationship is, Eva? Noise?'

'I'm looking after our interests,' Eva insisted. 'Someone had to.' She stood up to glare down at me. I also got to my feet. No one looked down on me. No one.

'Dan, you were busy elsewhere, so I had to take up the slack. And the only reason you aren't interested in Prop is because Tobey disapproves. Well, bollocks to that. *You're* supposed to be running this outfit, not him.'

'And I have been running it, Eva. Manufacturing and distributing Prop is a short-term proposition at best. Tobey has already said that he intends to crack down on illegal drug trafficking in Albion when he's in government and he's not bluffing. Pouring all our resources into Prop will bankrupt us within a year.'

'He's your friend,' said Eva with scorn. 'Warn him to back off.'

'He's my friend and I'll do no such thing,' I replied.

'Dan, I've been running our drug operations for almost two years now. Doesn't that tell you something? We now control the making and distribution of Prop, the best on the street. Our reputation for quality is second to none. Why d'you think Dowd is even considering a merger?'

'Eva, listen to me. One pack can't have two alphas. Sooner or later, Dowd and I would have to re-establish which of us was top dog – and there'd be massive nationwide fallout. Dowd can't be trusted. He'll wait till he has knowledge of all our dreams and schemes and then he or one of his minions will put a bullet in my head or stab me in the back. Literally.'

'It won't come to that,' Eva insisted, 'because we'd get to him first.'

'Eva, you are not to have any more dealings with Dowd, d'you hear me? Leave the running of my business interests to me. I know what I'm doing. You don't. From now on, you don't make a business decision without passing it by me first. D'you understand?'

'Yes. I understand perfectly,' Eva said quietly. She looked at me like a disappointed parent who'd just caught their child telling lies.

Such a shame, but in that moment I knew that our partnership, or mentorship, or whatever the hell it was, was well and truly over. A long pause, then the door opened quietly and closed the same way.

It was time to cut Eva loose – and, what's more, we both knew it.

thirteen. Tom Jeavons

'Dan, can I have a word?'

Another visitor to the study, my brother this time. I rolled my eyes. What I wouldn't give for just five minutes' peace. I'd already popped two paracetamol to tackle the pounding headache I now had. I swear it felt like someone were trying to drive a stake through my head.

'What is it, Tom?'

'I want to talk to you, but I need you in a calm, steady frame of mind,' he said.

'You have so picked the wrong night then,' I told him straight.

Though my brother was twenty, his wide-eyed, innocent grey eyes and gelled sandy-brown hair made him look at least five years younger. He was lean, verging on skinny. The taupe chinos he wore hung low on his hips and his black shirt was at least a size too big, as if he thought wearing a big shirt would fool people into believing he was larger than he actually was. He was so young.

'Dan, have you changed your mind about me coming to work for you?'

Oh Lord, not this again.

'No, I haven't, Tom. Now, if you don't mind—'

'I'd be more use helping you run things than stuck at university, studying for a useless degree,' my brother insisted.

I sighed. How many more times were we destined to have this same conversation?

'Tom, you will drop out of university over my dead body and not before.'

'That's not fair. It's my life. Stop treating me like a kid—'

'Then stop acting like one,' I snapped. 'A degree will open doors for you that I can't. No one will be able to look down on you with a decent education under your belt.'

'You didn't get a degree and no one looks down on you,' said my brother.

How wrong he was.

'Dan, you're rich and you have loads of people working for you, and you don't have to take shit from anyone,' said Tom.

'And I have very few real friends and have to constantly watch my back,' I told him. 'I'm also very unlikely to die of old age.'

'You have power—'

I sighed. My brother just couldn't hear me. All he could see were the bespoke suits and the plush apartments and those who asked how high when I told them to jump. The view from the outside was always sunnier than the view from the middle.

'Tom, what I have isn't life. Not a real life. I'm doing this for your own good. One day, with a good education under your belt, you'll thank me—'

'My entire arse!' said Tom. 'I could have fifty PhDs and that still wouldn't stop some Crosses from looking at me and seeing nothing but a blanker.'

'Then you out-argue them, out-think them, outsmart them,' I told him. 'A proper education gives you all the tools you'll ever need to do exactly that. Do it for you, not to please others.'

'Then how come I have to go to college to please you? It's not how I want to spend the next few years. I want to work for you.'

'Stop deluding yourself, Tom. You are not cut out for this life.' God knows I loved my brother, but he was seriously doing my head in.

'How d'you know? You won't even give me a chance—'

'Could you rough up some old woman who owes me money, or put a gun to someone's head and pull the trigger if necessary? You reckon you could do that, do you?' I asked deliberately. 'Or how about pulling a ten-year stretch minimum because you got caught burying a body or someone grassed you up? How d'you fancy staring at four walls, day in, day out, year in, year out. You could do that too, yeah?'

'I . . . I . . .'

'Exactly. Tom, keep your arse at college, d'you hear me? If you drop out, don't expect to see a single penny from me ever again. I'm not bluffing. I'm doing this for your own good and one day you'll see that. Now get out.'

My brother left the study, slamming the door behind him. The noise went straight through my head, amplifying my headache by several degrees.

Thanks, Thomas.

Proof, if any were required, that my brother was as young as he looked.

NOW

That was close. Too close.

One of Eva's minions actually opened fire like they thought they were in some mobster movie or something. Desperate or what? And totally lacking in class. Plus the bullet damn near took my ear off. It came that close. And as for me backing into the industrial bin like that . . . Stupid or what? I should've turned and walked away and no one would've been any the wiser. I could've been in that alleyway for any number of reasons: throwing up, taking a leak, looking for a dropped wallet. Mind you, they might've insisted on seeing some ID. And what if my name is already known to them?

Which leads to the question: what did Hedda tell them?

Obviously enough for them to deem me a threat – which is not good. And they both saw my face – which is even worse. They may not know my name and address, but, with a detailed description and all their connections, it won't take them long to track me down.

I've been scanning the news channels on my phone ever since the incident to see how it was reported. Was the shootout filmed on someone's phone? If so, did that person capture my face on their footage? I haven't seen anything on any news reports yet, so that works in my favour. The worst thing I could do now is panic. Panic gets you killed. All this means is I need to move faster than originally planned. I already have my to-do list.

And the new time frame? Less than twenty-four hours. Time to get to work.

Daily Shouter Online

Home. News. Politics. Celebs. Entertainment. Sport. Tech. Health. Science. Money. More.

BREAKING NEWS. Nought Lives Matter officially classified as a political party

Nought Lives Matter (NLM) has officially been declared a political party rather than a protest movement, allowing the government to block any future marches, fund-raising drives and advertising, as there are strict rules governing the way political parties conduct their activities.

'Last year's destructive protests showed the NLM's true colours. They are nothing but a group of looting, rioting thugs seeking to overthrow the legitimately elected government,' said Robert Lee, MP. 'It is absolutely right and proper that they should be labelled and seen for exactly what they are – a subversive, minority political party, intent on destruction and anarchy.'

Sharon Silver, an NLM spokeswoman, told the *Daily Shouter*, 'This is a despicable manoeuvre. The government knows full well that the NLM is a peaceful protest group made up of Noughts, Crosses and all right-minded citizens worldwide who despise bigotry and injustice. We have already offered proof that other groups with different agendas hijacked our peaceful demonstration. We in the NLM march for the right to hold the police accountable when they act unlawfully and to protest against systemic racism, which ultimately has consequences for us all. The government believes that, by labelling us a political party, they will be better able to control and ultimately silence us. It won't work. What is right, what is morally just, cannot be silenced or kept in the shadows. There is no stronger spotlight than the truth.'

THEN

Dan's Inner Party

fourteen. Sephy Ealing

A knock, then the study door immediately opened and Sephy Ealing swept in and strode up to my desk. She didn't waste time getting to the point either.

'Dan, why did you invite me to this . . . this farce?' She looked ready to breathe fire and burn me to a crisp.

'Farce?'

'I've introduced myself and spoken to all your friends. Quite frankly, I have more in common with George than any of your guests, so why am I here?'

I sighed inwardly. Yet another interruption. Hopefully this would be the last one. Once Sephy left, I had one more phone call to make and then I'd head back to my guests for my big reveal. It was finally time.

'Sephy, I invited you here because I'll be making an announcement after dinner and I wanted you to hear it,' I replied.

'As we're neither kin nor company, why on earth would I want to hear anything you have to say?'

'Because it will affect you directly. You and all the others here tonight have that in common.'

'Oh please. What do I have in common with your girlfriend—?'

'Ex-girlfriend.'

'Your patronizing, bloodsucking lawyer—?'

'I don't employ parasites with gambling addictions who owe me money—'

'Your wasted friend, Kellan Bruemann—'

'Whose one remaining ambition is to buy back his company from me. Never gonna happen by the way.'

'And your starry-eyed brother who is desperate to follow in your crooked footsteps?'

'Over my cold, dead body.'

Sephy started at my interruptions, rolling as they did over her objections. She looked more confused than ever. 'All right, so what exactly is it I'm supposed to have in common with these people? With Tobey?'

'Ah. An easy one.' I smiled. 'You both love Callie Rose.'

'Pfft! Love is just another weakness for you to exploit, isn't it? What a shame you came back into Tobey's life.' Sephy shook her head. 'Without you, he might've been a decent human being.'

To my surprise, that stung.

Sephy's brows lowered. She looked me up, she looked me down, like I was an arcane puzzle she was trying to solve. 'Dan, enough of your games. How does anything you have to say or do impact on me except negatively?'

I leaned back in my chair, twirling a pen with practised ease between my fingers. Sephy really was something else. She might be a lot of things, but a bootlicking, butt-kissing sycophant wasn't one of them.

'That's what I've always admired about you, Sephy. You don't roll over and play dead.'

'How many more times? That's Mrs Ealing to you.'

A tap at the door and George entered. When he saw I wasn't alone, he said, 'Excuse me, Mr Jeavons. I didn't know you had company.' He tried to retreat, but I beckoned him forward. Sephy's lips tightened, and I loved every second of prolonging her agony. She hated being anywhere near me and I was drawing it out deliberately.

'You know, you must've been quite the looker back in your day,' I said.

Sephy's eyes narrowed.

'You're a bit too mature for my taste though. I like my girls to be a little . . . fresher.'

Sephy made a great show of dry-heaving. She swallowed hard. 'Oh, I'm sorry. I just threw up in my mouth.' She dry-heaved again. 'And again. You are a creep, Daniel Jeavons. Am I supposed to be upset that I'm too old for you? Do me a favour. Can I please leave so I can escape you and your weapons-grade bullshit?'

'No,' I told her.

Behind me, George retrieved a couple of used coffee cups from the bookcase and left without another word. I kept my eyes on Sephy. She made no attempt to hide what she really thought of me. It was almost refreshing. Silence stretched out between us, taut and tense. I raised an eyebrow.

'So, as I said, *Sephy*, I have an announcement to make and I wanted you to hear it.'

'How about a sneak preview so I can go home?'

'And spoil the surprise?' I asked with a smile.

'What if I were to tell you to stuff your dinner party where the sun don't shine and defy you by walking out?'

'I wouldn't recommend that.'

Sephy's dark honey eyes threw continuous daggers my way. 'You deliberately placed me between Owen Dowd and Patrix so that my evening could be as uncomfortable as possible. You love your little games, don't you?'

'I'm sure you've found plenty to talk about,' I said, suppressing a smile.

'Yeah, right. You cast me in the role of perineum for the evening and you expect me to be all chatty?'

A moment, then I burst out laughing. 'Ah, Sephy, it's such a pleasure doing business with you. You have an original outlook. Tell me, which one of them is the arsehole and which the scrotum?'

'I was thinking female not male genitalia,' said Sephy sourly.

My laugh deepened. 'You are too salty. I like it.'

Slowly Sephy shook her head. 'Dan, five years ago, I was cooking something or other in my kitchen, I can't even remember what, and this annoying little fly kept buzzing round me. Tiny thing it was, but so aggravating. I could've ignored it, but I didn't want it landing in my food and contaminating what I was cooking. So I took off one of my slippers and I went after it. I chased that fly round and round my kitchen until I finally cornered it and I thought, *Got you now*. So I whacked at it with my slipper, just as hard as I could. Only I missed the fly and hit the wall with such force that my fingers bent right back and I dislocated one of them. My right index finger.' Sephy held up her hand, then showed it in profile. 'See where it's still crooked? It didn't set straight. Sometimes, when it's really cold, the joint still hurts. And all because I let a tiny fly distract me from what I should've been doing.'

'And I'm the fly, no doubt,' I said with scorn.

'No, you're the slipper,' said Sephy.

My frown was instantaneous. *What?*

Another knock at the door. Jesus wept! George entered without waiting for a response. He was carrying a silver tray on which was a fresh coffee pot, a mug and a cream jug. He placed them on my desk and left.

'Now, where were we?' I said. 'Ah yes, I believe you're about to do as you're told.'

'Screw you, Dan. I have neither the time nor the inclination to play your stupid games. Your minion Jarvis bullied me into attending this nonsense. No one said anything about how long I had to stay. I'm going home. If you've actually got something worthwhile to say, send me a text.' Sephy started to turn round.

'You leave now and Nathan's unfortunate accident could so easily turn out to be . . . infectious.'

Sephy froze. Slowly she turned back to me and, if I thought she'd displayed how much she despised me before, it was nothing to what she was showing me now. This woman was all hatred. The look on her face . . . I couldn't help it – I burst out laughing. Sephy really was so refreshing – a what-you-see-is-what-you-get woman. The best kind.

'I suggest you watch your back around me, you arrogant, murderous toad,' she said.

And, with that, she turned and left the room, my laughter still ringing in her ears.

fifteen. The Night That Would Never End

Even though I'd laughed off Sephy's hostility towards me, when she left the room, so did my laughter. What must it be like to have a woman like her at your side through thick and thin, good times and bad? Someone who'd tell you straight if you were being a dick, but would love you regardless? I'd never had that. Ever. There were women in my life, but they were there for what I could give them and for what I was, not who I was. Would I ever meet a woman who'd love me for me? Who would stick around if I were broke or ill? Someone to come home to? I shook my head. What on earth was I thinking? I'd made my bed and a bloody comfortable one it was too. When you got right down to it, I didn't have anyone permanent in my life because I didn't need anyone. It was as simple as that.

All the interruptions I'd suffered throughout the evening had obviously played on my nerves. My dinner guests were all people who wouldn't spit on me if I were on fire, except perhaps my brother, Tom, and George. For Shaka's sake! Of all the people present in my apartment, the only one who'd stayed out of my study was Jarvis. I was ready to give him a substantial bonus for that alone. The interruptions and the negativity had played merry hell with my mood. I was irritable, tetchy.

No more delays.

It was time to head back to the dining room and make good on my promise to Tobey. There was no way he could silence all those present, even as Prime Minister. I regretted that it had come to this, and that we were about to lose our friendship and decades of shared history, but so be it. I might lose, but at least this way I could ensure that Tobey wouldn't win.

The study door opened. Yet again. This was getting beyond a joke.

'For heaven's sake! You again? What d'you want?'

I watched as the door was closed carefully, quietly. This was turning into the night that would never end.

NOW

sixteen. Sephy

Sleep scares me.

It's got to the point now where my bed is the tangible manifestation of the enemy. I'm dog-tired all the time yet afraid to close my eyes.

I had the same dream again last night. The one I've been having regularly for a while now. I'm standing in an empty space, no people, no birdsong, no greenery. Just soiled grey tarmac beneath my feet and nothing else. The tarmac runs unbroken to the horizon in every direction. I'm at the centre of a deserted world and the loneliness inside swallows me like an ouroboros.

Where am I? I have no idea and yet the place seems so familiar. I turn my head, calling out, 'Hello? Hello?', but no one is there. I can't shake the feeling that there's something – or someone – behind me. Twisting round like a leaf in a gale gets me nowhere. So I stand absolutely still, close my eyes for a moment, then suddenly turn like I used to do as a child when trying to catch out my reflection to prove that it had a life of its own.

Only this time a few metres before me is a scaffold. Callum swings at the end of the rope hanging from it, a black hood over his head. I scream – and scream again.

Save him!

If I can get to him in time, I can prevent his death – hoist him up, cut the rope. Something. I have to save him. I walk, then run towards him – but I never get any nearer. I'm on a treadmill, a road to nowhere. I race until sweat pours from my forehead like a waterfall, stinging my eyes, running like ribbons of salt water between my lips and onto my tongue. My blouse sticks to me like a new plaster. And still I run, until my lungs burn in protest and my vision grows blurry. I'm moments away from passing out. Only then do I stop. My heart shatters like dropped glass because Callum is just as far away as he ever was. I reach out, but it's no use. Slowly my hand drops to my side. In despair, I turn away, and there he is in front of me again, gently swinging, the noose still around his neck. I turn left. He's there. Right. He's there. I turn my back. He's in front of me. I spin round: he's before me. My world view is a kaleidoscope of Callum dying. With tears streaming down my face, I fall to my knees.

'I'm sorry, Callum. I'm so sorry,' I cry. 'Forgive me.'

Without warning, his head jerks up like he's listening.

And I stumble back and scream.

Scream till my ears ring.

Scream myself awake.

And, for the rest of the night, sleep and I are strangers. So I sit on the edge of my bed, staring into the darkness as I rock slowly back and forth. Back and forth.

And remember.

seventeen. Libby

A cough I couldn't suppress woke me up. I was being held, and felt warm and safe, emerging from the most vivid nightmare I'd ever had. How bizarre! I'd dreamed I was stuck in a basement with – I opened my eyes and there was Troy looking down at me, his arm round my shoulder. My head had been tucked into his armpit like a sleeping penguin. With a jolt, I drew away, sitting bolt upright. Awkward! Troy's arm fell to his side. He smiled.

'Feeling better now?'

'What happened?' I asked, confused.

'You cried yourself to sleep.' Troy looked around. 'It feels late, like it's night-time, though it's hard to tell. I miss my watch.'

So not a dream after all.

Troy looked at me, puzzled. 'Are you OK, Libby?'

'Yeah, I—' I pinched the sleep out of my eyes. 'How long was I asleep?'

'Maybe an hour. Maybe longer.' Troy shrugged. 'Does it really matter?'

'I need to use the bucket.' I stood up.

Troy nodded. 'I'll turn my head to give you some privacy.'

'Why aren't you—? Oh.' Before, when one of us needed

to use the bucket, the other had headed for the furthest corner in the opposite direction. But Troy and his messed-up ankle were going nowhere. Having to announce when we wanted to pee or more was mortifying, but it couldn't be helped. It wasn't as if we hadn't used the bucket before, but my shyness about it hadn't faded, not even a little.

I headed towards the corner of the room where the bucket sat. The smell as I got closer grew more pungent. A few more hours and the stench would fill the entire room. Hmm . . . OK, so we were both going to choke to death on noxious fumes before we died of thirst. So many varied ways to perish down here.

'Troy, you should try to get some sleep yourself,' I said.

'Yeah, I think I might,' he said. 'I just didn't want to risk falling asleep with you leaning on me in case we both fell backwards off the crate.'

'Thanks!'

'You're welcome.'

I peed in the bucket, then dried myself off, using one of the last two remaining tissues I had in my trouser pocket. I didn't even want to think about what we'd do after I ran out. All I wanted now was a hot shower and a warm bed and to sleep for a week. But, failing that, I'd settle for what I could get. Even though Troy had turned his face away from my corner, in this sickly half-light I could see by his slumped shoulders and bowed head just how exhausted he was.

'I'm finished,' I announced as if he didn't already know.

'Don't forget to wash your hands – with soap,' said Troy. 'Don't slack.'

'Yeah, I'll get right on that.'

'My turn,' Troy announced. 'But I'll need your help to get there.'

With his arm round my shoulder and some, if not most, of his weight resting on me, we made our slow, painful way to the bucket.

Halfway there and Troy wasn't doing too well. Beads of sweat punctuated his brow like full stops. I asked, 'Troy, d'you mind if I watch?'

He stared at me, shock shaping every muscle in his face. '*What?*'

'D'you mind if I watch?' I asked as we carried on moving.

'Of course I bloody mind! Since when was peeing a spectator sport?' Troy's eyebrows were fast forming a knot.

'It would take our relationship to the next level,' I said.

'What next level? What relationship? Are you high on pee fumes or something?'

We were at the bucket.

'Gotcha!' I winked.

Troy's mouth fell open, then he reluctantly smiled. 'Yeah, OK. Payback for I spy earlier?'

I nodded gleefully. 'Plus it took your mind off your ankle.'

'You think you're slick, don't you?!'

'I know I am.' I laughed. Troy joined in. And for a moment, just for a moment, the sun came out.

'Do you . . . er . . . do you need me to unzip you or something?' My burning face had raised the temperature in the basement by a few degrees.

'No thanks. I can manage,' said Troy dryly.

'Thank God for that.' Leaving Troy leaning over the bucket, with one hand on the wall, I headed over to the far corner.

'Call me when you've finished and I'll help you back to the crate,' I called out.

'Will do.'

'And hit the bucket, not the floor around it,' I told him. 'The last thing either one of us needs right now is to slip on one of your deposits and crack our heads open on the ground.'

'You really are a glass half full kinda girl, aren't you?'

'Are you sure I can't watch you?' I asked, my back to Troy. 'It'll help you to focus if you know you've got an audience.'

'Libby, please take this in the spirit in which it's intended – bugger off.'

'Charming!' I chuckled, but the trouble was, now that I'd joked about watching him, the idea kind of took root in my head. I started to turn my head when I heard the sound of pee hitting the bucket.

Libby, you sad specimen. Don't you dare.

I turned back to the wall like a naughty child, cheeks flaming. Honestly! When he'd finished and had zipped up, Troy called me over.

'D'you think you could manage to sit on the floor with my help?' I asked as we headed back to the crate.

'Why?'

'So we can both get some sleep with no fear of falling off anything,' I said.

Troy nodded. We made our way to the wall closest to the stairs. Troy leaned against it before slowly sliding down, trying to control his descent. I did my best to help, but he waved me away. About twenty centimetres from the ground, his good leg, which had been taking all his weight, gave out and he dropped fast, his bum hitting the ground with a thud. Instantly Troy bit his lip to stop himself from crying out. Eyes closed, his head back, he took several deep breaths before he could even open his eyes again.

'Are you OK? I'm sorry—'

Troy glared at me.

'Oh, I'm sorry. Shit!'

'You just can't help yourself, can you?' said Troy, his voice, like his smile, weak.

I sat down beside him, wrapping my arms round his waist and resting my head on his shoulder.

'Libby?'

'Just for warmth. That OK?'

'Yeah.'

'Night, Troy.'

'It feels like we should be doing more than just trying to sleep.'

'We'll both feel better after a nap and, besides, it'll stop us thinking about being hungry and thirsty.'

'So we'll just dream about food instead – like fried flying fish splashed with lemon juice.'

'A cheeseburger and chips,' I said.

'Jollof rice served with tender, succulent beef and plantain,' said Troy, practically drooling.

'A cheeseburger and chips with tomato ketchup on the side.'

'I'm spotting a pattern here.' I heard rather than saw Troy's attempt at a smile.

'Cheeseburger is the food of the gods.'

'Lesser gods.'

'Nought gods.'

'Let's not get political,' said Troy with a sigh. 'I'm too tired.'

'All right. Let's call it the food of the haute-cuisine gods,' I said, compromising.

'Night, Libby,' said Troy firmly.

I closed my eyes, my smile fading. What Troy and I needed now was a miracle. I'd never believed in them before.

Now was a good time to start.

eighteen. Sephy

I am a Cross woman. More than the cliché of a woman who is always indomitable, never vulnerable. So much more than the stereotype of a woman who is fearless, never afraid. I just try to make sure that I don't live my life in fear; that would be no life at all. But there have been moments when I've silently broken down and cried, when I've seriously wondered if I had the strength to get out of bed in the morning. I guess most women have felt the same at some point – some more, some less. I'm a Cross woman with so many facets to my being that even I haven't discovered them all yet.

Some days I feel I could circumnavigate the planet in three strides max.

But then there are nights like this.

It's the last day of October, three o'clock in the morning, and my brain is ticking like a cheap, old-fashioned watch.

Where's my son?

Callie begged me to leave everything to her and Tobey, and God knows I'm trying, but it's so hard. I can't stop my mind from whirling.

That's my trouble, Callum. I think too much.

Maybe that's the reason for all these nightmares. They haunt me practically every night and I have no idea why. If anything, the bad dreams should've started when Nathan was killed, but that was over two years ago. And surely any nightmares should've been about what happened to him?

But they aren't.

The bad dreams I can just about cope with. Just about. It's the screaming myself awake that's messing with my head. It's the fear of the same nightmare happening night after night that has me too terrified to try and sleep unaided. Instead, I wait till my brain is zombified and zombie-fried enough to just pass out. Luckily for me, Troy's room is on the other side of the house near Meggie's bedroom suite where my outbursts can't be heard. That's one good thing at least.

But I can't go on this way. I'm going to have to seek medical help and soon, before I keel over from fatigue – or stress. In the small hours of the nightmare mornings, sleep mockingly snatches me up, and lifts me high, only to delight in suddenly dropping me. So I sit in the dark and wrap memories round me like a comfort blanket.

And I think.

Too much.

About you and me, Callum. But mostly about you.

D'you remember this photo? The two of us daring to hold hands in public, true happiness in our eyes. My face is in profile and there's more of the back of your head than the front in the picture. It shows the side of your face, though not your eyes, but it doesn't matter. I have the full image in my mind. You and I were at a funfair and you shot down five targets in a row to win a stuffed tiger for me. I was so proud of you. Five targets in a row. I hugged you so tightly as you laughed at my delight, and the stall owner offered to take our photo. How could we say no? But even then you weren't keen on having your picture taken so you turned to me and away from the stall owner at the last moment and ruined it. I printed and kept the photo anyway, and, when you died, I filed it – beneath clothes or books or at the back of the wardrobe. I can't really remember its exact last resting place, but it stayed buried for years.

When Nathan died and I was finally clearing out his things, there was our old photograph, hidden at the back of a drawer where I could've sworn I never put it. Using my smartphone to scan it, the photo became the image on my home screen. It's one of my lifetime favourite memories. In that moment when the photo was taken, we were both happy. Innocently ignorant and truly happy. I'm struggling to remember how that feels.

I swore I wouldn't do this any more: look at your photo and yearn for what might've been. What good does it do? You, the real you, are long gone. I'm talking to a man who is no longer here. You're dead. That's all there is to it.

Except it isn't.

In my heart, you live on, not speaking, never guiding, but always present. Watching. Waiting. You fill all the dark, empty spaces and places within me. Always have done. Nathan knew that. We never spoke about it – but he knew. There's a part of my heart that is yours and yours alone, Callum. That makes me feel so guilty. I loved Nathan – in my way. He knew that too. But it was nothing like the way I loved ... love you, Callum. You and I – we were beyond breath, beyond body, beyond reason. You and I were ... I can't think of a word big enough, wide enough, deep enough. Or maybe I can. We were ... love.

I miss you so much. Even after all these years, I miss you.

Falling in love with you was the easy part. Being in love with you? That's what tore my heart to shreds. If you had lived, would we still be together? Would we have faced all the enmity and adversity the world could throw at us and emerged bloody but unbowed, or would this world have found a way to drive an insurmountable wedge between us? I wonder about that. A lot.

But d'you want to know the strange thing? On this unkind October early morning, I've never felt closer to you. Perhaps it's fitting that it should be the festival night that Noughts call Halloween because it feels like, if I were to turn my head slightly, I'd see you sitting on the bed right behind me. It's as if you're out of sight, out of reach – but only just.

Wistful thinking?

Or wishful thinking?

Callum, the world has grown older and colder since we were together. Our daughter is in trouble and my son, Troy, is missing – and I don't know what to do about either. I want to scream, but I'm afraid that if I start I won't be able to stop because I can't help thinking that I somehow brought all this down on my children. I'm responsible for this. I thought I could take care of Dan Jeavons. Callie and Troy are both paying for that mistake.

Welcome to Karma Café. Sit anywhere you like. There is no menu. You get what you deserve.

The thing is, though I might deserve this, my children don't. Was my card marked from the day you died, Callum? I should've done more to help you. I should've shouted longer and louder. I should've done something, *anything*, to save your life. Except lose Callie Rose. I couldn't do that. Did you understand and forgive me for that, Callum, or did you die hating me? I know what you wrote in your second letter, that you loved me, that you would always love me, but I can't help but wonder about your thoughts in those final moments before death. I would understand if you blamed me, hated me, but I couldn't sacrifice our daughter to keep you alive, I just couldn't. She is the best of both of us, our hope for the future. I loved you so much, so how could I extinguish a part of you, any part of you? I wasn't strong enough to do that. Callum, she's so beautiful and smart. She's a fighter. You'd be so proud of her. Maybe you already are? My children are my world. I can't imagine my life without either of them in it.

But I will go to my grave wondering if I could've saved you. D'you know what my epitaph will be?

HERE LIES PERSEPHONE MIRA HADLEY.

SHE NEVER DID ENOUGH.

That's so telling, isn't it? I think of myself as Sephy Hadley, not Sephy Ealing. Inside, I'm still the young woman who watched her lover hang because of her. Well, I swear no one else is going to suffer because of me.

Callum, my children are in trouble. That weasel Tobias Durbridge is behind it, of course. I *despise* that man. If it weren't for him, our daughter would never have been shot. I've tried, but I just can't bring myself to forgive him for that. I held my tongue because Callie obviously felt more for him than he was worth. If ever there were a time-sink, useless construction project, it's that hollow excuse for a man. When it looked like their friendship had ended, that was one of the happiest days of my life. From the time he was knee-high, Tobey has been nothing but a giant pain in my backside. Always encouraging Callie to get up to all sorts. When they were kids, I could guarantee that, if Callie got into trouble, somewhere, somehow, Tobey would be behind it – lurking in the shadows and letting my daughter clean up his mess. Only this time the world of hurt we're in is on a whole new boss level.

God only knows what state Troy and Liberty are in now.

No! My son isn't dead. I'd know if he were dead. I'd *feel* it. Somehow, somewhere, he's still alive. Desperate. Terrified. But still alive. Still breathing. But for how much longer?

So here I sit, feeling grey and useless – and I pray. It seems like the only time I manage to do so is when death is knocking at the door of me and mine. I'm praying like I haven't in a long, long time that the kidnappers won't kill my son and Tobey's daughter outright, but will try to get Callie to see reason and dump Tobey's sorry arse.

Now that he's had more than a taste of power, he'll never give it up. Not for anyone. Power is addictive. Worse than alcohol, gambling and drugs combined. One taste is never enough. No sacrifice is too much. That's where Tobey's at now. I can see it in his eyes in every news bulletin or poster that features him. That lean, hungry look he can't quite disguise, no matter how hard he tries. I recognize it because I grew up with it. I saw it every day on the face of my father. Kamal Hadley was a politician first, last and every ladder rung in between. He let nothing and no one into his life that didn't serve his ambition. It was all about the optics. He had to be a family man because, back in the day, having a family played better in the world of politics than being single. He had to be independently wealthy because then he could sell the dream that anyone could have as much as him if only they worked hard enough. He had to turn his back on me to appease those Crosses who believed that Noughts were a subspecies. Tobey's agenda may be different to my dad's, but the result will be the same. His life, his world will chew up and spit out anyone who wasn't born with titanium armour surrounding their heart.

So what happens now?

Callie and Tobey are working together to try and find the kids – before it's too late. I'm trying so hard to hold on to hope, but the passing of time has taught me that hope flies on the finest of gossamer wings. Cling to it too hard and it's so easy to crush. Handle it too lightly and it darts away, then one blink and it's gone.

Oh, Callum, it's so strange. I don't believe in life after death. Yet sometimes, when it's late at night and I'm lying in the dark, I stretch out my arm, curl my fingers and pretend that you're lying next to me, holding my hand. Not Nathan. You.

The thought comforts me.

The feeling shames me.

How is this going to end, Callum?

How is this going to end?

The stillness of the cold night air was my duvet, memories were my pillows and, to be honest, I found it all soothing. So much so that I jumped when my mobile on the bedside table unexpectedly began to ring. Swinging my legs out of bed, I sighed when I saw the caller ID. If I didn't answer, she wouldn't give up. I accepted the call.

'Sephy.'

'What the hell, Minnie? You know what time it is, right?'

'Yes, but I wanted to be sure you wouldn't be too busy to pick up.'

'Is everything OK?' I asked my sister.

'I could ask you the same thing,' she sniffed. 'This is the third time today that I've tried phoning you. Why haven't you phoned me back?'

'I've been busy, Minerva.'

'What's going on?'

'Nothing, except me trying to get some sleep and you getting in the way of that,' I replied.

'Sephy, I know you. What are you not telling me?'

'Minerva, I haven't got time for your nonsense at the moment. I'll phone you at the weekend, OK? Bye.'

I disconnected the call. Almost immediately, my mobile started to ring again. I was all set to give my sister a blue mouthful when I saw it wasn't her.

I accepted the video call before it could vibrate a third time.

'Callie, are you all right? Have you heard anything? Troy?'

'No, not yet, Mum. Did I wake you?'

'No,' I said, sighing.

'I couldn't sleep either.' Callie echoed my sigh. 'I'm sorry to phone at this early hour, but I needed to talk to you.'

'That's OK, love. I'm always happy to talk with you. Just a sec.' I settled myself on the edge of the bed. My poor daughter. She sat, shoulders slumped, eyes red, mouth cast down. She looked like she hadn't slept in days rather than hours. 'I take it you haven't heard anything from the kidnappers?'

'No. Not a word.' Callie sighed again. 'I'm assuming you haven't either.'

I shook my head, admitting, 'This waiting around to hear from them is killing me.'

'Oh, Mum, don't say that. We'll get Troy back. You'll see.'

'Waiting twenty-four hours before calling in the police is a long time, Callie. I'd hate for it to turn into a lifetime.'

'Mum, I have faith in Tobey. I do. His daughter is missing as well, and he's a politician with connections. Can we trust him for just a few more hours? Please?'

I immediately felt contrite. Callie had her own worries to carry without loading my doubts about Tobey onto her back as well. I forced a smile, hoping it would help to honey-coat my words. 'Of course, but I'll do it for your sake – and Troy's – not his. Has Tobey heard anything?'

'Not that he's said, but, Mum ...'

'Yes?'

'He did tell me something else though ...'

Uh-oh ... Callie chewed at the corner of her bottom lip, a sure sign that I wasn't going to enjoy what came next.

'What did he tell you?' I said, bracing myself.

'Never mind. It doesn't matter. I shouldn't have mentioned it,' she said. 'I'm thinking that if we haven't heard from the kidnappers by midnight tonight we should definitely go to the police.'

'Callie, don't change the subject. You know that doesn't work with me. What did Tobey tell you?'

Silence.

'Callie Rose, spit it out,' I said, beyond exasperated.

'He said ... he said he had proof that you ... killed Dan.'

What the—? 'What kind of proof?'

'Look, Mum, I'm sorry I spo—'

'What proof?'

Pause.

'The letter opener used to kill him,' Callie whispered, though I knew she was alone. 'Tobey says your fingerprints are all over it. He says he took it and used an ornamental knife on Dan's desk to mask the original stab wound. In fact, his fingerprints on that knife are a major part of the reason why the police arrested him in the first place.'

'Son. Of. A. Bitch.' The words could barely escape my gritted teeth.

'It's not true, is it, Mum?'

'Callie, you listen to me. Whatever Tobey has, or thinks he has, I didn't kill Dan. It's important to me that you believe—'

'Of course I believe you. I argued as much when Tobey tried to insist you had something to do with Dan's murder,' Callie interjected. 'You're my mum. You wouldn't hurt a fly.'

Yeah? She should see me with a can of bug spray. Plus my never fully healed crooked finger shouted otherwise.

'Honey, if anyone tried to harm you or Troy, and I had to choose between them or you, they would lose – big time. But that doesn't change the fact that I did not murder Dan Jeavons. Wait a minute? Is that . . . is that the reason you're defending Tobey on this murder charge? Did he blackmail you into it or something?'

'Maybe I just believe in his innocence?'

'Callie Rose, this is your mother you're talking to. Don't bullshit me.'

'I'm sorry, Mum.' Callie sighed. 'It's just . . . it's been difficult.'

I bet. If Callie thought I didn't notice that she still hadn't answered my question, then she was mistaken. Tobey Durbridge was coercing my daughter into defending him. I'd put money on it. Just when I thought I'd run out of ways to despise that man, he found whole new avenues for me to explore. I wasn't a vindictive woman, but I was quite prepared to make an exception in his case.

'Mum, in all fairness to Tobey, he did tell me to recuse myself as his lawyer and walk away, but I wasn't prepared to do that.'

'Why not?'

'Old times' sake.'

Give me a break. 'What about new times?' I asked.

'Those too, I suppose,' said Callie.

A horrifying thought occurred to me. 'Are you and Tobey back together again?'

'No, Mum. Tobey and I are just working together to get Troy and Libby back home and that's all,' said Callie.

Which was some of the story, but not all of it. Callie should know better than to underestimate me.

'And I take it Tobey still has the letter opener?'

Pause. 'I think so.'

I *knew* so. And he'd keep it for as long as it was useful to him. The letter opener was his escape route from a murder charge. Tobey had me painted into a corner.

'That man is a piece of work,' I fumed. 'The only way to save him now would be for him to lose everything and I mean *everything*, but that's never going to happen.'

'What good would that do?'

'He could start rebuilding himself from the ground up as a decent human being.'

'Mum, don't stress. I can handle Tobey,' Callie insisted.

But could she? I sighed inwardly. 'Honey, I think we should both try to get some sleep or at least a nap. Something tells me that, when the day begins, it's going to be a long one.'

'Mum, are you all right?'

'Of course, darling. I'm fine. Or I will be when Troy is safely home.'

'I think we should both try to think about other things,' said Callie. 'Worrying won't help the situation.'

Like that was going to happen for either of us.

'We'll talk later, Callie. I love you.'

'I love you too, Mum. Very much.'

'Bye, love.' I disconnected the call.

Think about other things . . . ? Like what?

Oh, Callum, all I have in this world that I care about are Callie, Troy and Meggie. I'm even beginning to wonder why I'm clinging on so hard to my restaurant. Maybe it's because it's the last part of Nathan I have. Everything else has been taken away. But, if I close the chapter on Specimens, maybe a new chapter could begin? Guess what, Callum? Sonny has asked me to marry him. Isn't that something? I'm still trying to figure out what kind of something that is, but it's definitely something. I genuinely believed that there was nothing between us but friendship, like well-worn but still cosy slippers. I had no idea he still thought and felt about me that way. Isn't that something?! He asked for my answer and I asked for time to think about it. It's a big step. Colossal. I genuinely wasn't looking to get hitched again.

So what do I do?

If you'd ever asked me to marry you, the sentence wouldn't

have had time to get cold as it passed your lips before I said yes. And, with Nathan, it seemed the right thing to do at the time. Nathan and I didn't share the furnace of emotions that you and I did, Callum, but I think that was part of the reason I said yes to him. He was . . . restful. Solid. I don't mean he was boring – far from it. But I could relax with him. I could talk about music and art and politics and *living* without explanation or prevarication or apology. I didn't have to edit my thoughts or line up my words like naked, disarmed soldiers. There were no arguments about proper food seasoning! D'you remember those, Callum? The way you loved your food so damned hot that two mouthfuls were guaranteed to make my eyes water and my tongue catch fire. As for me, I always argued that good food seasoning didn't begin and end with curry powder and Scotch bonnet pepper sauce. Nathan and I didn't like overly spicy food, just well seasoned. Sonny reminds me of you, Callum, in a number of ways – but is that number enough? I don't know.

Callum, I still don't know what my final answer to Sonny will be. I want to make sure that, if I say yes, it isn't out of a sense of nostalgia. Does that make sense?

Do I love Sonny?

He was in my life when I really needed a friend.

But do I love him?

He loves me. That means a lot. I want to be loved. Maybe it's time to let you go, Callum. Pack up the past and put it away in a box labelled WITH ETERNAL LOVE.

Sonny makes me laugh. He's good to me. He won't ever let me down. So that's lots of reasons to marry him – right?

But do I love him?

The question echoes in my head, unanswered.

Another thing that's giving me pause is the business between Sonny and Troy. I mean, why would Troy accuse Sonny of complicity in Nathan's death? Why would he do that? As a joke? To deliberately throw a grenade between Sonny and me?

No, because Troy isn't like that. So why would he say such a thing unless he truly believed it? Sonny reckoned that Troy saw the Whitman Scorpius in the quarry on his land and put two and two together to make thirty-three and a third. A dark blue Scorpius killed his dad so the first same-coloured Scorpius Troy saw after that had to be the car that mowed down Nathan. Sonny reckoned that we just needed to give Troy some time to figure out for himself how ludicrous his accusations were. I'm prepared to do that.

I know Sonny. He couldn't and wouldn't harm anyone, much less mow someone down and flee like that. But I also know my son. Troy doesn't make stuff up and he doesn't let his imagination grab his hand and drag him all over the place.

Maybe . . . when Troy is found safe and well, I think it'll be time for Sonny and me to set a date for our wedding. It'll be by way of a double celebration. I like Sonny and he needs me. He's lonely. So am I. We'll be good for each other. You do see that, don't you?

Just give me a sign, any sign, Callum, that I'm doing the right thing.

Daily Shouter Online

Home. News. Politics. Celebs. Entertainment. Sport. Tech. Health. Science. Money. More.

BREAKING NEWS. Julliard claims general election was lost due to 'irregularities'

Mansa Julliard, leader of the Liberal Traditionalists and ex-Prime Minister, has called for a judicial review into 'irregularities' that occurred during the counting of votes in the recent general election, which she and her party lost.

'It is inconceivable that the people of this country would elect a man whose personal life and professional record have been in such a constant state of disarray,' said Julliard. 'We have evidence of several thousand votes cast in the names of deceased people in a number of key areas, including central London. The final result of the general election should be suspended until this matter is resolved.'

A spokesperson for the Democratic Alliance told the *Daily Shouter*, 'The Liberal Traditionalists won't admit that they lost and are brainwashing their supporters into believing that they were robbed of an election victory. This is not just undermining the judicial system in Albion, but democracy itself. Their rhetoric ensures that every election result from now on is questioned, doubted or ignored.'

I had just finished getting dressed after a quick shower when the phone inside my trouser pocket began to vibrate in a particular pattern. I took it out to check the alert. The tiny security camera above my front door was doing its job and alerting me to the presence of two people on my front-door step. Problem. It was the same two people who had cornered me in my car and tried to use me for target practice in the middle of a busy street late last night. Damn it! Well, they hadn't wasted any time. I turned up the volume of the external camera to hear what they were saying.

'. . . is in there. There's a light on upstairs. Go round the back in case it's him and he tries to make a break for it.' The brunette with her drawn-on eyebrows spoke, her voice low and grating.

'And if he does?' asked the blond man standing next to her.

She glared at her colleague for asking a stupid question. 'We have our orders.'

The guy set off at once, climbing over my side gate and out of sight of the camera to get to the back. The woman broke out a lockpick and a tension wrench and started fiddling with my front-door lock.

I pushed the phone back into my pocket. Time to make tracks. Flipping up the mattress, I pulled out the small metal case I had secreted beneath it. Spinning the numbered wheels of the combination lock, I clicked the case open and took out its contents – a fully loaded Glock 17 TB semi-automatic handgun and a suppressor, what used to be called a silencer. Screwing on the suppressor, I moved to switch off the bedroom light, then squatted down at the top of the stairs.

A tinkle of glass sounded from the kitchen. The blond arsehole had broken the window in my back door to get in. The scratching at the front door grew more urgent, then stopped as it clicked open. So much for my door lock – I'd been assured that was state of the art. State of the arse, more like. The brunette took a step into my house, her burglary tools replaced by a handgun. Silhouetted against the lamp almost directly outside my house, I had a better view of her than she had of me. Without hesitation, I opened fire. Three shots in quick succession – two to the body, one to the head. She pitched forward and hit the ground without a word. Her blood was going to ruin my beechwood floors. Blood was a bitch to get off a floor like that when it seeped into the joints.

Footsteps came running from the kitchen. I bunny-hopped to one side of the stairs. The blond guy paused momentarily when he saw his colleague lying face down on the ground. He gasped, then turned and charged up the stairs. Another three shots in quick succession. I lit him up. This fool had it coming. What was charging up the stairs meant to do? Put me off?! And his blood was going to ruin my oatmeal-coloured stair carpet.

So much for packing up a few belongings and getting the hell out. Time for a truncated plan A. Just go.

Gun still poised, I stepped over the body on my stairs and the one in my hall and closed the front door from my neighbours' prying eyes. I lived alone and owed my time and allegiance to no one – and I'd never been more grateful for that. I pulled first the woman's body then the man's into the downstairs toilet, piling one on top of the other. There! If anyone looked through the letterbox, their bodies wouldn't be immediately obvious. I spared about two more seconds of thought to cleaning the hall and my stair carpet, but what was the point? After I found Libby and Troy, I'd be on a plane to somewhere lush and green, with no extradition treaty with Albion, less than twenty-four hours later. I was never going to come back to this house, so let it smell and let the bodies fester. Not that they would do for long with the plan I had in mind. There was one last task to take care of in my garage and then this place was history.

How on earth had Eva's minions found me so quickly? There must've been a camera in the alleyway that I hadn't spotted, which helped them to identify me. Honestly! You couldn't walk anywhere in any city in Albion without some camera or other tracking and recording every move. So damned intrusive.

Once I had finished in my garage, I hopped into what had been my ex-wife's old car and drove off into dawn's early light, my mind racing. I had one more card to play, but it was a good one. If my plan panned out, I'd have Troy and Libby at my mercy before noon. Now was not the time to bolt or panic. If I kept it together, by this time tomorrow, I'll be Mansa Musa rich – courtesy of Tobias Durbridge.

And it couldn't happen to a nicer guy.

nineteen. Tobey

I stood at my tenth-floor bedroom window, looking out at all the mistakes I'd made and all the regrets to which they'd given birth from the time Callie and I first met.

It'd been a long night, but it was a longer list.

The buildings surrounding me stood in silent judgement, so I turned my gaze upwards to the purple-blue wash of sky being slowly softened by dawn's glow. Ha! I should've been a poet! Or maybe a musician. I used to play the keyboard, got quite good at it too. But no, none of those held the pull of politics. I actually entered this game truly believing I could do some good, make a difference. That's the reason I fought so hard to become Mayor of Meadowview. And when I finally made it? What a frustrating shock to find that any clout I had was strictly rationed and carefully controlled. I'd had to learn to play the game quick, fast and in a hurry to fight for more, or I would've been left out in the cold along with all those I was fighting for.

But, somewhere along the way, I'd lost sight of all those people who had put me in office. They became... irrelevant – except around voting time. Until it got to the point where I genuinely believed I didn't need them any more. Power required money, so I did what I had to do to acquire it. I'd quickly learned that where money was concerned there was no such thing as enough or too much. The things I'd instigated over the years, the wheels I'd set in motion, not giving a damn who those selfsame wheels were going to roll over and crush. I'd climbed higher and higher, discarding all those who had hoisted me up in the hope that I'd take them with me.

The phone in my trouser pocket vibrated once. Another news alert. I had my phone set to pick up notifications from all the major news channels worldwide. One of my ways of keeping my finger firmly on the pulse.

The last few hours had been a rollercoaster ride – and it still wasn't over. My head had been wrung and spun, and yet the world kept turning, and others got on with their lives, oblivious to how desperately hard I was trying to hang on to mine. My phone vibrated with regular irregularity, notifying me of the latest breaking story, the most recent nationwide event making the news, yet, uncharacteristically for me, it stayed in my pocket. What was I so afraid of? Missing a news item that might affect me or watching the world turn without me?

Here I was, looking out over the cityscape with the dawn creeping up like a thief. And I was watching it alone. Who did I have to share it with? No one. Who even gave a damn about me? I hadn't seen my mum and my sister, Jessica, in person in almost a year. Virtual face-to-face calls over the computer or my smartphone were as close as I'd come to them in too long. What was my answer to their every dinner or outing invitation? *I'm too busy, I can't get away, I have matters of state to attend to*. All excuses.

Here's the thing. Mum and Jessica made me . . . uncomfortable. There, I've admitted it. My family were a constant reminder of where I came from. Not the fact that I was born in Meadowview – I was proud of that. No, my sister and my mum were born in Meadowview and would die there, and they had no problem with that. Their lack of ambition irritated me. Embarrassed me, if I were honest. Too many times I'd offered both of them a way out of the area and their comfort-zone lives. They'd both turned me down, again and again, until I'd stopped asking.

So here I was.

My friends were few.

My true friends were fewer.

And the woman I had once killed for, and would gladly die for, hated my guts.

So come and greet me, dawn. I have an unwavering, ominous feeling that the next twenty-four hours are going to determine the course of the rest of my life.

Time to make a call from my burner phone. The first couple of times, the call went through to voicemail. It was only on the third attempt that it was accepted. 'Jarvis, it's me. What the hell is going on? Why didn't you answer the first time?'

'Tobey, Eva has forbidden any and all communication with you. It's generally accepted around here that you killed Dan, and Eva has made it very clear that you are no longer a part of the Outfit so I had to find some place private to speak to you. You don't have many friends left in the organization. Scratch that. You don't have *any* friends.'

Oh, so it was like that, was it? Well played, Eva. The woman was leaving me with decreasing room to manoeuvre.

'Including you?'

'Since Eva demoted me, you and I share the same boat,' said Jarvis sourly. 'Shane "the Weasel" Stoats is her new lieutenant and that leaves me nowhere. No one wants to be seen with me in case getting demoted is infectious. One way or another, my days are numbered.'

'What d'you intend to do about that?'

'Nothing – for the moment,' said Jarvis. 'Anyway, why're you phoning me? I thought we agreed you wouldn't for a while.'

'I need your help,' I admitted.

'No way. Forget it. I can't do any favours for you, not if I want to keep all my limbs attached. Eva doesn't trust me as it is,' said Jarvis.

'I wouldn't be contacting you if it wasn't essential.'

'What d'you want? And make it fast.'

All right then. 'What can you tell me about the kidnapping of two teens from Heathcroft High within the past twenty-four hours?'

'Two teens? Who are they?'

'Liberty Jackman and Troy Ealing.'

'Never heard of them.' Jarvis's response was immediate.

'Liberty Jackman is my daughter,' I said.

'Your *what*? You have a daughter now? When did that happen?'

I wasn't getting into it. 'Seventeen years ago. So you haven't heard anything at all?'

'Not a word. If this was some opportunist scratching for pennies, I would've had the full cast list by now.'

'That's what I'd figured, which means only one thing—'

'Eva or Owen Dowd planned the whole operation.' Jarvis got there quickly.

I had too.

'I can understand why you kept your daughter a secret, but if either Dowd or Eva knows about her, and is responsible for her disappearance, the chances are slim to none of seeing her again,' said Jarvis.

Not what I wanted to hear. At all.

'Thank you. I'd already worked that out,' I snapped. 'Whoever it was, they'll keep her alive till they get what they want.'

'Which is?'

'My destruction . . . They want me to announce to the world that I murdered Dan. Someone is moving heaven and earth to get me out of the way.'

'Damn. OK, I'll ask around. If I manage to get some intel, I'll phone you. Don't contact me again.'

And, with that, the call was disconnected. I glowered, but understood the caution. No one within the Outfit knew Jarvis reported directly to me. Not even Dan had known, which had proved incredibly useful over the years. Jarvis was a mean bastard who got up to all kinds of dodgy shit, but he was no fool. His loyalty belonged to me, bought and paid for. It was time to set more wheels in motion.

And, if they rolled over and crushed everything and everyone in their path, then so be it.

twenty. Sephy

'Morning, Jonny. It's Sephy Ealing, Callie's mum. Hi and all that. I need a favour.'

'What the hell, Sephy?! D'you have any idea what time it is?'

'Early. My apologies for disturbing you at this hour, but I really need your help.'

'For Shaka's sake. With what?'

Jon Duba didn't sound the least bit pleased to hear from me, and I couldn't blame him, but desperate times called for desperate, all-hours measures. Callie's investigator and I had met on a number of occasions and always greeted each other like old friends. He was one of the few people in Callie's world that I had any time for. He was an outrageous flirt, highly intelligent, and could always make me smile, but damn, he was grumpy this morning.

'Jon, I know you're aware of what's going on with Troy and Tobey Durbridge's daughter. Callie told me you're helping her to bring them home safely.'

'I don't have any progress to report yet, Sephy, if that's why you're phoning me. You've got to give me a chance to do my thing.'

'I know. I'm not phoning about that.' I sighed deeply. 'Jon,

I need you to look out for my daughter. She's relying too much for my liking on Tobey Durbridge. I trust that man about as far as I can pick up and throw a monster truck.'

'Oh, I see,' said Jon, somewhat mollified. 'And what d'you think I can do?'

'Just keep an eye on her, please. Don't let her get swept away by Tobey's smooth-talking façade. That guy is high on his own supply and where he goes trouble follows. I don't want Callie to be left spinning in his wake. So I need you to be the voice of reason when it comes to that man. Callie trusts your judgement.'

'Your daughter has it bad where Tobey's concerned. Has done for years.'

I frowned. 'How would you know that?'

'I have my ways,' said Jon enigmatically. 'Sephy, I'll do my best, but I can't guarantee anything. As long as you know that.'

'Your best is good enough for me,' I told him. 'Just . . . don't let her make a fool of herself over Tobey. He can't be trusted.'

'I hear that. Sephy, I—'

Pause. Jon had something on his mind. I could hear it in his voice.

'Jon?' I prompted.

'You didn't hear this from me, OK?' Jon began. 'Sephy, I have it on good authority that the CPS are close to dropping all charges against Tobey.'

'Based on what logic?' I frowned.

'Not logic. Power. He's the PM. The country is in turmoil, with more threats from the Arctic Rim on the horizon and heading our way. Fast. Without him, there's a power vacuum, so there's very real talk about dropping the charges so he can get back to business.'

'What about my son?' I protested.

'Only a handful of people know about Troy and Libby's predicament. Troy's kidnappers may want Durbridge gone, but the CPS are already lining up the sin-eater who will take the rap for Durbridge instead.'

His words hit like a clenched fist to my stomach. 'You mean me, don't you? I'm being set up to take the fall for Tobey?'

'Seph, the police received an anonymous tip-off that Tobey has the real murder weapon. They know both of Dan's wounds were made with a letter opener and they've been told that your fingerprints are on it.'

'No, they aren't because I—' I bit my lip. I almost blurted out that I'd wiped my fingerprints off the letter opener, but caught myself in time. I could just imagine how that would sound to Jon – like a bona fide confession that I killed Dan. 'Because I didn't kill Dan,' I finished weakly. Another thought struck me round the face. What if, in my panic, I didn't manage to wipe off *all* my fingerprints?

'How d'you know about the tip-off?'

'A friend in high places within the police service – and I believe him.'

Calm down, Sephy. Take a breath.

'Has Tobey handed the weapon over yet?'

'No, but the police will come knocking at his door within the next twenty-four hours, demanding that he hand it over and any other evidence he may have. If he doesn't, he'll be arrested for obstructing justice and this time the charge will stick,' said Jon. 'When push comes to shove, he'll give up the murder weapon and the recording he has of you – both of which are pretty damning.'

'What recording?' I asked sharply.

'The one of you standing behind Dan's slumped body with the murder weapon in your hand. Which one d'you think I'm talking about?' said Jon.

Oh. My. God. There was a recording of me in Dan's study? And Tobey had it? Why didn't Callie tell me? No wonder she'd been so upset. 'Damn it.'

'You don't know about the recording?' asked Jon, aghast. 'I'm sorry. I thought Callie would've told you about that too. Me and my big mouth.'

'It must've slipped my daughter's mind,' I said furiously.

'Well, please don't tell her that you got it from me or she'll kick my arse,' Jon pleaded.

'Tell me about this recording,' I ordered.

'Not much more to say about it really. As I understand, it shows you plunging the letter opener into Dan's back.'

'I didn't do it, Jon,' I protested. 'I thought it was one of Dan's stupid games so took the knife out of his back, then realized it wasn't so I put it back in a panic.' In my rush to explain, my actions sounded ludicrous, even to my own ears. It was the first time I'd admitted to anyone but myself what I'd done.

'If that's all the recording shows, then hopefully you have nothing to worry about,' said Jon.

Yeah, right. No two ways about it: I was up to my armpits in alligators.

'Why didn't Callie tell me?'

'You'll have to ask her that, but I'd rather you didn't,' said Jon. 'She'll know it was me who gave the game away.'

I said, stricken, 'So, if I've got this right, I have less than twenty-four hours to prove that Tobey murdered Dan or to find the real killer, or I'll be the one banged up for it.'

Pause.

'I must admit that's how it looks from where I'm standing,' said Jon.

The view was the same from my position. 'And you didn't think to warn me, my friend?' I asked. 'Suppose I hadn't phoned you?'

'I've only just had it confirmed, plus I'm going to do my damnedest to find out the truth too,' said Jon. 'I'm already on it. Sephy, trust me. You and Callie are the closest thing I have to family. I won't let you down.'

'I appreciate that, Jon, but you'll forgive me if I take my fate into my own hands.'

'Uh-oh. I'm not loving the sound of this.'

'Jon, I need you to send me the home and email addresses and phone numbers of all those who attended Dan's dinner party on the night he died. As Tobey's lawyer, Callie must have them.'

'Er, you do know that's classified information, right? If I give that data to you, both Callie and I could get into some seriously serious trouble.'

'Not if no one knows I have it. I won't be skywriting about it any time soon.'

'Sephy, I really don't think this is a good—'

'Please, Jon. I wouldn't ask if it wasn't vital.'

'Why don't you ask Callie?' Jon asked.

How to answer that? 'D'you want the truth?'

'Always.'

'Because she'd say no.'

'Which is what I'm going to say too,' said Jon.

'Look, I'm desperate and you're my only hope. Please.'

'You're not thinking of doing something stupid, are you?'

'You know me better than that. So will you send me the information?'

Pause. 'No one is to know you got it from me, OK? Including Callie.'

'It's a deal. I owe you one.'

'You're damned right you do.'

'And I don't suppose you could send me everyone's current location?'

'How on earth could I do that?'

'Oh, come on! We both know you can use their mobile phones to track people's whereabouts. Callie told me that you're an expert at that. You do it all the time.'

'Callie talks too much.'

'That's debatable. Jon, I'd really appreciate it.'

'D'you want my inside-leg measurement as well?'

'Hard pass on that. Just the stuff I asked for. I owe you two now. Oh, one last favour.'

'Oh my God. You're having a laugh now.'

'I need you to get a message to Jarvis Burton.'

Jon started coughing and spluttering down the phone. 'Are you k-kidding me? I don't have Jarvis on speed dial, you know. That man is lethal with a side order of sadistic and I have no intention of turning up as a blip on his radar.'

'Jon, I wouldn't be asking you this if it wasn't really

important. I need you to get a message to Jarvis and only Jarvis. It's vital.'

'Why do I like you?' Jon grumbled.

'Because I'm adorable.'

'Not so much at the arse-crack of dawn when you're asking me to get into illegal shit including with someone from the Outfit,' Jon argued.

'So will you do it?' I asked.

'What's the message?' he said with suspicion.

'I need you to tell Jarvis that I know who murdered Dan Jeavons.'

'What? Is that true? You know who killed Dan?'

'No, but I need him to believe I have that information.'

'Why?'

I ignored Jon's question. 'So will you do it?'

'Persephone, you're playing with fire here and I don't want to be in the firing line when you get burned.'

'That's a lot of fiery metaphors. Are they all leading up to a yes?' I said.

'I'm getting off the phone before you can ask me for anything else,' said Jon.

'So you'll do what I asked?'

'Yeah. Yeah. But that's the end of it.'

'If you follow my instructions, I won't trouble you again – for today at least. You can go back to sleep.'

'No, I'm wide awake now. Thanks for that. Bye, Sephy.'

twenty-one. Libby

I woke to a number of my senses being pummelled at once. The temperature in the basement had dropped from fridge to freezer, so never mind dying of hunger and thirst, hypothermia was going to kick our butts long before then. A foul stench squatting like a fat toad beneath my nostrils smothered my mouth. Even though the slop bucket was across the room, Troy and I had both used it in the night and the cellar wasn't wide enough for either of us to now escape the stink. Mind you, thanks to Troy and his junk-food habits, the moon wouldn't have been far enough away.

The single unadorned bulb lighting the room had begun to hiss and fizz intermittently. It didn't have long for this world. When it finally blew, Troy and I would be left in deep, cloying darkness. And then I would freak – I just knew it. I've never been a fan of the dark. The last couple of days definitely took the gold medal for being the shittiest of my life.

I glanced at Troy. He was still fast asleep, sitting with his back against the wall, his legs outstretched, his head now tilted back. At least he didn't snore. How I envied him. He had family who were probably trying to move heaven and earth to get him home safely.

I had no one.

My mind was spinning. I kept trying to stomp my lacerating thoughts into oblivion, but they sprang up like choking thorny vines, twining round me to *squeeze* the air from my body. Every so often, I managed to catch my breath, and with it some scrap of perspective, but such moments were few and far between.

My own mother arranged to have me kidnapped.

My own mother . . .

How much did she ask for me? A million? A couple of hundred thousand? A couple of thousand? Maybe a couple of hundred with a bottle of cider thrown in on the side. How much was I worth to her? My own mother let her boyfriend, Pete, and his scuzzy brother grab me off the street, bundle me into a van and bury me in this rank, dank cellar.

I didn't know what to do with that fact.

And now she's dead, shot full of holes.

I didn't know what to do with that either.

I didn't need to close my eyes to relive the moment Mum was shot, the bloodstains blooming across her top before she sank to her knees and hit the ground. She died right in front of me. Books, TV dramas, films – none of them had even come close to portraying what it's really like to watch someone die. There was something about the . . . *finality* of it that no one could prepare you for. I've never seen anyone die before. I never want to see it again. Ever.

Why did Mum do it?

Was that all I was worth to her? Some numbers to the left of a decimal point in her bank account? To buy what? A designer handbag? A beach holiday? A new car?

Mum probably justified it to herself by thinking my incarceration would only be for a day at most. Or two. The kidnapping would have needed to look real to anyone on the street who might've caught sight of what happened. That was probably the reason she hadn't just arranged to have me snatched from home – too easy to trace it back to her. It was risky but think of the money she'd make. And no doubt she'd promised herself that she'd make it up to me afterwards. Yeah, that's just how she would've convinced herself to go along with Pete's plan. It had to be her bastard of a lover's idea. At least he's dead now too. Not much consolation, but it was something. I don't mind so much that he's dead. Correction. I don't mind at all. But it doesn't matter who originally had the idea, does it? All that matters is that Mum went along with it. Blood may be thicker than water, but wads of cash are thicker than both. I know my mum. She wouldn't've seen it from my side; she wouldn't have thought about what effect her actions might have on me. She could never see anything from any other point of view than her own. She wanted money, I was a means to an end to get some – and that's all there was to it.

Troy was just collateral damage, in the wrong place at the wrong time.

He keeps telling me that I shouldn't feel guilty, that I'm not responsible, but I have enough guilt inside to sink an aircraft carrier.

And the worst thing of all? If my mum could do that to her own daughter, what does that say about me? What is it about me that makes me not just unlikeable but unlovable? Even my own mother thought so or she never could have done what she did.

I wonder where the ones who killed her and her accomplices are now? Upstairs? Or long gone?

Did they try to tap my dad for money too? Did he say no? Is that why they boarded up the door to seal us in here? Why should Dad pay a ransom for me? He doesn't even know me. He hasn't seen me since I was a baby and I certainly don't remember him. Strange to think of all those times I saw him on the news or on the TV and I barely paid attention. Why would I? Tobias Durbridge was nothing to me, or so I thought.

My mum didn't want me.

It looks like my dad doesn't either.

Proof positive that I'm complete poison. Toxic. Unlovable. I always knew it, so why did it feel like an ice-cream scoop had taken a massive chunk out of my heart? Why should I even care what happens to either of them? What good did it do to care about anyone? Seventeen years on the planet and I still didn't have an answer to that one – because there was no adequate answer. Using the back of my hand, I dashed away the unwelcome tears trickling down my cheeks.

'Libby, what your mum did, that's on her, not you.' Troy's voice came from far away, even though he was sitting right next to me. I hadn't even noticed that he'd woken up. I turned to face him, concentrating on his face, his mouth. What was he saying?

'Libby, this is not your fault.'

'I know.'

'Do you though?'

Troy's eyebrows were drawn together over dark brown

eyes which held concern and . . . sympathy. I couldn't bear it. I didn't want or need his pity.

I sat up straighter, glaring at him. 'Troy, I'm a survivor. I'll live.'

'We both will,' Troy replied pointedly. 'Remember that.'

I got the message. I'm not sure I believed it, but I got it. We sat in empty silence for a long while, neither of us speaking or moving. 'What time d'you think it is?' I asked at last.

Troy shrugged.

'How long d'you think we've been down here?'

'Rephrasing the question isn't gonna get you a fresh answer. Still no clue,' said Troy. 'And, for God's sake, stop scratching your arm.'

Surprised, I glanced down. I'd been rasping my lower forearm with my nails and I hadn't even realized.

My face reddening, I immediately stopped. 'There's not a lot else to do,' I said flippantly.

'Find something,' snapped Troy. 'Libby, I can't keep sheepdogging you away from sharp edges.'

'Who asked you to sheepdog me? I certainly didn't.'

'Yeah, but, as I said before, when you get gangrene, that'll be just one more thing on my plate.'

'Wow! You're all heart.' I scowled at Troy who scowled right back at me.

'I get it, Liberty. OK? You just lost your mum, and her boyfriend was a lowlife. You're stuck down here with no way out. But, if you could spare – oh, I dunno – maybe one thought for the fact that I'm down here with you, I'd appreciate it,' said Troy.

'You think I don't know that?'

'No, all you're thinking about is how me being stuck down here is making *you* feel. *You* feel guilty. It's all about you. Once in a while, why don't you just think about how others might be feeling? Try that one on for size.'

'Screw you, Troy.'

'Screw you right back, Liberty.'

I stood up and moved to sit on the crate, my back towards him.

'Mature, Libby. Real mature.'

'You should've jumped into the river when you had the chance,' I sniffed.

'Yeah? Well, you know something? If I could go back to that moment and I had it all to do again, I still wouldn't've left you alone. So suck on that.'

It took a moment for his words to sink in. Puzzled, I turned to face him.

Troy glared at me defiantly so what he'd said made even less sense.

I didn't get it. 'Why not?' I couldn't help asking.

'You figure it out,' said Troy.

But I just couldn't. 'I guess that's just another of life's mysteries that I'll take to an early grave, along with how to get out of this hellhole.'

'That's where you're wrong,' said Troy. 'Help me up.'

I walked over to him and held out my hands. Even in this half-light, I could see the gleam in those dark eyes framed by long, curled black eyelashes as he grabbed hold. Taking a half-step back, I pulled until he had enough momentum to stand upright on his own.

'Let me check your bandage to make sure it's not wrapped too tight.'

'Never mind the bandage,' Troy dismissed. 'I know exactly what we've got to do now, but I need you to trust me. Can you do that?'

Trust him . . . According to my mum, Troy was one of the people I should trust the least. But she wasn't here – and I wasn't her. Nor did I have to try to be to win if not her love, then at least her approval. Not any more.

'What d'you have in mind?'

Troy smiled. Just smiled. And, all at once, I felt not unburdened exactly, but strangely lighter. Whatever else might happen to us, we were in this together. I wasn't alone. At that precise moment, it meant everything.

'I have a plan,' said Troy. 'To get us out of here.'

'I'm all ears,' I prompted. What was he waiting for? A drum roll?

His smile broadened, displaying perfect white teeth. 'We dig!'

twenty-two. Troy

Libby blinked once and remained silent, as if waiting for the punchline.

'Hear me out,' I said eagerly. 'There's no way we can escape through the boarded-up door. The walls are brick so we aren't getting out that way. But this place is really old – some of the ground in here is just dirt.' This had come to me in that strange in-between of not asleep and not awake. Maybe it was worth a try – we didn't have much else.

I pointed to the far wall, illuminated by the solitary, now-flickering light bulb, but only just. With Libby's help, I hobbled over to it. The ground there was soft dirt and nothing else. Thumping with the side of my fist against the wall, the dull thud indicated it was solid. I'd need a pneumatic drill to get through that. But how far down did this particular wall descend? Half a metre? A metre? More? I looked around, trying to get my bearings. When we managed to escape and were being marched back at gunpoint, I'd noticed the basement door was on the left of the building and this house was next to an end-of-terrace. The basement ran directly beneath the kitchen, so I was relatively sure that this was an external wall leading to the back garden of the house. Would it be possible to dig through to the garden?

Who was I trying to kid?

Mostly myself, I guess.

The direction didn't matter. We'd die of thirst long before we managed to tunnel out of here. And the ground might be soft in the cellar, but the more we dug, the more compact it would become. The candle flame of an idea flickered and died. So much for that then. I turned, only to find Libby standing right behind me. And I mean right behind me. I plastered on a smile, like I'd just stumbled across a set of power tools, a fridgeful of food and fizzy drinks and a functioning bathroom.

'Dig where? Troy, speak to me! I'm not a mind-reader. Have you found a way out of here?' Anticipation threaded in and out of Libby's voice.

And that look in her eyes . . . the light of hope. How could I extinguish it?

'The dirt is soft here,' I replied, toeing the earth with the tip of my shoe. 'I was thinking maybe we could burrow under this external wall and escape through the back garden without being seen.'

'Will that work?' Libby's eyebrows drew together in a frown.

I shrugged. 'No idea. But doing nothing definitely won't get us anywhere.'

'What if we dig and find the foundation underneath is made of concrete?'

'Then we'll be no worse off,' I lied.

Silence.

Libby smiled and nodded. 'Let's do it.'

'Help me break up one of the crate lids. We can make

shovels out of the lengths of wood that will help speed things up.'

Libby was already turning away and heading for the nearest crate. I eyed the one-quarter-filled litre bottle of water at the foot of the stairs. That wasn't going to last long and, if we exerted ourselves digging, we'd get through it that much faster. But Libby, like me, needed to be *doing*. And, if we were going to die anyway, then better to die trying. Better to die doing. Better to die with hope than with none at all.

Daily Shouter Online

Home. News. Politics. Celebs. Entertainment. Sport. Tech. Health. Science. Money. More.

Hate crimes on the rise in Albion

According to official Department for National Statistics figures, there has been a sharp rise in the number of hate crimes reported to the police since the general election. It has been suggested that this is in direct response to Tobias Durbridge becoming the first-ever Nought Prime Minister. A Home Office spokesperson stated, 'The last government brought in some measures to improve the reporting of hate crimes and this government intends to build on that work. We want all sections of society to feel they can report such crimes to the police and their grievances will be taken seriously.'

A spokesperson at the DNS told the *Daily Shouter*: 'Though more hate crimes are undoubtedly being reported, our survey suggests that, for every one crime reported to the police, up to another twenty are going unreported by victims for a number of reasons. Our survey indicated that in the last year alone over 170,000 hate crimes went unreported to the authorities. It is disingenuous to state or believe that the sole reason for the rising numbers is that certain sections of society feel more confident reporting to the police. As for the spike in numbers since the general election last month, it is far too early to say whether or not this will be an ongoing trend.'

twenty-three. Libby

'This one has a little give in it,' said Troy. 'It's probably our best bet.'

I dropped the sturdy crate lid I'd been trying to flex and went over to him. The tongue-and-groove lid he was holding looked solid enough to me. Was that right? Tongue and groove? Like some floorboards? God knows how I knew that. Dubious, I looked at him.

'Just a very little give to it, but it's something,' Troy reluctantly added.

'OK then, let's do this.' I had no idea how we were going to do 'this' and waited for Troy to enlighten me.

He placed one edge of the lid on the floor, holding it at a forty-five-degree angle away from him. 'Libby, I need you to jump on the bottom bit.'

OK . . . 'Ready?' I asked, still dubious.

Troy nodded. I leaped forward, feet together, and landed on the crate lid, then immediately fell backwards onto the ground.

'Ow! Well, that bloody hurt.'

I wasn't the only one in pain. Troy shook out his left, then right hand, wiping them against his trousers. I wondered if it had jarred his ankle as the sweat beads on his forehead had come back.

He looked determined though. 'Try again, Libby, only this time more focus, less enthusiasm.'

Scowling at him, I scrambled up, setting one foot on the crate lid that Troy was still holding. Only then did I see the blood dripping from one of his hands.

'Oh my God.' I grabbed for it, horrified to see a deep gash in his left palm where the lid and my efforts to break it had caused more damage to him than anything else.

'For Shaka's sake! Why didn't you say something?' I asked.

'Like what?' asked Troy. 'I'm not going to whine about a couple of cuts and bruises.'

Which made me feel even worse. Maybe Troy was right – I did think about myself too much.

'We need to clean this wound,' I said. 'I'll pour a little of our water over it—'

'Are you drunk? What little water we have left is to go down our throats, not over my hand,' Troy argued.

'It could become infected—'

'If we don't get out of here soon, I'll be dead long before an infection can finish me off,' said Troy. If he said that to make me feel better, he failed epically. 'Come on, Libby. The sooner we get this crate broken up, the sooner we can dig ourselves out of here.'

I nodded, watching as Troy placed his good hand over his bad to steady the crate lid.

'Ready?'

'Ready.'

I put my foot back on it and stomped. Troy winced, but managed to keep hold of it this time. Deciding that it was best to do this as fast as possible, I stomped and stomped until the wood cracked and fractured into three pieces. My foot hit the floor, sending a jarring pain up my leg. Whoever built these crates wasn't mucking about. Troy's hands were a mess. He slowly wiped them on his trousers, wincing as he did so.

'Are you all right?' I asked.

'I'll live,' was all he said.

I was hot, thirsty, smelly and thoroughly pissed off, but I kept it to myself. If Troy could suck it up, then so could I. When we managed to escape and were at the harbour wall, how I wished I'd just pushed him into the river to swim and get help, but the truth was I'd been terrified of being alone with our kidnappers. That's how I'd lived my life – scared all the time.

But no more. The next chance we got to escape – if there were another chance – I'd make sure that both of us took it, no matter what happened to me. I owed Troy that much at least.

twenty-four. Tobey

'Sir, there's a Jon Duba down here at the front entrance. He insists he has an appointment with you, but he's not on the list.'

'Get out the way.' Jon pushed Michael to one side, his face looming into view on my video cam. The fisheye lens and the angle of his face meant I had a clear, unwelcome view up his nostrils. 'Durbridge, you wanker, you gonna let me in or what?'

Michael, my Cross close-protection officer, was too much of a professional to punch Jon's lights out. He did, however, firmly body-push him to one side until Jon was no longer in front of the lens. 'Do you know this man, sir?'

Keeping my expression neutral, I replied, 'My apologies, Michael. What with one thing and another, I forgot to inform you that he was coming. Please send him up.'

'Yes, sir.'

Michael's image disappeared off my phone. I opened my door, noting Deli, another of my close-protection officers, seated beside the lift. Her discreet earpiece meant that she'd heard every word of the conversation I'd just had with Michael. I nodded in her direction. She nodded back.

A minute later, Jon was at my front door, having taken the lift up to the apartment. We eyed each other without saying a word. His greying-brown hair was ruffled and untidy, and his glasses were cloudy and in need of a good clean. I stepped aside to allow him to walk past. Jon took a quick glance around, then made himself comfortable on my sofa, legs outstretched, shoes up on my cushions.

'Mine's a Scotch and ice – just one cube – since you're asking.'

I got him his drink, not bothering to comment on the hour. It was still early in the morning, for God's sake. Handing it to him, I sat down on the sofa opposite to the one he had claimed and waited. The look Jon openly cast me was speculative, to say the least.

'What's our first move?' Jon asked at last.

'I don't know what you mean or why you're here,' I replied carefully.

'Bullshit! Callie has filled me in and asked me to help you, so that's what I'm doing. I'm sure you have your own people, but you don't strike me as the sort of man to put all his eggs in one basket, or to sit back and wait for things to happen, so I'll ask again: what's our first move?'

Silence. I was impressed.

'Shane Stoats. He's Eva's new right-hand man so either he knows where Liberty is or he knows how to find out,' I admitted at last.

'You know about Shane Stoats?' Jon's eyes narrowed. 'Eva Foxton is very careful to keep him out of the public eye. He's her secret weapon.'

'That's the name I was given,' I said.

Jon raised an eyebrow, the corner of his mouth quirking at the same time. 'That makes you better informed than most cops in the Serious Crime Squad. Very few people even know his name, never mind that he's now Eva's second in command.'

'*You* know,' I pointed out. This guy knew a lot.

'It's part of my job to know,' said Jon. 'What d'you think I do all day?'

'Take photos of unfaithful spouses or of whiplash victims faking their injuries?' I ventured.

Jon's pursed lips and immediate frosty air let me know my assessment had been way off. 'None taken,' he replied. 'Actually, that's a lie. Definitely some offence taken.'

'Apologies if I've hurt your feelings. So would you be able to get me Stoats's home address?'

'You don't want much, do you?'

'Is that a yes or a no?'

'Of course I can get it.' Jon sounded affronted that I'd ever doubted his abilities. 'But why d'you want it?'

'I thought I'd pay him a visit and get him to help me find my daughter,' I continued.

'And if he says no?'

'He won't.'

'What makes you so sure?'

'I can be very persuasive.'

Jon nodded slowly. 'Yeah, I bet.'

Not a compliment. This man really didn't like me. He was trying his best to keep his expression amiably neutral, but my antennae were rarely wrong about such things.

'Let me come with you when you visit Stoats,' said Jon.

No way. I started to shake my head.

'Hear me out,' said Jon. 'I want to work with you until

your daughter and Callie's brother are found, so put me to work.'

'I don't think so. You—'

Jon raised a hand to interrupt me. 'You need me just as much as Callie does. I get things done.'

'I don't need—'

'Did you hear what I said? When I'm on the job, shit gets done. And I'm not above . . . shall we call it bending the law a little – or a lot – to get results. If I'm reporting directly to you rather than Callie, I'm sure you won't be as squeamish about how I get the job done as long as any fallout doesn't land on your head. D'you read me?'

'Like a baby's picture book.' We regarded each other. Jon's smile was slightly mocking. As I'd said, the man didn't like me much.

'Plus I owe it to Callie to try and help. She's been good to me.' At my raised eyebrows, Jon shook his head. 'For Shaka's sake, not in that way. We haven't slept together, if that's what your eyebrows are suggesting. I mean that she took me on and gave me a job when no one else in her position would. Cross lawyers prefer to use Cross investigators. Even now, some of the lawyers Callie works with still try to tell her that I can't be trusted, in spite of the fact that I've been working with her for years. Plus I messed up once, really badly, and she hauled my delectable butt cheeks out of the fire. I owe her. She's worried sick about her brother and I suspect that you, like me, are a man who doesn't let the grass grow under his feet. So here we are.'

I studied Jon. Though he was no spring chicken, he looked like he might be useful in a fight. And he clearly had certain connections and information at his fingertips, data I *could* obtain if I went through the proper channels, but only by answering a whole heap of questions and arousing a number of suspicions first. My hands were already being tied by Libby's kidnappers. I couldn't afford any of the delays that moving this to official channels would bring.

'Very well, let's do it. But let me tell you this: you get in my way and I'll step on you before I step over you,' I warned.

Jon smiled. 'I believe you'll try.'

I walked over to the wall cabinet and removed a smartphone from the left-hand drawer. Switching it on and entering the code, I turned to throw it at Jon who caught it one-handed.

'The code is six sixes, no thumbprint or face scan required.'

'What's this for?'

'I want to be able to talk to you, text you and leave messages without worrying about who may be tracking or hacking my calls. I know that phone is clean so that's the one I'll be using to contact you. It'll be just you and me using it.'

Jon pushed the phone into his jacket pocket. Good. I wasn't in the mood for an argument about it.

'Have you talked to Callie recently?' I asked, keeping my tone casual.

'Not recently. Spoke to her mum though.'

'Sephy? About what?'

Jon frowned. 'About none of your business.'

This man . . . I shook my head.

'What?' said Jon, swinging his legs round so his feet were back on the floor. 'You think, just because you're PM, I should bow down and kiss your buttocks?'

'I'll pass, but nicely put.'

'I have a way with words.'

'You know, given my title and status, most people are a little more polite when they talk to me,' I pointed out.

'That's why I don't like most people. And, Tobey, I shouldn't need to remind you that acquiring power and keeping it are not one and the same thing.'

'I know,' I said. I wasn't a complete fool.

'And, even if you are exonerated of Daniel Jeavons' murder, when it all comes out, there's plenty will say there's no smoke without fire. You want my advice?' Jon continued without waiting for confirmation. 'Get ahead of the chatter.'

'How d'you propose I do that?'

'You need to change your image. You're single and not even in a stable, long-term relationship.'

I shrugged. 'I can't really do much about that. My soulmate has proved to be . . . elusive.'

'My arse she has,' Jon snorted. 'Do yourself a favour, Tobey. Tell Callie exactly how you feel about her and put a ring on it to seal the deal.'

'Callie hates my guts.' I didn't even try to deny that's who we were talking about.

'Of course she doesn't. She's mad at you, sure, but a clever man like you can find a way round that,' said Jon. 'And think how it would play to the masses. Think of the headlines. Nought Prime Minister marries dual-heritage lawyer of renown. A lawyer whose grandfather was a respected politician. The traditional meets the modern in a new wave of change, and other such nauseating clickbait, tabloid bullshit. The press will view it as a marriage made in heaven and it'll spike the guns of all your opponents. You'll be seen as a representation of change, of the future. Anyone speaking against you will seem like dusty relics.'

'Just one problem with that,' I said. 'Callie would never go for it.'

'She will if you play your cards the right way,' Jon insisted.

'And what right way is that? I'm not exactly flavour of the month.' Or anywhere near.

'Listen, Tobias,' said Jon, leaning forward. 'Callie will have cooled down by now. She didn't mean what she said to you. It was heat-of-the-moment stuff, though you had it coming for blackmailing her into staying on as your lawyer. Real classy move there, Durbridge.'

This bastard actually had me blushing like a schoolboy. Callie had confided in him? I took a moment or two to digest that. 'Did she also happen to mention that afterwards I told her to recuse herself from being my lawyer?'

'Yeah, like that was ever going to happen,' Jon scoffed. 'Callie cares about you, Tobey, in spite of all your shenanigans. God alone knows why. She believes that there's still something decent deep inside you.'

'And you know that for a fact, do you?'

'Yes, because she told me so,' said Jon. 'Not in so many words, but that was the gist.'

Jon now had my full, undivided attention.

'When did she tell you all this?'

'Irrelevant. It's *what* she said that counts, not the exact hour and minute she said it. Anyway, enough chit-chat. Let's get down to it. For the third and final time, what's our first move?'

twenty-five. Troy

'History, Government and Politics, English and Chemistry.'

Libby paused her digging for a moment to stare at me. 'You're doing History? Seriously? What a waste of time.'

I straightened up. 'Excuse me?'

'History is pointless.'

'What the hell? How on earth is History pointless? It's our past and tells us how we got to be where we are today.'

Libby sniffed. '*Your* past maybe, not mine.'

I frowned. 'That's not true.'

'Of course it is. History is an erasure and an erosion of the truth about Noughts, so why should I care about it? It's not *my* history, it's yours.' Libby resumed her digging.

'History belongs to all of us,' I argued.

'Some more than others. Nought history shouldn't begin with Crosses colonizing Albion. What about all the centuries of stuff before that? What about the Noughts who fought for our rights during the time of the eighth Ashanti empress? Or the Noughts who fought and died in the Great War only to see their contribution deliberately ignored? If you only read Cross history books, you'd think we Noughts have been sitting on our arses for centuries, doing bugger all except slaving for you lot and, more recently, receiving handouts. History is bullshit.'

Libby's fiery eyes and raised eyebrows dared me to argue. I sighed. Life was too short. We both resumed our digging.

'Troy, history belongs to those who get to write it. How many Nought historians can you name?'

'I can't name any Cross ones either,' I told her. 'So what's your point?'

The wooden slat in my hand scraped my skin as I dug once again into the dirt by the cellar wall. When we'd finished digging, the blisters on my hands would be the size of beach balls. Dirt that had initially seemed soft underfoot was hard and unyielding now we were trying to clear it out of the way. I glanced behind me. We'd removed just a few centimetres of earth and we'd been at it for ages. Sweat was pouring off me, but with no fresh air or ventilation it didn't evaporate; it just ran down my skin, soaking into my shirt and trousers. God only knew what I smelled like. And, with each accelerated beat of my heart, my ankle throbbed with renewed pain.

Beside me, Libby dropped her wooden slat and examined the palms of her hands. 'This is shredding my skin.'

She wasn't wrong. Beads of blood, dark and brooding in the cellar's half-light, were dotted across her palms. As I took her hands in mine for a closer look, she winced. I immediately let go, but she pushed her hands back into mine.

'Go ahead,' she urged. 'How bad are they?'

'Not good. Let's take a break for a while.'

I released Libby's hands. After a quick glance, she wiped them on her trousers. My own palms felt like they were on fire, but at least after the first cut I hadn't broken any more skin. The last thing either of us needed was to get an infection.

'I have an idea.' I took off my shirt and began to pull at the sleeves.

'What on earth are you doing?'

'Protecting your hands,' I replied.

Except that was easier said than done. The bastard sleeves must've been sewn on with steel wire rather than cotton. After a lot of sweating and straining on my part, and suppressed giggles from Libby, the left sleeve I was tugging at finally began to give. It took far too long to rip it from the rest of the shirt and then tear it in two. By the time I'd finished, Libby wasn't even trying to hide her laughter. So embarrassing! My face flamed as I wrapped the two strips of material round her hands, careful to tie and secure them at the back rather than the front.

'What have you got in your upper arms instead of muscles? Overcooked noodles?'

'Thanks.' Lips pursed, I glared at her. 'Next time, sort out your own hands.'

'I'm just teasing, Troy. Thank you.'

Hmm!

'How's your ankle?' Libby said with an unsubtle change of subject.

'The pain has reduced from a roar to a dull growl,' I replied.

'Let me see it,' she said.

'Later. Can you carry on?' I asked, retrieving my makeshift spade.

Pause. At first I thought Libby was going to argue, but with a sigh she picked up her slat of wood.

'Yeah,' she said. 'Let's keep digging.'

It was slow going. Somehow I'd got it into my head that,

after an hour, the hole would be deep enough to stand in. I shook my head at our pitiful excavations so far.

I glanced at Libby. She was still digging, but the expression on her face spoke volumes.

'Let's play Truth or Dare,' I suggested. 'It'll help pass the time, unless you'd rather we sing?'

Libby sighed. 'Truth or Dare it is then.'

'I'll start,' I said quickly. 'Which one d'you choose?'

Libby considered. 'Truth.'

'What's the one thing you fear the most?' I asked.

'Wow! Start with an easy one.' Libby raised an eyebrow. 'You mean apart from being kidnapped and locked in a basement with a smelly bucket, no food and very little water?'

'Yeah, apart from that,' I agreed with a flash of a smile.

Pause. 'Dying alone.'

Long moments passed as Libby and I looked at each other.

'That's not gonna happen,' I told her.

'Why not?'

'Because.'

Libby was unimpressed. 'Is that all you've got?'

She still didn't get it, did she? We were in this together. 'Dying is bad enough, but dying alone . . . That's too lonely. No one should have to go like that.'

'Sometimes you don't get to choose,' said Libby. 'Sometimes you just— Oh God, I'm sorry, Troy. You're thinking about your dad, aren't you? What's wrong with me? I never get it right.'

'Don't beat yourself up.' I shrugged. 'And you and me and this situation we're in – we sink or swim, fly or fall together. That's just the way it is.'

Libby nodded. 'Thanks. So go on then. What d'you fear the most?'

'Aren't you supposed to ask me – truth or dare?'

'Truth or dare?' Libby said, exasperated.

'Truth.'

'For Shaka's sake, Troy! Why didn't you just answer my question the first time? What *d'you* fear the most?'

I thought about not telling the exact truth, but what was the point? 'Losing my Nana Meggie,' I said. 'She's . . . she's not doing too well at the moment. She doesn't drive any more and she sometimes walks with a stick. It's like I blinked and she was suddenly old. My other nana, Nana Jasmine, died before I was born.'

'You and Nana Meggie are very close?'

'Yeah. The two of us definitely have the most in common in my family,' I admitted.

'You'll just have to cherish every moment you have with her. Make new, happy memories every day you're with her that'll last a lifetime,' said Libby.

Silence.

'The truth kinda sucks,' I decided.

'Welcome to my world,' Libby agreed.

We carried on digging.

twenty-six. Callie

A sepia-grey sky threatened rain, and a great deal of it. How I would welcome that. Oh, to sit on this park bench and let the rain caress my face, flowing over me like a waterfall down a cliff. Enough rain to carry me away, along with all my fears and regrets. Whichever way I turned, I was being manipulated. Too many people were trying to label me helpless and treat me like a puppet, and it didn't sit well. At all.

These were the labels I owned:

Callie Rose Hadley.

Woman.

Dual heritage.

Barrister.

Loyal friend.

Passionate lover.

Gullible fool.

Why didn't I hate Tobey for what he'd done to me? His first instinct had been to blackmail me into continuing as his defence counsel. That right there told me so much about the man. I should've despised the tainted air around him. But I didn't.

I'd tried. I couldn't. Quite the opposite, in fact. How pathetic was that?

But one thing was certain – when all this was done, I never wanted to see him again. He and I were well and truly over. It had taken me all these years to finally accept what everyone else but me could see. He was rotten. Yeah, that was the word for it – rotten. And when I thought of how he'd used me to ensure my continued support as his lawyer . . . God, but I was stupid. Tobey was the only person who could reduce me to a giggling schoolgirl. Even when we'd been in bed together, with my piss-poor attempt at banter, I'd acted more like a teen than a grown-ass woman. It was to mask the nervousness I felt in his company. He'd done so much with his life, he'd reached the top, and he still wanted me. Oh God! I couldn't stop wincing at the memory of how deluded I'd been. Wanted me? Yeah, right.

Tobey Durbridge was a member of Nought Forever.

He said that was all in the past, and those days were behind him, but why then keep the NF tattoo on his chest? Because, even if those days were supposedly long gone, like his shadow, they were still a part of him, no doubt only emerging when in the company of others who thought as he did, but who also managed to keep it well hidden from casual view.

Across the street, children – with what seemed like every heritage represented – yelled and laughed as they ran round the wire-fenced school playground. Their movements were a riot of hats and coats and colour. Impervious to the chill in the air, they delighted in one another's company. No background, history or connections required. Joy shared is joy doubled, as Nana Meggie always says. Sitting on this bench, with my early-morning coffee warming my hands as I watched the children play, usually made my soul smile – but not today. Envious, I viewed them. All was right in their world. Nothing was right in mine.

Yesterday I'd failed to get the murder charge against Tobey Durbridge dropped.

And, in not backing out of his case, I was so scared I'd signed my brother Troy's death warrant as well as that of Tobey's daughter.

What was happening to them at this precise moment?

Were they already dead?

I closed my eyes, feeling physically sick. My imagination was flogging me. It'd been stripping the skin from my back from the moment I made the decision not to bail on Tobey – though every atom of sense in my head screamed at me to do just that.

Tobey Durbridge. Lots of labels for him too . . .

Ex-lover.

Player.

Manipulator.

Politician.

Blackmailer.

Iceberg.

Murderer?

Had he killed Dan Jeavons? I honestly didn't know. There was a time when my answer would've been an unequivocal 'of course not'. Not any more. I was *almost* certain he hadn't – but that 'almost' made bridging the gap to 'certain' impossible. What there was no doubt about was that Tobey had a ruthless streak a mile wide. He would allow nothing and no one to get in the way of what he wanted. Including me. But there was no force on earth or beyond that could make me believe that my mum had anything to do with Dan's death. I didn't care what Tobey said, or what so-called evidence he reckoned he had. Mum didn't do it. She wouldn't. She couldn't. Tobey was a son of a bitch to throw that one at me. Yet another example of his ruthlessness.

How ironic then that the qualities I had found abhorrent just a couple of days ago were the exact same ones I was now relying on to find Troy and Liberty and bring them home unscathed. What kind of hypocrite did that make me?

The worst kind.

Before Tobey came back into my life and threw a grenade into the middle of it, I'd had choices. Now my options were severely limited. The moment Tobey metaphorically knocked on my door, I should've slammed it in his face. What had I done instead? Fallen into bed with him.

Callie, you're far too smart to be this damned stupid.

And yet I obviously wasn't 'cause now look at me.

My career was in tatters.

My personal life was shattered.

And I couldn't even bear to catch sight of myself in the mirror.

Callie, you had no choice. You couldn't recuse yourself from being his barrister. You did the right thing—

How many times would I have to replay those words in my head before I started to believe them? Both Tobey and Jon, my private investigator, reckoned that this was a better strategy than immediately giving in to the kidnappers' demands. As Tobey had pointed out, what possible reason would the captors have for keeping Libby and Troy alive if we immediately gave them what they wanted? If they let

Troy and Libby go, either or both of them could identify their abductors right down to their shoe size. And, besides, if I recused myself from being Tobey's defence counsel today, what was to stop me from taking up his case again once Troy and Libby were home safely? Not a damned thing.

So, though it hurt me to admit it, I agreed with Tobey that it was best to defy the kidnappers' instructions and hope that still left us some wiggle room. A dodgy strategy, but, apart from going to the police, what other choice did we have? I must admit, my every instinct was still to get them involved, but Tobey reckoned he had too many enemies – political and otherwise – for the situation not to be exploited if it should become public knowledge.

So we were playing the game by his rules.

For now.

Why couldn't I shake the feeling that I was betraying Troy, as if somehow I was putting Tobey's career ahead of my brother's life? If anything happened to Troy, I'd never forgive myself.

Or Tobey.

We'd either bought Troy and Libby more time or we'd signed their death warrants, and dread of the latter was relentlessly choking me. I dug out my phone and made a call.

'Hi, Callie.' Tobey answered within two rings.

'Hello, Tobey. Have you heard anything?'

'Not yet, but we will,' he replied. 'It's good to hear your voice. Are you OK?'

'I'm holding on,' I said. 'Are you busy? What are you doing at the moment?'

'I'm thinking of going for a morning run while I wait for Jon to get back to me,' Tobey replied.

'Jon? My Jon? He's doing stuff for you?'

A moment's pause. 'Yes, your Jon. Aren't you the one who sent him to me earlier this morning to help out?'

What? 'Is that what he told you?' I asked sharply.

'Among other things. He knew all about our bust-up in the court building.'

My face began to burn. 'I didn't tell him everything—'

'Just enough.' The reproach as Tobey cut me off was obvious.

'Jon is my friend, Tobey. And, apart from my mum, he's the only person who knows what we're going through. He's been totally supportive.' I bristled, on the defensive and not keen on how that felt. Jon had provided some much-needed perspective, plus he'd been a shoulder to cry on. I really wasn't wild he'd been to Tobey but I'd deal with that later. Right now, we all needed as much help as we could get.

'Anyway, Jon is running a couple of errands for me. I hope you don't mind?' said Tobey.

'Of course not. Are you going to tell me what exactly?'

'I will if it pans out. Trust me.'

Silence. Tobey obviously wasn't going to divulge any more so, with an inner sigh, I headed back to neutral territory.

'So you're going for a jog?' I asked at last.

'I run. I never jog,' said Tobey with feeling.

'And you can *run* at a time like this?'

'What would you have me do? Sit and stare at the four walls? A number of people are out doing for me. Until we get feedback, we can't take the next step. That's why I need to go out, and running helps me think.'

I sighed. 'I'm sorry, Tobey. I'm worried and on edge, but that doesn't mean I should take it out on you.'

'If you can get here soon, you could come for a run with me,' Tobey suggested. 'I'd like that.'

'Pfft! Me? Run? Why on earth would I do that?' I asked, bemused.

'For the same reason I do – to stay fit and to clear your head.'

'To get all sweaty and smelly? Tobey, I will run if – and only if – something with sharp teeth or someone with an axe is chasing me and not until then.'

Tobey chuckled. 'All right. Message received.'

'Besides, I can think of other ways to stay fit,' I said, casting my mind back to my regular tennis matches with friends from chambers. Playing a game to compete and challenge yourself had a point and a purpose. Running and circuit training, nah!

'I can think of other ways too,' said Tobey, the silky tone of his voice making my face flame.

'I'm not touching that one,' I told him.

'Spoilsport!'

'Tobey, I'm on my way to chambers,' I said firmly. 'Promise you'll phone me as soon as you have some news?'

'Of course,' he said. 'You'll be the first to hear. D'you want to know one of the many things I love about you, Callie?'

'Go on then,' I said, ignoring the hyperbole.

'You're one of the few people in my life who speaks to

me like a normal human being without taking a detour to kiss my arse first. It's refreshing.'

'You're an idiot!' I disconnected the call, smiling faintly.

In spite of everything that was going on, and everything that had just run through my mind about Tobias Durbridge, he could still make me smile. I glanced down at my watch. Lingering on this park bench was no longer an option. In less than an hour, I had an early meeting with my head of chambers, Sol Camden, and I was a hair's breadth away from being unceremoniously bounced out of my job. Yesterday, in court, Sol had positively radiated disapproval. My rising golden star was now lead and falling fast.

With one last look at the children in the playground, I stood and started walking. The bag draped over one shoulder grew heavier with each step I took towards my car. Not for the first time today, I wished I'd tied my braided hair back into a ponytail instead of letting it fall loose round my shoulders. Everything was working my nerves today, even my hair. It was one of those days when I felt I was fifteen degrees out from everyone else, when nothing was quite aligned.

'Ms Hadley, I'm Ade Udo. We've met before. I'm a journalist with the *Okene Standard*. May I ask you a few questions?'

I spun round to confront the man behind me. Adeyemi Udo. Our paths had crossed before to the mutual dissatisfaction of us both. Ade wore his designer fade with the same poise that he wore his off-the-rack suit. His clothes, his haircut, his demeanour were all meant to give off a man-of-the-people, sympathetic air, but I knew better. This Cross was born with a platinum spoon in his mouth and had spent his entire career sniffing out stories and hounding interviewees like they should be grateful for the attention. He wasn't above spinning the truth for juicy clickbait either. He was about my age with a chiselled face that was all angles. His dark brown eyes sparked with an alert gleam that currently bordered on hungry. That made him dangerous.

My mouth said, 'No, Mr Udo, you may not.' My thoughts said, *Bugger off!* I turned away and carried on walking.

Uninvited, Adeyemi fell into step next to me. Irritated, I glared at him, but it was water off a duck's butt.

'Ms Hadley, do you believe in equal justice for all?'

Like I couldn't see where this was going. 'No comment.'

'You have a reputation for integrity and scrupulous fairness,' Ade continued. 'How do you square that with the suppression of the public's right to know about the charges against Tobias Durbridge? The man who runs the country is a criminal and you're making sure that we in the media can't report that fact.'

I stopped and turned to fully face him, my gaze narrowing.

'Now you listen to me, Mr Udo,' I said softly. He moved in closer to hear my words, waving his smartphone under my nose so he could record every word. 'In this country, the law states that a person is innocent until proven guilty, not the other way round. The super-injunction is still in place so, if you try to print otherwise, I will personally see to it that the full force of the law hits you like a heavyweight boxer. Now, if you'll excuse me.'

'No, I won't excuse you,' said Ade. 'You lawyers with your suppression of the truth are helping to ensure that there's one set of rules for the rich and powerful and another set for everyone else.'

'Happy you got that off your chest, Mr Udo? I have places to be.' I glared at him, daring him to follow me further. Let him try it.

He got the message and turned to crawl back under whatever toadstool he'd emerged from. I carried on walking, my heels stabbing at the pavement with the brisk pace I set. Bastard! I didn't need him and his nonsense. Not now. Nearing my car, I pressed the button on my car-key fob. The doors clunked open.

'Miss Hadley?'

Now what? I spun round. To my surprise, two male, uniformed Cross police officers moved to stand on either side of me. One was my height and stocky, with short locs. The other officer was at least a head taller than his colleague with dark, almost black eyes and a trim precision beard with no moustache.

'Can I help you?'

'Are you Callie Rose Hadley?'

'Yes, I am. Is there a problem?'

'Miss Hadley, we have a warrant for your arrest,' said the taller cop.

The words picked me up and dunked me head first into a vat of ice water. Chilled to the bone, I asked, 'Is this some kind of joke?'

'I'm afraid not, Miss Hadley,' said the taller cop doing all the talking.

'On what charge?' I asked.

'Perverting the course of justice. You do not have to say

anything, but it may harm your defence if you do not mention when questioned something which you later rely on in court. Anything you do say may be given in evidence. Do you understand your rights as I have explained them to you?'

Was this guy having a laugh? 'I'm a lawyer. Of course I understand my rights.' *Dickhead!*

'If you could turn round.'

'Why?'

'We need to put handcuffs on you.'

No way. A quick look around. We were already attracting attention. The last thing I needed was for that shit-fish Ade Udo to take photos of me being handcuffed and blast them all over Albion's media channels.

'Officer, I am not resisting arrest and I will accompany you to the police station to get this sorted out, but I would ask, as a courtesy from one judicial officer to another, that you don't put handcuffs on me like I'm a common criminal.'

The two officers exchanged a studied look.

'I'm sure my head of chambers, Solomon Camden, or my friend Anika Morgenstern, the Attorney General, will be happy to sort out what is obviously a grave misunderstanding.' I was dropping names like wedding confetti, but desperation was nipping at my heels. What the actual hell? I was being *arrested*?

Just when I thought things couldn't get much worse.

'If you'd like to accompany us to our car,' said the shorter cop, pointing along the road. A squad car. They'd sent two uniformed officers in a common squad car to pick me up. That right there was sending a message.

I walked to their car and got in the back without saying a word. The officers sat in the front, a mesh grille between us. The cracked leather back seat smelled of bleach on distant keyboards, and vomit and piss on upfront bass and drums. Within moments, we were in motion.

I addressed the cop in the front passenger seat rather than the driver. 'Officer, how exactly am I supposed to have perverted the course of justice? And who was it who brought that charge against me?'

'It'll all be explained when we get to the police station.'

I sat back. Arrested . . . If I were formally charged, I'd be suspended and probably disbarred. The scum-sucking son of a bitch who'd wanted me to drop Tobey's case was obviously trying a different approach, hoping for the same outcome. And, if it was the same person or persons, then once I was charged and automatically suspended, they'd have no further use for Troy and Libby. That meant the person responsible knew their way round the judicial system and had clout. Tobey and I had gone from buying ourselves more time for our loved ones to having no time at all.

I dug into my jacket pocket and pulled out my phone. With one eye on the men in front, I pressed the two icons to dial Sol's private number. It was only when I lifted my phone to my ear that the cop in the driver's seat protested.

'You're not meant to be making any phone calls. You can make one from the police station.'

Ignoring him, I launched in before Sol had finished the first syllable of, 'Hello?'

'Sol, it's Callie. I've been arrested for perverting the course of justice. They're taking me to—Where are you taking me?'

'Blackfriars Police Station, but you really shouldn't be on the phone,' said the driver.

Then stop the car and try to take it from me, bitch.

'Blackfriars Police Station,' I repeated for Sol, while eyeing the cop scowling at me in the rear-view mirror.

'Callie Rose, what the hell?' Sol exclaimed.

'Sol, I'm being stitched up. Obviously. I need you to come and bail me out, please,' I said.

'I'm on my way.'

He disconnected the call. I stuffed the phone back in my pocket, never taking my eyes off the cops before me. Sol would help me sort this out. I didn't doubt for a second that he was actually on his way.

And then what? One by one, my options were being snatched away.

As a lawyer, it was my job to give a voice to the voiceless, power to the powerless. While I was at university, studying law, I'd devoured every word I could about my dad's trial and his subsequent conviction. One thing was clear: he never stood a chance. There was never any real proof that he'd kidnapped and harmed my mum. I suspect his so-called confession had been coerced out of him and the prosecution had played on the prejudices of the all-Cross jury. I also suspected that my grandfather Kamal Hadley had had more than a little something to do with the outcome.

Analysing my dad's trial had made me even more determined to become a lawyer, to help anyone who was innocent and might find themselves facing the law coming at them like a wrecking ball. The trouble was, to be a working lawyer meant providing a defence for the innocent and the guilty alike. In my time, I'd defended too many like my Uncle Jude who were prepared to watch the world burn even if it meant they burned right along with it. That in itself had been a revelation and an education. Evil was a real thing, a living, breathing entity that gatecrashed some, but was invited in by too many others. I didn't want to become as jaded as some of my colleagues, but I was beginning to realize that ship had sailed.

Yet there was always one thing I held sacrosanct above everything else – the law. I believed in the rule of law. Without it, there would be chaos. Now, though, the law was being used as a battering ram to knock my life way off course and the person wielding it was doing a stellar job.

Whoever it was, they had just made a big mistake. A huge mistake. There was no force in the universe that would stop me hunting them down and bringing them to justice. The person or persons responsible were about to learn the hard way that they were screwing with the wrong woman.

Daily Shouter Online

Home. News. Politics. Celebs. Entertainment. Sport. Tech. Health. Science. Money. More.

Oliver Bigson condemns 'constant poverty-porn images of Noughts'

Oliver Bigson, famous Nought actor-director, has condemned what he called the 'constant poverty-porn images of Noughts bombarding our screens'. Bigson, star of blockbuster films such as *Mr Greenrock*, *Angel in Denim* and *Vampires of Drea*, spoke out yesterday while a guest on *The Robert Pierre Show*. He said, 'It's a shame that here we are in the twenty-first century and yet Noughts and Nought children in particular are very rarely onscreen unless it's in recordings for various charities where they are seen to be suffering. The constant trickle of poverty-porn images of Noughts is demeaning. Is it any wonder that most Crosses in all the countries in Zafrika believe that Albion is a third-world, second-class country full of Noughts who can't exist without Cross aid?'

Stella Sharples, a patron of Albion Aid, condemned Bigson's statement, saying, 'We are not trying to give the impression that every Nought in Albion is suffering, but the fact remains that there are many Noughts who struggle every day to not just make ends meet but to put a roof over their heads and food on the table. The basics. All we're requesting is a little help from those who have a lot for those who have too little.'

twenty-seven. Tobey

Hellsake! I'd already made a couple of phone calls and was now pacing up and down the sitting room. A caged tiger had nothing on me. Confinement was really doing my head in. A run would help, otherwise I was stuck in my apartment, cooling my heels until Jon Duba got back to me. That man was something else, coming to my apartment so early and uninvited.

Reluctantly, I was willing to take all the help I could get. I'd given him every bit of information I had and he'd promised that, with his contacts, he'd know Troy and Libby's whereabouts by lunchtime. That didn't stop me sending him a text message, nor him replying in his inimitable style.

Today 08:12

I want you to update me on the hour every hour until my daughter is found.

Are you kidding me? Do you want me to actually do some work or should I just

play text volleyball with
you all day long? Pick one.

OK, but when you find out
their location you are to
immediately inform me.

When I find them, my first
priority will be to get them
to safety, then I'll contact
you. You've got to trust me
to do my job or this isn't
going to work.

You are a rude pain in the arse.

Back atcha. Some advice.
Find a less arrogant tone
when you text people. If
you spoke to me the way
you text, you and I would
be trading bitch-slaps by
now. Now stop texting me
and let me do my thing.

It wasn't that I doubted his abilities, especially after Callie had spent a fair proportion of our night together singing his praises. *J this* and *J that*. As somebody Callie valued so highly, I didn't expect Jon to be anything else but on top of his game. But that wasn't going to stop me from making my own arrangements too. I had a few contacts of my own I could call upon.

And, if Jon didn't deliver, then Jarvis would. Even with his demotion, he was still my eyes and ears within Eva's organization. What was once Dan's was now all hers – or so she thought. She'd declared herself Dan's successor, with Shane and the rest of Dan's old crew backing her all the way. What had she promised them to buy their loyalty? Their own operations? Had she carved up the country like a Sunday roast and promised them all a slice? Eva would soon discover that it took more than a proclamation to wear Dan's old crown. Owen Dowd would be making his move, and soon, to take over all of Eva's territory and then she'd have a gang war on her hands. But let her enjoy her moment in the sun. It wouldn't last long.

Bollocks to this!

I opened my front door. 'Deli, I want to go for a run. An hour will do it. Please inform Michael downstairs that he'll be joining us.'

Deli raised her eyebrows. 'Sir, is that wise?'

'It's run or lose my damned mind.'

'Yes, sir.'

There was no more to be said.

A quick change into my running gear and, a couple of minutes later, I was travelling down in the lift with Deli. Michael was front and centre the moment the lift door opened, running shoes already on his feet. A quick nod to acknowledge him, then we headed for the exit. But the moment I stepped out of my apartment building I was met with a barrage of flashing lights and waving mics in my face. Had my super-injunction been overturned? My heart thrashing against my ribs, I headed down the steps with my protection officers at my side, a plastic smile sitting uneasily on my lips. The reporters moved with me, making it hard to get past them. I was surrounded.

'Prime Minister, is it true that you were once a member of Nought Forever?'

What the actual hell? My mouth fell open before I quickly pasted on a more neutral expression.

'Prime Minister, do you, in fact, have a tattoo on your chest that reads *Nought Forever*?'

Hellsake!

'Are you now or have you ever been a member of the terrorist NF?'

My eyebrows knitting together, I stopped walking to face the reporters who all pushed their microphones further forward into my face. Better to face them now than let the speculation run for days, ruining what was left of my reputation.

'Where on earth did you get that garbage?' I asked.

'Your ex-lover Bella Monroe will be on the programme *This Morning Albion* in less than an hour saying that she split up with you because you used to be a member of the banned NF and have a tattoo on your chest proudly stating it. Is that true, Prime Minister?'

What the hell? Bella! This bitch!

'And you believe the word of a jealous ex who is trying to discredit me because I called time on our relationship? Are you all really that gullible?' I asked, adding a pitying smile to my expression.

'Miss Monroe is adamant that the tattoo on your chest exists.'

I looked round the mob of reporters circling me like sharks sensing blood. With an exaggerated sigh, I unzipped my running jacket and lifted up my T-shirt. Photographers' cameras flashed, TV cameras moved closer. I pulled my top up higher to reveal my naked chest. If the camera flashes were blinding before, they were like fireworks celebrating the New Year now. I resisted the urge to smile as I lowered my shirt. That would make the online news within the hour, the TV news tonight and be on the front page of every newspaper by morning.

Screw you, Bella, and the taxi they sent to pick you up. Without saying another word, my protection officers and I started at a serious pace towards the local park. I ignored all the questions being fired in quick succession at my back, not properly relaxing until the reporters had been left far behind us. I had no time for Bella's jealous nonsense. I had other more important things on my mind.

The sky, a strange mix of grey and brown like a toddler's finger-painting, threatened imminent rain. Rain or shine – nothing was going to stop me today. I hit the park and was off, my detail matching my pace. They got paid handsomely to keep up with me and anyone who slacked didn't last long in my employ. I ran round the park perimeter twice, keeping up the punishing pace.

But, no matter how fast my legs ran, my thoughts outpaced them. Thoughts that goaded, that relentlessly mocked. After all these years, and the wistful memories, I'd had Callie in my arms only to lose her once more.

Blackmailing her into staying on as my lawyer . . .

Smooth, Tobey. Real smooth.

Once she'd discovered my tattoo, every word that came out of my mouth had emerged wearing a grotesque clown mask. Every move I made after that had just served to push her further away. So much for my renowned fast thinking and my reputation for being ninja-quick on my feet. Not when it came to Callie. She was my nemesis, yet in spite of that I needed her like I needed to breathe The only trouble was she hated my guts and I had no idea how to rectify that. There was no point even trying until Troy and Libby were found safe and well. That was the other thing that had me bewildered. The depth of love I felt for a daughter I barely knew. But it didn't matter. Liberty had reached out to me – she wanted us to meet after all this time. Surely that meant she and I had . . . potential? Yet now that too had been snatched away.

My plan of action was simple – find my daughter and teach a hard, painful lesson to the ones who had dared to abduct her. Whoever they were, they had no idea who they were messing with. But they would learn. I'd personally see to it. And, if that retribution paved my way straight through the gates of hell, then so be it.

No one else I cared about was going to get hurt.

So, from now on, I'd do what I had to do. Whatever it took.

What I especially needed was to get out from under this ridiculous murder charge that hung over me like a heavy boulder suspended by a single fraying thread. I'd spent a sleepless night figuring out how to do that until I'd finally come up with a stratagem. It was risky – bollocks to that, it was perilous – but it was all I had.

Each time my feet pounded the path, my thoughts jumped and slid and slotted into place like jigsaw pieces. Running always did that for me, helped straighten out my thinking. I didn't have all the answers, but I had more than twenty-four hours earlier. I didn't know where my daughter was right now, but I would by early afternoon. My hands were about to get very dirty and I had to make sure that Callie was nowhere near when that went down.

If anything happened to her . . .

Somehow I had to get Callie to forgive me. One night with her wasn't enough. I wanted her face to be the last thing I saw before I closed my eyes each night and the first thing I saw each morning when I woke up. I'd thought I was over her. She was a memory that walked like a shadow behind me. Occasionally, that memory would walk in step for a moment, for a minute, but no longer. Jon – damn him – was right. When the kids were safe, I'd apply all my energy to having her back in my life. Permanently.

I turned to head back to my apartment. Activating my earbuds, I issued a command to the smartphone in my pocket to phone Jon Duba on the burner I'd given him.

He picked up within two rings.

'You told me not to text you so I'm phoning for a progress report,' I said, getting straight down to it.

'For Shaka's sake! When I know something, you'll know something. Besides which, I'm only lending you my services. Don't forget Callie is my boss. I still don't like you.'

'Godsake, man, will you back the hell up?' I asked,

exasperated. 'We all want the same thing here. I'm not your enemy. And you came to me, not the other way round – remember?'

'Was there anything else? I'm busy,' snapped Jon.

'D'you know where Eva Foxton is? I want to pay her a visit,' I said, reining in with difficulty my irritation at his tone. 'I've already spoken to George, Dan's old butler, but he doesn't have a clue.'

'Why would George know Eva's whereabouts? What's it got to do with him?'

'Eva has sacked him and given him until this Friday lunchtime to clear out. She intends to move into Dan's penthouse apartment at the weekend. As all the moving arrangements are being sorted between the two of them, I thought George might have a clue. Good butlers know everything, and George is a very good butler. One of the best.'

'But he didn't have an answer for you.'

'Being one of the best doesn't make him all-knowing,' I conceded. 'So do you know or not? You're not the only one who's busy.'

'You're convinced Eva had something to do with Libby and Troy's disappearance?'

'I'd put money on it. No one else has the clout, resources or, quite frankly, the titanium balls. Dowd wouldn't care one way or the other if I'd killed Dan. In fact, he'd be grateful that I removed his rival. Which leaves Eva.'

'And the motive would be – apart from sticking it to you, which I can understand and fully appreciate?' said Jon.

Hellsake! This man just wasn't going to let up.

'One of the first things I promised to do when our party got back into power was to obliterate the illegal drugs trade in Albion, particularly sales of Prop, from the top down. No more county lines and using children to run the stuff up and down the country, no more corrupt cops inflating their bank accounts by looking the other way, no more bosses like Owen and Eva raking in a fortune over the broken lives and bodies of their victims.'

'I thought that was just smoke and mirrors to get you elected,' said Jon.

'It was a manifesto promise and I intend to make good on it,' I replied. 'Eva and Owen have the market for Prop pretty much sewn up between them, but not for much longer. Not if I have anything to do with it. Are you prepared to help me or not?'

'Give me an hour.'

And, with that, Jon disconnected our call.

Rude.

He had the upper hand right now because I needed him, and we both knew it, but once I had Liberty home safe and sound then Jon and I were going to have a full and extremely frank exchange of views.

twenty-eight. Troy

Digging was painful, not to mention tedious, and our progress was slow to non-existent. I was beginning to wonder if I'd actually already died and this was some kind of purgatory where I'd only get to heaven once I'd dug my way out of this frickin' basement, but it would take several millennia to do so.

We'd been digging in silence for a while when Libby hit me with an unexpected question. 'Troy, which girl or guy in our year would you ask out on a date?'

Eyes wide with dismay, I stared at her. She chuckled. 'And you have to answer truthfully. No lies in this basement. That way we can both build a shared stairway to heaven.'

Face burning, I admitted, 'I . . . er . . . well . . . I quite like Meshella—'

'Meshella Musenga? Are you kidding me? She's a total bitch. Believe me, you can do better.' Libby looked me up and down. 'You need to raise your standards.'

'So who would you pick out for me then?' I asked, annoyed.

'Hmm. How about Ramona?'

'I don't think so. Besides, Zane has his eye on her so she's off limits.'

'Terri?'

'The one who's always going on about her latest fashion this and her exclusive fashion that? I'll pass.'

'Have you ever been on a date with anyone from our school?' asked Libby.

Cheeks on fire, I shook my head. 'I've asked out a couple of girls over the last year, but they both said no.'

'Are they stupid or what?' Libby frowned.

I grinned. 'Thanks for the compliment!'

Bright red now crept across Libby's cheeks as she realized what she'd just said. 'Don't get all puffed up. Why did they say no?'

'They didn't tell me and I wasn't going to ask them to write an essay,' I replied. 'To be honest . . . I find it hard to know what to talk to girls about.'

'You're doing all right with me. We're not an unfathomable species from another planet,' said Libby. 'Just talk to us like normal human beings.'

'So have you been on any dates?' I asked.

'One. With Dominic Slecker, but that was a disaster.'

'Why?'

'His views were too much like my mum's.'

Enough said. I always thought Dominic was an arsehole. Libby had just confirmed it.

'If you could change one thing about your life, what would it be?' She kept the out-of-nowhere questions coming. 'The one thing you regret doing or not doing.'

She was making a big deal out of checking the makeshift bandage around her palms rather than look at me.

I sighed. 'I wish I'd tried harder to persuade Mum that her friend killed my dad.'

'But there must be something you can do?' Libby frowned.

'You believe me now?'

Her frown deepened. 'Of course I believe you. This isn't a wind-up, is it?'

I shook my head. 'It's not the kind of thing I'd joke about.'

'Well then,' said Libby. 'So what're you going to do?'

'Short of persuading Sonny to confess, there's not a lot I can do. And I guarantee he won't be declaring his guilt any time soon. He's got the thing he wanted – my mum. Nothing I say or do will make him give her up.'

'Then you'll have to get him to admit it,' said Libby decisively.

'And just how d'you reckon I should do that?'

'Did you take photos when you were at the quarry?'

I shook my head. 'No. I was too shocked and shook up to do anything – and, by the time I thought of it, Sonny was right behind me on his quad bike, so I didn't get the chance.'

'That's a pity. With the car now gone, Sonny probably thinks he's home and dry.' Libby shook her head. 'What we need to do is get him so riled at you that he'll blab about the whole thing and you must record it. As long as he thinks he's got away with it, his guard will be down.'

'That kind of thing only happens in bad TV dramas. And where did "we" come from?'

Libby looked taken aback. 'Of course – we! You don't seriously think I'd let you try and do this on your own, do you? We have to find a way to get him to confess.'

'Thank you.' My voice was gruff. I hadn't realized till that moment just how much I needed someone to believe me and be on my side when it came to Sonny. The thought of him someday marrying my mum when he'd killed my dad had been eating away at my brain like steady drops of battery acid.

'If we can get him to agree to meet you at a restaurant – no, too noisy – or a library or somewhere relatively quiet, we can set it up beforehand so you can come straight out and accuse him and then see what he says.'

'I did that before, in front of Mum and in private. All he said was, *prove it*. Sonny's not an idiot, Libby. It won't be that easy to set him up.'

'Yeah, but there's only one of him and there's two of us.' Libby smiled. 'I know we can do this.'

'One slight problem . . .'

'What's that?' She frowned.

'Er, we're stuck in here. Remember?'

Libby looked round in surprise, like she'd forgotten we were locked in a cellar with no way out.

Lips pursed, she said, 'Give me ten minutes for the pain in my hands to subside. Then we'll get back to digging.'

'But you said—'

'I know. But we need to get out of here so you can stop Sonny marrying your mum. We can't give up.'

In that moment, I was so grateful for Libby. Her positivity that we could escape and then do something about Sonny was almost infectious. *Almost*.

'What about you? What one thing would you change?' I asked.

'One thing when I have so many to choose from?' Libby scoffed. 'Well, if I can only change one thing, I would hang on to my best friend in Year Seven and I wouldn't let my mum or my pride or anything else come between him and me. Ever.'

My face began to burn again as Libby looked me in the eye and carried on speaking. 'Then I would've had someone to tell about my mum's put-downs and abuse, how her boyfriend Pete wouldn't leave me alone and how they both made my life a misery. I would've had my best friend to share all that with. And I would've been in his life to tell him how sorry I was when I heard his dad had died. That's what I would change.'

Damn it! What was wrong with me? Every time this girl opened her mouth, I had to swallow real hard to stop myself from doing something really embarrassing.

'You and me? We could start over from here if you like,' I suggested.

'I would like that. Very much.' Libby put out her bandaged hand. I shook it.

We shared a smile, tentative but real. The years since we were both eleven didn't melt away exactly, but they didn't sit quite as awkwardly between us.

'Troy, your dad dying the way he did,' Libby began. 'How long did it take you to get over it?'

I knew what she was asking. 'I didn't get over it,' I admitted. 'I just stopped living with grief and instead let grief live with me.'

'What does that mean?'

'It's like an unwanted visitor that I'll never be rid of. Sometimes it comes into my head and outstays its welcome, but there are days when it . . . fades, and I can think of my dad and smile without feeling like someone is throwing darts at my chest.'

'How long did that take?'

Pause. 'It's a work-in-progress.'

Libby nodded. 'Fair enough.'

Daily Shouter Online

Home. News. Politics. Celebs. Entertainment. Sport. Tech. Health. Science. Money. More.

BREAKING NEWS. Nought workers at Albion Isle Bank earn a quarter less than their Cross colleagues

Albion Isle Bank's recent survey of its 30,000 employees has revealed that its Nought employees on average earn 25 per cent less than their Cross colleagues on the same grade.

Colbi Obi-Reacher, CEO of Albion Isle Bank, told the *Daily Shouter*, 'Yes, the discrepancy figures are disappointing, but we have been taking active steps over the last few years to rectify this anomaly. This survey will ensure we redouble our efforts to ensure no such gap exists within five years.'

A Nought bank employee who did not wish to be named stated, 'The bank has known about this for decades. The survey was just concrete proof of what we Nought employees already knew: we are not being treated equitably and too many of us have permanent head scars from bouncing off the glass ceiling. In five years' time, it wouldn't surprise me in the slightest if we're having this same conversation.'

twenty-nine. Callie

I stared out of the rain-splattered window as Sol and I sat in the back of a white cab on our way back to chambers. Droplets wove meandering patterns down the window and the sky above was a sombre misery-grey. The late-morning London traffic was appalling. The journey was more stop than start with the taxi driver trying to spark up a conversation when it was obvious that neither Sol nor I were in a particularly chatty mood. Or, more accurately, I was seething and ready to decapitate someone and Sol was trying to keep out of the line of fire by saying as little as possible.

'Sol, who was it who had me arrested? Was it Gabriel?' I asked quietly when I could trust myself to speak.

'I don't know for sure yet, but that's where I'd put my money,' said Sol. 'That man is such a loser.'

My lips tightened. 'If it was him, then I'm going to rip his balls off.'

'I suggest you obtain incontrovertible proof before you start shredding testicles,' said Sol dryly.

I barely heard him. Gabe . . .

Gabriel Moreland was not just the prosecutor in Tobey's trial, he was also my ex whose ego had taken a severe pummelling when I'd dumped him. He'd never forgiven me for it. When I discovered he was to be my opponent in Tobey's trial, I knew I'd have a fight on my hands. I'd found out since that he'd specifically asked for the case when he learned I was defending Tobey. He'd made Tobey's forthcoming trial personal. Gabe couldn't handle losing at anything. So I knew he'd try to use the court case to rub my face in the dirt.

It turned out that my arrest had arisen from not informing the court that my mum had been present at Dan's dinner party on the night he died. Though all the witnesses had confirmed that Dan was still very much alive when Mum left his apartment that evening, it didn't alter the fact that I should, at the very least, have informed the prosecution about her involvement. The Bar Council took the view that just because my surname was Hadley it did not negate the fact that I should've been the one to inform them that Sephy Ealing, one of those present on the night of Dan's death, was my mother. Apparently, the information had been 'brought to their attention' and I'd been informed that further enquiries might well result in me being formally charged. My conduct was being investigated. Even if I were to be exonerated, any and every prosecutor worth half a damn would bring up my arrest as a reason why I should not be allowed to work as a court advocate. As a defender, any one of my future clients found guilty could appeal against their sentence on the grounds that they had had a lawyer likely to prejudice the court based on past conduct – and I'd be screwed. Any future clients found innocent could have their sentences appealed against by the prosecution on the same basis and I'd be screwed.

Let's face it, I was screwed.

'So what happens now?' As if I didn't know.

'Let's discuss it in my office,' said Sol, his brown eyes sombre in the dim light of the cab.

I couldn't wait that long.

'Sol, thank you for standing by me, but we both know what this means,' I said quietly. I glanced at the cab door. The lit red light on the panel of buttons and switches beneath the window indicated that the driver could hear every word we said. I switched it off, but knew that didn't guarantee that we'd have absolute privacy.

I'd already done some quick thinking to form a plan. 'Sol, here's what I propose,' I said quietly. 'I'll hand my case files to others in the office to take over – except for the one case that is responsible for all this. Let me continue to act as defence advocate in that and when it's all over – no matter what the outcome – I'll resign.'

'Let's not get ahead of ourselves. It doesn't need to come to that,' said Sol.

He was a good man. 'I think we both know that ship has disappeared over the horizon.'

'We have to get to the bottom of this to make sure it goes no further, then we apply to have the arrest expunged from your record,' said Sol.

'Expunged or not, my guess is the word is already out.'

Sol didn't reply. He couldn't, and his silence confirmed my worst fears.

Like I said – screwed.

'There is, of course, someone else who could've orchestrated all this,' said Sol.

'Who?' I frowned.

Sol eyed our cab driver. 'The man you're c… defending.'

My mouth fell open. 'Why on earth would he have me arrested?'

'Because, with you out of the picture, he would have up to six months to find another lawyer, and any lawyer who knows what they're doing could delay the trial for up to a year after that. That would put him back in office and able to pick up where he left off, super-injunction in place in perpetuity.' Sol gave me a solemn, conspiratorial wink to make sure I got the point. 'With you in the frame and his court-case date set and imminent, he's effectively benched from politics.'

Already I was shaking my head. 'No. He wouldn't do that to me. No.'

'Are you sure about that?' asked Sol. 'I mean one hundred per cent sure?'

I opened my mouth to answer, only to slowly close it again. While sitting on the park bench earlier, hadn't I too wondered whether or not I could trust Tobey?

'Can anyone ever be totally certain about anything?' I hedged.

Sol raised an eyebrow. Damn him. Would Tobey really stoop so low as to have me arrested just to get back to his job, even temporarily? The sad, worrying answer was – I didn't know. But even ninety-nine per cent sure still left one per cent of doubt.

And that one per cent was enough to kick the hell out of my heart. I had to put my feelings aside and get on with the business at hand. Taking out my phone, I sent a text to Jon.

Today 11:07

Hi, J, any progress?

llie, it's only been a minute. Give me a chance. I'll tell you what I told Tobey – when I find Troy and Libby, I'll get them to safety, then let you know our location. You and Tobey need to stop phoning/texting me every two seconds. Let me get on with my job without the constant interruptions.

All right! All right! My head is now bouncing round my feet where you just bit it clean off. I was only asking. I'm worried sick and scared, OK?

I understand. No need to get sniffy with me. You know I love you.
Durbridge? Not so much.
Keep your chin up xx

I'm trying, Jon. God knows I'm trying.

thirty. Sephy

As I drove to my first appointment, my phone rang. A glance at my dashboard indicated that Sonny was phoning me. With a sigh, I pressed the control on the wheel of my car to connect the call.

'Hi, Sephy. I'm at your house, chatting to Meggie, and wondering where you are?' said Sonny.

Shoot! I promised him we'd spend the morning together. I'd completely forgotten.

'Sonny, I'll be home soon. I've just got a couple of stops to make first and they won't take long.'

'Sephy, what's going on?'

'I will tell you everything when I get home, I promise,' I replied. 'Trust me.'

Pause. 'D'you trust me, Persephone?' Sonny's question was serious verging on solemn. There were more than just words behind that question: there were thoughts and feelings as well.

'Of course I trust you, Sonny,' I said. 'I'm marrying you, aren't I?'

'*Are you?* Do you want to marry me, Sephy?' Sonny asked.

Pause.

'I do.'

'At last!' said Sonny, the grin evident in his voice. 'I love you, Sephy. Very much.'

'That's because you have excellent taste,' I teased. 'See you soon.'

I hung up before Sonny could say anything else, like asking me to say the words back to him. I cared about Sonny a great deal. I had now said I'd marry him. But I had yet to say the three words I knew he was waiting for.

Callum, what's wrong with me? Why do I find it so hard to say them? I'm still waiting for a sign from you that I'm doing the right thing. Yes, I know that's ridiculous, but I swear I can feel you near me, watching over me. So please, just one indication that I'm doing the right thing. Then I can live the rest of my life knowing that you're happy for me. Please.

Specimens. I stood before my restaurant, waiting for the usual sense of pride, of accomplishment when I looked at it, to warm me. But I felt nothing. Its smoky windows and simple awning were classy without being ostentatious. This place had been my haven when Nathan died, something to keep going in his name. No wonder I'd fought Dan so hard when he tried to take it from me.

I walked through the eerily empty dining room on my way to the kitchen. Most days we opened for lunch and dinner – except Sundays. On Wednesdays, Specimens only opened in the evening, so the place was always like a ghost of itself until the dinner customers began to arrive.

When Nathan and I had run this place together, it had been more of a nightclub that served food on the side. Now it was the other way round. It was an upscale restaurant with live music most evenings. After Nathan's death, in my naïvety,

I had thought that a restaurant would be easier to manage than a nightclub. No more bouncers. No more drunk people arguing to get in or puking all over the bathroom and the dance floor, in the pitiful belief that getting bombed off their faces was the only true way to have a good time. I didn't miss any of that at all. But running a restaurant had brought its own set of problems. From customers who cleared their plates, then complained about the food, hoping to get their meal for free, to those who actually brought in vermin, hoping to discredit me and my restaurant, and others who wanted a free meal for them and their thirty friends in exchange for a positive online review. Feel free to sod off and die with that one. And, Callum, don't even get me started on the never-ending complaints . . .

'My soup is too cold.'

'It's gazpacho, ma'am. It's meant to be served cold.'

'Gazpacho? What backward country is that from?'

A suppressed sigh. 'Would you like to try it, ma'am? I can assure you it's delicious.'

'No, I don't want to bloody try it. Foreign muck. Bring me some sweet-potato soup or some cou-cou – if you even know how to cook that properly.'

'Yes, ma'am.'

'My pie is too hot.'

How about you wait a couple of minutes before cramming it in your mouth then?

'Yes, sir.'

'My fruit crumble is too dry.'

See that little pot of custard next to your bowl of crumble? Pour that over your dessert and snap! Problem solved.

'No, sir.'

'I don't like the colour of these egg yolks.'

I didn't lay them.

Three bags full, sir.

The complaints ranged from the invalid to the downright ridiculous. Thank goodness for Amari, the restaurant manager, who was adept at dealing with difficult customers. She had oceans of patience.

Increasingly, I'd been thinking about selling Specimens and having done with it. It wasn't like I hadn't received offers over the years – mostly from legitimate sources; some from the likes of Dan Jeavons. I could only hope and pray that his pernicious soul was rotting in hell where it belonged.

Daniel Jeavons . . .

His name sat on my tongue like needles and pins. I didn't send him off, but that didn't mean I was sorry about it. He was the deceased author of the play my family and I now found ourselves cast in. His reach extended even from the grave.

But I was going to put a stop to that.

The moment I walked into the restaurant kitchen, all eyes were on me, albeit momentarily before the staff got back to work. On the kitchen radio, there was a news story about Tobey Durbridge, but one of the kitchen staff turned the volume down as I entered the room. I liked to see the kitchen busy, everyone moving with a point and purpose. With Saul, my head chef, in charge, there was no way any of the staff would get away with slacking.

'Mrs Ealing, is there a problem?' he asked. He was a stocky guy, but it was all muscle, a hangover from the days when he used to be a professional wrestler before a broken back forced him to look for another line of work. Saul was the blondest Nought I'd ever met. His eyebrows, even his eyelashes, were blond.

'Mrs Ealing?' he prompted. His frown had now tipped over into a full-on impatient scowl. He wanted me out of his kitchen so that he and his staff could get back to working without scrutiny. I was holding him up. Tough!

Amari raised a quizzical eyebrow too. She was a Cross with thin locs dyed copper, beautiful full lips and an eyebrow piercing above shrewd, dark, honey-brown eyes. 'Is everything all right, Sephy?'

I forced a smile. 'Of course. I'd just like a word with Devon.' I turned to the tall, bald Nought guy behind one of the counters, noting his surly expression, which was a permanent fixture. 'Dev, may I see you in my office, please?'

'But Saul's going through our roles for the evening. I'll miss it if—'

'You'll catch up. Now, Devon – if you don't mind.'

Now, Devon, even if you do mind. I made my way through the staff-only swing doors and walked towards my office at the end of the corridor. I didn't need to glance behind to know that Devon was walking behind me, truculence in every step. He was fine taking orders from Saul. From Amari and me? Not so much. That was his problem – I didn't intend to make it mine. I held the door to my office open, waiting for him to walk past me, which he did, slightly closer than was strictly necessary.

I sat on the edge of my desk, not bothering with a chair. I indicated the chair in front. 'Take a seat.'

'If you're going to fire me, I'd rather stand,' Devon replied.

I studied him, taking my time before answering. 'Any particular reason why I should fire you?'

Devon pursed his lips together as he glared at me.

OK, let's try something else. 'You're still on parole, right?'

Devon nodded.

'How's your wife and family?'

He took a deep breath. 'Look, Mrs Ealing, don't fire me. Please. I need this job. I know I can be . . .'

'Surly? Belligerent? Moody? A pain in the arse?'

A slight smile flitted across Devon's lips. 'All of the above,' he agreed. 'But I'm a good chef and I'm determined to be a great one. Saul has faith in me and that's all I need – someone to believe in me.'

'Does Katie believe in you?' I asked of his wife.

Devon shrugged, a whole world of meaning in the lift of his shoulders.

'You think she's waiting for you to . . . let her down?'

Devon sighed. 'I know I don't have a good track record and yeah, I've messed up before, but I'm not going back to prison. I can't. Not again. I'd rather die first.'

That I could use. Needs must.

'Devon, I need some info from you,' I said.

'Oh yes?' Devon eyed me, on his guard again.

'Now that Dan Jeavons is dead, who has taken his place?'

A stillness descended over Devon that wasn't hard to decipher. His ice-blue eyes narrowed. 'How should I know? What makes you think I have anything to do with that world?'

The belligerence was back with a vengeance.

'Dev, I wish I had the time to bat this back and forth with you, but I don't. I wouldn't be asking if it wasn't a matter of life and death – literally.'

'I don't know what you're talking about—'

'For Shaka's sake! You think anyone gets taken on at my restaurant without a full background check first?' I straightened up. 'You think I don't know about your time in prison because you took the rap for your brother who worked for Jeavons? How long has it been since your brother's disappearance? Nearly three years, isn't it? Word is he's propping up a motorway or bridge somewhere for bringing the House of Jeavons into the public gaze and disrepute. So don't treat me like a fool. I've neither the time nor the patience.'

Shocked, eyes wide, Devon's mouth dropped open.

Remorse washed over me. That was well out of order. And coming out with it so brazenly too, but I pushed any and all regrets to one side. They were a luxury I just didn't have time for. I was being a bitch, but so be it. My son needed me.

'You don't know that. Dave might still be alive for all you know,' Devon proclaimed, his eyes spitting lava. 'That's a hell of a thing to say.'

'You're right and I'm sorry. Of course he might still be alive,' I say, acknowledging the extremely remote possibility. Giving Devon a few seconds to calm down, I carried on. 'Dev, I really do need your help. So let me ask you again: who has taken over from Jeavons?'

'I don't hang around with people like that – not any more.'

I raised an eyebrow, waiting for him to get to my point.

'But the word on the street is that Dan Jeavons only trusted two people with all the details of his many operations,' Devon said reluctantly. 'Eva and Shane.'

'Eva Foxton and Shane who? Not Jarvis Burton?'

A speculative gleam lit Devon's eyes. 'How come you know about them? How d'you even know their names?'

That was my business.

'Well, what I heard is that Eva has taken over and demoted Jarvis. She got a new lieutenant, some guy called Shane Stoats. He's a psycho by all accounts. Takes no prisoners,' Devon continued. 'But Owen Dowd has practically declared all-out war on her and anyone who throws their lot in with her. There'll be a turf war soon, and it's going to get bloody.'

I digested Devon's news in silence.

'So Jarvis no longer works for Eva?'

'He does, but in name only. Everyone's taking bets on for how much longer. In fact, we're all surprised he hasn't already picked up his toys and walked. For someone like Jarvis, being demoted from vice-president to foot soldier must be hellish humiliating. His pride has taken a severe kicking, if nothing else.'

Now why would a guy like Jarvis still be hanging around Eva if he were no longer in a position of authority? Maybe he just had bills to pay like everyone else. But I'd met Jarvis. He wasn't the kind to take an insult like that lying down. In Eva's shoes, I'd watch my back.

'Where do I find Eva?'

Devon's eyebrows shot up until they practically disappeared beneath his hairline. 'How the hell would I know? I told you, I don't hang around with that sort. My wife would kill me, not to mention Saul.'

'I'm not saying that you're inside her pocket,' I replied. 'But she must conduct her business from somewhere that isn't her home, so where might that be?'

Devon glared at me. 'Dan owns . . . used to own Ava's on Habari Street in Soho. I've heard that Eva has set up shop there, but that's all I know.'

A starting point. It would do.

'Thanks, Devon,' I said. 'Don't let me keep you.'

Eyes narrowed, Devon cast me one last speculative look before he headed for the door of my office. At the last moment, he turned back. 'Mrs Ealing, I don't know what you're up to and it's none of my business, but just be careful, OK? The likes of Eva Foxton and Stoats don't play by any rules you and me have ever heard of.'

I smiled faintly. 'Thanks for the heads-up, Devon. And sorry for what I said earlier about your brother.'

Devon nodded and left the room.

Eva Foxton and Shane Stoats.

My worst fears were confirmed. Eva's reputation preceded her. There would be no respite from the demands for money. If anything, a bigger slice of the Specimens pie would probably become obligatory. The time to just sell up and have done with it was drawing ever closer.

There came a tentative knock at my door. Without waiting for an invitation, Amari entered my office.

'Sephy, I . . . is everything all right? You didn't look too happy when you came into the kitchen.'

I dredged up a smile. 'Everything's fine, Amari. I need to

go out for the rest of the day and I probably won't be back until tomorrow. You can handle anything that comes up, right?'

Amari nodded. 'Of course.'

I didn't doubt it for a second. Amari was a very competent manager. She and the rest of the staff were now my only reason for not wanting to give up this place. They had worked their arses off to make Specimens a success. Giving up would feel like letting them down.

But Specimens and my staff would have to wait. I had some thinking to do, some plans to make and a meeting to prepare for. Eva didn't know it yet, but she and I had an appointment.

I straightened up and followed Amari out of my office. We both headed towards the front entrance in silence. She needed to check the late dinner bookings on the computer at the front desk, and I had places to be. I turned to her, only to find her already looking at me, her eyebrows drawn together in concern.

'Amari, I know I don't tell you this often enough, but thank you for being an amazing manager who always has my back. And thanks for handling Noah.'

Noah had been the deputy manager given the boot by Amari the previous month.

Amari's eyes widened. 'You knew about that?'

'About him stealing from the restaurant? Yeah, I knew. I think I found out the day before you did. I also knew you'd handle it – which you did.'

'Thanks,' Amari nodded. 'It was . . . unpleasant. I didn't like sacking him, but he was stealing food and silverware and over-egging the restaurant's expenses so he could pocket the difference.'

'You did what you had to do. Though I have to warn you, we may end up having to report Noah to the police after all. I've been warned we're about to be investigated by the tax authorities.'

'Oh no. If it gets out that one of our managers—'Whatever else Amari was about to say was cut short by the front door opening. 'I'm sorry, but we're not open until five thirty.'

'I'm not here for lunch,' came the reply. 'Unless she's buying.'

And there, looking me up and down, stood the last person I'd expected to see today. My sister, Minerva.

thirty-one. Libby

Troy took a sip from the one remaining water bottle and handed it back to me.

'Have some more,' he said.

I shook my head. For every sip he took, he was letting me have two. And, to my shame, I'd only just noticed. I screwed the lid back on and examined the contents. We had about one-eighth of a bottle left. I doubted if that little would see us through the night.

'How long can we survive without water?' I asked.

'Three to four days,' Troy replied immediately.

'The shit you know.'

'I think you mean the *useful* shit I know,' Troy corrected.

'I don't suppose you know of a way of making water down here in this cellar?' I said. Now that really would be useful.

He sighed. 'If I'd known we'd be down here this long, I would've suggested that we didn't pee and poo in the same bucket. We should've pooed in a far corner and peed in the bucket so we could drink it.'

'Ew! You've got to be kidding me.'

'Pee is mostly sterile, but it does contain some waste stuff so it should only be drunk in small doses and as a last resort, but, I don't know if you've noticed, we're rapidly reaching that point.'

He didn't have to tell me that. My nerves had been on a rolling boil since we'd been chucked down here in this cellar, but there was only so much panicking I could do. Panic was exhausting.

'Well, that's all academic as our pee has been contaminated now,' I said with some relief.

Drinking pee? And not even just mine, but Troy's as well? *Ewww!*

'Where's your sense of adventure, Libby?' asked Troy, trying to suppress the smile threatening to take control of his mouth.

'I left it at home next to the kitchen tap,' I told him sourly.

He laughed – and I was surprised by just how much I liked the sound. So much so that I couldn't help smiling too, albeit reluctantly.

'We'll find a way out of here, Libby. One way or another.'

'I know we will,' I replied.

Troy leaned forward. So did I. Forehead against forehead, eyes closed, we both considered our words.

Together we would rise or fall.

But at least it would be together.

thirty-two. Sephy

'Minerva? What on earth brings you here?' I frowned.

'And hello to you too, Persephone,' Minerva replied.

Amari looked at me and Minerva and decided she had things to do elsewhere. She retreated like her toes were on fire and I can't say I blamed her. Minerva and I stood awkwardly, taking each other in. No hug, no kiss, nothing that might smudge her make-up.

My sister was one of those annoying people who aged like vintage wine. Even now, I still secretly admired her effortless poise. If anything, she was leaner and more toned than when we were teenagers. An hour each morning in her home gym saw to that. She was never less than immaculate and was impatient with anyone around her who didn't set themselves the same impossible standard – which included me. My sister had her family and her career and, as they had flourished over the years, so our relationship had diminished. Minerva was now the editor of one of those glossy magazines, all horrendously expensive clothes and accessories worn by tall, stunning, mainly Cross models with long necks and sneering expressions.

The truth was that Minerva and I had very little in common and, over the years, we'd become high-days-and-holidays sisters. I'd accepted the truth a long time ago, but that didn't stop me from being wistful for the relationship we should've had. Our conversations rarely strayed away from:

'Happy birthday, Minerva.'

'Merry Crossmas, Seph.'

'How are Zuri and Taj?'

'Good. How are Troy and Callie?'

'Fine.'

'How are you?'

'Never better.'

That was usually the gist of our painful, mercifully short phone calls.

Even after all these years, I couldn't shake the belief that Minerva had never quite forgiven me – and Callum – for tarnishing the family brand. Invitations to family dinners extended by me were rarely turned down, but they were seldom reciprocated. Minerva lived in a gated estate for the super-exclusive who wanted to stay that way. It made me wonder if any of her neighbours even knew she had a sister, much less who her sister was . . . is. I doubted it. But then why should they? My fifteen minutes of fame was a long time ago.

Minerva flashed me another critical look. In a second, she had taken in my black jeans, my mustard-yellow jumper, a couple of sizes too big for me, and my fawn-coloured sheepskin boots, made for warmth and comfort rather than style. The tiny flicker of her top lip signalled her disapproval. Anyone else would've missed it. I didn't. My clothes had been bought from the local department store, not an exclusive boutique like hers. If she had a problem with that, she could file it under 'tough'.

'How is everyone?' I asked.

'Fine.'

I winced inwardly at the inevitability of our usual tepid conversation. Minerva hadn't come all this way to exchange platitudes, but I'd learned over the years that if my big sister, Minerva, wanted something it was best just to stay silent and let her get to the point.

'Sephy, I've been hearing rumours,' she began slowly.

What? Had she heard about Troy? If she had, then everyone knew.

'Oh? What kind of rumours?' I asked carefully. Warning bells pealed in my head.

'About Callie and Tobias Durbridge. Is my niece getting involved again with that blanker?'

I winced. I couldn't help it. The B-word . . . Even though it was never addressed to me, I hated it. Mind you, in my time I had been called a 'blanker-lover'. Unpleasant.

'Minnie,' I began, deliberately shortening my sister's name to its detested moniker to prick her skin. 'My first love and your niece's dad was a Nought. Don't say that word in front of me.'

'You know I didn't mean anything by it,' Minerva dismissed.

'If you don't mean anything by it, don't use it. And, if you can use it in front of me, knowing everything I've been through, then that doesn't make you much of a sister, does it?'

'OK. I'm sorry. Happy now?'

I glared at Minerva. If she didn't get it after all this time, then she never would.

'Look, I'm truly sorry,' Minerva said with a sigh. 'I've had a crap day. Between you and me, *Essentials* isn't doing so well. I've been told I have three months to turn the magazine's fortunes around or the publication is no more and I'm out the door.'

'I'm sorry to hear that.' And I was. Being the editor of *Essentials* was the entirety of Minerva's professional world and three-quarters of her personal life.

'Sephy, to cut a long story short . . .'

'Too late!'

Minerva frowned for a second, then rolled her eyes. 'As I was saying, I've heard rumours that Tobey Durbridge is in trouble, serious trouble, and that Callie is defending him in court, but there's a super-injunction stopping the story from being reported. Is any of that true?'

But wait! Is that why Minerva had turned up on my doorstep? For an exclusive? For Shaka's sake. I shook my head.

Me and my family's woes were all very well, but Minerva had a magazine to save. She was after an exclusive, juicy story – and that made her extremely dangerous.

'I'm surprised at you, Minnie, listening to gossip. Is that what *Essentials* is now? A gossip rag?'

Minerva bristled. 'No, it is not. But an exclusive would help the magazine out enormously.'

'And it wouldn't do you any harm either, right? Well, I'm afraid you've been misinformed. You're barking up the wrong tree.'

'Is that true? It feels to me like you're protesting rather too much.' Minerva's eyes narrowed.

'Suit yourself.' I shrugged. 'You want to waste your time chasing an illusion, go for it. Now, if you'll excuse me, I have an appointment. I was just heading out the door when you arrived.'

'Where are you going?'

Oh hell, no!

'Minnie, the days of reporting my movements to you were over when we were teenagers. No . . . wait . . . there never were any such days. I'll follow you out.' I indicated the door.

Minerva frowned, but did as requested and headed for the door. 'There's no need to be quite so salty. And you do know how much I loathe being called Minnie, right?'

'You do know how much I hate you minding my business, right?' I shot back.

Reluctantly, Minerva smiled. 'You and me, we always could start a forest fire with the sparks we strike off each other.'

A smile tugged at the corner of my lips. 'Maybe one day we'll manage to hold a conversation without snapping at each other.'

My sister and I looked at each other. 'Nah!' we said in unison. And we laughed.

Once out of Specimens, we had our obligatory goodbye hug and I watched and waited as Minerva walked back to her car, which must've been parked in the next street. Only when she turned the corner did I head for my own car. I wouldn't have put it past my sister to try to follow me. Sad but true. Even when I'd started the engine and was on my way to my destination, I still checked my rear-view mirror more than usual just to ensure Minerva wasn't trying to pull one of her stunts. After driving along a couple of random streets, when I saw no sign of her, I headed for my next appointment.

Callie would be appalled if she knew what I was doing, but sitting on my hands, waiting to hear from her or Tobey, wasn't ever going to happen. What kind of woman, what kind of mother, what kind of human being would I be if I did nothing? I had done that once before and the man I loved more than life itself had died.

That was never, ever going to happen again.

The front door opened. I stood up, my hands buried in my jacket pockets. Luckily for me, Shane Stoats was a man of regular habits. He had risen up the ranks to become Eva's second in command, ousting Jarvis. My original intention had been to go after Jarvis, but that was pointless now. He was no longer part of Eva's inner sanctum. Shane was now my best bet to get what I wanted. And, as someone within Eva's sacred inner circle, I'd been observing him for a while.

Being a belt-and-braces kind of person, a month ago, wearing overalls and under the guise of installing a compulsory smart utilities meter in his five-bedroom home, I'd managed to obtain the wireless-network name and password of the house router from his wife, Jill. She'd let me in, given me the information I requested and left me to it with a pitiful lack of curiosity. After fifteen minutes of banging on this wall and tapping at that wall in the garage where the utility meters were, I'd informed her that the wireless signal from her house was not strong enough to install the smart meter, but that the technology was improving all the time so she should expect to hear from us within the year when the hardware had sufficiently improved.

Of course, once I had the wireless name and password, neither Shane, his wife nor his two teenage kids could use their phones, their laptops, the computers within their house without me being able to log in and track every call made, every Internet page visited, every password input.

And, like most people once they'd used the given router password, they never changed it. I had access to all Shane's emails, bank accounts, even the texts that he sent and received in his home.

So I knew he could tell me what I needed to know.

With his wife and kids away on an impromptu holiday and not due back until the weekend, there had been no time like the present. Shane liked to head home every Wednesday between eleven and four thirty. The 'official' explanation was so that he could tend to any household chores that needed doing and spend some quality time with his family. The truth was he wanted privacy so he could gamble on the stock markets and organize his many bank accounts, including the offshore ones. He syphoned funds from here and paid in sums with a lot of digits from there to augment his bank balances. If it weren't for the fact that he had two-factor authentication on his accounts, which meant he needed to input a real-time code sent to his phone each time he wanted to access one of them, I could've and would've cleaned out every bank account he owned weeks ago. But, even with all his bank accounts, what he had was nothing compared to what I intended to get within the next twenty-four hours – with his help, of course.

As Shane's footsteps echoed in the hall, I waited patiently. I'd been cooling my heels in his kitchen for at least twenty minutes after I'd broken in and disabled the router so that the external and internal cameras around his house wouldn't pick up my image. Shane entered, shuffling through the many envelopes he'd picked up from the doormat to see if any of them were worth opening immediately. I stood watching him for a second or two, taking in his sky-blue shirt, his cream-coloured slacks and his bare feet. He must've kicked off his shoes somewhere in the hall. Some instinct had obviously kicked in because his steps slowed then stopped as he looked up. The letters in his hand fell to the floor.

I straightened, my hands still in my jacket pockets. Shane looked me up and down, his eyes missing nothing. He was assessing just how much of a threat I was to him. From the slight tug upwards of one corner of his mouth, I'd been weighed and found wanting – which was fine by me. Being underestimated always gave me an edge. Shane tilted his head to one side, still appraising me.

Not one hair of his immaculate plaited ponytail shifted out of place. This guy passed six foot five in height easily, and pulled off the lean, mean, don't-mess-with-me persona he was undoubtedly going for. I was doing some appraising of my own. I knew his kind. Shane was a guy who liked to dish it out and had no qualms about doing so frequently. Taking it would be a different proposition. If this man got the upper hand, even for a moment, I'd be history.

'Well, you'll know me next time,' I said dryly as Shane continued his scrutiny.

'I know you now,' he said gruffly. 'And you're gonna regret that.'

'What are the chances of you telling me the location of Liberty Jackman and Troy Ealing and the two of us then just going on our merry way?' I asked.

'Slim to none.'

I sighed. 'Yeah, that's what I thought.'

The words were barely out of my mouth before Shane pounced, and I do mean pounced. A starving lioness leaping on a wildebeest could've learned a thing or two. Luckily for me, I'd been expecting him to do just that or I'd've been toast. My hand was already wrapped round the gun in my jacket pocket, my finger on the trigger, and the moment Shane made his move I made mine. And even then the son of a bitch still managed to land on top of me, knocking every last bit of air out of my lungs.

Winded and gasping, I shoved him aside onto his back, a bullet wound in his upper chest, my gun now out in the open and it couldn't have been more firmly planted in my hand if it'd been superglued. I scrambled to my feet. Shane didn't. He lay groaning on the floor, coughing up blood.

'I'll ask you again: where are Libby and Troy? And don't bother lying because we both know you know where they are.'

'Screw you.'

'I've had worse offers,' I taunted. 'But that's not on this week's to-do list. Where are Libby and Troy?'

Another cough. I squatted down next to him. 'Tell me what I want to know and I'll phone for an ambulance.'

Even though he must've been in a great deal of pain, Shane still managed to give me a withering look. I didn't blame him. I wouldn't have fallen for that one either. Worth a try. 'Please don't make me work my way through your nearest and dearest to get the information I want.'

Another cough, this time deliberately aimed at me. Blood splattered all over the lower leg of my trousers and my shoes. Gross!

I jumped up and backed away. 'Tell me what I want to know or I swear I'll be back here bright and early on Saturday morning to make sure your wife and kids – Jill, Abby and Stephen, isn't it? – join you in the hereafter. But not before I've had my fun with them first.'

The flicker in Shane's eyes revealed his first moment of fear since he'd seen me in his kitchen. It never failed. Kids could turn the hardest man's toughest armour into so much soggy, snotty tissue paper.

'They . . . they . . .' Cough. 'Next to . . . end house. Mbizi Street. East Gurendah Harbour.' Cough.

Really? They hadn't bothered to move Libby and Troy to a new location? Arrogant or what?

'If Troy and Libby aren't where you say, I'll be back to take out my disappointment on your family. Understand?'

Shane nodded. 'Th-they . . . are there . . .'

I believed him, which meant coming to Shane's home had been a complete waste of my time. Pissed off, I levelled my gun at his head.

'Don't hurt . . . my family . . .' he whispered.

'Lucky for you, that's not on this week's to-do list either.'

I pulled the trigger.

thirty-three. Tobey

Today 12:32

Jarvis, WTAF? Why have you not got back to me? Have you found out anything about L or T yet?

I've only just had it confirmed that Eva ditched the original clueless morons who snatched those two and has taken over the operation herself. Her plan is to get rid of you once and for all. What d'you want me to do about it?

Find out the location and get them to safety. BY ANY MEANS NECESSARY.

I hear you. BTW, I hear Sephy knows who really killed Dan. Is that true? Is it connected to this?

I'll get back to you on that. Now go do what I pay you for.

thirty-four. Sephy

I was sitting in my parked car, ignoring the rain slapping at the roof and off the windows as I observed the guy on my screen who had only just accepted my invitation to a video call.

Patrix Ellerman, Cross lawyer and all-round lowlife, was far too busy to see me in person and could only spare a couple of minutes on a call. What a shit-fish!

I'd not laid eyes on him since the night of Dan's dinner party and now I took him in as he sat in his high-backed brown leather chair, leaning forward with his hands clasped and his index fingers steepled in what was obviously a power pose he'd no doubt practised in front of more than one mirror. He wore a charcoal-grey jacket with a pale pink, collarless, buttoned-up shirt. His hair was short at the sides with mini locs on top. The whole ensemble had been picked for maximum effect, as was his affectation of tapping his steepled fingers against his bottom lip. Patrix was a guy who appreciated the finer things in life and didn't mind who knew it. He also liked his props – to be treated with what he felt was the proper respect. My daughter, Callie, had introduced me to a number of lawyers, Crosses and a few Noughts, who – like her – deeply cared about not just the law but justice. Patrix wasn't one of those.

'Mr Ellerman, thanks for agreeing to talk to me.'

'Like I said, Mrs Ealing, I'm a very busy man,' said Patrix.

'Of course. Well, I'll get straight down to it. I have reason to believe Tobey Durbridge will soon be cleared of Dan Jeavons' murder and the police will come gunning for one of the rest of us who were present on the night that Dan died. I'm trying to establish incontrovertible proof that none of us did it.'

Silence. Patrix stared at me like I was sprouting horns right before his eyes.

'Mr Ellerman?'

'What makes you think that's the case?' Patrix was wary, to say the least.

'A friend in the police service told me as much.' Which wasn't a million miles away from the truth.

'I don't see what that has to do with me. Obviously I didn't kill Dan Jeavons.'

'Is it obvious?' I asked.

Patrix leaned forward in his chair, his faux power pose abandoned. 'Of course I didn't kill that blanker.'

'You had every reason to.' I was unable to keep the frost from creeping into my voice.

'What d'you mean?'

'I heard about you and Dan and your gambling issues,' I said. 'If *I* know, it's only a matter of time before the police do too – if they don't already.'

'So I owed Jeavons a few hundred thousand. So what?'

A few hundred thousand . . . Whoa.

'I heard Dan was tired of waiting for you to pay it back.'

'You heard entirely too much,' said Patrix. 'Listen, Jeavons was nothing but a greasy, jumped-up social climber with ideas above his level who thought he could use me to progress. So

I returned the favour. What was he going to do? Take me to court and sue to get his money back? And just where did his money come from in the first place? Drugs and extortion and people trafficking. Not a penny of it was legally obtained. In Albion courts, the rule of "clean hands" applies. He couldn't use the law to recover money from me when it was obtained illegally in the first place – and I told him as much. So what if I took money off that unctuous, no-class lowlife? A bit of quid pro quo here and there never hurt anybody.'

Quid pro quo? Is that how this sorry excuse for a man got to sleep at night? He knew Dan's money was dirty and covered in blood, but that hadn't stopped him helping himself. And now he thought he was off the hook. Patrix Ellerman . . . My instincts hadn't steered me wrong as far as this scum was concerned.

'On the night we're talking about, I understand you spoke to Dan in his study? That was before the first course, wasn't it?'

'I wish I hadn't bothered. Kellan had already put Jeavons' back up so, by the time I saw him, he was in a stinking mood that he then took out on me. I asked him for a loan of a few thousand, nothing Jeavons couldn't handle, but he wasn't as forthcoming as he might've been. He told me he'd think about it.'

I played a hunch. 'I have it on good authority that he turned you down. Isn't that right?'

'How on earth did you know that?' Patrix was seething.

'Your conversation was overheard.' I shrugged, hoping my tone was convincing.

'By who? I'll bet the butler, George? Nosy, blanker son of a bitch. That man has the ill-bred habit of appearing out of nowhere when you least expect him. No doubt he had his ear to the door throughout my entire conversation with Jeavons. But then what else can you expect from a Nought?'

'I believe he's dual heritage.'

'Dual heritage, my arse. One drop of Nought blood makes you a blanker as far as I'm concerned.'

What a repulsive, odious turd. Enough of this bullshit.

'Mr Ellerman, I don't appreciate you using that slur in front of me,' I stated.

'Oh, excuse me all over the place. One drop of Nought blood makes you wypipo as far as I'm concerned. Is that better?' Patrix said with sarcasm.

Keep it together, Sephy. Deep breath. And another . . .

'So Dan wasn't in the mood to forgive your debt?' I continued.

'Are you kidding? I really should've known better than to see him after Kellan,' muttered Patrix, shaking his head.

No, your mistake was being a money-grubbing, despicable excuse for a human being, I thought, while deliberately keeping my expression neutral.

Poker face, Persephone. Inhale. Exhale. Extreme poker face.

'Do you remember what was on Dan's desk when you spoke to him?'

Patrix frowned, thrown by the question. He took a moment, then said, 'A sixteen-inch laptop computer, an opened A4 brown envelope, a bronzed female hand holding a silver-coloured letter opener, a lamp that was switched on, an ornate knife with a silver-coloured handle mounted on a plinth, a couple of books, desk speakers, a phone, a notebook, a glass paperweight that looked like it had lava flowing inside, a stapler, an expensive set of blue and silver pens standing up in a shark's mouth penholder and a framed photograph.'

Impressive memory. A lawyer's attention to detail.

'Did anything strike you as out of place or odd?'

'About Jeavons or his desk?'

'Either. Both.'

Patrix shook his head. 'Jeavons is . . . was a neat freak so everything on his desk had been carefully placed. I tried to come round his desk to look at the photograph. You know, faking an interest in him and his loved ones to grease the money-giving gears, but Dan slammed it face down, swung round in his chair and waved me away like he thought I was about to attack him with the stapler. Moron! He really didn't like people standing behind him, so I backed off and left soon after.'

'But that's not strictly true, is it? Dan threatened you. He wanted back the money you owed and you weren't happy about that,' I bluffed, based on what I knew of Dan, to see what Patrix would do. The explosion was almost instantaneous.

'What the hell? Who told you that?' Patrix's eyes narrowed. 'It *was* George, wasn't it? That shit-stirring snake. Listen, if you think I would let Jeavons get to my sons or my ex-wife for that matter, then you're way off. How dare that bastard threaten my family? I told him I'd pay him back every penny within six weeks with all the interest he'd tacked on without telling me. And I warned him just what I'd do to him if he ever threatened me or my family again.'

Ah! I was right. Dan obviously made a habit of threatening people's families to get what he wanted. Families, friends, loved ones – to a hagfish like Dan, they were all armour chinks to be exploited.

'Did he back down?' I knew the answer to that one. No way could Patrix make a man like Dan take a seat.

'Of course.' Patrix sat back in his chair, blinking heavily. Could it be any more obvious that he was lying? No wonder he was so shit at gambling. Anyone watching him would figure out whether or not he was bluffing in less than five seconds.

'Dan really was a piece of work, wasn't he?' I replied evenly.

'Pfft! Anyway, why were you there that night?' asked Patrix. 'Did he have something on you too?'

There was no way I was going to answer that.

'Did you speak to Dan in his study again that night?'

'Hell, no. Once was more than enough,' said Patrix sullenly.

'Thank you for your time, Mr Ellerman. Oh, just one last thing. What's your opinion of Tobey Durbridge?'

Patrix's expression twisted with scorn into something ugly and chilling. 'I can't believe that maggot is our Prime Minister. I never thought I'd live to see the day that this great country of ours elected a blanker as its leader. Well, I and a number of my friends in high places will be working tirelessly to make sure his every move is blocked and his every proposal is dismissed while he's PM. This will be the one and only term he gets to serve. And, when his five years are up, I will make it my personal business to make sure he can't even get elected rat-catcher of East Fluffyfuck.'

What. A. Dick.

'He may surprise you and be good at his job,' I ventured.

'Oh please. He's a blanker. That's all I know or need to know.'

Wow! What must it be like to constantly see the world

through the prism of bigotry? His world view was so blinkered, so . . . petty. Patrix had lived with it for so long that he couldn't even see how much his hatred had distorted and corrupted his vision. Every person who didn't look and think like him was the enemy. It was so pathetic. So . . . tiny. And the saddest thing of all was that it was self-inflicted.

'Well, thank you, Mr Ellerman,' I said. 'It's been . . . illuminating.'

After a conversation with this guy, all I wanted to do was go have a shower and scrub his poisonous words right off me. Patrix Ellerman was totally beneath contempt.

'Hold on, Mrs Ealing. You own Specimens Restaurant, don't you?'

'I do.'

'I don't suppose I could persuade you to offer me a short-term loan?' said Patrix. 'I would, of course, pay it back with interest.'

Was he frickin' kidding me?! It took all my inner reserves not to burst out laughing. As it was, I could feel my lips quivering!

'No, Mr Ellerman. I have no interest whatsoever in lending you money.'

As if.

'We're both Crosses. Where's your sympathy for what Jeavons did to me?' asked Patrix, eyes narrowed. The marrow-deep sense of entitlement was strong with this one.

'Mr Ellerman, if you're looking for sympathy, you'll find it between symbolic and syphilis in the dictionary. Goodbye.'

I disconnected our call.

Well, there it was. The last but one house at the end of Mbizi Street, East Gurendah Harbour. I'd been watching it for over an hour. In that time, a bearded man had come out of the building and driven off in a black, sporty vehicle whose licence plate I'd already photographed. It'd be a bit much to hope that Libby and Troy had been left alone. That would make my job too easy.

I couldn't wait any longer. If I was going to make my move, it had to be now, before any others left in the house could be warned that I was coming. I got out of the car and discreetly checked my gun.

Show time.

thirty-five. Troy

Libby and I had been digging for who knew how long and our progress was embarrassing. I could stand in the hole we'd spent hours digging and not get my shins dirty. However, I'd be standing on one leg 'cause my ankle was still throbbing like a bastard. Libby's tights wrapped round my leg were bulky and uncomfortable and meant I couldn't put my legs together. I felt like and probably moved as if I was stuck on an invisible horse – I couldn't run off now if I tried.

I glanced at Libby. Her face was filthy where she'd been constantly pushing her hair back with dirty hands. Her lowered eyebrows and pursed lips gave her a look of bullish determination as she dug her makeshift spade into the dirt, scooping it up with the nailed end, throwing it against the adjacent wall. Libby caught me watching her. We didn't smile, didn't frown, didn't speak. What was there to say?

Pop!

Pop! Pop!

Pop! Pop! Pop!

The unexpected noise came from somewhere above us, towards the back of the house, I think. Libby and I exchanged a look. What on earth was that? One or two pops and I might've thought maybe I'd imagined them, but there were too many to believe that.

'Hello?' I called out. 'If you're up there, we need more food and water. And toilet paper! Hello?'

Silence.

'Why would anyone up there care about us?' asked Libby softly. 'If they boarded us up in here, they couldn't give a damn about our welfare.'

She had a point. We waited another minute or two, straining to hear any further noises. Nothing. With a sigh, we both got back to digging. I told myself that our way out of here lay in our own hands.

Now we had to make that come true.

'I need a space
That's mine alone.
A view, a hue
To call my own.
When I'm lonely,
Deep shades of blue,
I close my eyes
And what I do
Is think of home,
Where I belong.
I dream of home
And sing this song.'

I sang softly to myself, needing to break up the silence of the basement. Plus I was feeling the words. I didn't look up from digging, but I knew Libby was watching me. I braced myself for a tirade of abuse, but that wasn't gonna stop me.

'*I think of home where I belong.*'

Defiantly I sang a little louder.

'*I dream of home, and I grow strong.*'

Libby opened her mouth, but – to my surprise – it wasn't to complain. Instead, she belted out, '*I close my eyes, I'm almost there. My home is with me, everywhere.*'

With a grin, I joined in.

> *'I think of home,*
> *Where I belong.*
> *I dream of home*
> *And I grow—'*

Then there came the sound of wood splintering. Libby and I were instantly silent. Metal nails were dragged, creaking and grating, from old wood, the noise echoing round the basement.

Libby helped me to my feet before retrieving my excuse for a spade and handing it to me.

She stood beside me, her hand tightening round mine as we both stared up at the door. She needn't have worried. I wasn't about to let her go.

More wood splintering. The noise came from high up on the door, steadily working its way lower. After hours of nothing but our own whispered voices and the dull thud of our digging, the noises from above were raucous, shocking.

'Quick, grab something,' I hissed.

A moment's confusion, then Libby nodded. Letting go of my hand, she reached for her improvised shovel. Primed and ready, we both watched the door as the sound of wood splintering intensified. Was more than one person working on removing the boards? It was hard to tell. All Libby and I could do was stand.

And wait.

thirty-six. Callie

I sat in my office, drinking in the solemn aspect: the leather and furniture-polish smell, the case files stacked on my desk beside my computer, representing all facets of life. I loved my office, with its small wooden desk tucked into one corner, and the large, leather-bound law books lining two of the four walls. This place was my home from home, my sanctuary of justice – but not for much longer. With my phone notifications and alerts except from Tobey, Mum and Jon switched off, I'd spent the last couple of hours handing over my forthcoming trial cases and bringing Simon and Nyota, the lawyers taking them over, up to speed. Every case on my desk had now been reassigned – except Tobey's. Sol had made noises about 'once I was exonerated blah blah', but that's all it was – noise.

Arrested—

My career was well and truly over and everyone in chambers knew it. The only reason I kept Tobey's case was because I was his advocate of record. Standing up in court and declaring that I was Tobey's lawyer meant I was now duty-bound as well as legally obligated to represent him, plus I doubted if Tobey would allow anyone else to take over from me. That said, it was time for a video call.

Tobey answered his private phone within a couple of rings. His smile was immediate. 'Hey, Callie. What's what?'

'Tobey, did you have anything to do with me being arrested this morning?' No preliminary pleasantries.

Tobey stared at me in stunned silence. My eyes narrowed. If his expression was fake, then he was a damn fine actor.

'Well? Did you?' I said with impatience, needing to hear him say it.

'What the hell, Callie? Of course I didn't. You were arrested? For what?'

I took a deep breath, trying to push down the cold wrath inside. It wouldn't be fair to take it out on Tobey if he really had nothing to do with this.

'I'm sorry, Tobey. It's just that I was picked up by two police officers this morning and charged with perverting the course of justice.'

'Perverting the course of justice – how?' Tobey's frown deepened.

'By not letting the prosecution or the court know that my mum was at Dan's flat on the night he died.'

'I'm not with you. The police interviewed everyone who was there that night, including your mum.'

'They interviewed Sephy Ealing. No one put it together that she was my mum because we have different surnames.'

'So why didn't you say something if you knew it would be a legal problem?'

Seriously? 'Because it wasn't relevant. She was exonerated. Mum had nothing to do with it.' *At least that's what I'd thought until Tobey told me otherwise*. 'I don't care what you or anyone else says. Mum didn't do it,' I reiterated. 'Look, can

I come and see you? You asked me to be patient, but I need a progress report. D'you know where Troy and Libby are yet? I need to be *doing*, not sitting here being done to.'

Tobey nodded. 'I'm at my apartment. I'll be waiting,' he said softly before disconnecting the call.

A moment, then I grabbed my bag and headed out the door just as Sol was trying to come in.

'Where are you going?' Sol frowned.

'To see Tobey,' I replied, not breaking my stride.

'Callie, wait. I don't think that's a good idea. Have him come into the office if you want to discuss the finer points of his case. Seeing him alone is . . . inadvisable.'

'Don't worry, Sol. I know what I'm doing,' I argued. 'If I'm not back today, I'll see you tomorrow.'

'Wait, Callie, I've got news,' said Sol, trailing behind me.

I turned.

'I have it on good authority that the CPS is looking into all the evidence against Tobey Durbridge again.'

'How come?' I frowned. 'They obviously thought they had enough to bring him to trial in the first place. Why are they taking a second look?'

Sol looked around to confirm we were indeed alone. Even then, he still lowered his voice. 'Apparently, they were assured that Tobey would confess to Dan's murder should the case ever come to court.'

More pieces of the puzzle were being slotted into place. 'Is that right?' I asked stonily. 'Assured by who?'

Sol shrugged. 'That's the sketchy part. No one seems to quite know. You get how these things work. A word dropped in this ear. Encouragement dropped in that ear. There are those at the top who are still not comfortable with the idea of a Nought being our Prime Minister and they will do what they can to either remove him or discredit him.'

'I said from the beginning that the case against him was flimsy at best,' I reminded Sol.

'Yes, well, without an uncomplicated, straight-up plea of guilty from Tobey, maybe the Chief Prosecution Service are coming round to your way of thinking. I don't recommend you tell Tobey yet just in case the CPS decides not to back down. You don't want to raise his hopes for nothing.'

Silently fuming, I nodded my agreement. Whoever it was who had set all these wheels in motion, Tobey being found innocent, or the case being dropped, evidently wasn't the endgame they had in mind. And, with the possible evidence Tobey had against her, where would all this leave my mum?

'Sol, if you need me, I'll be with my client,' I said. I spun round and headed for the exit.

'Callie, please be careful,' Sol called after me. 'Yes, there are political manoeuvrings against Durbridge going on, but that doesn't mean that he can be trusted. If he goes down, like a drowning man, he'll grab hold of you and try to drag you down with him.'

Which stopped me in my tracks. I turned my head. 'Sol, believe me, I know that.'

I kept on walking.

thirty-seven. Tobey

I buzzed round my apartment, making sure there was nothing untoward that would rain down Callie's disapproval upon me. No knickers stuffed behind the sofa cushions. No lipstick or earrings 'carelessly' discarded by past acquaintances, hoping to use the absence of their personal items as an excuse to visit me again. I used a cleaning service who came every other morning to see to the place, but my usual cleaner was on two weeks' holiday and I had declined the offer of a replacement. Once in a while, it did me good to fend for myself as a reminder of where I came from.

Look at me! What the hell was I doing? Trying to make a good impression on a woman who found me deeply unimpressive. And, with her mum whispering in her ear, what chance did I have? On the night of Dan's party, when George announced that dinner was served, Sephy and I'd had a brief chat – if you can call it that – as we headed for the dining room. If I'd vomited gold bars and pooped pearls, that woman would still give me the serious side-eye. I remembered every word of our conversation.

'What's what, Sephy? How's Callie Rose? I haven't seen or spoken to her in too long.'

'Not long enough,' Sephy replied.

My lips twisted into a wry smile. 'Same old Sephy.'

'Same old Tobey. And that's Mrs Ealing to you.'

I tried again. 'I've been following Callie's career. You must be so proud of everything she's accomplished. I know I am.'

Sephy looked me up and down. 'I've been following your career just as closely, Tobey,' she told me. 'The smart money says you'll be the next leader of Albion.'

'And what d'you say?'

'I say I was smart enough not to vote for you. You know as much about public service as I know about the dark side of the moon.'

Well, I did ask. 'Mrs Ealing, that's hardly fair. Why d'you think I got into this game in the first place?'

'You see, Tobey, you just gave yourself away there. You're in the position to change the course of people's lives for good and yet you call it a game. Yes, the drug rehabilitation centre you set up back in the day was to help others. Everything after that has been to help yourself,' she replied.

Why was I even arguing with this woman? Nothing I said or did was ever going to win her over. But that didn't stop me trying. 'I know it's hard for you to believe, but I genuinely want to do some good.'

'Then start by staying away from my daughter,' said Sephy.

'Why is it so hard for you to believe that I care about Callie?'

'Care about her?'

Pause. 'Yes, care about her,' I repeated. Damn it! I was blushing. A grown-ass man who made other world leaders nervous, yet this woman had me blushing! That's what Sephy had reduced me to, what she always reduced me to.

'Tobey, you wouldn't know an honest emotion if it bit you on the left bum cheek. You don't really love my daughter; you've just

persuaded yourself that you do because you think that makes you a better person. It doesn't. You're the biggest fake and I'm going to use every breath in my body to get Callie to see the truth about you.'

Slowly I shook my head. This wasn't indifference or general dislike: the woman truly loathed me. 'Mrs Ealing, I didn't make the rules, but I know how to play the political "game". So maybe you're semi-right and I am a fake about most things. But not about Callie. Never with her nor about my feelings for her.'

'Tobey, are you even capable of real love? I've watched you over the years and I've also heard things, none of them flattering. You and your act have a lot of people fooled, including my daughter, but not me.'

I straightened up, recognizing a losing battle when I saw one. 'Whether you believe me or not is your choice – but I would never do anything to hurt Callie, and that's the truth.'

We both stood watching each other as the other guests flowed around us giving us curious looks. Without another word, Sephy turned and walked into the dining room. I had been dismissed.

I sighed as I looked round my apartment. I could wish I had Sephy on my side when it came to winning Callie back, but never mind. I'd just have to do it without her help. Once I was sure the apartment was ready to welcome visitors, I changed into black jeans and a long-sleeved burgundy T-shirt before phoning Jon Duba. No answer. I tried again. Still no answer. Where the hell was he? Where was my progress report? I hated this helpless feeling – like sitting on top of the world and watching it slowly disintegrate beneath my feet – and there wasn't a damned thing I could do about it.

I had to admit that, in spite of not knowing how to answer phone calls, Jon Duba was no amateur. In the space of a couple of hours, he'd provided me with the information I'd requested. I now knew Shane Stoats's home address, something I hadn't even known when Dan was alive. And, according to Jon, Shane was going to be home for at least the next couple of hours. Also, according to Jon, Eva would be at Ava's until midnight. Ridiculous name for a nightclub. It used to be called the Kettle Honey Club, but Dan had renamed it about six years ago. When I asked why, he just shrugged and said, 'Why not?' I was sure there was more to it than that, but at the time I didn't push. After all, what difference did it make to me what he called his club? It was none of my business. I now wondered if it had something to do with Eva. Strange how all roads, all routes, all motives seemed to lead right back to that woman.

First things first. Number one on my list was to pay Shane a visit. Jon had asked me to wait until I heard from him so that he could come with me. He had something to take care of first, but I wasn't prepared to wait a second longer than necessary. No one but me knew what I was prepared to do to get my daughter back in one piece, the lengths that I would go to. I didn't doubt for one second that before the day was over there would be blood on my hands.

The fewer people who witnessed that, the better.

Back in the day, I'd cultivated dubious friends, dodgy deals and wheels within wheels – all the things I needed to rise, but which I thought I could just dust off when the time was right. Karma was laughing at me because I was going to have to embrace all of that again.

I had something to ask Callie first. Once I had her answer, then I could get to work. No protection officers, no police. No witnesses. I began to pace, waiting for her to arrive. But that wouldn't do. I headed out of my apartment and down to the foyer, protection officers following silently in my wake. I wanted – no, I needed – to be with Callie from the moment she entered the building. And yeah, I had it bad. There was no point in trying to deny it any more.

The thing of it was, if anything bad happened to Troy, it felt like it would be happening to me and Callie as well. I couldn't have that. Yes, I was being selfish. I needed my life back on an even keel, with Libby and Troy in school again, and Callie by my side, and this ridiculous murder charge hanging over my head erased once and for all. So I was strategizing, figuring out exactly where to place my pieces on life's chessboard.

And there could only be one outcome.

I wouldn't settle for anything less.

thirty-eight. Callie

When I arrived at Tobey's apartment building, to my surprise he was already in the foyer, waiting for me. He must've had a previous meeting and just seen someone off the premises. The moment I appeared, he came over to greet me, flanked by two close-protection officers at a discreet distance. Tobey kissed my cheek before I could stop him. The warmth of his lips on my skin lingered.

'Hello, Callie,' he began. 'Listen, I'm so sorry about what happened to you this morning, but you must believe that I had nothing to do with it.'

I pushed the ghost of a smile onto my lips. 'Sorry, Tobey. I realized that as soon as I'd calmed down.'

Which was the truth. If Tobey had been responsible for my arrest, he would've named it and claimed it long before now. He placed a hand on the small of my back and escorted me to the lift.

'Have you heard anything? From the kidnappers?' I asked softly, though so, so eager to hear good news.

Tobey shook his head.

'Mum and I haven't either,' I said, my hopes deflating. 'It's too long.'

'Callie, we'll get them back,' said Tobey.

'How d'you know that? What exactly are you doing to make that happen?'

'Everything I can.'

'Is that going to be enough?'

'I hope so.'

'You hope so? That's all you've got?' I said.

'Isn't that all any of us have? Hope?'

'Spare me the philosophizing. I hoped you'd have more for me than just faith.'

'I know you're worried, Callie Rose, but . . . Never mind.' Tobey bit back what he wanted to say, clearly with difficulty. 'We will get them back,' he said again, this time with more certainty.

He shook his head at his protection officers. They didn't enter the lift with us. I closed my eyes, took a deep breath and told myself to give Tobey a break. He was right. Troy and Libby would be rescued – one way or another. I had to believe that. It was all I had to hang on to.

The two of us travelled up to his apartment in a silence that sank its eagle's talons into my skin. I should've taken the stairs. All ten flights of them. It would've been less stressful than standing next to my ex-lover in this expectational, almost confrontational quiet.

Tobey stared resolutely straight ahead. I looked at him, the truth slapping me round the face. Being so adversarial with him was my way of trying to keep my emotional distance. I didn't trust who I was or who I became in his company. It was my problem, but I was making it his.

'I'm sorry, Tobey.'

He turned to me, relaxing only slightly. 'You're forgiven.'

Years ago, if the wind had blown in another direction, things might've been very different between us. I sighed. I needed to get my head on straight. I was Tobey's lawyer – and that's all I was. And that's all I would ever be.

And yet . . .

This was ridiculous.

Get it together, Callie Rose.

'Is it OK to talk freely in your apartment?' I asked.

'My apartment is swept for listening devices daily,' Tobey replied. 'I would never risk our conversations being overheard or recorded.'

'What about Jon then? Have you heard from him yet? Is there any news?'

'Not yet, but I choose to see that as a good sign.'

I lowered my head, my shoulders sagging. God, but I was tired. Tears, as sharp as pins, jabbed at my eyes. 'Tell me honestly, Tobey, d'you think . . . they're still alive?'

Unexpectedly, Tobey stepped forward to take me in his arms, pulling me close. 'Don't say that. Don't even think it. Of course they're still alive. They've got to be.'

A moment's pause, then, just as unexpectedly, I wrapped my arms round his waist. We both needed this, to take comfort from each other. Apart from my mum and Jon, no one else knew what we were going through. In this, we were all the other had. Tobey's arms tightened round me as I buried my face in the curve of his neck, my eyes closed. I drank him in, the fresh smell of him, the hard yet gentle feel of him. It felt good. Comforting. In his arms, I didn't feel so alone. Sometimes, like now, I felt so close to Tobey, as if I could just step inside him and we'd merge, becoming the one entity we were always meant to be. And, as one, we'd be stronger, smarter. Practically invincible. Blushing at the way my imagination was running away with me, I stepped back out of his arms.

'Callie—'

A ding, and the lift doors hissed open. His hands dropped to his sides as he reluctantly let me go. Two close-protection officers I'd never seen before stood on either side of his front door.

Tobey acknowledged them with a nod, then opened the door to his apartment, standing to one side to usher me in.

Once the door was firmly closed behind him, I took a moment or two to compose myself before turning round.

'Why d'you live here when you have a huge official residence you could be using?'

'Until the case against me is dismissed, it was decided I should stay here.'

'Why?'

Tobey shrugged. 'I'm officially taking some time off to handle private matters, so it's only right I do that from here, working behind the scenes. Besides, sometimes it's easier to distinguish between political friends and the back-stabbing bastards from a distance. Some of those appointed by me in my government are already scheming to take my place.'

The landline phone on the side table beside one of the sofas began to ring. On the laptop computer on the desk in one corner of the room, email after email kept arriving. Luckily, Tobey had either the sound down or his audible alerts off, otherwise his laptop would be pinging constantly. He answered the phone, listening carefully before turning his back on me to speak. I moved away from him, not wanting to eavesdrop.

A knock at the door. I opened it.

'A package just arrived for Mr Durbridge. It's been scanned and is safe,' said one of Tobey's protection officers. 'May I leave it on the post table?'

'By all means,' I replied, hoping she knew where that was because I didn't.

The woman brought in a small parcel and put it on a table on the other side of the door. The table already had a number of envelopes and packages waiting to be perused. By the time the protection officer had left the apartment, Tobey was off the phone. But almost immediately it started to ring again.

'I'll let it go through to the answering machine,' he told me. 'Or we'll be here all day.'

How on earth did he do it? The world of party politics was like wrestling with crocodiles in a sewer. How did those who entered the vat spotless and full of good intentions stay clean in that environment? I shook my head. Rather Tobey than me.

Across the room, his laptop screen was still visible. The emails kept on coming.

'Jesus, take the wheel!' I exclaimed, staring at the non-stop emails. 'I hope you have good people watching your back. Who's looking out for you? Don't you get any peace from all this? It must feel like being pecked to pieces.'

Unexpected sympathy filled me as I looked round the room. But why? Wasn't this what Tobey had always wanted? I became aware of him standing like a sentinel less than a metre away, watching me.

'What?' I asked when Tobey's unblinking stare started to burn.

'Callie, is there any chance, when all this is over, that you and I could start again?' he asked quietly.

'We're already friends, Tobey. Nothing will ever change that.'

'I'm hoping we can be more than that.'

Blinking in confusion, I opened my mouth to reply, but Tobey got in first. 'I know this isn't the time or place, but I need to put it out there. I want to be with you. The two of us. Together.'

I gawped at him. Closing my lips, I endeavoured to come up with an appropriate response. Strangely disappointed, I said, 'Tobey, what on earth makes you think that I'd be interested in being your side chick?'

'Callie, I'm not asking you to be my side chick,' said Tobey. 'I'm asking you to be my wife.'

Shit! What? *Wife?*

The shocks just kept on coming. I stumbled to the closest sofa to sit before I fell down.

Start again by getting married? Was he for real?

'You . . . you want to *marry* me?'

Tobey came over to sit next to me. 'Yes.'

A weighty silence pressed down hard upon both of us as we looked at each other. Tobey's gaze never wavered from mine.

'Why?'

'We'd be good together.'

Frustration flared within me. His proposal had unexpectedly lit a flame of something close to joy inside me, only for it to be almost immediately snuffed out by his reply and common sense. Is that what our relationship had been reduced to, the politically convenient?

'I don't understand you, Tobey. I'm trying, but failing epically. You bedded me to ensure I stayed on as your lawyer and, when that didn't work, you blackmailed me into it. You even threatened to take our so-called relationship to the press and Bar Council to get me disbarred if I didn't do what you wanted. Which part of that spells out *marry me*?'

Tobey regarded me, then nodded, strangely calm. 'Like I said, this is neither the time nor the place.' He got to his feet. 'While we wait for Jon to get back to us, let's pay Eva's friend the weasel a visit. If we get nothing from him, I'll take you home, then I'll go see Eva by myself.'

If Tobey thought he was going to see Eva alone, he had another think coming, but now was not the time to argue about it. I too stood up, not keen on Tobey looming over me. The abrupt subject change had thrown me momentarily. I hadn't liked the look on his face, a look that said he thought I would eventually come round to his way of thinking. For now, though, all right – we'd play this his way. 'Why are we visiting Shane Stoats?'

Tobey's eyebrows shot up. 'You know about him?'

Oh please! 'Tobey, I'm a lawyer and a bloody good one. You think I don't know about organized crime in the capital and the players involved? Don't insult me.'

'My bad.' Tobey held out a placating hand. 'I heard a rumour that Shane has taken over from Jarvis Burton as Eva's lieutenant. And Eva has taken over all of Dan's . . . enterprises so, if anyone knows where Troy and Libby are, it'll be Shane or Eva.'

'What makes you so certain?'

'The ransom demand.'

Fair enough. If the ransom demand had been solely about money, it would've been much harder to pin down its source.

'And you have Shane's address?' I asked.

Tobey shrugged. 'Perks of the job. I'll just go get a jacket.'

With that, he entered his bedroom, leaving me frowning and suspicious. My thoughts whirling, I followed him as far as the open bedroom door. Tobey stood at the window, his back towards me, his shoulders slumped, his head bowed. His whole attitude was one of defeat. When he thrust his fingers through his hair, I darted backwards out of sight.

Heading over to the sitting-room window, I looked up at the grey-toned sky. I was genuinely confused. Tobey wanted to marry me. Why? He hadn't mentioned love, not once, but the way he'd looked at me . . . It would be so easy to believe what my eyes were telling me and all I had to do was remove my own common sense from the equation. I tried to think like a chess player trying to fathom the strategy of her grandmaster opponent. What did Tobey have to gain from marrying me? Not much as far as I could see. I was the granddaughter of Kamal Hadley who'd been a prominent Member of Parliament back in the day, but it was no secret that he'd disinherited my mum and had nothing to do with me. His bigoted feelings towards Noughts were a matter of record. Still, optics-wise, being with me wouldn't do Tobey any harm, would it? Was that his thinking? What would look good politically? After all, sooner or later, Tobey being charged with Dan's murder would become public knowledge.

These things always did – it was just a matter of time. So what better advertisement and endorsement of his innocence than the fact that his own barrister was now his wife? Lips pursed, I shook my head, not loving the direction my thoughts were taking. Was I overthinking this? Probably.

'D'you want a drink or something to eat before we leave? It'd be no trouble.'

I turned and shook my head. Tobey now wore a worn black leather jacket over his burgundy T-shirt. His hair was slightly ruffled where he'd dragged impatient fingers through it. One of his old habits. He always did that whenever he was frustrated or upset.

'So for now we're still keeping the police out of it?'

'Yeah, for as long as possible.'

'Why did you need Jon's help? What's he doing that you couldn't?' I asked.

'He can go to certain places and ask particular questions that I can't. Sometimes having a public persona throws open doors, and sometimes it's a real pain in the arse and gets in the way of any kind of private endeavour.'

'I would've thought you could go anywhere, do anything, get anything you wanted.' I raised an eyebrow.

'Then you'd be wrong,' said Tobey quietly.

My smile faded. Uncomfortable silence descended, begging to be filled. 'So you were telling me more about what Jon is up to.'

With a shake of his head, Tobey sighed, my persistence finally wearing him down. 'He's checking out a couple of my suggestions, starting with Owen Dowd. Dowd's the only other person besides Eva who would know where Troy and Libby are, though taking them would bring him no advantage. First of all, how would he even know about my daughter? And, if he had learned of her existence, why would he want me out of the way? Dan would be his target, not me. If he thought I was responsible for Dan's demise, he'd be more likely to send me a Crossmas hamper than try and put my arse in prison.'

I nodded. That made sense.

'Jon said he'd join us after he's spoken to Dowd. In the meantime, we'll go and talk to Shane.'

'Why would Owen Dowd answer any of Jon's questions?' I asked with a frown. Owen and Dan Jeavons were two sides of the same coin – ruthless and mercenary. So why would Owen help Jon, unless there was something in it for him?

'Jon told me that he can get things done and I believe him,' said Tobey.

Uh-oh. 'I don't allow Jon to break the law when he works for me. Not even a little bit.'

'That's why he's currently reporting back to me,' said Tobey.

I didn't need to be a rocket scientist to know what that meant. 'As PM, aren't you meant to set a higher standard?' The judgemental words spilled from my mouth.

Tobey gave me a pointed look. 'Not at the expense of my daughter. This is precisely why I didn't want to include you in my conversation with Jon. I wouldn't want to put you in the position of having to compromise your oh-so-precious ideals.'

'Meaning?' I frowned.

'Well, you never were one to let human faults, failings and frailties get in the way of your principles.'

My mouth fell open. Wow! That was quite some bitch-slap.

A moment of silence, then Tobey said, 'Do you ever think about the day you found me with Misty? Does it cross your mind once in a while or do you pick at it every day like a scab that never heals?'

Oh hell, no. 'I'm not going there. Hard pass,' I declared. 'Crazy hard pass.'

'Neither of us will ever get past it if we don't confront what happened. It's the great sky-high wall between us.'

'And you think discussing it after all these years will break down that wall?'

'God knows I've tried everything else.'

Tobey's vehement words made me start. How dare he make me feel so uncomfortable, as if I was the one in the wrong?

'You don't get to do this, Tobey,' I bristled. 'You don't get to turn this round on me like I was the one who screwed you over.'

'Callie—'

'No! I'm not doing this again. This is all water under the bridge so can we let it go – please?'

'You're renowned for a lot of things, Callie, but a forgiving nature isn't one of them. You could give a masterclass on bearing a grudge.'

'So your inability to keep your trousers zipped up is my fault?' Indignation gripped me.

Tobey sighed. 'No. I take full responsibility for my actions. But, if you could've forgiven me for what I did, I would've been your slave for life.'

'I did forgive you. I forgave you at the time.'

'Yeah? You know what? Your forgiveness has a real bitter aftertaste to it.'

'I forgave you, Tobey. That doesn't mean it was easy to forget what you did. You slept with Misty at my birthday party to spite me.'

'It wasn't to spite you. Not everything is about you.'

'That was. You deliberately set out to hurt me and you succeeded.'

'And I've apologized – more than once. You threw away everything we had and could've had over something that meant nothing, Callie. Less than nothing.'

'Don't you get it? It meant something to me. And it meant something to Misty because she became pregnant with Libby.' I slow-clapped. 'Congratulations. You got to walk away with the fewest scars.'

'You couldn't be more wrong,' Tobey said. 'You broke up with me to punish me at the time and, by cutting me out of your life, you've been punishing me ever since. Callie, you once told me you hoped my child would die. Well, congratulations – you might just get your wish.'

Every part of me froze – except the unbidden tears that immediately flowed over my cheeks. Stricken, I looked at Tobey, scarcely able to believe what he'd just said to me.

'Hellsake. I'm sorry, Callie,' Tobey said, running unsteady fingers through his hair again.

'Y-you really believe that of me?' I whispered.

'No. Of course not. I'm sorry.' He hugged me to him and I didn't push him off. Instead, I buried my face in his shoulder and cried my heart out – for the hurt then and the pain now and all the lost years in between. Tobey stroked my back, whispering words of apology over and over.

It took too long, but I finally heard them.

When at last the stream of tears ceased, I wiped my face with the back of my hand, noting how one side of Tobey's burgundy T-shirt was now considerably darker.

'You're going to have to change your shirt,' I said, embarrassed.

'Not until you say I'm forgiven,' said Tobey.

I looked him in the eyes. 'I forgive you, Tobey.'

He smiled. I smiled back, feeling strangely lighter, but then I had just cried half a bucket of tears all over him.

'I'll wash my face while you change your top,' I told him.

In the bathroom, I splashed water on my face, drying it with a plush Egyptian-cotton towel from the rail beside the basin. I looked at myself in the mirror. Tobey had painted quite an ugly picture of me and I hated it. Mostly because he was right. I was hurt and jealous and had abandoned our friendship because of it, punishing us both. Holding onto my hurt feelings was like carrying a ton weight on my back.

If Tobey and I were to stand any kind of chance, it was time to let all that go. So I needed to honestly answer one question. Did I want Tobey and me to have a second chance? The surprising truth was yes, I did. Very much.

A couple of minutes later, I was back in the sitting room, as was Tobey in another identical burgundy T-shirt. At my raised eyebrows, he mumbled, 'I like this colour so I have more than one.'

I wondered at his awkwardness until the reason hit me.

'Some woman once told you that colour suits you. Am I right?'

Two spots of colour appeared on Tobey's cheeks, answering my question.

'Thought so! And then you went out and bought a job lot of the same shirt in the same colour. Well, whoever it was, she didn't lie.'

'Time to go,' said Tobey, not even trying to be subtle about changing the subject. We'd barely taken a couple of steps when he turned to me. 'Callie, before we go to see Shane Stoats, I need to warn you that this could get messy. In fact, I'd prefer it if you stayed here till I have some news.'

'Tobey, this is my brother and your daughter we're talking about and I need you to believe that I'll do whatever it takes to get them back.'

'Anything?'

'*Anything*.' As Tobey raised a sceptical eyebrow, I said, 'I mean it. My family comes first. Nothing else even makes the list.'

'I wonder if you truly know what that means, Callie. You are first, last and always about the rules, about the law. I fully expect to get my hands dirty on this one. If you're going to have a problem with that, then you should stay here,' said Tobey. 'That way you can deny all knowledge. I don't want you getting in my way when your feet catch a chill.'

'I'm not gonna get cold feet. We're in this together or not at all.'

'Damn it, Callie Rose, I'm trying to protect you.'

And the strange, sad thing was I knew he meant it.

'I'm a big girl now, Tobey. I can look after myself.'

Besides, I had nothing left to lose. Not any more. The circuit judge opportunity that I'd been up for had been quietly withdrawn. Refusing to drop Tobey's case and then being arrested had been the final nail in my career coffin, but Tobey didn't need to know that.

'I'm trusting you, Tobey. Now I'm asking you to do the same and trust me. We're in this together and, if we both need to get our hands dirty to bring Troy and Libby back home safely, then I can live with that.'

'Can you though?'

I shrugged. 'I guess we're both about to find out.'

thirty-nine. Sephy

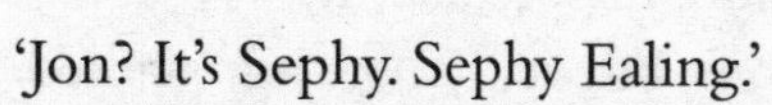

'Jon? It's Sephy. Sephy Ealing.'

'Oh God,' he groaned.

'None taken!' I said dryly. 'Did you pass on my message to Jarvis Burton?'

'I did.'

Should I ask how he managed to do that? I decided against it. 'And you're sure that he and he alone received the message?'

'Positive.'

Jon's pursed lips and folded arms spoke volumes. My phone might not have been on the bleeding edge of technology, but the video image of Jon was still sharp enough for me to see that he wouldn't be happy if I asked for yet more favours. Hell, he wasn't happy now.

'Are you going to answer every question with monosyllables?' I asked.

'Yes.'

'How did Jarvis seem when you told him?'

Jon sighed. 'I caught up with him as he was buying himself a coffee. I passed on your message word for word and then I scarpered. I didn't stay to take in the minutiae of his facial expressions, the nuances behind any changes in body language or the intricacies of—'

'OK. OK. I get it. Don't pummel the point to death.'

'*Pfft!*'

'Well, that's another one I owe you. How many is that now?'

'I've lost count,' Jon replied.

'Thank you for your help, Jon. I appreciate it.'

'I'd say you're welcome, but I'd be lying,' Jon replied. 'Sephy, please be careful. I don't want to see you get hurt.'

'That won't happen.'

'Hmm. I hope you know what you're doing.' Jon hung up without another word.

His last words to me kept playing in my head.

I hope you know what you're doing . . .

So do I, Jon. So do I.

forty. Tobey

Callie had no idea what getting her hands dirty really meant, but it would be pointless to argue. 'Let's go.' I was already heading for the door.

'Tobey, before we leave, I need something from you.'

'What?' I asked.

Callie straightened to meet my gaze. She looked like she was ready to do battle. What was she up to?

'I'd like to see this recording you have of my mum allegedly holding the weapon that killed Dan.'

'What? Why? What purpose would that serve?'

'I'd like to see it,' Callie said quietly. 'Please don't make me beg.'

A sigh, a shake of my head, but I took out my phone, calling up the relevant app, and selected the appropriate recording. I'd taken the backup flash drive from Dan's laptop on the night of his death, making sure to permanently delete the only other copy of the recording from Dan's cloud storage. Later that same evening, I transferred the flash-drive contents to my private phone before completely wiping and reformatting the drive. Belt and braces. I was confident I had the one and only recording of the study at the time Dan died, and that was the way it was going to stay.

Fast-forwarding to the relevant section, I handed the phone to Callie. She immediately sat down on the sofa, her attention entirely focused on the recording. I sat beside her, waiting for the inevitable fallout. Callie pressed play and brought the phone closer, her gaze intense.

The short clip showed Sephy, wide-eyed and open-mouthed with panic, plunging a thin-bladed letter opener in Dan's back before wiping the handle clean.

Callie frowned at me, her downturned lips twisting in puzzlement. Without saying a word, she played the clip again.

'What's the issue?' I asked. 'It seems pretty straightforward to me.'

'You kept this because—?' asked Callie.

Damn it. My face burned red. Callie nodded knowingly.

'Whatever you may think of me, Callie, I tried to shield your mum, but as you can see she—'

'Mum didn't do it,' she said softly.

'Callie, come on. You can clearly see—'

'How many times did you watch this, Tobey?'

I frowned. 'Once with George present. Once by myself to make sure I'd transferred the recording properly.' What difference did it make? The recording wasn't going to change, no matter how many times I viewed it.

'You thought you knew what you were looking at so you didn't bother to watch it properly.' Callie pressed play again, only to immediately press pause. 'The recording starts with the knife in Mum's hand, but look at it. The blade is already bloodstained. And look at Mum's face. She's horrified.'

'Because she's just realized what she's done,' I prompted as gently as I could.

Pursing her lips, Callie again hit play then pause in quick succession. 'Dan was stabbed twice, once in the jugular, once in the back, but check the knife blade. Only one drop of blood falls from it onto the back of Dan's dark jacket.'

Callie touched play once more. We both watched as Sephy stabbed Dan with slow deliberation, then used the inside hem of her blouse to wipe the handle of the letter opener.

'So the recording only started after she'd already stabbed him once,' I said. 'It still shows she did it.'

The scowl Callie was directing my way was beginning to chill my bones. 'OK, tell me what I'm missing?'

'Mum wasn't the one who did the initial stabbing. She took the knife *out* of Dan's back. The fact that it's already covered with blood smears shows that. According to the coroner's report, Dan was stabbed once in the jugular and once straight through his heart, from the back. Whoever stabbed him would've been covered in blood. You can't stab someone in the jugular and not get blood over the weapon and all over your hands. The single drop of blood falling from the blade indicates that Dan's heart wasn't beating when Mum removed the knife or there would've been blood all over her. Look. There isn't a speck of red on her.'

Frowning, I took a closer look. Callie was right . . .

'I was there, remember? No one at that dinner table had blood on their hands.' At least not literally. 'Callie, all this proves is that your mum washed her hands first before returning to the rest of us.'

'Tobey, we're watching Mum replace the knife and try to wipe her fingerprints off it, but there's nothing here to show that she stabbed Dan in the first place. Look closely. There's blood on the handle, but none of it was transferred to Mum's blouse when she wiped it, so the blood must've dried by the time she tried to remove her fingerprints. And this is before any trip to the bathroom to supposedly clean up.'

I pressed rewind and played the clip at half-speed.

'Why doesn't your recording start from the time Mum entered Dan's study?' asked Callie, interrupting my viewing.

'I asked the same question of George. He told me the security camera must've been set to restart at a certain time, which turned out to be when your mum had the letter opener in her hand,' I replied.

'How convenient for the killer,' said Callie.

'Well, they couldn't've known Sephy would be in the room when the recording restarted. That was just bad luck on your mum's part,' I replied.

I took back my phone to watch the recording again from the beginning. 'It's not conclusive proof of your mum's innocence though,' I argued.

'Tobey, there would've been blood spatter from the neck wound. It would've been on the assailant's hand and sleeve at the very least. I've defended and prosecuted enough knife-crime trials to know what I'm talking about. Mum doesn't even have a drop of blood on her. I think she came in, saw Dan slumped over his desk with a knife in his back and – for whatever inexplicable reason – removed it and then replaced it. And, what's more, that's a case I could win in court. There's enough doubt to guarantee Mum wouldn't be convicted.'

I watched the footage yet again. Callie was right.

'Why are you so determined to believe that Mum killed Dan?' Callie asked, genuinely hurt.

'I'm not. Hellsake! Everything I've done since I discovered the recording and the murder weapon has been to protect your mum, not drop her in it.'

Callie smiled, her gaze softening as she looked at me. She believed me – thank God.

'And you're right,' I said. 'There's no blood anywhere on her, including her hand. I saw your mum stab Dan in the back and thought—' I trailed off.

Callie nodded reluctantly. 'Understandable. And your first instinct was to protect her so thank you for that,' she said.

'Callie, I'm sorry if I jumped to conclusions about Sephy.'

'If?'

'Scratch the "if",' I said. 'Forgive me?'

'Find my brother and bring him home safe and well and I'll forgive you anything,' she replied.

And the way she said it . . . More incentive, if any were needed, to bring Libby and Troy home. 'Fair enough. Let's go get our loved ones back.'

Just as we stood up, a ping came from Callie's jacket pocket. A text alert by the sound of it. She took out her phone and glanced at it. I headed for the door to give her some privacy, only to stop after a step or two when I heard her gasp. I turned.

Eyes narrowed, Callie was frowning at me.

'What now?'

'May I see your chest, please?' she asked.

'Excuse me?'

Callie raised an eyebrow – and then I knew what this was about. Pulling my T-shirt out of my trousers, I rolled it up to my neck. I was doing that a lot today.

'Oh. My. God! It's true!' she breathed.

The day after Callie discovered my tattoo, I'd had it taken care of. I went to see Feenix, a Cross tattoo artist of repute who had been recommended to me. I'd promised to pay her five times her usual fee if she didn't balls up the end result. After she'd signed a non-disclosure agreement, I showed her my chest and explained what I wanted done. A true professional, Feenix hadn't commented on my original tattoo. She'd just got down to business, listing the pros and cons of my proposed replacement.

'The only way to make this work is to use dark inks to reinstate the word "Forever" and to overwrite the word "Nought". The simplest way to do this would be to reinstate the red heart as the background. If I do this, there's no going back or changing your mind,' Feenix warned. 'Laser surgery to remove any new tattoo I give you won't work and will be extremely painful into the bargain.'

'I know what I'm doing,' I tried to reassure her. 'And I'm not going to change my mind.'

'If you say so,' she said as she got to work.

Forever, the word that it had taken five painful laser treatments over the years to try and eliminate, was reinstated. *Nought* was replaced with a new word written in the same cursive black ink, shadowed to look like the word was three-dimensional and bursting out of my heart. Feenix was a true craftswoman and I couldn't fault her work when she'd finished.

Unexpectedly now, fingers trailed gently across my new tattoo. I smiled behind my raised T-shirt as Callie explored each letter with her fingertips, her touch making my skin tingle. She placed her palm over the tattoo, over my heart. I stepped back.

'Can I pull my top down now?' I asked, lowering it slightly.

Callie nodded, her hand falling to her side. 'I can't believe you did that. Your next girlfriend won't be too happy with it.'

I shrugged. 'Shall we go?'

Callie followed me towards the door. I glanced at her to find her studying me, total bewilderment on her face. The painful reintroduction of my tattoo was worth it just for that expression. Two simple words that had definitely given the woman beside me food for thought.

Callie Forever.

I'd barely set foot outside my apartment when my private mobile vibrated yet again. There were times when being a public servant, and therefore in theory always contactable, was a considerable pain in the arse. I took it out and tapped on the screen to read the newly delivered text message – from a number I did not recognize – in its entirety.

> *Today 14:28*
>
> Tobias Durbridge,
> I hope today finds you in a loving mood because your daughter Liberty and her Cross boyfriend are now under new management. If you'd like to see them again, you will carry out the following instructions to the letter.
> 1. Inform your bank that you will be transferring a considerable sum of money

later tonight. You will instruct them not to block or query the transfer.
2. This evening, I will send you an account name, number, sort code and amount. You will have exactly ten minutes to transfer all the money requested.
3. The amount of money to be transferred will consist of eight digits. I know it's only a fraction of what you're worth, but I'm not greedy.
4. Once the money has been successfully transferred, I will provide the location of your daughter and her friend. Then we'll all have what we want.
You have one chance to get this right. If you don't answer your phone, if you hang up, if the police are listening at your end, if you try to trace this text or tonight's call, if you refuse to follow any of these instructions, there will be no second chances. This is your opportunity to prove your daughter means more to you than your money.

My blood ran icy-cold as I read the text again. *Under new management*—What did that mean? I had questions. Like how the hell did this new person get my phone number for one? And how did they know I had anything like eight digits in my bank account?

'Is everything all right, Tobey?' asked Callie.

'Yes, everything's fine,' I replied, ushering her into the lift.

I turned to the two protection officers who were

making moves to accompany us. 'Michael, Deli, tha

I'll be out with Callie for the rest of the day incog

your services won't be required.'

Deli and Michael exchanged worried looks.

'But, sir—' Michael began.

'I'll be fine,' I reassured them as I pressed the button for the basement level. 'I want to be alone with Miss Hadley, and four would definitely be a crowd. If I need you, I'll phone, OK?'

'Sir, I really think—' The lift doors shut, cutting off Deli's thought.

'That was rude,' Callie informed me dryly.

'But necessary,' I replied.

After a moment's further deliberation, I showed the text to Callie. She needed to know that I wouldn't hold anything back nor hide anything from her, even though that had been my first instinct when I initially got the text. I would do whatever it took to get her to truly trust me.

She read the message and handed back my phone, her expression stony. 'Whoever sent it could be one of the kidnapper's associates or just someone who's heard rumours. Or it could be someone who knows about the kidnapping, but who doesn't have Libby and Troy and is just trying their luck for a huge payout.'

'Yeah, I'd thought of that myself. I'm not handing over a damned thing without real-time proof that they're both still alive.'

'Do you have that kind of money?' asked Callie.

'I can get it,' I said carefully, adding, 'This one transfer uld well wipe me out, but that's not my primary concern. The thought of giving in to this blackmailing filth doesn't sit well with me.'

Callie studied me speculatively, then nodded. 'Thanks for showing me. How did the sender get your phone number?'

'Your guess is as good as mine.' Something else I was wondering. The number of people who had my personal digits could be counted on the fingers of two hands excluding the thumbs: Callie, of course, as my lawyer, members of my family and a very few friends and trusted colleagues. And all those who did were under strict instructions not to pass my number on without my express permission. I wasn't into this 'so-and-so gave me your phone number, I hope you don't mind' bullshit. Yes, I did mind – very much.

'Oh God! Troy and Libby must be so scared. I can't bear it.' Turning her head, Callie wiped a swift hand over each eye. I moved to stand before her, carefully brushing away any remaining tears with my fingertips.

'Callie, we're not beaten yet,' I told her. 'They are still alive. I refuse to believe otherwise and so should you.'

She graced me with a tentative smile, before leaning forward to kiss me, her lips so soft against mine. I wrapped my arms round her, returning her kiss with interest. All I wanted to do was hold her tight and reassure her that everything was going to be all right. I tried to tell her as much with my lips on hers, loving the way she felt in my arms, loving the way her tongue felt playing against mine.

Yet, with each moment that passed, I couldn't shake the impression that we weren't going to see out the night unscathed. I'd never been one to value feelings over rational thought, but this mood was gripping me tighter and tighter with each passing minute.

This time tomorrow, would any of us be the same? Somehow I doubted it. When at last we both came up for air, the lift doors were on the verge of closing again. I reached out a hand to halt their progress.

'Are you OK, Callie?' I asked tentatively.

She smiled. 'Yeah. I'm just grateful for you, that's all.'

Damn it. It was those sorts of declarations that had me – and kept me – wrapped round her little finger. We stepped out into the underground car park where I kept my three private cars – a compact, a luxury saloon and an SUV, all black, of course. I led the way to the SUV. The sender of the ransom note was right about one thing. I'd give anything and everything I had to get Liberty and Troy safely home again, even if the cost was great. Even if the cost was *everything*. But we still had a few hours before the deadline.

Time enough to put a plan of my own into motion.

Daily Shouter Online

Home. News. Politics. Celebs. Entertainment. Sport. Tech. Health. Science. Money. More.

BREAKING NEWS. Prime Minister reveals all after being accused of having an NF tattoo

Prime Minister Tobias Durbridge today revealed his chest to the world after being accused by an ex-girlfriend of having a Nought Forever tattoo over his heart. Nought Forever are a banned militant group who have been responsible for a number of atrocities over the last few decades, though their popularity and influence have declined in recent years.

Bella Monroe stated this morning that the Prime Minister used to be a member of Nought Forever and had a tattoo to commemorate and celebrate that fact. Tobey Durbridge showed his chest to *Daily Shouter* reporters earlier today to disprove that claim. Indeed, he does have a tattoo on his chest, but the writing inside a red heart reads *Callie Forever*. Who is this mysterious Callie? Sources close to the PM have suggested that it may be Callie Rose Hadley, barrister and granddaughter of the late Kamal Hadley, MP, though this has yet to be confirmed.

The *Daily Shouter* has reached out to Bella Monroe for a comment.

Do you know who Callie is? Phone or email us using the contact details below. We pay!

forty-one. Sephy

'George, thanks for letting me do this.'

The butler nodded as he led the way to Dan's study. I don't know what I'd been expecting, but the place was immaculate and the sweet, distinctive smell of leather polish and vanilla hung in the air.

'The police have gathered all the evidence they can so there's no reason not to let you look around,' said George.

'Did the police leave everything as they found it?' I asked, glancing about me as we walked.

George's snort of derision was immediate. He instantly looked contrite. 'I'm sorry, Mrs Ealing. That was very unprofessional of me.'

'But human.' I smiled. 'And please call me Sephy.'

'That wouldn't be appropriate, Mrs Ealing,' he said.

I didn't push it. I wasn't sure what to make of the middle-aged man before me with his irregular smile and his cool, watchful, hazel-brown eyes. I suspected George didn't miss much – if anything. Crow's feet crinkled the corners of his eyes and furrowed frown lines had taken up permanent residence on his forehead. The creases cupping his mouth spoke of a man who knew how to laugh, but who also knew how to cry. His moustache was carefully groomed and discreet, his black hair short and precision-cut, framing his face.

'Is there something wrong, Mrs Ealing?' George asked, his eyebrows raised at my undisguised scrutiny. Embarrassed, I quickly shook my head. He opened the study door and ushered me inside.

I guess I'd kept my eyes trained on him just a tad too long. 'Er, George, I was just wondering why you became a butler in the first place. You strike me as the type of person who could do anything you put your mind to.'

George nodded. 'It's kind of you to say so, Mrs Ealing. After my wife died, I needed a job that would provide for me and my daughter, Chima. When a friend told me how much butlers could earn and what the job entailed, I decided that would suit me down to the ground. After my training, I was lucky enough to find a position with Mr Jeavons and I've been with him ever since.'

'I'm sorry about your wife. How did she die – if you don't mind me asking?'

'Cancer.'

'I'm so sorry. My sincere condolences.'

'Thank you.' George held himself rigid with remembered pain.

'How did you come to work for Dan Jeavons?' I couldn't help asking.

'Mr Jeavons contacted the agency I work for. He wanted a butler rather than a housekeeper to manage his household. He had rather old-fashioned ideas like that.'

'Is there much call for butlers these days?' I wondered.

'You'd be surprised. To the very rich, we're a fashion

accessory like the latest sports car and the best schools. If you have money, your home is not properly dressed without a butler.' The tone may have been neutral, but the words most certainly were not.

'How long had you worked for Dan?'

'Eight years,' George replied. 'He had one butler before me, a Nought, but he proved to be unsuitable. Mr Jeavons specifically requested a Cross butler and I was happy to be interviewed where some of my colleagues were not.'

A Cross butler? George was clearly dual heritage. I guess that made him Cross enough in Dan's eyes.

'Really? Did Dan's reputation precede him even then?'

'Oh, nothing like that,' George dismissed with a wave of his hand. 'But some of my Cross colleagues were most insistent that they didn't wish to work for Noughts.'

'Ah, I see. But you didn't mind?'

'I was prepared to work for anyone who would pay me what I'm worth and treat me with respect.'

'And Dan did that?'

A slight pause. 'Yes, he did. I'm a single parent who wanted the best for his daughter and Mr Jeavons helped with that.'

'How old is your daughter?'

'Chima was seventeen yesterday.' George's hazel-brown eyes softened at the mention of his child. 'She's going to study medicine at university. One day she'll be a world-famous neurosurgeon and save countless lives. She's so smart . . .'

George's voice trailed off, his gaze cloudy and withdrawn. His lips thinned as if painful memories were washing over him. He was hurting, but I couldn't be sure if it was for himself or someone else.

'Where is Chima now?' I asked softly.

'She's been staying with me for the last year. She used to board at her school, but . . . anyway, she's here with me.'

'I thought you were a live-in butler?' I said.

'I am. I mean, I *was*. Mr Jeavons' apartment suite occupies the whole top floor of this building including the annexe apartment through the kitchen which is where I live. Mr Jeavons wanted me to be available at all times. My apartment has two bedrooms with en-suite bathrooms, an open-plan sitting room and a kitchen-diner. It's not huge, but it was all I needed.'

George spoke like he was being interviewed, pleasant enough but very formal; he didn't let his guard down for a moment. 'Anyway, that's all academic now. Mr Jeavons owns . . . owned this building and left it to his brother, Tom. Mrs Foxton, who is administering the estate until Tom comes of age, has already served me with one month's notice. Chima and I will be leaving on Friday.'

'You're losing your home? Couldn't she at least have given you longer than four weeks?'

'It was to be expected, ma'am. I had hoped to have a little longer to find another situation, but Chima and I will manage.'

'I'm so sorry. Dan didn't mind your daughter living with you?'

'Oh no. In fact, it was his idea. He suggested Chima joined me while she revised for her mock exams. Mr Jeavons said he'd do anything he could to help her career, including pulling some strings to get her into university when the time was right.'

Really? 'You believed him?'

'Oh yes,' said George. 'Mr Jeavons was a man of his word if nothing else.'

Hmm . . . 'May I ask, what's your opinion of Tobey Durbridge?'

A cold flash sparked in his eyes. 'I'm sure he'll make a competent Prime Minister.'

I smiled. 'That's not what I asked.'

George nodded ruefully. 'Mr Durbridge and Mr Jeavons were very alike. Birds of a feather.'

True, but still not what I asked.

'Did you like him?'

'Liking either of them was never in my job description.'

'You're a master at not answering the question,' I stated with a wry smile.

George nodded, his mouth quirking at one corner. 'Very well. No, I don't particularly like Mr Durbridge. He's too hungry for success for its own sake. You know the way a robber will steal from banks because that's where the money is? Well, Mr Durbridge was hungry to become a politician not to serve the public, but because that's where power lies if you're not born into it. Mr Durbridge wants power and he can't escape the feeling that he constantly has something to prove, and in my opinion that's a lethal combination. He was fully prepared to use Mr Jeavons to get to the top, but, once there, Mr Durbridge wanted to swap horses and suddenly run a clean race. Mr Jeavons wasn't going to have that. He wasn't going to allow Mr Durbridge to just turn his back on him like that. There! Is that honest enough for you?'

I nodded, adding, 'Tobey and Dan appeared quite chatty at the dinner party.'

'Yes, they did indeed put on a very good show,' said George.

Hmm . . .

'Was working for Dan what you expected?'

'It was . . . an eye-opener,' said George carefully.

I bet it was. 'You never . . . sought a change of scene?'

'Mr Jeavons paid me very well,' George replied. 'Thanks to him, my daughter went to a very good boarding school and will be going to a top university in Zafrika with her full tuition already paid for, provided she gets the required grades.'

'Good for her.' I tried to serve him a smile. It was not returned.

George shrugged. 'Anyway, I should get back to work. Is there anything else you require?'

'There is one last thing, George,' I began. 'I understand there's some kind of recording taken on the night of Dan's dinner party. Is that true?'

'Yes, ma'am. There are motion-activated cameras in all the rooms in this apartment except the bathrooms, and of course not in my living quarters,' George explained, adding, 'Mr Durbridge took the flash drive containing the evening's CCTV recordings. He also made sure to delete the backup copy from the cloud.'

My stomach took on the weight of a bowling ball. I looked around, but could see nothing attached to the ceiling or the cornices. 'Where's the hidden camera in this room?'

George pointed to the half-bookcase against the wall adjacent to the door. On it sat a number of ornaments: a couple of paperweights, a sculpture of a dancer that looked like the genuine antique article and a modern art piece that was dull gold and polished black spheres and sculpted angles.

'The gold one is the camera,' said George.

Shit! 'Did you watch the recording?' I asked.

George's eyes danced away from mine for a moment before he deliberately looked me in the eye and spoke. 'Yes, ma'am. Before the police arrived, Mr Durbridge and I both watched the footage of that night for around the time of Mr Jeavons' demise.'

'What did you see?' My breathing was getting faster.

George's gaze didn't falter as he kept his expression carefully neutral. 'A section was missing. The image jumped from Mr Jeavons looking up as his door opened to him slumped over his desk with you standing behind him, the letter opener in your hand, just before you stabbed him in the back.' The butler announced this like he was giving a weather report.

Shit!

Silence.

My thoughts were spinning coins on a table, which I could do nothing with until they noisily settled and were still. As well as the murder weapon, Tobey had a recording of me with it in my hand.

Jon was right: I was going to be framed for Dan's murder, and the worst thing of all was I had no one and nothing to blame but myself.

'George, for what it's worth, I didn't kill Dan. I was stupid enough to take the knife out of his back because I thought he was playing some asinine prank. When I realized he was really dead, I replaced it and wiped the handle so I wouldn't have anything more to do with it.' My face began to burn. 'Not my finest hour. I wasn't thinking straight.'

'Yes, ma'am,' said George non-committally.

I shook my head. Even now I couldn't believe I'd done that. When they used that cliché in films or TV dramas, I used to laugh at how ridiculous it was. As if anyone would be brainless enough to really touch or pick up an obvious murder weapon like that.

I wasn't laughing any more.

The thing was, when I walked into Dan's study that night, I couldn't believe what I was seeing was real. I thought it was another of Dan's mind games. One of his nasty little tricks to gain the upper hand. It was just the kind of insidious bullshit he'd get up to and it certainly wouldn't have been the first time.

After pretending to leave the dinner party for the evening, and telling George that I'd see myself out, I loudly closed the front door, then hurried down the hallway away from the dining room to wait in the bathroom opposite Dan's study, praying that no one would want to use it while I was in there. I reckoned that I should be safe as there were two other bathrooms closer to the dining room than the one I occupied.

Thirty minutes. That's how long it took for Dan to finally be alone. With the door slightly ajar, I heard a number of people enter and leave his room, but that's all I heard. Every time I tried to leave the bathroom to see Dan, someone else would round the corner to demand his attention. Waiting, waiting, waiting had been a lesson in frustration, and instruction in the art of patience. And, when I finally entered the study, there was Dan, slumped over his desk with a knife sticking out between his shoulder blades, a pool of dark liquid beneath him.

'Dan, you're not funny,' I hissed at him.

When there was no reply, I walked further into the room. And still Dan remained slumped over his desk.

'Dan, I know this evening is about you bleeding me for more money. Well, I'm not giving you another penny – and I'm not giving you my restaurant either. So you can do your worst—'

And still he didn't move.

'Oh, for heaven's sake! Dan, could you look at me, please? What d'you hope to achieve with this stupid-assery? Am I supposed to run screaming from the room?'

I walked round his precious desk to confront him. He'd gone all out on this one, right down to the fake blood pool beneath him. He couldn't know I was still in his apartment so this charade had to be for someone else's benefit. Who? His brother? Bella? Patrix? I didn't care. I'd had it with Dan and his juvenile idiocy. That's when I grabbed the knife and pulled it from his back. Except the joke was on me. A drop of real blood dripped down from a real blade. Only then did I notice that Dan had more than one puncture wound in him. My attention went back to the knife in my hand.

And, in that moment, I knew I was in a shit-ton of trouble.

Panic is a strange thing. It grabs you and redwashes your thoughts. It plays tricks with time, speeding it up and slowing it down and turning it on its head, but all within a single moment. I thought I was acting rationally as I replaced the knife in Dan's back, aiming at the exact same spot I took it from. Then I used my blouse to wipe the hilt. All I could think about was removing my fingerprints in case the police thought I'd killed him. It only occurred to me afterwards that, in creating an escape route for myself, I'd also provided one for Dan's murderer if their fingerprints were also on the murder weapon. And, to be honest, I couldn't even be sure I'd wiped off all my fingerprints as I was in such a state by then.

So stupid.

I regarded the room as it was now. 'And there was no clue as to who really *did* kill Dan?' I asked George.

'No, ma'am. When Mr Durbridge and I watched the recording, there was just a jump in the footage as I said.'

'How exactly could that happen?' I frowned.

'Mr Durbridge asked me the same question. The only thing I can think of is that someone, the killer, erased the minutes that revealed his or her identity, then set the recording to restart when they knew the coast would be clear. You see, the camera can be both motion or time activated.'

I thought for a moment. 'How hard would it be to wipe the part of the recording that showed the murder and then restart it?'

George considered. 'Mr Jeavons' computer was on the desk in front of him when he was killed and the program to monitor each camera feed in the apartment was running, so . . .'

'So anyone who knew about the cameras and was familiar with the program could've deleted the appropriate section of the footage?' I finished for him.

'Yes, ma'am.'

'How hard would that be?'

'Not hard at all, ma'am. You open the program, click on the appropriate room, scrub back to the approximate time of the incident and delete the relevant section of the recording. The app would then allow you to specify when recording should begin again. Plenty of time for the killer to make good his or her escape before then.'

'Who knew Dan had a camera in this study?'

'I believe Mr Durbridge did, Patrix Ellerman knew as Mr Jeavons' ex-lawyer and friend, as did his brother, Tom, Eva Foxton, Jarvis of course, and maybe Bella Monroe if Mr Durbridge or Mr Jeavons told her.'

I raised an eyebrow, feeling deprived. 'Basically, that's everyone except Kellan Bruemann, Owen Dowd and me.'

'It would appear so, yes, ma'am.'

'And erasing the footage didn't require a password?'

George shrugged. 'No. Mr Jeavons' computer required both facial and fingerprint recognition or a two-tier password to start up and he believed that was sufficient.'

'If computer access required facial recognition or a fingerprint to start, how did you and Tobey get to review the recording? That must've been considerably after the event.'

'Mr Jeavons set up his laptop's security so that his face or fingerprints were only required after a complete computer shutdown. While it was up and running, and even in sleep mode, no such biometrics were required. Since he never took the laptop out of this apartment, he considered it perfectly safe here.'

'I see. George, who d'you think murdered Dan?'

George shrugged. 'It's not my place to speculate, ma'am.'

'There's no clue as to whether or not the killer was a Nought or a Cross, a man or a woman?'

'No, ma'am. After you left, the next person in the study was Mr Durbridge and that was over an hour later. He checked to see if Mr Jeavons had a pulse and, after viewing the recording, called the police.'

Hmm. The day after the dinner party, the police interviewed me as someone who was present and after that they hadn't bothered me again. I figured I'd successfully managed to escape detection. I'd assumed I was safe. Big mistake. Tobey had proof on a recording that not only was I there, but that I'd handled the murder weapon. Proof he'd have no choice but to hand over to the police when they came knocking at his door. Why hadn't he done anything with this yet?

'Did the police remove the letter opener on the night of the murder?'

'I believe Mr Durbridge might've taken the letter opener and swapped it for the ornamental knife on the desk instead. He carefully wrapped up the letter opener and took it with him.'

'And you let him?'

'It wasn't my place to stop him,' George replied. 'He was most keen that no hint of suspicion should fall at your door.'

'Dad, where did you put my . . . ?'

A girl's voice unexpectedly sounded behind us. I spun round. Standing in the doorway was a striking Nought girl with a cloud of wavy chestnut-brown hair, large, quizzical, dark amber eyes and full lips set in an oval face. She wore tropical sea-blue trousers and a dark blue T-shirt with a couple of tiny darker stains over her left breast. She must've spilled something and not realized. Her feet were bare. She was facing her dad and side-on to me.

'Oh, you must be Chima,' I said, smiling. 'I'm Sephy

Ealing. Your dad has been telling me about your plans to go to university. Congratulations.'

A quick glance at her dad, then Chima turned towards me and slowly nodded.

'Hello. I'm sorry. I didn't know Dad had company,' she said.

'No problem,' I said. 'Your dad was just telling me that you're going to study medicine.'

Chima forced a smile. 'It's all Dad and I have ever dreamed of. I'm hoping to be a surgeon one day. I want to make him proud of me.'

'I'm already proud of you, princess,' said George.

Chima shared a smile with her dad and I was momentarily forgotten.

'Well, good luck,' I said warmly.

'Thank you. Dad, can I borrow you when you've finished?'

'Of course, angel. I'll be right there.' As Chima left the room, George turned to me, his smile fading. 'If there's nothing else, ma'am?'

'I don't suppose you have a spare copy of the recording for that evening, do you? One you might've kept surreptitiously? I'd love to see it for myself,' I said, having one last try.

'I'm afraid not, ma'am,' said George.

He gave me a studied look that I had no trouble interpreting. He'd wanted to keep hold of the recording, but Tobey took over, not prepared to take any chances. As far as I was concerned, Tobey was Dan Jeavons in a bespoke suit and with better manners, but he was still just as toxic.

'Thank you, George.'

'Ma'am.' And, with that, George left me alone in a room I'd never expected to see again.

forty-two. Troy

Libby and I stood statue-still. The squeaky groan of nails being pulled from old wood continued above us. A harsh creak, then a loud rasp and the clatter of wood being dropped carelessly to the ground. The clatter happened again, and then a third time, followed by the screech of rusty bolts being drawn back – metal scraping against metal.

Then silence.

If the harsh, grating noise of the door being unbarricaded was bad, the profound silence that followed it was far, far worse. It was like having my neck on the block and waiting for a guillotine blade to fall. Libby was squeezing every drop of blood out of my hand – but I wasn't about to pull away. I was squeezing right back.

'Troy—'

'I'm here.' My voice was equally soft. 'Libby, if you get the chance, just run. Don't wait for me. I'm not going anywhere with this ankle.'

Libby turned to me. She opened her mouth to argue, then thought better of it. She nodded reluctantly. Good. She was seeing sense.

I nodded. With a crack and creak that echoed in my heart, the door above us began to open.

forty-three. Callie

Tobey and I looked up at the mock-Tudor detached house before us with its stylish blend of Zafrikan and Albion influences. This house couldn't be more than ten years old, but it was working hard to seem centuries older. A black WMW was parked on the spacious paved driveway, wide enough to cater for at least three SUVs.

'Shane isn't going to be happy to see us, is he?' I said.

'Tough!' Clearly Tobey wasn't about to lose any sleep over that.

'Let me handle this,' I told him as we approached the front door.

I went to ring the bell, but Tobey grabbed my hand, my finger mere millimetres away. He shook his head, issuing a soft 'Shush!' He pointed to the front door and I now saw what had made him pause. The door was slightly ajar, only wide enough to be seen from close up, not the road. His expression sombre, Tobey turned to me, mouthing, 'Wait here.'

As if.

He pushed at the door with the back of his hand. It took a second for my brain to click as to why. No fingerprints. He stepped into the hall; I was right behind him. He cast me an irritated look, but I wasn't going anywhere. Tobey went into the first room on the right, a sitting room with pale yellow walls, a mid-grey carpet and two cream leather sofas placed in an L-shape. Against the far wall was the biggest flatscreen TV I'd seen outside a cinema. A quick look around, then back out into the hall. The next room on the right was a dining room. Cream-coloured walls, the same grey carpet and a large french-polished wooden table that seated ten people with ease. Shane Stoats was clearly doing all right for himself. Back into the hall and through to the kitchen. Tobey had only taken one step when he froze. I only just avoided walking into his back. Looking round him, I saw the body at once. A Nought guy lay on the floor, his unseeing eyes open and staring up at the ceiling. Dried blood decorated his lips like clown's make-up. A large burgundy stain covered one shoulder of his sky-blue shirt. In the middle of his forehead was a bullet hole, a pool of blood beneath his head. Nauseous, I turned from the sight, eyes closed.

Do not throw up, Callie Rose. Don't you dare!

I didn't want another look and yet my eyes were drawn back to the body on the floor. All the photos and videos of dead bodies I'd seen over my career, yet nothing had prepared me for the sight of a real one. There was something so still, so final-page about death. I kept swallowing, determined not to throw up, though my stomach was heaving.

'Callie, have you touched anything since we came in this house?'

I couldn't answer. I just kept staring at the body until Tobey took me by the shoulders, placing himself between me and the dead man. He repeated his question.

'No. No, I didn't,' I said.

'We need to leave. *Now.*'

'Shouldn't we phone the police? We can't just leave him like that.'

'Callie, we can and we must. D'you want to spend the next few hours answering questions and writing statements? Hours that could be spent looking for Libby and Troy?'

My silence reluctantly conceded that he had a point. Tobey ushered me out of the house. Using his foot, he eased the door till it was almost shut, leaving it as we'd found it.

'Was that . . . was that Shane Stoats?'

'Yes, it was,' said Tobey grimly. 'Someone beat us to him. Let's get out of here.'

We got back into his car and sat in silence. His expression was stormy. Unexpectedly, he thumped the dashboard with the palm of his hand, making me jump. Then he started the engine and took out one of his phones, tapping on a couple of icons before putting it to his ear.

'Who're you phoning?' I asked, when no explanation was forthcoming.

'Jarvis Burton.'

Dan's old lieutenant. 'Why?'

'To see if he or Eva ordered the hit on Shane.'

'Would he tell you?'

'Yes.' Tobey was barely paying me any attention. His focus was on the phone call he was making.

'Would Jarvis even order such a thing?'

'That's what I'm going to find out.'

I gave Tobey a cursory glance before turning to look out of the passenger window. There it was – proof, if any were needed, that Jarvis was in Tobey's pocket as I'd suspected for some time now. Tobey had the guy on speed dial. How long had Jarvis been working for him, I wondered? Had their dealings started when Dan was alive? I still had Tobey's case to present and win, so I needed to be careful what I learned about him. It was against the rules for advocates to wilfully deceive the court. I couldn't very well present Tobey as squeaky clean if I knew otherwise.

I glanced at him. He might be a lot of things, not all of them savoury, but was he capable of murder? I wondered if Jarvis was the same informant inside Dan's outfit who Jon sometimes worked with? Over the years, Jon had received some really useful information from his contact, information that had helped me to win more than a few cases. Till this moment, I'd deliberately never questioned Jon too rigorously on the source of the info. Bending the law was one thing, knowingly snapping it in two was quite another. The former I could just about accept as sometimes the only way to get justice, but never the latter.

Tobey hung up, frustration creasing his face. 'It went straight through to voicemail. He must've switched off his phone.'

'D'you think he had something to do with Shane's death?'

'I don't know,' said Tobey reluctantly.

'Maybe he did the hit or at least ordered it because Shane took his place?' I ventured.

'Maybe,' Tobey said evasively.

A quick glance behind and we were off. Once we were on our way, I asked, 'OK, what do we do now?'

'We need to let your friend Jon know what's happened.'

I took out my phone and started keying in a message to Jon. A quick glance from Tobey was followed by a sharp rebuke. 'Godsake! You're texting him? *Seriously?* You're going to leave a message that we've just found Shane's body and are fleeing the scene? Callie, are you actually actively trying to put a noose round my neck?'

Stricken, I stared at him.

Tobey's frown at my reaction was chased away when he realized what he'd said, remembered how my father died all those years ago. 'Hellsake! I'm sorry, Callie. I shouldn't have said that.'

'It's fine,' I lied.

'I really am sorry.'

I took a steadying breath. 'Honestly, it's all right. And you're right about trying to leave Jon a message. That was stupid. I wasn't thinking.' Chastened, I phoned Jon instead, using speed dial. It went straight through to his voicemail. 'J, it's Callie. I have some news. Could you phone me, please?'

Neither of us was having much luck getting through to people on the phone. I glanced at Tobey. Yeah, I got that he was a top-slot, hotshot politician and his every action since I'd turned up at his apartment earlier just emphasized the gap between us. Protection officers, constant updates via emails, texts, phone calls, documents to read, news bulletins to be aware of – Tobey's every moment was spoken for. Yet he'd shaken it all off to try to track down the daughter he barely knew and my brother. I don't know what I would've done if I hadn't had Tobey at my side throughout this. Every time I thought I knew how he might act or react, he did something to surprise me. Look at the way he'd risen to the top. OK, so he might've taken a short cut or nine to get there, but, as he hadn't been born with a palladium spoon in his mouth, maybe short cuts were the only way he had to get to the top. Or was I just making excuses for a man who still occupied a space and place in my thoughts – and my heart – however much I might not want him to?

'Shane is dead, Jarvis isn't answering his phone, Jon's not answering his phone, so we've got one choice left,' said Tobey.

And he didn't say anything else. I mean, really?

'Stop being so damned mysterious,' I said. 'What do we do next? Or would you rather keep that to yourself too?'

Tobey glanced at me, but let my snide comment slide. 'Enough with the pawns. Let's try cornering the queen herself.'

'Eva Foxton?'

'The one and only. And, Callie, take my advice. When we're with her, watch your back.'

forty-four. Sephy

Well, Callum, here I am in Dan's study, sitting in his chair. A shudder grips me, chilling, like a malignant ghost walking through me. The last time I was in here, Dan's body lay slumped over the desk, a knife between his shoulder blades. I'd refused to believe what my eyes had been telling me. Telling me? Screaming at me, more like. But I really had believed it had been one of Dan's pathetic games. See! I didn't even trust him to be properly dead.

Even before Nathan's death, Dan made our lives a misery. You couldn't run a pub or club or restaurant in this town without some mobster or other demanding a thick slice of a pie they had no hand in making or baking. For them, extortion was a quick way to make a whole heap of money. But for Nathan and me it wasn't just standing up to the substance of what they were trying to do; it was the principle behind it as well. Giving in to the Owen Dowds and the Dan Jeavons of this world would mean no going back. We'd be the victims of whichever bully boys thought they could employ such tactics.

Nathan stood up to all of them, even though they'd put him in hospital twice. When he died, they then turned their attention to me – both Dowd and Jeavons – each demanding a hefty proportion of my monthly profits. Well, I wasn't going to take that lying down, sitting up or in any other position, and that's what I told the beefed-up minions each of them sent, warning them that, if they tried anything, I would sing like a songbird to the police and the press and anyone else who'd listen. Dowd had backed off when I hit him with a fact or five I knew about not just his organization but him personally – courtesy of dinner-table conversations with my lawyer daughter. But not Dan Jeavons. No, he took it to the next level. If he'd threatened just me, I would've told him to go to the devil and instructed him on what to do when he got there, but he was shrewd. He wasn't stupid enough to directly threaten Meggie, Callie and Troy. No, he just insinuated that bad things could happen to my loved ones. What were his exact words? 'Incidents and accidents happen, Sephy; that would be entirely your fault.' Loathsome bastard. I could've and should've killed him for that alone.

I defied Dan to do his worst. So he did. Callie was almost knocked over while crossing the street to get to her law chambers. Within a couple of weeks of that happening, Troy was mugged by two young Noughts on his way home from school who pushed him against a wall, slapped him a couple of times and demanded, 'What have you got for us, dagger?' before taking his phone and smartwatch and running off.

The same night Troy was mugged, I drove round to see Dan at his club, Ava's. Jarvis tried to stop me from going into Dan's office, but I was so spitting mad I kneed him in his tenders and marched past while the beetle clutched his groin and rolled on the floor.

'Dan, if you ever come near my children again, I swear I will kill you,' I told him without preamble.

'You can't hold me responsible for incidents and accidents, Sephy,' said Dan silkily. 'Don't blame me if you can't or won't take better care of your brats.'

The time for talk was over. Lips pursed, eyes blazing, I was about to leap across Dan's desk to slap him into a new postcode when I was unexpectedly lifted off my feet and carried out of the room.

'Ah, Jarvis. Had enough of rolling on the floor then? If one middle-aged, dried-up old trout can take you, maybe I need to rethink who should be my lieutenant. What d'you reckon?'

Jarvis's arms tightened considerably round my waist. I should've kneed him harder.

'Let me go!' I yelled.

With Dan's laughter pealing in my ears, Jarvis ignored me and carried me not just from the room, but from the club to dump me out back among the bins and the rats.

Two days later, Troy's watch and phone were sent to me in the post with no letter, no note, no explanation. None was required. Dan was demonstrating just how easy it would be to get to Troy and do something worse than shove him into a wall a couple of times. And, to my shame, his actions were enough to make me capitulate. Capitulate, hell! I collapsed like a house of cards. And, as much as I despised Dan, I despised myself more for giving in to his threats.

But, Callum, what choice did I have?

From that moment on, when Jarvis turned up at the beginning of each month, there was an envelope waiting for him containing one-quarter of my restaurant's monthly takings. And Jarvis wouldn't let anyone but me hand it to him. Oh, Callum, if you only knew what giving that turd-weasel my money did to me each month. The absolute humiliation and seething, silent fury that ate away at me as Jarvis smirked before pocketing my cash.

So there was no way I had any intention of attending Dan's dinner party when Jarvis passed on the invitation. In fact, I invited Jarvis to relay my four-word answer of 'Sod off and die' back to Dan verbatim. Jarvis had already anticipated my answer and replied with four words of his own.

'Incidents and accidents, Sephy.'

So I turned up on the date, on the dot, to be met by a barrage of Dan's bullshit. And, even though he was dead, he was still proving to be a ginormous pain in my backside.

Yet here I sit in his chair, wondering what I'm doing.

Honestly, Callum! I'm looking around this study like I think the walls are going to start talking to me, telling me who did it. I check out the ornament holding the camera on top of the half-bookcase. Even close up, it's impossible to see that it's a camera. State-of-the-art spyware – which, ironically, had done nothing to stop Dan's murder.

That letter opener in Dan's back . . .

Who would Dan let get close enough to stab him in the back? A lover? A mother figure? A brother? I'd had conversations with most of them at the dinner party, but was no further forward. Somehow I had to find a way to talk to all of them, plus Jarvis and Eva. With the full facts, surely I'd be able to work out who murdered Dan? That was the only way to protect myself and my children.

The question was how?

Daily Shouter Online

Home. News. Politics. Celebs. Entertainment. Sport. Tech. Health. Science. Money. More.

Flu vaccination take-up among WAMEs at lowest point in decades

People from the Nought community in particular are significantly less likely to take up the flu vaccine compared to Crosses. Every Albion citizen over 60 is annually offered the vaccine, but, whereas the take-up among Crosses has consistently been over 82 per cent, that among Noughts so far this year has been less than 48 per cent.

A study from the National Public Health Authority (NPHA) found that a number of Noughts distrust the vaccine and have actively decided against taking it. Mei Dupone of the NPHA warned that a concerted effort must be made to counter false rumours and targeted misinformation.

'I've seen websites which claim that the vaccine contains microchips to track Noughts and their movements throughout the country, that the vaccine is a way to sterilize Noughts or render them impotent, that the vaccine is not to counter flu at all, but is a way to weaken or kill off Noughts at a designated time or place. None of these claims is true. I would encourage all Noughts to read the independent and peer-reviewed research data available on the NPHA website to get the truth about the flu vaccine.'

Gareth Johnstone, chair of NLM, stated that there's a reason for the reluctance of the WAME community to take the vaccine: 'For decades, drug companies have experimented and tested their new drugs on Noughts throughout Europe, using us as guinea pigs and treating Noughts like expendable cannon fodder. Yet, when it comes to advanced clinical trials, we are excluded. Every Nought has a story to tell of Noughts who have been adversely affected by the flu vaccine. How many Noughts were included in the latest clinical trials? For example, was it tested on Noughts with cystic fibrosis, a predominantly Nought disease? These drugs are clinically tested on Crosses, and passed for Cross use, and then rolled out as effective for everyone, which may not be the case.'

A spokeswoman for the NPHA stated that the low take-up is particularly worrying as there have been as yet unsubstantiated reports of a new strain of flu emerging from some Far Eastern countries – a strain as yet unseen in Albion.

forty-five. Libby

Hand in hand, Troy and I had been staring at the open door above us for ages. My senses were on red alert, waiting.

Waiting.

But nothing.

We looked at each other warily.

'Help me up the stairs,' Troy whispered.

He placed an arm round my shoulder as we made our way towards the bottom of the stairs. He grabbed the banister with his free hand and hopped up each step, biting his lip against the agony of each jarring movement. When at last we reached the top, he was bathed in sweat. I held onto him, as there was no handrail at the top to grab hold of any more, and waited for the pain he was going through to relax its grip on him. Several moments later, Troy motioned for me to step back down the stairs and wait.

Not a chance.

Giving him an impatient look, I moved ahead of him. A wary, deep breath later, I darted through the open door into the hall, the slat of wood ready in my hands. Hopping, Troy followed. A rapid look around revealed the hall was empty. A single sickly light bulb with no lampshade hung from the hall ceiling. Silence echoed round us.

'Troy?' I whispered.

'Shush!' said Troy, listening intently.

'Put that piece of wood down before you hurt someone.'

The voice had Troy and me spinning round, the makeshift spade in my hand raised to strike. A man with brownish-grey hair and glasses was standing in the derelict kitchen doorway, leaning against the door frame, his thick arms crossed. Behind his round glasses, which made him look like an owl, were the greenest eyes I'd ever seen. Green like moss.

'Please don't swing that at me,' he said, pointing at the length of wood in my hands. 'You might not miss.'

'Who the hell are you?' said Troy. 'Start talking.'

'My name is Jarvis. Jarvis Burton. I've come to get you out of here, but we need to hurry. I've dealt with the two arseholes who were guarding you, but I know for a fact that they have friends. When the two in the kitchen don't report in, more will arrive – and soon. And, Libby, that piece of wood and my good looks won't hold them at bay for very long.'

'You've only told us your name. We still don't know who you are,' Troy said.

'Libby, I work for your dad and I'm here to rescue you,' said the man, straightening up with a grin. 'I suggest we get the hell out of here first and you can both thank me later. Let's go.'

'No,' said Troy. 'Not until you prove you're not another arsehole using us to get rich quick. I've had it with being passed around like an unwanted Crossmas present.'

Jarvis shook his head. He turned in the kitchen doorway

to stand sideways on. 'Check the kitchen for yourselves if you don't believe me.'

'I'll check,' said Troy. 'Libby, brain him if he tries anything.'

'You got it,' I said. I checked my stance and distance so Jarvis couldn't unexpectedly grab my improvised weapon from my hands.

'Jarvis, could you go stand further into the kitchen away from us?' asked Troy.

Muttering an obscenity-ridden rant about unappreciative, spoilt teenagers, Jarvis did as Troy asked.

Troy limped forward, never taking his eyes off the man across the room. I was only a step behind, just in case Jarvis thought he'd try something. Troy got to the kitchen doorway and looked around, then froze. He held out his arm to stop me from taking a look for myself.

'Happy now?' asked Jarvis.

'What is it?' I tried to move round Troy's arm, but he wouldn't let me.

'Libby, no.'

'But I want to see,' I protested, attempting to push past him.

Troy turned to me and said quietly, 'It's two bodies, Libby. Haven't you seen enough death?'

I froze. So Jarvis really had got rid of two of the men holding us hostage. Troy was right. I'd seen enough death to last me five lifetimes. We stepped back.

'Now that's sorted, can we please get the hell out of here before we end up on the kitchen floor beside them?' said Jarvis. 'I used the gun belonging to one of them against them both and it's now out of bullets. If their friends arrive, my winning smile isn't going to make us suddenly bulletproof.'

I shuddered. Jarvis pushed past us to lead the way, but we were only halfway along the hall when a key sounded in the front-door lock.

We had company.

forty-six. Sephy

'Have you made any progress at all?' I asked my daughter, my mobile phone squashed between my ear and shoulder as I searched through the drawers of Dan's desk.

'We're definitely moving forward, Mum,' said Callie. 'Tobey is confident we'll bring Troy and Libby home soon.'

Hmm. 'Is he there with you?'

'Yes. We're on our way to a meeting.'

'Callie, tell me something. When Tobey told you about the letter opener, did he say anything else?'

'Such as?'

'Is that the only so-called proof he has of my guilt?' I asked.

'Mum, let it go. You had nothing to do with Dan's death and there's nothing Tobey can say or produce that could make me think otherwise.'

Which didn't exactly answer my question. 'Callie, how are you and Tobey getting on?'

'What d'you mean? We're working together.'

I knew my daughter and I knew when she was being evasive. 'Is there a chance of the two of you getting back together?' I asked straight out.

Pause. 'Who knows? Unlikely. But never say never, I suppose,' Callie replied.

'Is that what you want though?'

'I've got to go, Mum. Talk to you later.'

'Love you, honey.'

'Love you too, Mum.' Callie disconnected our call, making me smile wryly.

Whenever I asked Callie about her love life, she always had other places to be, other things to do, other conversations to have. She wasn't exactly forthcoming, but it didn't matter. I had eyes. After all these years, she still wasn't completely over Tobey. Would she ever be? Just another of the reasons why I'd asked him to stay away from my daughter.

After examining every drawer, every book, every ornament, every part of Dan's study for almost an hour, I finally admitted defeat and went in search of George. Even now, I wasn't sure what I hoped Dan's study would give me. Answers? Insights? What I had was a whole lot of nothing. George wasn't anywhere in the apartment, but there was a door on the other side of the utility room off the kitchen so I knocked on that and then opened it. A short hallway led to another door, this one slightly ajar. As I approached, I heard raised voices.

'Dad, this isn't fair. You can't tell me what to do. Not any more.'

'I can while you're under my roof,' George replied, adding with exasperation, 'Chima, you have your whole life ahead of you. Don't let one mistake ruin everything. You've got to put this behind you.'

'That's easy for you to say. You're dictating all my choices, Dad. Don't I get to decide anything about my own life?'

A phone began to ring, interrupting their conversation.

A moment, then: 'Look, I need to take this. I'll be right back,' said George, his footsteps receding.

I knocked on the door, plastering on a smile. Moments later, Chima stood there, effectively barring my way.

'Can I help you?'

'Ah, Chima, I'm sorry to intrude. I was just looking for George to tell him I'm leaving now.'

'I'll get—' Chima's words were interrupted by the sudden, unexpected sound of a baby crying. The dark, damp bloom on her T-shirt grew slightly larger.

'I'm babysitting,' she explained quickly.

'How old?' I enquired.

'Three months today.'

'What's his name?'

'Zelie. Her name is Zelie. She—'

'Can I help you, Mrs Ealing?' George strode into view, moving his daughter back with one hand, to stand directly in front of her. His expression tightened almost imperceptibly as he looked at me. I was in his space now and he wasn't happy about it, and what's more he wasn't bothered about letting me know that.

'Oh, George, I just came to tell you that I'm going to head off now. Thank you for letting me see Dan's study.'

'Did it help, Mrs Ealing?' His tone was soft, but those brown eyes of his were giving me ice burns.

'Not much, but it indicates a possible route forward.'

'Well, I hope it works out for you.'

Ever the butler, George didn't ask for further information.

'Thank you, George. By the way, I don't think I caught your surname?'

'Davison. George Davison.'

'Thank you for your hospitality today, Mr Davison. I appreciate it. It was a pleasure to meet you, Chima.'

I turned round and the smile fell off my face. I left the apartment, troubled.

forty-seven. Troy

Jarvis turned to us, a finger to his lips. He beckoned to Libby to pass him the slat of wood she'd dropped. Her expression, her whole body, tense, Libby picked it up and handed it over without a word. Jarvis waved us to one side with his free hand, indicating that we should get out of the way before he switched off the light. Whoever it was outside, they had obviously gleaned that something was wrong. A shadowy figure, illuminated by the street lamp, stepped back from the door, their shadow retreating. Libby and I moved into the sitting-room doorway out of harm's way, watching as the shadow advanced slowly and the front door was cautiously opened.

A man stepped warily into the darkened hallway. The street light outside revealed the outline of a gun in his hand. Jarvis waited for him to take a further step before darting out from behind the open front door and bringing the wooden slat down hard on the gunman's hand.

'Oof!' He dropped the gun, but wasted no time in bending to retrieve it. Jarvis brought the slat down on the guy's head and he immediately hit the ground, sprawled and out for the count. Jarvis picked up the gun and stepped over him to head out of the front door. Libby put my arm round her shoulder as we moved to follow him. Jarvis held out a hand behind him to stop us coming any closer. Libby and I froze. Warily, Jarvis looked up and down the street.

'Quick!' he urged.

Libby and I waddled forward.

'Can't you move any faster?' asked Jarvis impatiently.

'We could if you bothered to help,' said Libby. 'Troy's hurt his ankle. We're going as fast as we can.'

'For heaven's sake.' Jarvis strode back to us, grabbed my free arm and placed it round his shoulder, his hand on my waist.

'Let's go,' he snapped.

'Wait,' I said, pulling away from him. 'We still don't know who you are?'

Jarvis's eyes widened. 'You have got to be kidding me.'

'For all we know, you could be the accomplice of these guys and you've now decided to cut them out and take the ransom money for yourself.'

'We don't have time for this,' Jarvis argued.

I hopped back, removing my arm from around Jarvis's shoulder and ignoring the pain that flared through my lower right leg. Libby moved to stand beside me.

'Troy has a point,' she said. 'Show us some proof that you are who you say you are.'

'Bollocks to this!' said Jarvis, digging through his jacket pockets. 'D'you want to be rescued or d'you want to rot in this dump? Your choice – and the door to option one is rapidly closing.' But, with a huff, he did pull out his phone and start tapping on the screen. Turning it round, he showed a text-message exchange between him and Libby's dad. Libby and I both leaned forward to read it. Then he played the start of a voicemail message left for him by Callie. My sister's voice rang out: '*J, it's Callie.*'

'Happy now or would you like a DNA sample as well?' asked Jarvis.

'There's no need to get snide. We had to check – you could've been anyone,' I replied.

'Troy, I'm working on behalf of your sister. Libby, I'm working with your father to bring you two home safely and, just so you know, I'm not loving the ingratitude. Now, are you two coming or not because I am *this* close to driving off and leaving both of you behind?' Jarvis moved past us and returned to the front door to check if the coast was still clear.

Libby and I hobbled after him, a few steps behind. Jarvis beckoned to us to follow and we spilled out of our prison. The first thing I did was look up at the sky, which I admit I never thought I'd see again. Sombre dusk-blue brushstrokes were darkening it by degrees. Early evening and I'd never seen anything so beautiful. The air was burgers and onions, river smells and petrol fumes – and had never smelled sweeter. From far away came the rumble of traffic, the odd car horn drifting towards us on the wind like a distant song. It started to drizzle, raindrops brushing against my cheeks. It took everything I had not to put out my tongue to catch one of them like a little kid.

'Move now, admire later,' Jarvis ordered. 'Come on! Shift!'

'Troy's ankle hasn't miraculously been fixed in the last minute. D'you wanna help?' Libby frowned.

Jarvis took another quick look around before heading back to us. Ignoring my grimaces, he half carried, half dragged me to his car. I didn't bother to argue that I was going as fast as I could.

When we got to his car – a mid-range transporter with dark, tinted windows – Jarvis held open the back door. Libby tumbled in, reaching out to help me inside. It was too high up to hop so I had to put my right foot down, however momentarily, to hoist myself in. Pain flared like fireworks throughout my entire body.

The moment my legs were clear, Jarvis slammed the door shut behind us before running round the front to sit in the driver's seat. Moments later and we roared off with Libby and I still fastening our seat belts. Only then did I notice the steel-mesh grille on the inside of the back windows. That wasn't all. There was a mesh grille, running floor to ceiling, acting as a bulkhead between the front and back seats.

'There are a couple of bottles of water and some snacks in the lower side pockets of the back doors,' said Jarvis.

He didn't need to point them out. Libby was already glugging down water like her stomach was on fire.

Never mind that. 'Is this your car?' I asked.

'No, I borrowed it,' Jarvis said.

'Where are we going?' asked Libby. 'I want to see my dad.'

'Your dad wants me to take the two of you to my home,' said Jarvis.

Wait. What? 'No. Take us home, *please*.' I needed to see my mum and my sister almost as much as I needed my next breath.

'I can't do that,' Jarvis argued. 'If you both go home, what's to stop your kidnappers from trying again? And we can't get the police involved yet because some of them are on the payroll of the one who ordered the kidnapping. We're not going to do anything that puts you in jeopardy.'

'So when will I see my dad?' asked Libby.

'And when will I see my mum and Callie?' I said.

'Soon, I promise. Once we get to my house, you can both have a shower and freshen up and phone whoever you want. Deal?'

Libby and I exchanged a look. I wasn't feeling this plan – at all.

'Where d'you live?' Libby asked.

'In Norwood, Meadowview. It's not far,' said Jarvis. 'You two must be starved. I can order a takeaway while the two of you clean up if you like?'

'Oh yes, please.' Libby was all relief. Why weren't her insides tumbling like mine? 'Can I have a ham-and-pineapple pizza, please, with a side order of garlic bread and then something like chocolate cake or cheesecake for afters? Can you make that two side orders of garlic bread and both puddings?'

Jarvis laughed. 'You got it. And you, Troy?'

I met Jarvis's eyes in the rear-view mirror. The hairs on the back of my neck were bristling.

'Troy?' Jarvis prompted.

'I'm still thinking. First meal of freedom – important choices.' I hoped my smile made it look like food was all I had on my mind.

Jarvis eyed me without blinking. In the driver's mirror, I couldn't see much more than his eyes, but the expression in them was intense. This guy had just killed two people, but from his demeanour you would never have guessed it. Yes, he was keen for us to leave the scene, but surely he should be more . . . shaken by what he'd just done? Or was shooting people an occupational hazard?

I shook my head. I'd definitely been in the basement too

long. I was being overly suspicious and cynical. Libby and I were on our way home. OK, so we'd have to spend some time at Jarvis's house first, but Callie had made a plan for us. We'd have food, hopefully a bed, and I could phone her and Mum. Mum must be worrying herself sick. She got nervous if I was half an hour late from school without explanation. School. How I longed for my normal, boring life.

'What's today's date?' I asked.

'The thirty-first of October. Halloween,' Jarvis replied. 'Why?'

'It feels like we spent weeks down in that basement,' I said.

'It must've been a terrible ordeal, but you're safe with me,' said Jarvis.

But, if we were so safe now, why was Jarvis driving like the devil himself was behind us? I guess he was afraid the friends of the three men we'd left behind in the kitchen and the hall were following us. The neighbouring houses were a blur as we passed them. Pretending to lean my arm against the window, I felt the steel mesh with my fingers, surreptitiously pulling at it. There was no give to it at all; the edges were sharp, biting into my fingers.

'Troy, are you all right?' asked Jarvis.

'I will be when I talk to my mum,' I said.

'I sense you're not entirely convinced about me. You two can trust me. Look at this face.' Jarvis briefly twisted round to us before turning back to the road. 'These are trustworthy eyebrows.'

Was this man for real? Libby and I exchanged another look.

'Thanks for rescuing us,' I said.

'You're welcome, but don't just thank me – thank your sister and Liberty's dad,' said Jarvis, his eyes still on me in the rear-view mirror. 'They've been moving heaven and earth to bring you home safely.'

Well, that was good to know.

'How long d'you reckon we'll have to stay at your house?' asked Libby.

'Not long,' Jarvis replied. 'A few hours, a day at most. This time tomorrow you'll be back in your own beds.'

I sat back, holding on to that hope with everything I had. Without warning, a well-known song from a couple of years ago sounded on the car radio. Jarvis turned up the volume, but then came a sound that had me sitting forward, alarmed – an ominous clunk as he locked the car doors.

'Childproof locks. Just a precaution. I wouldn't want either of you to fall out of the car,' Jarvis said, chuckling. 'Tobey and Callie would kill me!'

'How old d'you think we are?' asked Libby with disdain.

Even though he'd engaged the childproof lock, I pulled at the door handle anyway. Nothing. Is that what turning up the radio had been about? To mask the sound of the locks being engaged?

'Troy, are your ears ornamental?' Jarvis asked me, not missing what I'd done. 'Sit back and relax. Like I said, I'm taking you where you'll be safe.'

An alarm bell inside my head began to jingle softly. Something was definitely up with this guy and this situation.

Libby leaned towards me, her lips almost against my ear, her breath warm. 'Troy, what's wrong?'

I shook my head, finding it hard to put my concerns into words.

'Don't you believe him?' asked Libby.

'Not sure,' I replied softly. 'Something about this whole thing is . . . off.'

'He seems OK,' Libby said. 'Maybe we were in the cellar too long. We can't treat everyone like the enemy.'

Which was the same thing I'd just told myself and yet . . . 'That's not why I'm not buying his story,' I replied.

'Then why?'

But that was the trouble: I didn't know why. Jarvis was chatty, smiley and very friendly. Yet he struck me as trying too hard to be all those things.

'What do we do?' whispered Libby.

'There's nothing we can do but watch and wait,' I said quietly. 'When he stops the car, if you see or hear anything at all that rings warning bells, run. Run and don't look back.'

Libby frantically shook her head. 'We should stay together.'

'My ankle is trashed – remember? If you need to scarper, I'll distract him, hold on to him or something, and I want you to leg it. Run and don't look back. Promise?'

Reluctantly, Libby nodded. I stared at the back of Jarvis Burton's head. Even if he was who he said he was, this man was hiding something. For now, Libby and I had no choice but to wait. I turned to look out of the window, trying to figure out where we were and where we were going. A glance at Libby showed that she was doing the same. I was sick and tired of being treated like a lowly pawn on a chessboard. If Jarvis wasn't who he said he was, he was going to regret not taking us to the police or to my sister.

forty-eight. Tobey

Ditching my protection officers had been the easy part. Getting Callie to sit this one out? Not so much. As I drove, a huge part of me wished I'd been more insistent about her staying in my apartment until all this was over. Rain pattered and splattered on the car roof, its arrhythmic pulse strangely soothing. What had started a while ago as drizzle was now a downpour. Rain usually calmed me, but not today.

'Tell me about Jarvis,' said Callie unexpectedly.

I glanced at her. She was watching me, her expression set.

'Jarvis is part fixer, part enforcer and all barracuda. When Dan was giving the orders, Jarvis was the second in command who made sure those orders were carried out. His real value is in what he knows. Nothing happens in the capital or any major city in this country without his knowledge, and what he doesn't know he makes it his business to find out.'

'Why didn't he step up to fill Dan's shoes then? Why take orders from Eva instead?'

'Jarvis maintains that he is strictly lieutenant, not captain, material. He had no interest in taking over from Dan and that's why Dan trusted him. He knew Jarvis wasn't going to . . . stab him in the back to get to the top. Besides, uneasy lies the head that wears the crown. But, like I said, I could be wrong. Dan was my friend. Jarvis isn't.'

Callie looked at me curiously. 'You're not a Jarvis fan then?'

'It's mutual. He's not exactly my number-one admirer either,' I said with a wry smile, adding, 'probably due to the fact that I once threatened to put him in the ground.'

'When?'

'Years ago.'

'Why?'

'Business.' I shrugged. No way was I going to expand on the reasons.

'Did you mean it when you said it?' asked Callie.

'I did.'

'Did Jarvis believe you meant it?'

'Oh, he knew I did. I don't make idle threats, Callie, or false promises.'

Silence.

'When you're around him, d'you need to watch your back?' Callie said seriously.

'I watch my back around most people,' I told her.

'Including me?'

I shook my head, my eyes back on the road. 'No. You're one of a handful of people in this world that I trust.'

Which was the truth. I glanced over to see she was still watching me, concern clouding her eyes.

'Tobey, do you have lots of friends?'

I smiled. God, she was so innocent. What a question. 'Callie, I have lots of colleagues, acquaintances and sycophants. *Friends*, on the other hand, are few and far between.'

'Sounds lonely.'

I shrugged. 'My life is what I made it.'

'So you're happy?'

'Happy?' I rolled the word round my mouth, trying it out for size. It was a bad fit. 'That's not a requirement for my job.'

'What's the point of it then, if it's not making you happy?'

'It's that simple, is it?'

'I love being a barrister. I can't imagine doing anything else,' said Callie. 'If being an MP makes you miserable—'

'Callie, don't put words in my mouth. I never said I was miserable. I am where I've worked hard to be. I wouldn't want to do or be anywhere else . . . minus the forthcoming court case of course.'

Callie raised a placating hand. 'Sorry. My mistake. Tell me about Eva Foxton.'

Another quick glance from me before returning my attention to the road. Where was she going with this?

'Eva is a woman in her late fifties, I guess. She's been a background figure in Dan's life for quite a while, but I only met her for the first time at Dan's dinner party. I think she was his mentor, advisor and surrogate mother. She was one of the few people Dan spoke about without scorn, but he kept her very private.'

'And now she's taken over from him?'

'It would appear so. She used to run certain parts of Dan's empire before he died, so maybe she thought it only right that she take over the lot,' I said.

'What parts?'

'The parts I made it my business never to ask or know about,' I replied.

'And burying your head like an ostrich worked for you?' asked Callie, judgement rippling through her tone.

'And all your lawyer friends are pristine, are they? You and they never put a foot wrong?' I said pointedly. 'And every person you've defended in your career has been truly innocent? Tell you what: bottle your perfect life with your perfect decision making and your perfect morals and sell it online. See how you do.'

Silence.

Hellsake! That had been laced with more hostility than I'd intended.

'Tobey, you said you wanted to marry me. I have no idea why when you obviously don't like me very much,' said Callie at last.

I glanced at her, but she was now looking out of the car window. I sighed. 'I'm sorry. That was uncalled for.'

'But honest,' said Callie.

The truth but not the whole truth. If only she knew—

forty-nine. Sephy

The moment I stepped through the front door, Sonny had me in a bear hug, making me squeal with alarm then delight. We'd exchanged spare front-door keys a while ago for convenience, but I didn't expect him to be waiting in my hall.

'What the hell, Sephy?' he said after a kiss. 'You said lunchtime.'

'I know. I'm sorry. The stuff I had to do took longer than I thought.'

'I've been worried.'

I placed one hand against his cheek, stroking it gently. I needed to stop treating Sonny as if he were a commodity in my life that I could take or leave as required. 'I'm sorry, Sonny. I missed you.'

'Missed you too,' Sonny replied, only slightly mollified. 'I'll make you a sandwich and a cup of coffee. You eat, then tell me just what's been going on.'

I quirked an eyebrow at his imperious tone. But Sonny's lips tightened. He wasn't going to apologize for going complete caveman on me.

'Sephy, I've been worried sick and thinking all sorts. You've got to put me out of my misery.'

'I was going to. I've been racing around since I got up and

I'm shattered,' I admitted. 'No doubt I look every minute of my age.'

Sonny gently took my chin in his hand and looked into my eyes. 'Behave yourself. You still look exactly the same as when I first saw you,' he said, before giving me a short, gentle kiss. We exchanged a smile.

'You're such a liar, but I love you for it,' I teased. The words rolled out before I could stop them.

'Do you, Sephy? Do you love me . . . for it?'

My heart began to bump inside me. I placed a hand on Sonny's face, caressing his cheek. 'I'm marrying you, aren't I?'

A grin split Sonny's face, the light in his eyes blinding. 'Yes, you are.'

This man had placed his entire happiness in my hands and it was heavy and hot, and it was a struggle not to turn my palms and drop it. Sonny loved me. He deserved nothing less in return. And I would do my best, but would it be enough? If I even had to ask—

Sephy, you're not being fair to him—

I quelled the whispering voice in my head and followed him into the kitchen. We had a lot to discuss.

'While you're making the coffee, I need to check something on the General Records Office website.'

'Check what?'

'I'll tell you if it pans out, otherwise it's not worth wasting your time.'

'How d'you want your coffee – black or latte?'

'Black with a lemon slice, please.'

I flipped open my laptop and got to work at the kitchen table as Sonny busied himself fiddle-faddling with the new coffee machine he'd bought me. The General Records Office held the details of every birth, marriage and death in Albion, available online for a 'reasonable' fee. By the time Sonny figured it out and had made my coffee, I'd submitted my credit-card details and received the information I was searching for. Now I had to decide what to do with it. Sonny plonked a cheese and sun-dried tomato sandwich and a steaming mug of coffee in front of me.

'OK, let me have it,' he said, pulling up a chair.

I took a deep breath and did exactly that – both barrels. As I spoke, his eyes grew wider and his expression stormier. Each time he tried to interrupt me, I raised a hand to ward him off and continued. I had to get everything out at once or it wouldn't come out at all. The only thing I kept from him was the info I'd just retrieved from the General Records Office because I still wasn't sure if the information was something or nothing. When I finished speaking, there was a stunned silence. I knew it wouldn't last.

'No! No! NO!' Sonny exploded. 'Sephy, have you lost your entire mind? We have to phone the police.'

'No. We were given explicit instructions not to. Troy has been kidnapped and I know exactly how he's feeling – terrified and helpless. I wouldn't wish what he's going through on my worst enemy. Plus I'm front and centre for Dan's murder. Involving the police is out of the question – at least for now.'

Sonny began to pace up and down. 'What you're doing is a really bad idea. The police—'

'Sonny, didn't you hear what I just said?' I sighed. 'The moment Troy and Libby are home safe and sound, then I'll be giving the police the full story with footnotes and an index, but not until then. Don't make me regret telling you.'

Sonny stopped pacing to glare at me. 'That's not fair, Sephy. The police have the resources to handle this situation, you don't.'

'But Tobey, Callie and Jon working together do,' I pointed out. 'If it was anyone else but Tobey's daughter with Troy, I probably would've gone to the police by now, but Callie pleaded with me to give Tobey twenty-four hours and that's what I'm doing.'

Even though it was killing me.

'If anything happens to Troy . . . well, it doesn't bear thinking about.' Sonny shook his head. 'I know your son doesn't like me much, but I care about him. I don't want anything bad to happen to him.'

'I know – and I'm grateful.' I wrapped my arms round him. 'So will you come with me to talk to Eva Foxton?'

Sonny drew back, his expression resolute. 'Sephy, you are not going anywhere or doing anything for the rest of the night without me by your side. That's a promise.'

I raised an eyebrow, but he wasn't going to back down. He wasn't happy about what I was doing. I knew he wouldn't be, which was why I'd tried to do as much as possible without him knowing, but if I was going to go and see Eva then I'd rather not do that on my own. Eva Foxton's reputation cut a lethal swathe as it preceded her.

'So you've made a suspects list?'

'Yep, and I've been updating it all morning, based on previous conversations with the suspects and some more research.'

'Let's have a look,' said Sonny.

'Well, it's not much of a list – just the people present at Dan's dinner party and my impressions of the ones I've spoken to today or on the night Dan died.'

Sonny beckoned for me to hand over my tablet, which I did reluctantly. I really didn't need him disparaging my efforts.

Dan Jeavons – dead piece of shit, roasting in hell.

Kellan Bruemann – ex-CEO of Bruemann Construction, eternal victim by all accounts.

Bella Monroe – Tobey's ex. Scorned and bitter, unappreciative of her lucky escape.

Tom Jeavons – Dan's brother. As naïve and as clueless as he appears?

Patrix Ellerman – scumbag elitist. Bad gambler. Would sell his granny for a slice of cheesecake.

Eva Foxton – mother figure to Dan. Reputation for being ruthless. Dangerous.

Owen Dowd – living piece of shit. Special circle of hell being constructed just for him. Enough said.

Jarvis – Dan's ex-second in command, apparently recently demoted. Vicious bastard. Watch your back.

Tobias Durbridge – biggest piece of shit on the planet.

George – Dan's butler, sweeping up shit.

Me – up to my neck in shit.

Sonny raised his eyebrows as he read. 'That's a lot of excrement flying about.'

'As long as none of it lands on Troy. That's all I care about.'

'Well then,' said Sonny, 'let's go see Eva Foxton.'

Daily Shouter Online

Home. News. Politics. Celebs. Entertainment. Sport. Tech. Health. Science. Money. More.

BREAKING NEWS. Two bodies found in abandoned house near East Gurendah Harbour

The bodies of two Nought men were found earlier today in a terraced house near East Gurendah Harbour, each man shot dead by an unknown assailant(s). A police spokesperson told the *Daily Shouter* that both were notorious underworld figures who were known to work for Dan Jeavons, also recently deceased. Their identities have yet to be formally released.

One source close to Dan Jeavons' organization told us: 'We're all just hoping this isn't the start of a turf war because, if it is, then this country is about to erupt in a way no one has ever seen before.' When pressed, the source could not or would not name Dan Jeavons' successor.

fifty. Libby

The landscape of yellow street lights and modern office buildings shrouded in the late October evening had given way to stretches of dark fields to our left and tall hedges to our right on the narrow, unlit road we drove along. I looked around, but had no clue where we were nor where we'd been. I didn't recognize the area at all and, judging by the look on his face, Troy was just as clueless. Neither of us could see further than the illumination provided by the car's high-beam headlights.

'Where are you taking us, because this sure as hell isn't Norwood, Meadowview?' Troy said, breaking the silence in the car.

I looked from Troy to Jarvis and back again. What was going on?

'Of course it's Meadowview,' Jarvis argued.

'My nan was born in Meadowview and I still have relatives who live in Norwood. Nana Meggie used to take me to see them during the holidays when I was younger. I spent a number of years being dragged all around by my cousins.' Troy pointed out of the window. 'And this isn't it.'

'You think you know every street?' said Jarvis, eyeing us in the driver's mirror.

'Not every street, but every other one. You're not working for Libby's dad and my sister, are you?' said Troy.

His words made me start. Jarvis didn't even turn round to look at us.

'I'm taking you somewhere safe,' he said. 'Then you can borrow my phone to—'

'Stop lying,' Troy demanded.

Jarvis didn't bother to answer. My heart, like my hopes, began to slowly sink.

'Are you gonna kill us or are you doing this for money?' Troy asked.

'If I was going to kill you, I could've done it back at the house by the harbour,' said Jarvis.

'Not if you have to prove we're still alive to get any money,' said Troy.

'But, Troy, he showed us a text from my dad,' I whispered. 'And played a message from your sister.'

'Which would be easy to fake. And, even if they are real, that doesn't mean he's not out for himself.' Troy turned back to Jarvis. 'Am I right? Is that what this is about – money?'

Jarvis didn't answer. I met cold green eyes in the driver's mirror. I didn't need lessons in telepathy to know what Troy was thinking because it had to be the same as me. Had we escaped from the frying pan only to land with a thud in the middle of the fire?

After driving for the best part of an hour, Jarvis turned into the driveway of a private detached house surrounded by fields on one side and woods on the other. I peered around as much as I could, but there were no other houses nearby.

Jarvis pressed some kind of small device in his hand and the up-and-over garage door began to open. Moments later, he reversed into the garage and the door shut behind us. So much for legging it at the first sign of trouble. The garage light was on, activated by the door opening I guessed.

Jarvis switched off the engine and opened his door. I tried mine. Still locked. Jarvis moved to Troy's side of the car. To my surprise, he opened the back door. Ohmigod! We'd been wrong about this guy. He was on our side. Jarvis beckoned for Troy to get out.

'You're letting us go?' Troy asked, stunned.

'Just you,' said Jarvis.

Those two words put saliva in my mouth and sent an arctic chill down my spine.

'Hang on.' Troy frowned. He stayed seated next to me. 'What about Libby?'

'Liberty has to stay. You can go.'

'T-Troy—?' Was that really my voice, so shaky and filled with dread? Troy and I had made a pact that if just one of us had the opportunity to get away, then we would take it. Here was Troy's chance. But why would Jarvis keep me but allow Troy to leave? All kinds of scenarios ran through my mind, every one of them petrifying.

'Don't worry, this is part of the plan,' said Jarvis, turning his attention to me. 'The kidnappers were after you, Libby. Not just your mum and her lover and his brother, but the ones who took over from them.' Jarvis answered the question in my mind. 'So, until the actual person who ordered the kidnappers to kill your mum and her accomplices is uncovered, you're not safe. I'm just following your dad's orders. Troy, you need to leave.'

I was really confused now.

Slowly Troy shook his head. 'Libby and I leave together or we stay here together until my sister and Libby's dad come for us.'

Troy wanted to stay with me? After everything he had said about when one of us got the chance we should grab it with both hands and run with it? Literally.

'Troy, go. This is your chance to get away,' I told him.

'I'm not leaving without you,' Troy said firmly.

'Don't be ridiculous. Look, I haven't got time for this.' Jarvis was getting more aggravated by the second. 'You need to go. Now.'

'No. I don't think so.'

'You fool! I'm doing you a favour here.' Jarvis's face was beginning to turn not just red but puce.

'You've brought us to the middle of nowhere and I'm supposed to walk home from here? I don't know where we are and I've wrecked my ankle. How far d'you reckon I'll get? Or would you put a bullet in my back before I'd even gone one hundred metres?'

Jarvis glared at Troy who returned the hard stare.

'Jarvis, are you one of the kidnappers?' Troy surprised me by saying.

'What? What the hell—?'

'Are you?' Troy persisted.

'Of course not,' Jarvis denied.

'If you're not one of the kidnappers, how did you know one of the people who originally abducted us was Libby's mum? And how did you know the other two were Libby's mum's boyfriend and his brother?' said Troy.

Shock held me rigid. Troy was right. They might've known the woman who was shot was my mum, but neither of us had mentioned anything about Mum's boyfriend, Pete. Or that it was them, in masks, who'd grabbed us outside school.

Silence.

Without warning, Jarvis slammed the car door shut, activating the remote in his hand to lock the doors again. Troy immediately pulled at the door handle, but it was futile.

'Childproof locks,' Jarvis said. 'Troy, you should've headed home when you had the chance.'

He took out his phone and aimed it at us, pressing it right up against the tinted windows. It took me a couple of seconds to realize what he was doing – filming us. That meant only one thing.

I shouted, 'What're you gonna do with us?!'

It was now crystal clear that this man was after a payout, not our liberation. Troy scratched his ear while he stared at Jarvis. Then his hands started fluttering like birds. When I realized what he was doing, I flung myself at the grille and started pounding on it, careful not to obscure Troy's hand gestures, but to distract our kidnapper.

'Let us out of here right now!' I yelled. 'When my dad gets hold of you, he's gonna rip you apart! You let us out of here this minute! I need to go to the loo! Let us out!'

The grille was scraping against my hands as I pounded, but I didn't care. I wasn't sure what Troy was up to, but if he had a plan I was all in. Though taken aback, Jarvis still carried on filming, raising his hand slightly. A quick sideways glance revealed that Troy was still signing, though he did his best to make his hands appear as if they were just making random, desperate movements rather than sending a message. He'd told me about his ability to do sign language after the first time we'd been filmed, an ability that had helped keep the small flame of hope alive within me. All I could do now was pray that his sister would somehow get to see Jarvis's recording. I carried on banging on the grille and shouting. Jarvis walked round the front of the car, filming us and the garage. I didn't take my eyes off him. He finally nodded, satisfied, and put his phone away.

'Nice try, Troy, but I know all about you and your sign language,' said Jarvis. 'I'll make sure your twitchy fingers are cut out of any recording I send to your sister and Tobey Durbridge. Now you two won't mind staying put while I run a couple of errands, OK?'

Troy gave him the finger, no decoding required. Eyebrows raised and a smile on his lips, Jarvis removed what looked like a green jerrycan from one of the metal shelves by the garage door. Taking off the cap, he started splashing its contents all over the car – front, back, sides and roof. The smell hit me after a few seconds, but I knew what it was before that. Petrol. We were being doused with petrol.

'NO! Don't do this. Please!' I screamed. 'We've never done anything to you—'

'We've seen his face and can identify him.' Troy's voice was quiet as we watched the clear liquid running down the car windows like deadly rain.

'Jarvis, please don't do this,' I pleaded. 'Troy, do something—'

'Don't beg, Libby. Don't give him the satisfaction,' said Troy, his gaze never once moving from Jarvis and what he was doing.

When he had finished, Jarvis carelessly threw down the can. We watched in silence as he moved to the up-and-over garage door and started connecting up something, though I couldn't see what it was as his back was to us. After about a minute, he dug in his pocket and retrieved a key. Flicking a switch on the wall, he unlocked the internal garage door and entered the house.

'Well, at least he left the light on.'

'What?'

'The light switch by the door.' Troy pointed. 'He could've just left us to stew in the dark.'

'In case you hadn't noticed, we're stuck in a locked car covered in petrol, in a garage, in the middle of nowhere with no means of escape,' I pointed out.

'Believe me, I'd noticed,' said Troy quietly. 'But we're still standing – and that counts for a lot. And, if he is gonna use that recording he just made to squeeze money out of my sister or your dad, then hopefully Callie will be able to see what I signed.'

'Jarvis said he was going to cut out your fingers,' I reminded him.

'He may delete some of my message, but he can't delete the whole thing, not without cutting our faces out of the recording as well,' said Troy. 'I made sure of it.'

'In a half-full mood, I see.'

'A half-full mood means you live life with hope rather than just endure it with an empty heart,' said Troy.

Yeah, but for how long? I pulled at the car door again. It didn't budge. We were going nowhere. Flinging myself back in my seat, I took a proper look round the garage. It was lined with shelves on which sat cans of paint and old bits of junk like discarded toasters and hairdryers, a fan heater on its side, a number of boxes of assorted sizes, bits of metal and wire and . . . oh my God! Only then did I see it. What the hell?

'Troy, is that what I think it is?'

He turned to see what I was pointing at. 'What is it?' he frowned.

I contorted my body to get a proper look. On a shelf just behind us and to my right sat an orange-coloured block about the size of a box of fifty Crossmas cards. Next to it was a phone with a lead coming out of it and into a small black container that had been pushed into the orange-coloured block. Mum's boyfriend before Pete, a lowlife who liked to call himself Wolf, had been a tanks, guns and weapons nut. He'd also been into explosives. He was always reading about them, talking about them, spouting on about how explosives and conflict were the only ways for Noughts to win against the Crosses. Wolf and Mum only split up because he was caught by the police trying to blow up some government building or other and imprisoned for life. But, while he and Mum were together, he'd tried to bond with me by explaining how to make and use explosives. Some of her boyfriends were weird, some were nasty, all were lowlifes. But Wolf? He was in a class down there with Pete. He was a fanatic – and deadly dangerous. Wolf gave off mad, bad and dangerous vibes like a stinky cheese gives off fumes. It was one of the happiest days of my life when he was put away.

My happiness was short-lived because, within a few months, Mum took up with Pete. But at least Wolf was gone. But that's why I recognized the radio-controlled IED when I saw it. And, if I was right, as soon as the phone next to the plastic explosive was called, it would initiate the firing circuit of the IED. With that and the petrol Jarvis had thrown over the car, it was guaranteed that this garage and everything in it would be blown to smithereens in a fireball that would be visible from the moon.

I twisted to look up at the garage ceiling through the side window. Lurching forward, I strained to make out the ceiling rigging and the garage door through the front windscreen.

'Oh God! I'm right.' What little hope I had left inside fluttered, flickered and all but died.

'What? What is it?' Troy moved beside me.

'Jarvis has set up an IED with a mobile-phone trigger and he's also rigged it to the garage door,' I said. 'See! Those two wires on the door are linked to the device at the back of the garage. If anyone opens the garage door, this place will go up like a rocket.'

'So if anyone tries to rescue us . . . ?' Troy left the rest unsaid. 'If your dad and Callie come to rescue us . . . ?'

I stared at him. I hadn't even thought of that.

'God, we can't catch a break,' said Troy.

'Why didn't he just put a bullet in our heads and have done with it?' I said with disgust.

'Because he needs us alive until he gets whatever ransom money he's demanded. After that, we're history,' said Troy. 'I think . . . I think this is it.'

It wasn't just what he said, but the way he said it. The

half-full mood had dissipated. Did Troy really believe that it was over, that there was nothing we could do but wait for death to escort us out of the garage? I'd thought I had no hope left, but Troy's words had a strange effect. They fanned the tiny, dying spark that remained within me back to life. Troy had spent our time together shoring up what little hope I had inside me. Now it was my turn.

'Troy, we're still alive now, and you know what they say about where there's life, there's cake. So I'm going to need you to get it together, pull your head out your arse and help me find a way to get us out of here in one piece. If we can get out of the car, we can go through the internal door into the house and escape that way, so all we have to do is work out how to escape this car.'

Troy glared at me.

'Please don't fade on me now, Troy Ealing,' I pleaded. 'You're the one who said that while we're still standing we're still in the game. Did you lie?'

Slowly but surely, Troy's glower morphed into a slight smile. 'No, I didn't lie – and you are rude.'

'But right!'

Troy nodded. 'But rude.' He took another look around the car. 'Maybe if we worked together and timed our movements we could kick out the back window, grille and all.'

I smiled. 'I know we can. Let's do it.'

Daily Shouter Online

Home. News. Politics. Celebs. Entertainment. Sport. Tech. Health. Science. Money. More.

Synthetic Prop is responsible for a 62 per cent rise in all crimes committed in Albion

The National Public Health Authority (NPHA) stated that synthetic Prop use has resulted in a 62 per cent escalation in crime over the last nine months.

An NPHA spokeswoman noted that, 'Accelerating Prop use has resulted in a rise in drug trafficking, county lines, "cuckooing", robbery, domestic violence, assaults, abuse and murder. Over the last ten years, governments of all stripes have ignored calls to get a grip on the drug problem in Albion. They have stuck their fingers in their ears and sung *la-la-la* while various rehab and anti-drug agencies have tried to warn them of the looming crisis. The last government even cut funding to state-run rehab and anti-drug agencies, stating that they were not "cost-effective".

'I know of one elderly tenant living alone who has been subject to "cuckooing", where a group of drug traffickers took over his flat and ran part of their drugs operation from his home for over two years. He was threatened with knives and other violence should he go to the police or alert any housing officials to his plight.

'I know of children as young as nine and ten who are being used to ferry drugs around the country as they're much less likely to be stopped and searched by the police. Lives across all strata of society are being ruined. I hope the new government gets a grip and quick or we'll be back here next year, and the year after that, discussing the breakdown in societal cohesion as a result of drugs and drug trafficking.'

According to a government spokesman, 'The Prime Minister has made it his personal mission to bring those who seek to profit from Prop production, distribution and use to justice. Their days are numbered.'

fifty-one. Sephy

There it was – the infamous Ava's. Prickles of alarm were already scratching at my skin. Leaded stained-glass windows adorned either side of black, solid, wooden double doors clearly visible behind the steel security roller shutters. A very clever way to preserve the privacy of those inside while still looking upmarket. The entire facade managed to sing out while standing back. Very clever indeed. Ava's had been the haunt of on-the-way-up actors and on-the-way-down models a few years ago. A couple of raids too many had put an end to most of its true celebrity clientele. Now it served mid-listers and wannabes. Those who were desperate to be seen by those desperate to report and photograph anyone in the public eye.

Dan Jeavons had been so proud of this place. He'd been wanting to expand, his eyes looking in the direction of Specimens, my restaurant. He wanted to 'buy' it from Nathan and me and rename it Ava's – Part Deux. The two establishments were close enough to each other to be a set, far enough apart so that his proposed new restaurant couldn't be tainted by his club's more notorious reputation. Nathan's one-word answer to Dan's proposal was swift – and he had spoken for both of us. The only trouble was Dan was allergic to no. Nathan and I had learned that to our cost. That *no* had started all this.

Only a couple of weeks after we'd unequivocally turned down Dan's proposal for the umpteenth time, my husband was knocked over and killed by a hit-and-run driver. I didn't need to be Benjamin Banneker to figure out who was responsible. That's why I couldn't understand it when Troy got the ridiculous notion into his head that Sonny was responsible for Nathan's death. As if. No, I had Dan Jeavons to thank for that. He might not have done the dirty work himself – that was more likely to have been Jarvis or another of his brain-dead minions – but there was no doubt in my mind that Dan had ordered it. And, after Nathan's death, Dan carried on seeking to blackmail my restaurant out from under me.

Now he was dead.

And I still wasn't free of him.

'Sephy, are you OK?' asked Sonny from beside me.

I gave a fleeting smile in answer to his question. 'Sonny, could you give me a minute?' I took out my mobile and hit the icon to phone my daughter. It went straight through to her voicemail inbox. Disconnecting the call, I decided to record a voice memo and send that to Callie instead.

Sonny frowned at me. 'What're you doing?'

I raised a hand to stop his questions, concentrating on what I was going to say. 'I'm leaving Callie a message.'

'About what?'

'The truth.'

'I don't understand.'

'Sonny, just a sec – OK? I've got some private things to tell Callie. Would you mind waiting for me outside the car?'

Sonny turned to stare out of the windscreen, his expression stony. I placed a placating hand on his thigh, dismissing the tiny voice inside me asking me why I was doing so. There were places and spaces within my life that were mine and mine alone or reserved for my children. I didn't need him to fill every part of my existence. I didn't want to completely disappear into Sonny's life any more than I wanted him to try and disappear into mine. Sharing a life wasn't about subsuming myself to him. Did he understand that? If not, then we didn't stand a chance. When I had Troy home safe and sound, Sonny and I would need to sit down and talk, really talk, about our expectations of each other.

Giving me a tight smile, Sonny did as I asked and left the car, slamming the door behind him.

With a sigh, I activated the messaging app and recorded what I needed to say to Callie, setting out facts and giving her strict instructions. My voice memo was last-minute insurance and I needed to make sure that Callie knew that. The message sent, I stepped out of the car.

'Ready?' I asked Sonny.

He nodded.

'Then let's do this.'

We walked up to the unassuming side door next to Ava's, and Sonny pressed the buzzer. This was the discreet entrance that led directly to the club's offices on the first and second floors.

'Yes? Can I help you?' came a woman's impatient voice through the intercom.

'My name is Persephone Ealing. I'm here with Sonny

Devlin. We'd like to see Eva Foxton.' I bit back the 'please' at the end of my sentence.

'Just a moment.'

A moment turned into a minute. Exchanging a look with Sonny, I raised my finger to press the buzzer again when the intercom crackled back to life.

'Come up.'

A click as the door was unlocked. Sonny pushed it open immediately. Before us was a staircase covered in a well-worn indigo-blue carpet, a white wall to one side of it and a set of barred, windowless, steel double doors that led directly into the club on the other side. One steadying deep breath later, I started up the stairs, Sonny close behind me. We were well and truly putting our heads in the lion's mouth, and all I could do was pray it wouldn't bite.

The door at the top of the stairs contained a small frosted-glass panel at head height and no handle. It swung open easily when I pushed it, revealing a plush, deep-blue-carpeted reception area. A swift look around revealed two solid, wood-panelled doors, one behind the receptionist, the other to her left. The panelling was only on the surface, masking but not hiding each steel door beneath.

The receptionist, a Nought woman with short blonde hair coloured pink at the front, looked me up and down, not a trace of a smile on her face. 'Take a seat, please.' She indicated the charcoal-grey leather sofa to her right. The moment we sat down, so did she. She picked up a tablet from her desk that immediately had her full attention.

We sat and waited in silence. No phones ringing. No fingers tapping on a computer keyboard. No voices, no outside street noises. The room was soundproofed, which made sense given that we were sitting on top of a nightclub. I glanced at Sonny. He nodded at me questioningly. I smiled. Yes, I was fine and, to be honest, extremely grateful that Sonny was with me.

So we waited.

And we waited.

Just as I was on the verge of getting vexed, the phone on the receptionist's desk rang, making us all jump. She answered it on the second ring. 'You may go in,' she said, indicating the door to her left.

Sonny and I got to our feet just as a click came from the door. Moments later, we found ourselves in an unexpectedly spacious room with oak floors, a huge dark wood desk and at least three couches dotted around the place as well as a few upright chairs. Bookcases lined the wall behind the desk, but I couldn't see a single book. Instead, the shelves contained all kinds of ornaments, sculptures and framed photos. To the right were two leaded-glass windows, at least three metres between them.

My attention was drawn to Eva Foxton who sat behind her desk flanked by two Nought bodyguards, a sandy-haired man and a taller woman with auburn hair tied back in a ponytail and steel-grey eyes. Both bodyguards wore jackets to try and hide the fact that they were armed. And, as for Eva, she wasn't what I'd been expecting at all. Her silver-grey hair had been cut short at the sides and left longer on the top to form a fringe that was partly swept back from her forehead. Her face was devoid of make-up apart from the grape-purple lipstick that carefully defined her mouth, especially the Cupid's bow of her top lip. I wasn't quite sure what look she was going for. Fierce? Cyanotic? Eccentric? Whatever. I wasn't here to dwell on her lipstick colour choices. If this woman knew my son's whereabouts, then I wasn't going to leave until I knew as much as she did.

'Mrs Foxton, we came to see you because—'

'Call me Eva, and I know why you're here,' she said. 'You think I know where your son Troy is.'

I eyed her keenly. 'And do you?'

'Not any more.' Eva shrugged.

I frowned. 'What does that mean?'

'It means I knew where he was a few hours ago. Now I don't.'

My eyes narrowed. If this woman was playing games with me, she'd quickly learn that I wasn't in the mood. I was just about to open my mouth to tell her so when she got in first.

'Sephy, if I may call you that, let's put all our cards on the table, shall we?' Eva began. 'Liberty's mother, Misty, and a couple of her moron friends kidnapped Libby in the first place. Troy just got swept along for the ride. I found out about the original unambitious plan and took over, but I was double-crossed and now I have no clue where Troy and Libby are.'

By the time she'd finished, the tramlines between my eyebrows were fathoms deep. 'Let me get this straight – you were planning to take over and hold my son and Tobey's daughter for ransom to get what you wanted, only someone else beat you to it?'

'That's about the size of it.'

'How dare you? What gives you the right to play with

people's lives like that?' I said furiously. 'My son, Troy, is a human being, not a carved wooden figurine on a chessboard.'

She shrugged. 'Sephy, it wasn't personal. Just business. Troy and Libby were a means to an end, that's all.'

'What end?' asked Sonny, just as angry as I was.

'I wanted something from Tobey Durbridge and this seemed like a guaranteed way to get it,' said Eva.

'You're the one who wanted him to plead guilty to Dan's murder,' I realized. 'Why are you so keen to pin the blame on him?'

'I'm not pinning any blame where it doesn't already belong,' Eva snapped, her amiable mask finally beginning to slip. 'Tobey did kill Dan so it's only right that he should pay for it. And, if his incarceration also works to my advantage, then it's all good.' Eva ended her argument with a silky-smooth smile.

This woman was too basic. My previous assessment of her had been spot on. She was a shark, salivating at the first hint of blood in the water.

'D'you know who took Troy and Libby?' I asked. 'Tell me you know that much at least.'

'I have a pretty good idea actually,' said Eva. 'In fact, he's on his way here now.'

Only a few words, but they stopped me cold.

'Pardon?'

'I'm expecting more company within the next ten minutes or so, and one of them knows exactly where Troy and Libby are at this precise moment.'

'Who's coming?' My voice was as sharp as pins, only to be countered by another of Eva's oily, ominous smiles.

'Patience, Sephy. Everything comes to those who have patience.'

'Don't try me, Eva. I am more than ready to kick your arse,' I told her.

'I believe you,' she said with a smile. 'I always could recognize a kindred spirit when I saw one.'

One of her bodyguards stepped forward. If it was meant to be menacing, then it failed. I was too angry to care how many steps forward the woman took. Damn, but Eva was good. What a master manipulator. And she was loving this, making me play her game when my son's freedom and perhaps his very life were at stake.

'Eva, be honest. If Tobey had given you everything you asked for in your ransom demand, would you have let Troy and Libby go?' I asked.

Silence.

Sonny and I exchanged a look. I had my answer. I nodded at Eva, just the once, strangely grateful that she hadn't tried to bullshit me.

Eva nodded back, again just the once. She and I understood each other perfectly.

'However, that's academic now, isn't it?' said Eva smoothly. 'Until the other guests arrive, I suggest we all get comfortable. Would either of you like a cup of tea?'

fifty-two. Callie

Tobey's phone vibrated in his pocket just as he was parking the car. After he applied the brake, he took out his phone and immediately started checking it.

Without looking up, he said, 'Callie, where does Jon live?'

'My Jon?'

Pause.

'Yeah, him.'

I shrugged. 'He has a flat in Zeneca.'

'That's in the city, less than fifteen minutes from your office, isn't it?'

'That's right. Why?'

'He's just left Lusaka Green.' Tobey studied his phone as he spoke.

Lusaka Green was a posh, leafy suburb south-west of the capital. It was at least thirty-five minutes from central London.

'That's where his ex-wife lives. What on earth is he doing there? Is that where you sent him?'

'No. Nowhere near there.'

'How d'you even know where he is?' I asked.

'I gave him a burner phone, but made sure to activate location tracking on it first. I wanted to be able to track his movements twenty-four-seven.'

'Why?'

'So I'd know where to send help if shit hit the fan and he got into trouble. I can't take anyone else's misery on my conscience. It's already overloaded as it is.'

Before I could reply, my phone started to beep too. Taking it out of my pocket, I saw I had a text from Jon. At last! Hopefully he had some good news for us. Maybe that's why he was in Lusaka Green. Assuming he'd sent the text to Tobey and me simultaneously, I opened it and began to read.

> Callie, don't say anything to Durbridge about this text. Don't even let him know we've been in contact. Don't trust him or anything he tells you. He's been lying to you. I'll explain when I see you.

I gasped. I couldn't help it.

'Is something wrong?' asked Tobey.

I shook my head, unable to look at him. Without warning, Tobey snatched the phone out of my hand.

'Hey!' I protested. I tried to grab it back, but he used one arm to ward me off as he read the message. Without a word, he handed the phone back. We glared each other.

'How dare you? That was out of order,' I fumed.

'No more secrets between us, Callie. Not today of all days.'

'Then answer this, Tobey. If something were to happen to Eva, who would take over from her?' I asked, still annoyed.

'Who knows? Jarvis, I suppose, if no one else steps up.

That's if Owen Dowd doesn't try to assume ownership of the whole outfit first.' Tobey's expression, like his tone, was relentlessly neutral.

'And those who used to work for Dan and Eva would go for that? They'd accept Jarvis as their leader?'

'I imagine they're used to constant changes at the top. It's not exactly a role that provides job security,' Tobey quipped.

'You said Jarvis wasn't captain material,' I reminded him.

'Because he doesn't want to lead, not because he can't,' said Tobey. 'Big difference. Jarvis is a known quantity so most of Dan's old crew trust him.'

'Including you?'

Tobey's eyes narrowed. 'Callie, why don't you ask me what you're burning to know?'

Deep breath. 'Tobey, is Jon right about you?'

'I don't know what he was referring to in his text, but I promise that if you ask me a straightforward question you'll get a straightforward answer. I need you to believe that, Callie.'

'Then tell me the truth,' I said. 'Does Jarvis work for you?'

Pause. And then: 'Jarvis has been my eyes and ears within the Outfit for years. Dan was bankrolling my political career. I thought it might be wise to know exactly where the money was coming from, that way I could make it clear to Dan what I would and wouldn't tolerate – like drug and people trafficking.' Tobey had answered more than one of my questions.

'As mayor or as a politician, were you working for Dan? Were you on his payroll?'

'No. I have never worked for or reported back to Dan. That's the truth.' Tobey's gaze didn't fall away from mine, his face didn't go red, his breathing rate didn't increase – none of the usual indicators of someone telling lies were present. The truth or just masterful manipulation? I got out of the car. Tobey did the same.

'Callie, do you believe me?' he said.

'I want to, Tobey,' I replied. 'I really do. Do you know who's trying to get rid of you?'

'I suspect Eva, but I don't know for sure,' said Tobey.

'If you believe that Eva's behind all this, why are we going into Ava's to see her? Isn't that reckless, to say the least?'

'I want my daughter returned home safe and sound, and Eva needs to know I'll do whatever it takes to get Libby back. If Eva is responsible for all this, she needs to understand that she's messed with the wrong man. So when we get in there, whatever happens, follow my lead and trust me – OK?'

I reluctantly nodded. In spite of our chequered history and our sketchy present, I still considered Tobey my oldest friend and, as such, I owed him the benefit of the doubt, at the very least. Or was this just my way of trying to prove to both of us – but mostly myself – that I wasn't the judgemental, unforgiving excuse for a woman he thought I was? After slamming the door shut, I looked up to see Tobey watching me.

'Ready? Let's go,' he said.

As we walked towards the nightclub, my heart was in my mouth. This was such a bad idea, but what choice did we have? I told myself that each step brought me closer to finding Troy and bringing him home. So why did it feel like I was stepping into the path of an oncoming express train?

fifty-three. Tobey

Another beep sounded on my phone as we walked towards Ava's. Now what? It was a text message with a video recording attached from a mobile number I didn't recognize. How had the sender got my phone number? Opening the message, my eyes widened as I watched.

'Is that news about Troy and Libby?' Callie asked from beside me. 'May I see?'

I beckoned her closer. Standing next to me, she watched the recording, her mouth falling open only to snap shut. The clip only lasted about five seconds, but that was long enough. Libby and Troy were in the back of some kind of vehicle with wire mesh over the windows. Troy was scratching his ear, but then the recording zoomed in on his face, followed by my daughter's.

Callie took the phone from my unresisting hand and played the recording a second and then a third time, bringing it closer to her face to scrutinize it. She started shaking.

I leaned in closer, my arm instinctively moving round her shoulder. 'What is it? Did Troy manage to sign something?' I asked.

Callie replied, 'I just got one letter – J.'

She stared at me, bewilderment writ large all over her face, before she exclaimed, 'Jarvis! It has to be him.'

A frown chiselled away at my face. No, that couldn't be right. Jarvis had taken my daughter? He wouldn't dare. He knew what I'd do to him if he ever tried such a thing. And, anyway, why he would he?

'I thought you said Jarvis had been demoted and wasn't Eva's second in command any more?' said Callie.

'He isn't . . . wasn't.'

'Maybe Eva reinstated him once she heard about Stoats's death and he's following her orders?'

'He wouldn't do that,' I argued. 'It doesn't make sense. Jarvis wouldn't—'

'Of course he would,' Callie interrupted. 'If it's true about his demotion, Jarvis has nothing to lose now. Maybe he considered it was time to go freelance – or retire on your money – and your cash would certainly help finance that. And, if no one suspects him, so much the better.'

A chill crept right through me. Was it true? Had Jarvis betrayed me? Is that why I'd been unable to get in touch with him? Jarvis was a strange one. Even after all these years, I still hadn't quite worked out what made him tick. I mean, he was one of the most ruthless people I'd ever met. He'd reverse over his granny in a tank if he needed to, and yet I'd watched him tear up at a nature film where a fox had been shot by a farmer.

'Jarvis values honour and loyalty above most everything else. If he'd done this, I would know.' Who was I trying to convince – Callie or myself?

'I'm sorry, Tobey, but what's loyalty and honour when you could have several millions at your disposal for the rest of your life?' said Callie.

'There's something wrong here,' I said, perplexed.

'You think?' Callie raised her eyebrows. 'Perhaps it has a little something to do with the fact that Jarvis, who everyone says is a psycho, has our loved ones?'

'If he has, he just made the biggest mistake of his miserable life,' I told her. 'But wait a minute . . .' Playing a hunch, I checked the metadata of the recording. The location was given as Lusaka Green – where Jon had just been. I traced his current location, using a separate app.

'Jon's on the move, heading back into town. I'll text him to meet us here at Ava's. Then I'll get Jade, my PA, to arrange to have the location in Lusaka Green checked out.'

'How will you do that? They can't search every building there.'

'They won't have to. My app can pinpoint a location down to one square metre. I can track every place Jon has been, and for how long, since I gave him the burner phone. He visited a location in Lusaka Green for just over fifteen minutes.'

'But Troy said Jarvis has them,' Callie insisted, looking devastated. 'It can't be Jon. He's one of my best friends. He wouldn't do this.'

'Hellsake! Callie, I admire your loyalty, but the facts speak for themselves,' I reminded her. 'And Troy gave us the letter J only.'

'Are you able to track Jarvis's whereabouts in the same way?'

Reluctantly, I shook my head.

'So Jarvis might've been there at some point this evening as well. Maybe Jon followed him,' said Callie.

'Which is why I'm going to assume they're both guilty until I know otherwise.'

Grudgingly, Callie nodded.

'If Libby and Troy have been stashed in Lusaka Green, then my people will find them. We'll know one way or another before Jon gets here. And, if it is him, then knowing he had Libby and Troy gives us an edge. For the first time, we'll be one step ahead of him. If he's up to his neck in this, we need to find out whether he's working alone or with Eva.'

'That's one helluva lot of "ifs". I hope you have a massive apology ready and waiting when you find out that you're wrong about Jon.'

'I'll kiss his feet if I'm wrong, but if I'm right . . .'

Callie shook her head, unwilling to believe her friend could have anything to do with Troy's disappearance. I stepped away from her to make a phone call.

'What if the address at Lusaka Green is perfectly innocent?' Callie called after me.

If Callie were to send just a fraction of the faith she had in her colleague my way, I'd be a very happy man. 'Callie, if Lusaka Green is a red herring, then we're no worse off, are we?'

She nodded, again reluctantly. I got on with my phone call. Lowering my voice, I launched in the moment Jade answered her phone. 'Jade, I want you to send an armed response unit to the address I'm about to text you. I believe there are two kidnap victims being held at that address – and one of them is my daughter.'

'Oh my days! Your daughter? Yes, sir. At once.' After her

initial outburst, the calm, collected, ultimate professional Jade took over.

'Once they've secured the building, let me know immediately if they find anyone,' I said.

'Yes, sir. Of course. I won't let you down.'

I hung up, then texted her the location. Jade immediately texted back to tell me she was already in contact with the Commissioner of the Metropolitan Police Service. That's what I admired about her. She got the job done. I wasn't going to half-arse around with a couple of beat coppers checking out the place first. If Libby and Troy were in Lusaka Green, and whoever had taken them had accomplices, I didn't want to give them the chance to harm my daughter or escape my justice. Better to employ shock-and-awe tactics than the softly-softly approach. If I was wrong, it would be easier to apologize after the fact than seek permission beforehand. I could only hope I'd got it right and my decision wouldn't prove costly to my daughter. But what else could I do?

As I walked back to Callie, she asked, 'What now? Wait here until the Lusaka Green address has been checked out or go in?' She pointed at Ava's. I looked at the nightclub, drinking it all in. The doors were closed and locked behind a security grille, the stained-glass windows on the ground floor dark, but I could see lights shining from the first floor. Eva was at home.

'We go in.'

As we headed towards the side door that led to the first and second floors of Ava's, I glanced at Callie who wore her stunned disbelief like a thin coat in a blizzard.

She caught me looking at her and slipped her hand into mine to give it a reassuring squeeze. Comforting me was uppermost in her mind. When she tried to pull away, I held on to it. She tilted her head, puzzled.

'Callie, whatever happens, I want you to know that my feelings for you haven't changed. I never lied about that.'

'What did you lie about then?'

'Ever the lawyer!' I said ruefully.

Callie raised an eyebrow. 'What aren't you telling me?'

I sighed. 'Eva is not a fan of mine. She may say some things . . . Just take what she says with a bucket of salt. And don't let her intimidate you.'

Callie leaned forward to give me a warm if brief kiss on the lips. 'I believe in you, Tobey.'

'You do?'

'Yes, I do.'

Was she . . . was she trying to tell me something? That look in her eyes . . . she hadn't looked at me like that since . . . since the very first time we ever made love. A man could live fully and die happy within that one look. Dread took root and mushroomed inside me. If it were for anyone else but Libby and Troy, I would've taken Callie by the hand, got back in my car and driven us the hell out of there. Callie and I had rarely felt closer than at that moment and I was loving it. So much so that my guts had turned to water at the thought of Callie and Eva being in the same room together. Eva knew enough to ensure that Callie never again looked at me except with utter contempt.

'I have faith in you,' Callie told me with a smile.

I stepped forward just as Callie did – and we kissed again.

This time a kiss that could restart my heart should it stop beating. We clung to each other, pouring our hopes, our yearning, our very souls into it. When at last we came up for air, I felt like I'd been drowning, but – dear God – I wanted to drown again and again.

'Callie—'

'We should go in,' she said, gently pulling her hand away from mine.

I nodded. 'This isn't over.'

She slowly smiled. 'No, it isn't. When this is through, you and I have a lot to talk about and a lot of wasted years to make up for, but for now let's go speak to Eva.'

Simple words that lifted me up only to slam me back down to earth. This was it. The moment of truth had arrived. Eva was about to ruin my life and there wasn't a damned thing I could do about it.

fifty-four. Sephy

'*Mum?* What on earth are you doing here?'

I shook my head. This was not the time. 'Not now, Callie.'

'Callie Rose, how lovely to meet you in person at long last,' said Eva, playing the gracious host. 'Please take a seat.'

Callie headed for the sofa furthest away from Eva. Tobey sat beside her without saying a word.

'Hello, Tobey.'

'Hello, Mrs Ealing,' said Tobey, his tone sombre.

We regarded each other for a moment or two. Tobey's unblinking gaze as he looked at me was entirely wretched, like the bottom was about to fall out of his world. What had he done? My gaze moved to my daughter. No hurt. No angst. Callie merely looked puzzled.

'Well now, isn't this cosy? I've never been so popular.' Eva looked round the room, a wry smile tugging at her lips. She stood up and poured herself a glass of something amber from a decanter on a shelf behind her. 'I'd offer this round,' she said, 'but why waste the good stuff?'

'Can we get this show on the road?' I asked with impatience. 'I want my boy back.'

'We're just waiting for two more, then we can begin.'

'Two more?' I asked.

'Jon Duba and Jarvis Burton,' said Eva. 'I've sent them both a very special invitation.'

Jon was coming here? Why on earth would he do that? Callie and Tobey exchanged a look.

Sonny took my hand in his. 'Sephy, what's going on?' he asked softly.

I shook my head. 'Ask Eva.'

'Eva, d'you mind if I have a quick word with Sephy?' asked Tobey.

'By all means, be my guest,' Eva said amiably.

Tobey crossed the room to squat down before me. He leaned in to whisper in my ear. 'I hear you think you know who killed Dan. I strongly recommend you keep it to yourself until you can tell the police directly. D'you understand?'

Slowly I nodded. Tobey stood up to retake his seat next to my daughter. Earlier I'd asked Jon to pass on a message to Jarvis. It had been a ploy to see who Jarvis might then pass the memo on to, because then I'd know for sure who he was working for. It had been my way of trying to find out just who was in charge. Well, I guess that was one mystery solved. Jarvis worked for Tobey and, like a dutiful soldier, had reported back to him every word I'd said. I now knew for certain exactly who – and what – Tobey was. I wasn't surprised, but was strangely disappointed – more for Callie's sake than my own. She still thought of him as one of the good guys.

One burning question answered. Time for another query to be resolved.

'Eva, while we're waiting, could you tell me who it was who had my husband killed – you or Dan?'

'Mum!' Callie exclaimed, but I ignored her.

'Sephy, don't.' Sonny tried to take my hand, but I shrugged him off.

I focused on Eva. Eyes narrowed, she looked me up and down. 'What makes you think it was either of us?'

'Because I'm not a fool,' I said stonily. 'My husband Nathan Ealing, owner of Specimens Restaurant, was killed in a hit-and-run incident nearly three years ago. Who ordered that? Was it Dan, you or maybe Owen Dowd?'

'Sephy, stop,' Sonny urged. 'This is hardly the time or place—'

'I know one of them was responsible for my husband's death,' I snapped. 'If it was Dan, then I hope his chestnuts are roasting in hell.' Now it was my turn to look Eva up and down, my gaze dripping with a contempt I didn't even try to hide.

'Dan had nothing to do with your husband's death,' Eva frowned. 'He would've told me if he'd ordered it.'

'So it was you?'

'Not me either. I know of your restaurant, and I know Dan was keen to acquire it, but he didn't kill to get it.' There was something about her calm, everyday tone that had me believing her, even though I didn't want to. 'Why would Dan want your husband killed? That's not good business,' Eva continued. 'You can't negotiate with a dead man and all that would do is piss you off and make you far more likely to go to the police. I taught Dan a long time ago to beware of people with nothing to lose. It makes them dangerous.'

Was she telling the truth? If so, was it just one of those things, a random hit-and-run with Nathan in the wrong place at the wrong time?

'I know you don't know me and have no reason to trust me, but I give you my word: neither Dan nor I, nor anyone else who worked for us, had anything to do with your husband's death,' said Eva. 'And I wouldn't lie about that. And if Dowd was responsible, I would've heard. My condolences.'

A strange chill swept over me, bringing stillness in its wake. I had no reason to believe Eva and yet I did. Stunned, I turned to look at Sonny. His eyes were clouded with guilt, his lips turned down. A single bead of sweat ran down the side of his face.

'Persephone, I'm so sorry,' said Sonny softly. Only a few words required to unwrap real remorse.

Oh, Nathan . . .

'Sephy—'

'Let's talk about it later, Sonny,' I said. 'At this moment, all I want is my son back.'

'Sephy, listen—'

'Not now. Please,' I said through gritted teeth.

I turned back to Eva who was watching Sonny and me with a great deal of curiosity. A glimmer of understanding played across her face. She tilted her head and nodded slowly. Now we both knew who was responsible for Nathan's death. And inside . . . inside, my heart was being fed through a shredder.

A beep interrupted the stillness of the room. Tobey took his phone out of his pocket and read the screen. His body tensed and a strange expression swept over his face, only to be quickly masked. If I didn't know the man of old, I might've missed it. As I watched, he put his phone away, but the tension stiffening his muscles didn't lessen. He sat up straighter and moved to sit closer to the edge of his seat. I did the same. Something was about to go down and I wanted to be poised and ready for it. Sonny tried to take my hand in his again. I pulled sharply away, unable to even look at him.

The door opened and in walked Jon wearing a green shirt, black jeans, a black leather jacket, black gloves and trainers, closely followed by Jarvis dressed in denim jeans, a round-necked dark blue jumper and black boots. Jarvis strode over to Eva and stood just behind her, clearly a position he'd taken many times. He nodded at Eva's male bodyguard, who immediately left the room, closing the door quietly behind him. His services were no longer required.

Jon looked around, casting a smile my way when he caught sight of me. I tried, but I just couldn't dredge up one of my own. 'How are you, Sephy?' he asked.

'Surviving.' But only just.

Oh, Sonny, how could you . . . ?

'These days that's all any of us can hope for.' Jon shrugged.

Well, Callum, you gave me a sign. Just not the one I was hoping for.

'Take a seat, Jon,' Eva interrupted. 'Then we can begin.'

'Whatever you say, Eva.' Jon sat down in an upright chair. Glancing at Tobey, alarm bells began to peal in my head immediately. The way Tobey was looking at him—

That look wasn't even directed at me and yet dread pierced my body.

We were in for a bumpy night.

Daily Shouter Online

Home. News. Politics. Celebs. Entertainment. Sport. Tech. Health. Science. Money. More.

Nought model speaks out against 'tokenistic TV ads'

Top model Darlene Grimes, 33, spoke out today against what she called 'tokenistic TV ads'.

'I'm fed up with being the token Nought who is only included in ads so that various organizations can tick their diversity box. Forget that! I've been in perfume ads where I'm the sole Nought among a number of Cross models and I'm always placed at the back. When I've appeared in non-tokenistic ads, such as a series of recent supermarket ones with a pretend Nought family, both the retail chain and I were blasted for promoting an unrealistic depiction of a Nought family – because apparently we Noughts don't have families who eat dinner together or shop at supermarkets. I've even had people drag me on social media, saying there are too many Noughts on TV and every other ad has a Nought in it – all of which is so much racist rubbish. We Noughts exist, whether the complainers like it or not. These petulant bigots are not used to seeing Noughts in normal roles in TV dramas and in ads, so even a single face is one too many for them. It's so tiring. To the bigots and the haters, my message is this – from the bottom of my heart and from the heart of my bottom, f*** you.'

fifty-five. Troy

After at least twenty minutes of Libby and I kicking at the back window, then the right-hand-side back window, I was ready to throw in the towel. The back window grille had bowed, but it was still intact. We hadn't made even a dent in either window. Plus every time I kicked out at the window, a jolt like dirty lightning ran up my body, gathering momentum before racing down to my busted ankle, jarring it mercilessly. Maybe if we had another few hours we might've been able to kick out at least one of them, but we didn't have that kind of time and we both knew it.

'Is there some non-obvious way to get past the childproof locks?' Libby asked, examining her door more closely. 'Don't some vehicles come with a latch or a hidden bolt, or something that—'

Sirens! Getting louder, closer . . . They were probably going to flash right by us. I opened my mouth to answer Libby when the noise of the sirens stopped right before the garage door. Libby and I exchanged a look of terror. How was it possible to feel such relief and yet such dread at the same time? Of all the moments since we'd been snatched off the street, this was by far the worst. We were mere metres away from being rescued and mere seconds away from being blown to bits.

'DON'T COME IN HERE! DON'T OPEN THE GARAGE DOOR! THERE'S A BOMB!'

Libby joined in, screaming out her own warning. Between the two of us, all we were doing was making a noise. I put a hand on Libby's arm.

'Shout the same as me or they won't be able to make out what we're saying,' I told her. She nodded.

'DON'T OPEN THE GARAGE DOOR! THERE'S A BOMB!'

Libby joined in, calling out the same thing at the same time. With the car doors locked and the windows up and the garage door closed, could they even hear us? Probably not, and yet we didn't stop shouting. We couldn't stop. This was our only chance to save ourselves.

But it wasn't working. Before us, the wide garage door began to open as it was pulled upwards.

fifty-six. Libby

'DON'T OPEN THE GARAGE DOOR! THERE'S A BOMB!' I yelled until my throat felt like it was being rubbed with sandpaper. I yelled against my mum and Pete and the world that had brought me to this point, mere seconds from my death. Troy grabbed hold of my hand as we both kept yelling.

The door stopped opening about half a metre off the ground. The wires leading from it to the back of the garage were as taut as hell. If the door opened even one more centimetre, Troy and I were toast. So we kept shouting the same words, over and over.

We heard a number of voices, some calling out, some urgently speaking, and the strobing lights of the cars out front were being reflected up at us from the driveway. There came a smash that made both Troy and me jump. It sounded like the front door to the house was being rammed. Moments later, the internal garage door handle began to turn. I grabbed hold of Troy and pushed my face into his shoulder, my eyes tight shut. Troy wrapped his arms round me and held me close as we waited for our world to either start spinning or to stop turning for good.

Daily Shouter Online

Home. News. Politics. Celebs. Entertainment. Sport. Tech. Health. Science. Money. More.

BREAKING NEWS. It's 14 May! Date finally set for Zafrikan Trading Alliance referendum!

It's official. Next year, on 14 May, Albion will have the chance to vote on whether or not to stay in the Zafrikan Trading Alliance. Nick Allumina, the Business Secretary, informed the *Daily Shouter* ahead of this afternoon's official statement that 14 May would be a historic date for Albion, a chance for the country to stand on its own two feet. 'We are delivering on the main manifesto pledge made by our Prime Minister, Tobey Durbridge. The people of this country expect and deserve no less. This is our chance to take back control.'

Julian Soga, Shadow Business Secretary, stated, 'This is a tragic day. As a member of the ZTA, Albion enjoys free trade, travel, education, work and domicile with most countries in Zafrika. Outside the ZTA, the vast majority of Albions will find themselves worse off, with less freedoms and the inevitable price rises of most goods and services, including food, clothes, raw materials and manufacturing. Hundreds of thousands will lose their jobs and struggle to find another. Our manufacturing industry will die as organizations leave our shores and set up in other countries with better trading terms. Everything we as a nation buy from Zafrika will become far more expensive. Everything we sell to Zafrika will be subject to tariffs, making our goods more expensive and less attractive. This is a lose–lose situation for Albion and, if we leave the ZTA, we will be feeling its adverse effects for not just months but years to come. The campaign begins today to convince the Albion electorate to remain a part of the ZTA.'

Nick Allumina accused Julian Soga and the Liberal Alliance of 'scaremongering'.

fifty-seven. Callie

What was going on with Mum? She had a strange look on her face, like she was in pain. Did she believe Eva about Nathan? I didn't even know she suspected Eva or Dan of being behind his death. Why didn't she tell me? And what was in the text Tobey just received? He hadn't shown it to me, but its contents now had him perched on the edge of the sofa and coiled like a spring. Tension and something far, far colder were positively vibrating through him. I could've been sitting right across the room from him and I still would've felt it. Was he about to race over and pounce on Jarvis? Lord knows that's what I wanted to do. That man over there, standing behind Eva, was responsible for all the heartache everyone I cared about in this room had gone through in the last thirty-six hours.

Placing a hand on his knee, I steeled myself to whisper, 'Are you OK, Tobey? Bad news about Troy and Libby?'

'No.' That was the full extent of Tobey's reply.

'Tobey—'

'Trust me, Callie,' said Tobey. He turned to give me a fleeting smile. 'Please just trust me. OK?'

I nodded, my lips pursed together so tightly they were in danger of going numb. Why did it feel like I was fifteen minutes behind everyone else in the room? It was not a sensation or a situation that I was finding easy to digest. In fact, it stuck in my throat.

Was Tobey lying? Had something happened to Troy and Liberty and he was trying to find a way to tell me? He'd asked me to trust him, but it was so hard with all the secrets he liked to keep.

What wasn't he telling me now?

fifty-eight. Sephy

'As we seem to all be assembled, let's start with you, Tobias,' said Eva, like a queen on her throne. 'What brings you here?'

'My daughter, Liberty,' said Tobey, his tone curiously even. 'I just received instructions regarding a proposed money transfer of several millions from the person who kidnapped her and Callie's brother, Troy. The kidnapper sent me a video of my daughter locked in a car with Troy as proof that he has them both, along with their offshore account details. Would you know anything about that, Eva?'

Eva and Tobey regarded each other. I swear, you could've heard a feather drop.

'Not a thing,' Eva replied at last.

I neither knew nor cared what was going on between these two. All I wanted was my son home safely.

'The men who killed Libby's mother, and the demand that I publicly admit to killing Dan, I suppose you don't know anything about those either?' said Tobey.

Eva shrugged. 'Well, that was just business, sweetie. Just business.'

Tobey nodded slowly. 'That's the reason you turned on me? Business?'

'With Dan dead and you neutralized and neutered, I can

run things my way without interference. Simple logic,' said Eva.

'Did you kill Dan?' asked Tobey.

'No, of course not, but I've always been a woman who could recognize an opportunity when it slaps me in the face.'

'Dan told me that about you,' Tobey agreed. 'So you heard about Libby and Troy's abduction and decided to take over. Do you know where my daughter is now?'

'No idea. That's the truth,' said Eva. 'The people I had guarding them were killed and Libby and Troy were taken. I did wonder if maybe you'd found them and that's why you're here? Revenge?'

Pause. Tobey watched Eva without blinking once. The tension in the room ratcheted up several notches, like heat being turned up beneath a pan of already simmering water.

'No, I didn't find them,' said Tobey. 'Who d'you think would have the nerve to take Libby and Troy away from you?'

'I'd like to know that too,' Eva said, shrugging. 'I've been assured it wasn't any of Dowd's people.'

'You genuinely don't know where my daughter is?'

'I give you my word – for what it's worth.' Eva seemed very keen for Tobey to believe her.

She and Tobey had forgotten about the rest of us. In that moment, we were all irrelevant.

Eva shook her head. 'Look, Tobey, at this point, if I knew, I'd tell you. Then I'd have something to barter with. You're looking at me like I'm not your favourite person and it hurts.' She ended with a mocking smile, but I wasn't fooled. This woman was bricking it, in spite of the bodyguards behind her.

'Dan always said you were good at reading people,' Tobey

said coolly. 'But don't worry, I know who took Libby and Troy – and where our kids are at this precise moment.'

'You do?' Callie asked sharply, getting in before I could. 'Where are they?

'The police have them safe,' said Tobey, his tone softening as he turned to look directly at my daughter. I watched as he took her hand in his and caressed it. 'They were locked in a car in a garage that was rigged to blow up the moment the external garage door was opened. Luckily, the inner door leading into the house wasn't rigged, so the police were able to rescue them and defuse the bomb before any damage was done. But the person who made the IED tried to make damned sure that Libby and Troy wouldn't be around to identify him.'

'Troy's safe? He's really all right? Oh please, where is he?' Relief flowed through me, headier than cheap champagne. 'Where was this garage? Whose is it? Do they know?'

Tobey looked round. 'Why don't you tell everyone?'

Who was he speaking to?

'Well, Jon? We're all waiting.'

All eyes in the room shifted to Jon's stunned expression. Without warning, he took a phone of all things out of his pocket and pressed the screen twice.

Tobey stood up. 'Thanks for confirming that you were the one responsible for making the bomb, Jon, even if you did give Troy and my daughter Jarvis's name rather than your own. Your phone won't activate shit though. Didn't I just say that the bomb has been defused?'

Tobey stalked towards him, his fists clenched. Now everyone was on their feet, including me.

Jon leaped up and pulled a gun from his jacket pocket. 'That's close enough, Durbridge.'

Jon and Tobey were less than two metres apart. Callie immediately put herself between them. Stupid child! Sonny tried to stop me, but I shrugged out of his grasp and ran to stand before my daughter, pushing her back.

'No, you don't.' A thwack from behind us. Eva cried out. I turned to see the gun she'd been holding clatter onto her desk. She collapsed back into her chair, cradling her forearm. Jarvis had hit her with the retractable steel baton he was putting back in his belt. He retrieved the gun off the desk at once. Eva's other bodyguard swore and drew her weapon. Jarvis opened fire. A deafening shot made me cry out in alarm. The bodyguard dropped to the ground without making a sound, a rosette of red in the middle of her forehead. Tobey took a determined step towards Jon, who took a step back, his gun arm outstretched.

'I said that's close enough, Tobey,' said Jon, freezing Tobey in his tracks.

Unexpectedly, Eva started to laugh. 'Isn't this jolly?' she declared with delight.

'Jarvis, put the gun down,' Jon demanded. 'I won't ask twice.'

Reluctantly, Jarvis placed the weapon on the desk out of Eva's reach.

'Now how about we all just take a deep breath and chill?' said Jon. 'Go on. You heard me. Everyone sit back down.'

'Jon, no—' Callie's heartbroken whisper filled the room.

Jon cast her a look of real regret, but the gun in his hand didn't waver for a second. I perched on the edge of a couch,

Sonny beside me. Across the room, Tobey and Callie sat next to each other. Tobey's expression was carefully neutral, but he never took his eyes off Jon. Not once. I could only hope that he wasn't about to do anything stupid. Eva was still cradling her arm, while Jarvis stood behind her, watchful.

I couldn't help glancing at the Nought woman lying dead on the ground. I'd seen violent death before and it never failed to horrify me. Sonny took hold of my hand and squeezed it, drawing my focus away from the dead woman. I jerked it away.

'Jarvis, go and sit by Callie. You too, Eva,' Jon ordered. 'In fact, why don't you all sit together? Nice and cosy.'

He waited until we did as directed. Sonny gathered up two single chairs and placed them either side of the couch Callie was sitting on. I sat as far away from him as I could get. Sonny deliberately took up residence in the single chair next to me. On the other side of me was Callie, then Tobey, then Eva. Jarvis sat himself down in the other single chair.

After making sure we were all properly seated, Jon made his way to the desk to retrieve Eva's gun, never taking his eyes off any of us. The man now had two weapons, one in each hand. Pocketing his own one, he swapped Eva's gun to his right gloved hand, quickly examining it as he did so.

Tobey rocked forward, but he was at least three metres away from Jon. There was no way he could cross that gap before Jon put a bullet in him. Tobey obviously reached the same conclusion because, though he was still leaning forward, he didn't stand up or move further. Thank God. Any bullets that missed him were more than likely to hit my daughter.

'If there's any more shooting to be done, I'll use this gun,' said Jon.

The one with Eva and Jarvis's fingerprints on it. Jon was no fool. I couldn't help wondering how many more would die before we left this room.

'Why, Jon?' Callie asked, bewildered.

Jon shrugged. 'For the money, of course. What other reason is there?'

fifty-nine. Tobey

Stupid. Stupid. Stupid. I'd let myself get distracted and missed my chance to disarm Jon. God only knew if I'd get another. And, now that we were all seated, it made it that much harder to take him by surprise.

'Tobey, Eva was going to shoot you in the back just now,' said Jarvis quietly.

I turned to her. She looked at me with defiant contempt.

'Why would you do that?'

'Because I despise you and your kind.' Eva shot me a look of pure loathing, the mask finally removed.

'My kind?'

'You think you're something, don't you? You think you've got it made in the shade. You're the same as me, but you think you can be Prime Minister of the entire country?' Her every word dripped with scorn. 'You're nothing but a jumped-up blanker who's forgotten who and what he is. You're a sell-out.'

What the actual hell? Had I heard this woman correctly? 'That's why you hate me? Because I worked my arse off and did something with my life? Seriously?' Was she for real?

'Who d'you think you are, Tobey? You're a nought. Nothing more,' said Eva.

Hellsake! She meant *n*ought – with a lower-case *n*. That's how far gone she was. Nothing much surprised me any more – maybe the odd football score, but that was about it. Yet I had to admit that this woman and her vitriol did – and all because I was a Nought who dared to have ideas above his supposed station. Damn!

'You know something, Eva? That shit is old and tired when Crosses spout it. As a Nought, you should be celebrating every rung of the ladder that other Noughts manage to climb, 'cause when one rises we all do. Instead, you choose to wallow in hatred, like the worst racist dickhead, because that's all you know and that's all you're capable of. I actually feel sorry for you.'

'Screw you and your pity. You and your minion Jarvis are living on borrowed time.'

'Maybe, but that won't stop you from getting what you deserve too,' I assured her.

'Er . . . d'you two mind? Man with a gun here,' said Jon.

'And I'll make it my life's work to make sure you also get what you deserve,' I told him.

'Yeah, yeah!' Jon dismissed. 'Well, now we're all here and I've got your attention, I'll need you to transfer that money pronto, Tobey.'

'You must be joking,' I scoffed. This man was delusional if he thought I'd give him the steam off my piss, let alone any of my hard-earned cash.

'I never joke about money,' said Jon. And he very deliberately aimed his gun at Sephy. 'Your choice. Your money or your lover's mother. Let's see how she'll feel about you if you let her mum die. And, if you do decide to choose your money over Sephy, my next target will be Callie Rose.'

sixty. Callie

Jon looked around at us all, a forced, fake smile playing across his face, but his gun was steady and still levelled at Mum's heart. A muscle in his cheek ticked and jumped irregularly. He was caught between a rock and a hard place and he was feeling it.

As was I.

The pain in my chest as I looked at Jon was getting worse. His betrayal was drilling holes into my heart. His gaze settled on me, a hint of regret tingeing his green eyes. Or was that my imagination?

'Jon, how could you?' My voice wobbled but stayed upright.

Jon sighed. 'Callie, I like you. I respect you – and there are probably only three people on this godforsaken planet I can say that about. I tried to let Troy leave, I really did, but he refused to go anywhere without Liberty.'

'What am I supposed to say to that? Thank you?'

Jon shook his head. 'Why didn't you leave this to me like I asked you to? You would've had your brother back, I would've been rich and no one would've been any the wiser.'

I stared at the man I'd considered one of my dearest

friends. The man whom I'd confided in over the years as if he were my confessor. I didn't know him at all.

'You must've known your plan was doomed to failure,' I told Jon. 'Did you really think that, with all of Tobey's resources and connections, he wouldn't find his daughter before the ransom was due?'

Jon shrugged with false nonchalance. 'Once I knew Eva had taken over my kidnapping scheme for some nonsense political agenda, it was my duty to take it back. I couldn't give a shit about Tobey and Dan and who did what to who. All I want is my money.'

'Why did you even come here?' asked Tobey. 'You must've suspected that your plans had been shot out of the water.'

'You're right. I knew there was a risk that my involvement was now known, but I decided to follow the cash.'

'So you're only here because you knew I would be?' asked Tobey.

'Don't flatter yourself,' said Jon. 'You and I could conduct our business over the phone from different continents if necessary. No, I needed to be where Callie is. She's the only one I could use to force you to transfer money into my bank account. So here we all are.'

'You're the one who killed my men at Gurendah Harbour, aren't you?' said Eva evenly.

'Unavoidable, I'm afraid,' said Jon.

'I'll be sure to thank you and yours properly for that.' The wink Eva bestowed on Jon made my blood run cold. I stared at my friend, even now unwilling to believe it of him. I'd read the online story of the two bodies found in a house at East Gurendah Harbour a few hours ago. *Jon* did that?

'Who are you?' I asked him.

'Says the woman who's never had to scratch for money a day in her life,' said Jon with bitterness. 'What would you know about going without? I read all your online journals and they were a joke. Yearning for and harping on about trivial bullshit. You've never struggled to pay a bill or put food in your stomach.'

I stared. 'How did you access my password-protected journals?' I asked sharply. I hadn't updated them in years, but the mere fact that he knew about them, let alone had read them, made my cheeks burn fiery hot.

Jon shrugged. 'When I decided to work for you, I accessed your house on the pretence of updating your utility meter and you gave me your router name and password. After that, I could access every file and password you had on your computer. How d'you think I knew all that stuff about your fears and regrets that I told you about at my interview?'

Well, that explained a lot.

'I asked you after the interview how you knew so much about me, but you never said,' I remembered.

Once Jon started working for me, for months afterwards I'd asked him where he got his information from, but he'd always reply, '*A good magician never reveals how their tricks are done*.' I'd been impressed enough to finally let the topic drop and leave it alone. If he had told me, I might have had to question how he'd obtained his information on some of my clients over the years. So I'd deliberately looked the other way. As long as he got results, I could fool myself into believing he acquired his information reasonably legitimately.

Now I knew otherwise.

'I was in your house for over twenty minutes, Callie, and you still didn't recognize me when I came for an interview a month later,' Jon said with contempt. 'People like you never notice those who serve.'

Ashamed, I hung my head. I remembered an engineer who'd come to update the utility meter when I was working at home, but I'd barely given him a first glance, never mind a second one. I could recall that he was a Nought, wearing a black woollen hat, and he'd had a moustache. That was it.

'You're right and I'm sorry. Please, Jon, don't do this. You can't get away with it. Even if you get Tobey's money, you'd never be free to spend it.'

'Let me worry about that,' said Jon. 'Tobey, start the money transfer. I'm not going to tell you again.'

Beside me, Tobey took out his smartphone.

'Jon, you think you're the only one who has to work for a living?' asked Mum from beside me. 'If so, then you're a fool.'

I gasped. What was Mum playing at? The last thing any of us should be doing was antagonizing this man.

'I've known what it's like to be broke and I've known what it's like to be hungry, day in, day out. You think you're the only one who's ever had to go without?' said Mum, standing up.

She shrugged off Sonny's hand on her forearm. I recognized her expression. She was unimpressed and wasn't afraid to tell Jon about himself – gun or no gun. Terrified, I got to my feet too. Tobey stood up beside me.

Mum, please. Don't do this. Don't piss him off.

The thought played on a loop in my head. If only Mum

could read my mind. She was backing Jon into a corner and that made him not just unpredictable but volatile.

He looked Mum up and down. 'You know what, Sephy? I believe you. I think you do know what it is to go without, even if you are a Cross,' Jon replied. 'But people like Tobey get away with murder – literally. So why shouldn't I grab something for me in the meantime? Why should people like Tobey always win and people like me always lose?'

'If you tried removing your head from your arse, you'd be able to see that Tobey had nothing to do with Dan's death,' Mum said, taking another step forward.

Once again, Sonny tried to pull her back, but she wasn't having it.

'To hell with this man and his pity party for one,' Mum told Sonny, before turning to face Jon again.

'Mum, please—' I pleaded out loud this time.

'And, Sephy, you know that for a fact, do you?' mocked Jon.

'Yes, I do actually,' said Mum. 'I know exactly who killed Dan and it wasn't Tobey.'

sixty-one. Sephy

Now all eyes in the room were on me. I had everyone's attention, but I only had eyes for Jon. This man was fully armed and extremely dangerous and I wasn't going to let him start shooting up the place, not with my daughter present.

'Tobey's innocent? Who told you that? Your daughter? Your establishment friends? You've bought into their lies,' said Jon scornfully. 'You're letting them use you as part of a cover-up. I thought you were smarter, or at least had more conscience.'

'Oh hell, no!' Was this guy for real? 'You're standing there with a gun pointed at me and you're gonna lecture me about conscience? Jonny Duba, you are a dickhead of multidimensions. The truth doesn't stop being the truth just 'cause you don't like it.'

'Who was it then?' asked Jon. 'Who killed Dan?'

I resisted the almost overpowering urge to look at my daughter. 'What's the point of telling you, Jon? How would that change anything?'

'I want to know.'

'Then want must be your master,' I replied.

Jon's face tightened. He raised the gun, his hand tightening round the stock. 'Tell me.'

'No!' Sonny tried to move in front of me, but I blocked him. I wasn't going to let him or anyone else for that matter get hurt because of me. I needed to distract Jon so that Jarvis or Tobey could make their move. Sonny couldn't, Eva wouldn't and Callie shouldn't.

'Jon, you've already admitted that this is about money, not justice, so what's your problem?' I asked.

'Sephy . . .' Sonny warned softly.

'And if your desire for money leaves bodies in your wake and blood on your hands then so be it?' I continued. 'Is that how it is?'

'I didn't choose this path; it chose me.'

'Bull. Shit! Every step of the way, you had a choice. The path you decided to take is yours and yours alone. Own it.'

'Says she who was born with a lifetime dose of affluenza.'

'Oh, give me a massive frickin' break, please,' I said with disdain. 'It's been a hellish long day and I'm seriously too tired for your nonsense. What makes you so special that you shouldn't experience what most other humans on the planet have to go through?'

Though my eyes were trained on Jon, I could see Tobey slowly moving forward, one softly planted step at a time. I too started moving towards Jon. He needed to focus on me.

'I was a public servant for decades and what do I have to show for it?' said Jon, anger flaring like a gas jet in his green eyes. 'A gold watch that runs slow and a stomach ulcer. No more wife and no one to give a shit if I live or die.'

'Oh, boohoo! My haemorrhoids bleed for you. There are plenty of people – Noughts and Crosses – who were born with little and have a lot less than you do now and have never resorted to the carnage you've created to get what you want.'

'And the Noughts who have nothing will likely die as they lived – poor. Nothing ever changes. Well, I won't live like that,' said Jon.

I shook my head. Jon couldn't see beyond what he thought he needed. Nothing and no one else mattered.

'You have a Nought Prime Minister now. Doesn't that prove how much things are changing?' I said.

'Tobias Durbridge? Are you having a laugh?' Jon mocked. 'The man is as crooked as a dog's hind leg.'

Jon started to turn his head to look at Tobey. I took a deliberate step forward to draw Jon's attention back to me.

'If Tobey was dirty, it would've come out by now,' Callie added from behind me.

Jon stared at her before he burst out laughing. 'For Shaka's sake. Are you new to life, Callie? Who d'you think was the mastermind behind Dan's whole criminal organization? You seriously think Dan had the smarts to run a nationwide operation? Dan took care of the day-to-day stuff, but Tobey was the strategist, the brains. How else was he going to finance his political ambitions? Why d'you think Eva was so keen to get rid of him? When Durbridge got to the top, he wanted to hand it all over to Dan, wash his hands of that world and get out. And, as PM, he fully intended to keep his promise to come after any and all criminal organizations dealing in Prop. And, what's more, Dan – and Eva – knew it. Without Tobey, Dan knew he didn't stand a chance against Owen Dowd and all the other sharks circling round him.

And, without Prop, Eva knew the Outfit would be obsolete within a year.'

'I don't believe it.' Callie's words were boldly said, but a trace of uncertainty was already clouding her eyes.

'Why would I lie?' asked Jon.

'For what it's worth, that was going to be Dan's announcement to all of you on the night of his dinner party – how Tobey was the puppet master, the one at the top really running things,' Eva piped up. 'He was going to permanently crash and trash Tobey's political career.'

I looked at Tobey. His expression was unreadable as he watched Eva. Was it true? Was Tobey running the Outfit this entire time? I'd thought him capable of a lot of things, but not that. Never that. I'd underestimated him.

'Tobey?' Callie said softly, seeking some kind of assurance that Eva was wrong.

Tobey glanced at her and shook his head, before turning back to Jon. He still hadn't spoken a word in his own defence. Nor had he denied it.

'What purpose was my presence at the dinner supposed to serve?' I frowned.

'The guests that night were picked to ensure maximum damage. There's no way Tobey would've succeeded in stopping all of you from spreading the word. By scuppering Tobey's political career, Dan was trying to ensure that their crooked empire would live on,' said Jon. 'He wanted to make sure that Tobey had nothing else in his life but the Outfit.'

'And how d'you know all this?'

Jon gave me a pitying look.

I shook my head, the truth slowly dawning. 'All the time you were working with my daughter you were secretly working for Dan.'

Behind me, Callie gasped.

'I was strictly freelance, working for whoever paid me the most,' said Jon unapologetically. 'That just happened to be Dan most of the time. He used Callie and the courts to get rid of his enemies who couldn't be got at any other way. And, Callie, you did a first-rate job. Dan loved working with you.'

I could only imagine what this news was doing to my daughter. She loved the law. To hear that she'd been used by Jon and a man like Dan Jeavons for their own ends had to be devastating.

'So you were on Dan's payroll and then you decided to get a little something-something for yourself,' I said. 'You are so pathetic, Jon.'

'And this time tomorrow I'll be pathetic on an island eating flying fish and sipping vodka martinis.'

Look at this man. Look at all the pain and hurt he's caused. Look what he's done to our daughter, Callum. She believed in him. She trusted him. So did I.

I took another step forward, but big mistake – I got too close. Jon grabbed hold of my arm and spun me round, pulling me against his body, his gun to my head. The barrel was hard and oh so cold against my temple. 'That's far enough, Durbridge.'

Tobey froze, still over a metre away from Jon. Everyone else was behind him. Tobey was close to Jon, but not close enough.

'No more talk. Transfer my money now, Tobey. And don't insult my intelligence by telling me you can't do it from your phone because we both know you can.'

The barrel of the gun was being stabbed into my temple as a reminder to the whole room that he meant business. Callie was only a step behind Tobey. Sonny was still the furthest away. Jarvis stood at Eva's side. All eyes were on Jon and me.

'All right. Calm down. I'll do as you ask,' said Tobey. 'Just don't hurt Sephy.'

He raised the phone in his hand and started tapping at the screen.

'All this to get money,' I said with contempt. 'You disappoint me, Jon. I thought you had more imagination.'

'Since when does imagination pay the bills? Thanks to Tobey, I'll be getting a great deal of money. What other reason is there to do anything in this world?' Jon's breath was warm and unpleasantly moist against my ear. 'The moment the money hits my bank account, *adios* and I'm gone. I don't think that's too much to ask.'

'You're lying, Jon. You're not going to leave any witnesses, are you? Is that why you're pointing Eva's gun at us rather than your own?' came Callie's voice quietly. 'You'll get your money, then kill us all and arrange it to look like Eva and Jarvis did it and died in the attempt.'

Behind me, Jon jolted. And, in that moment, I knew then that Callie had called it. None of us were going to leave this room alive. Callie . . . my baby . . . To my horror, and before I could stop her, Callie started moving towards us.

'You and I are friends, Jon. You won't shoot me,' said my daughter.

Tobey tried to pull her back; she tried to wrest his hand off her forearm. Tobey moved in front of her, determination on his face.

Jon immediately pointed his gun at Tobey, though his other arm was still round my neck, hauling me closer, choking me. Callie took another step towards us. With a furious glare at her, Tobey stepped in front of my daughter again. Directly behind me, Jon's agitation ratcheted up several notches. His arm round my neck tightened; his breathing rate increased.

'Durbridge, stay where you are,' Jon warned.

'Or what?' said Tobey, taking another step forward. 'What will you do, big man?' he mocked. 'Shoot me? You haven't got the guts.'

Jon's body stiffened as his finger began to tighten on the trigger.

'Tobey, no.' I stomped down just as hard as I could on Jon's left foot while I spun round, stepping between him and Tobey. I could only hope . . .

BANG! BANG!

A white-hot lance ploughed through my body, setting my whole being on fire. Clutching my abdomen, I dropped like a stone.

sixty-two. Tobey

The moment the gun sounded, I leaped forward to tackle Jon. We both crashed to the floor, his gun between us. Kicking out at me, Jon fought to point the gun at my chest. I battled to mirror his intent. Jon brought a fist up and round to punch the side of my head. Pain exploded inside my skull like fireworks. He struggled to bring his finger back to the trigger as I fought to get the gun away from him. Another punch to my head, this time with more impact. A high-pitched whistling noise instantly assailed my ears. Neon lights flashed before my eyes, but I couldn't let go of Jon or the gun. If I did, we'd all be dead. Jon and I were so close together on the ground that there was no room to turn the gun fully so that the barrel was against the chest of either of us. Jon drew his foot back and kicked my right shin. Agony flared up my leg. Instinctively, I pulled away and headbutted him, my forehead to his nose. A crack. Jon grunted. Blood spurted from one nostril, but his grip on the gun never faltered. We both fought to reach the trigger first. I could feel it, the metal cool beneath my index finger.

BANG!

The gun going off was like a simultaneous punch to both eardrums. Instinctively, one of my hands flew to my ears, my head ringing louder now.

Jon—

I launched myself at him, praying he was just as dazed as I was. I couldn't let him fire off another round. But Jon lay perfectly still, his eyes open and staring up at the ceiling. I looked down at his body. A bloom of red, smaller than a saucer, spilled like a watercolour over the left side of his green shirt. I checked for a pulse. There was none. My ears still ringing, I scowled at Jon. Fucker. He'd got what he deserved.

My thoughts were interrupted by a scream from Callie – a racked, wretched scream ripped from the depths of her soul.

'MUM! Mum, please . . .'

I turned to see a sight that stole all the breath from my body. Sephy had been shot.

sixty-three. Sephy

Christ! This hurts . . . so much. I can't bear it. I clutch at my stomach with both hands, writhing as agony hits me and grips me and rips me apart. Release. Catch. Release. Catch. Catchcatchcatch. Never before have I felt anything like the white-hot, searing pain now blazing through me. So intensely hot that it scorches all the air in my lungs. I can't catch my breath. It hurts too much. There's no respite. I'm in a tornado, being lifted up and up as the pain intensifies. And, though the pain in my abdomen is star-hot, the rest of my body is icy cold and getting colder by degrees.

'MUM . . .'

From far away, I hear Callie calling to me. At me. Shouting my name. Why is she shouting? When will this pain stop? Please make it stop. I can't take much more of this. It's too much.

I think . . . I think I'm in trouble . . .

'Callie . . .' Forcing out the one word exhausts me.

'Mum, hang on. You're going to be all right. An ambulance is coming. Just hang on.' Her words sound so muffled and far away. My heartbeat is so fast, so loud in my ears.

'Callie . . . Tobey did—'

It's no good. Trying to speak makes me cough and the cough sends agony ricocheting round my body.

I mouth my daughter's name. She looks so scared, bless her. I want to take her hand and tell her everything will be OK. I long to take away her fear, her hurt – but I can't. She bends her head, her ear close to my mouth.

'Tobey . . . needs you . . . S-save him.' My voice is softer than a whisper yet I know my daughter can hear me. Her and her alone. Callie looks at me, tears running down her cheeks like winter rain on a windowpane. She nods. My baby. My beautiful baby.

Callum, just look at our beautiful daughter . . .

'Where the hell is the ambulance?' Callie jumps to her feet to ask.

I struggle to turn onto my side. It takes every ounce of strength I have left. A jolt as sharp and fast as lightning rips through me, robbing me of all breath. Instinctually, I know that turning has done more damage.

I can't feel my legs. I can't feel anything past the pain in my stomach, which is slicing me in half.

Please, God, please, someone – make it stop.

I close my eyes and press harder against my stomach as if to push the pain away – right through my body and out the other side. I try to inhale, but it hurts too much. I can't breathe in or out. Why can't I feel my legs? Eyes still closed, I tell myself to wiggle my toes, or just one toe. Did it work? I can't tell.

God, don't let me die. Not like this. It hurts so much.

Warm fingers touch my cheek – and the pain fades. I open my eyes – and smile.

It's him—

He's lying on his side, facing me. His fingers are still on my cheek. I raise my hand to place it on his. And his fingers, his warmth, they don't fade away like they usually do. I open my mouth to ask, 'Am I dreaming again?' but the words won't come. I cannot speak.

But it doesn't matter. He's still smiling at me. I'm so happy to see him again. So happy. Taking hold of my hand, he places it back at my side.

Don't leave. Please don't leave. It's not even hurting any more now you're here with me.

The words exist in my head. They won't leave my mouth. They can't. Why can't I speak?

Please let him know what I'm thinking.

Please, God.

If you're up there.

Somewhere.

'I love you, Sephy,' he says softly.

I love you too, Callum.

I think it over and over, just as hard as I can.

I love you too. So much.

Am I hallucinating again? Conjuring him up from memories? I must be. Wait a minute . . . he spoke to me. He actually spoke. He's never done that before. And, in all these years, his hands have never touched me.

This dream while I'm dying is the best one I've ever had. I never want it to end.

Can I go with you? Let me go with you. Please, I plead silently.

He stands up and reaches out to me. I place my hand in his. There's nothing I can't do when my hand is in his. I get to my feet. We smile and hold each other. Just hold each other. I exhale slowly, pain-free. And when we kiss, I'm finally warm again.

sixty-four. Tobey

Tears streamed down Callie's cheeks as she gathered her mum in her arms. I squatted beside her, my arm round her shoulders. Callie needed to know that I was there for her. I'd always be there for her.

'Tobey, what should I do?' Callie pleaded.

'Keep applying pressure to the wound.' Looking around, there was nothing I could use for makeshift bandages. Shrugging off my jacket and my long-sleeved T-shirt, I balled up the top to press against Sephy's wound. She'd been shot twice and was bleeding, front and back. I knew from past experience that the prognosis wasn't good. At least one of the bullets had passed straight through her.

Callie turned to me, her stricken expression a study in pure fear mixed with grief. Her anguish was shredding my heart. My shirt against Sephy's wound was already drenched in her blood and my hands were sticky with it.

Not good.

'Where the hell is the ambulance?' Sonny raced out into the street to meet the paramedics when they finally arrived.

Sephy gave the tiniest of sighs. Her hands fell away from her abdomen – and then she was still.

'Mum, please. Hang on. Please.' Fresh sobs wracked Callie

as she spoke. Sephy's eyes were closed, her hands at her sides were covered in her blood, but it was her expression that got to me. She looked . . . peaceful. For the first time, I truly understood the phrase 'at peace' when someone had died. Before, I'd considered it a euphemism. No one I'd seen die had ever been at peace.

'Tobey, help me,' Callie begged.

'Let me try CPR.'

Reluctantly lowering her mum to the ground, Callie shuffled over to let me get closer. Kneeling over Sephy, I started chest compressions, two sets of five, before trying to breathe air back into her lungs. And, all the time, I knew it was useless, but I had to try. I kept it up for a couple of minutes even when my wrists began to ache.

'Tobey, please, don't let her die,' Callie begged. '*Please.*'

But it wasn't my call. I searched for a pulse and put my ear to Sephy's mouth to see if I could feel or hear her breathing. Nothing.

Sitting back, I said quietly, 'Callie, I'm so sorry. She's gone.'

'No, she isn't. Don't say that. She can't be.' Her tears flowing like a waterfall, Callie laid her head on her mum's chest. I wrapped my arms round Callie, trying to gently pull her away. Sephy had been shot in the stomach and I already knew the damage the bullets of a .45 semi-automatic Dhoruba handgun could do. The two bullets Sephy had taken had surely shredded her insides.

At last the paramedics arrived. I stood up, pulling Callie with me to her feet. She clung to me, sobbing. My heart cracked in two for her. We stepped aside to give the two paramedics – a clean-shaven Nought man with sandy-brown hair tied back in a ponytail and an older bald Cross woman with flawless make-up – room. With no time for pleasantries, they immediately got to work. Sonny came to stand beside us, tears streaming down his cheeks as we watched the paramedics do all they could to revive Sephy.

To no avail.

Finally the Nought paramedic turned to us and shook his head regretfully. Callie buried her face in her hands.

'No!' Sonny's cry was ripped from him. He sank to his knees beside Sephy, seeking out and taking hold of one of her bloody hands in both of his.

'Tobey, what can I do?' said Callie, her every word jagged and anguished.

'There's nothing we can do, Callie, except let her go,' I replied softly.

I held her tighter, tears pricking at my own eyes at the grief radiating through her in waves as she wept. In that moment, I would've given anything, given up everything, even my own life, to take her pain away. But I couldn't. All I could do was hold her.

After the paramedics had taken Sephy away but before the police arrived, Callie went to the bathroom next to Eva's office. While she was gone, I used the opportunity to have a private word with Jarvis over by Eva's desk. Eva was back in her chair, her hands resting on the desk before her. When she saw me looking at her, she self-consciously dragged her wounded arm onto her lap.

'Jarvis, Eva is sunset. Tonight.' I kept my voice low so that only he and Eva could hear me. I wanted her to hear. How could I show her mercy when I knew she'd view it and exploit it as a weakness, using it to come after me and mine again? I couldn't risk that. I'll say one thing for her, she didn't cry or scream or beg. She just sat up straighter and smiled.

'Nothing personal, Eva,' I told her. 'Just business.'

Eva nodded. 'Touché.'

Prickles began to scratch at my nape. I looked across the room. Callie was watching me intently, her eyes still red from the tears she'd shed. I tried to smile at her. She didn't smile back. She scrutinized me for a moment or two longer before turning away. There's no way she could've heard what I'd just said from where she stood. There had to be at least four metres between us. I headed after her without another word. I knew Jarvis would get the job done. He always did.

'Callie, wait,' I called out.

She turned her head. 'Shall we go?'

'Yes.'

Leaving the building, we headed for my car and were pulling out just as the sound of police sirens reached us. If we waited, we'd have to spend all night answering questions at a police station and I knew Callie wanted to go to the hospital to be with her mum. As a number of squad cars screeched round the corner, I was already driving away. It was time to pull some strings and call in some favours.

The police caught up with us at the hospital as Callie sat with Sephy's body, ceaseless tears running in rivulets down her face. Though the officers were sympathetic, they insisted on interviewing us there and then. Callie, Sonny and I told the same story. Jon had pulled a gun on all of us. He'd shot Eva's bodyguard, shot Sephy and, in an ensuing struggle between him and me for the gun, it had gone off again, killing him. And all because he'd kidnapped my daughter and Callie's brother to try and extort money from me. Detective Inspector D'Souza, the officer in charge, had assured me that it was a clear case of self-defence. Once we'd given formal statements, no further action would be taken.

Just over an hour later, the police finally left us alone with our grief. I struggled desperately for the right way to act, the appropriate thing to say. I had nothing. I took Callie's hand in mine and held it tight, hoping she could somehow absorb a fraction of what I was feeling from moment to moment.

'Tobey, I want you to listen to something,' said Callie after many minutes of silence.

Before I could reply, she handed me her phone. The messages app was open and showed a number of texts from her mum.

'Mum's last message,' Callie informed me softly.

I took a closer look. The last one from Sephy was an audio message. Godsake! I didn't know how to even begin to process that. This was a voice message from someone who was no longer with us. How must Callie be feeling, to hear her mum's voice like this?

'Callie, love, are you all right?' I asked with concern.

Callie shook her head. 'No, not really. Not even close. But listen.'

Unease, like nails being dragged down a chalkboard, began to scratch at my skin. I pressed play and held the phone closer.

Hi, angel,

I'm not going to beat about the bush because Sonny is waiting outside the car and we're heading into Ava's to see Eva Foxton and I want to make sure that someone besides me knows how many blue beans make five. This message is insurance, just in case.

OK, Callie, here it is.

George Davison murdered Dan Jeavons. George is . . . was Dan's butler. I don't have any proof, but I'm convinced of it. George's daughter, Chima, is seventeen and she has a three-month-old daughter named Zelie. I checked Zelie's birth certificate online with the General Records Office and Jeavons is Zelie's dad. That man is . . . was a son of a bitch who told me that he liked his girls 'fresh'. Ew. Just thinking about it makes my skin crawl. I think Dan's mistake on the night he died was saying it when George was present, plus George was the only one Dan would allow to get behind him. I saw it with my own eyes. George gathered up coffee cups or some such from one of the bookcases behind Dan and Dan didn't even twitch. When I spoke to Patrix earlier today, he said Dan wouldn't even let him move round his desk, never mind get behind him. If you speak to the other guests at Dan's dinner party, I'm sure they'll have similar tales to tell. I guess Dan thought he had nothing to fear from someone who worked for him. Just shows how wrong a man can be.

But here's the thing, Callie: I don't know what to do with the information.

I've been warned that the case against Tobey is about to be dropped and that the police are going to come after me. Tobey still has the murder weapon that's bound to have a partial print of mine or other forensic proof that I handled it, like fibres from the blouse I wore on the night. I tried to wipe it clean with my blouse, but I know that in my haste and panic I did a lousy job. And, thanks to an anonymous tip-off, the police now know that Tobey has the real murder weapon. That juicy titbit could only have come from George. He was the only one apart from Tobey and me who knew about the letter opener. I believe this is his way of making sure the police only look in my direction in their search for Dan's killer. Well, I have no intention of going to prison for something I didn't do, nor am I going to let myself get locked up for being stupid – which yes, I was. I admit it. But, if stupidity were enough reason to lock someone up, there'd be no one left on the outside. But here's the problem – I don't want to land George in prison either. His daughter and his granddaughter need him, now more than ever. Plus, if I'm honest, I don't blame him. Dan was all kinds of wrong for what he did to Chima.

That man was always a lowlife, no-class, scum-sucking creep.

Mouthing off to me about how he preferred younger girls when George was in the room with us at the time . . . Well, it makes me wonder if Dan had some kind of death wish or was he just sticking it to George because he could? Am I sorry Dan's gone? Hell no, I am not.

Anyway, I know Zelie is Chima's child because I met them both earlier today. As soon as Zelie began crying,

Chima started to lactate and it stained her T-shirt. Been there, done that. Particularly with breast pads that don't work and get saturated within a minute and a half, rendering them pointless.

So I'm letting you know the truth, but you are NOT to do anything with this information without my permission. D'you hear me, Callie? Do not take it to the police or any other authority without passing it by me first. And please, please don't let Tobey know about my suspicions. I still don't trust that man, nor what he'd do with this knowledge. Nor do I want him retaliating against George and Chima for the death of his best friend Dan and, quite frankly, I wouldn't put it past him.

Damn but I'm tired.

This has been one hell of a day and it's not over yet. I need to get Troy home safely and then I can apply my mind to what to do about George. And I'll tell you something else, honey. Dan was going to die that night one way or another. He spent the whole evening antagonizing his guests so the atmosphere by the time the starter was served was positively febrile. George just got in first. Anyway, let's talk later when hopefully Troy is home and asleep in his own bed.

I love you, Callie. You're still my favourite daughter. Ha! See you soon.

Callie watched me intently as the message finished.

'I don't understand,' I frowned. 'George killed Dan?'

'So Mum says,' said Callie. 'What happens when the police ask you to hand over the murder weapon?'

'Then I will, but unfortunately it's been dishwashed quite a few times since Dan's party.' I shrugged. 'I left it in the kitchen and my cleaner thought it was just another piece of dirty cutlery. It's been washed regularly ever since.'

'But you still have the recording?'

'What recording?'

'The one of Mum in the study with the letter opener in her hand,' said Callie.

'What recording?' I repeated pointedly.

Callie and I looked at each other. A brief, tremulous smile flitted across Callie's lips. It didn't last long, but it was there.

'Thank you,' she said softly.

'You're welcome,' I replied. 'Though I have no idea how your mum worked out who the murderer was after just one day when the police and I have been trying to figure it out for weeks.'

'So you believe her?' asked Callie.

'Your mum wouldn't accuse anyone unless she was one hundred per cent certain,' I said.

'So what're you going to do?'

And only then did it click. Was Callie using this as some kind of test?

'If George says nothing to the police about me taking the murder weapon, then I'll keep my mouth shut,' I said. 'But, if he does try to drop me or Sephy in it, then I'll have no choice but to present the police with your mum's counterproposal.'

'Seems fair,' said Callie. 'We leave the ball in George's court, for now.'

'For now,' I agreed.

DI D'Souza had cautioned us that, even though the bodies of the female bodyguard and Jon had been removed, Ava's was now a cordoned-off crime scene. We were warned we wouldn't be able to return, which was fine by me. I didn't care if I never saw the place again. The detective didn't mention Jarvis and Eva so they must've been long gone by the time the police had secured the building and arrived at Eva's office. At least I didn't have to worry about any blowback from that.

No, the only thing I had on my mind was the woman in the chair beside me. After she shrugged away my first few attempts to put an arm round her shoulder, I gave up. But I wasn't going to leave her. She shouldn't be alone at a time like this. She needed me.

'Can I get you a tea or coffee?' I asked gently.

Callie didn't speak. She just shook her head. I took her hand again. This time, Callie didn't pull away. Her fingers were cool as they curled round mine. And there we sat, with the body of Persephone Hadley lying on the hospital bed before us, as I struggled in vain to find some words, some way, to take away Callie's pain.

sixty-five. Troy

Home. I was finally back home and it had never felt sweeter. My house. My room. Nana Meggie. I would never take any of them for granted ever again. Now I just needed Mum and Callie to return to complete my circle of relief. After a visit to the hospital to check us both and to strap up my severely sprained ankle, Libby and I sat at the kitchen table, eating the mountainous mass of scrambled eggs, plantain and beans on toast that Nana Meggie had insisted on making for us, despite the late hour. Libby was just picking at it. I was tucking in. And damn, it tasted good. One of the best meals of my life.

Nana Meggie insisted that we both fill her in on every moment from the time we were kidnapped to the time we were rescued. I let Libby do most of the talking while I carried on eating, and Libby didn't leave anything out. She even told Nana Meggie about her mum's involvement in our abduction and what had subsequently happened to her. If I'd been telling the story, I might've glossed over that bit. When Libby was finished, Nana Meggie turned to her, her expression thoughtful.

'Libby, you are welcome to stay with us until your dad sorts out a proper home for you.'

'Thank you, but I couldn't impose like that—'

'It's not an imposition,' Meggie insisted. 'It's an invitation. You certainly can't go back to your mum's house and, as you've only just reconnected with your dad, he won't be geared up to have a teenage girl staying with him permanently. Plus he'll probably be resuming his political duties soon and you shouldn't be alone. It's not healthy. So I insist that you stay with us for as long as you like.'

Libby smiled, tears shimmering in her eyes. 'Thank you, Mrs McGregor,' she whispered.

'Oh please. Call me Nana Meggie,' said my nana, smiling. 'After everything the two of you have been through, this is the best place for you, Libby. It'll be hard for anyone else to appreciate exactly what you've both had to endure over the last couple of days.'

Libby nodded, turning her head away to dash the back of one hand over her eyes. I carried on eating my plantain.

'When I think what might've happened to you,' Meggie said to us for the umpteenth time. After moving my crutches from where they were leaning against the kitchen table, she told me not to try and retrieve them myself, but to ask her to get them for me when I was ready to move. In between mouthfuls, Meggie kept giving both Libby and me spontaneous hugs. And I didn't shrug her off or complain like I might've done just a few days ago.

I couldn't believe that so little time had elapsed since Libby and I were grabbed and bundled into the back of that van. It felt like an eternity had passed, should've passed. I guess the world never stopped turning. It was what Nana Meggie called a life lesson. As she went off to get another carton of orange juice from the fridge, I took the opportunity to get a word in edgeways.

'Are you OK?' I asked Libby.

'Are you sure your mum won't mind me staying here for a while?'

'Nana Meggie doesn't mind, I don't mind and Mum won't mind – I guarantee it,' I told her. 'In fact, Mum will probably insist on it too, so just say thank you and then we can talk about something else. OK?'

'OK.' Libby smiled.

'It's not a big deal, Libby,' I told her. 'We've got more than enough space.'

'I've already given you the bedroom next to Troy's. There are fresh sheets on the bed and fresh towels in the bathroom.' Nana Meggie placed an orange-juice carton on the kitchen table between me and Libby. She added, with a frown, 'You two won't be getting up to any hanky-panky, will you?'

Libby's face whooshed red.

'First of all, Nana, no one says hanky-panky any more. And, second, no, we most certainly will not. Libby and I are friends and nothing more,' I said, putting her straight.

Honestly! Nana Meggie was so embarrassing. She had no filter. She just spoke her mind as she saw fit. 'One of the few perks of being old,' she always said.

'Well, if you decide you want to be more than friends, remember to use contraception. No glove, no love,' said Nana. 'I'm sure I could find you the odd condom or two knocking about the house if you ask nicely.'

Libby's face turned beetroot. My face was burning.

'Oh. My. God! Nana, will you please stop?'

Nana cupped my face with one hand, pinching my cheek and giving me a kiss on the forehead. 'You know I'm just teasing – though not about using contraception if things between you two head in that direction. Now, d'you two need anything else before I go back to bed?'

'No, thank you,' Libby mumbled politely.

'No. Just go. Please,' I begged.

With a chuckle, Meggie left the kitchen and headed back to her room.

'I'm sorry about that. My nana has a peculiar sense of humour when she gets going.'

'That's OK,' said Libby, her face only just resuming its original colour. 'I like her. You're lucky you have a family who tease you.'

I couldn't argue with that.

'What will you do when the dust has settled?' I couldn't help asking. 'Will you live with your dad?'

'I don't know.' Libby's fork clattered onto her plate. 'I don't know anything any more. I just want to sleep for a week and wake up to a world full of answers.'

I knew what she meant.

The front door opened. Hopefully that was Mum and Callie. One of the police officers who'd brought us home told us that Mum, Callie and Libby's dad, Tobey, had worked to secure our release. I owed each of them a big hug.

Libby retrieved my crutches and handed them to me. After she'd helped me to my feet, I headed for the hall with Libby right beside me.

Callie and Tobey were in the hall. I looked past them. They were alone. I took a closer look at my sister. She was crying. My heart dropped. A tight band started to contract round my chest.

'Callie, where's Mum?'

My sister slowly shook her head.

'Callie, answer me. Where's Mum?'

sixty-six. Callie

Beyond exhausted, I watched a watery sun rise from behind the treetops to the east of our garden. I was in Mum's house in my old bedroom. Troy had finally gone to bed, distraught and worn out from crying. And all I could do was hug him and cry with him. My eyes, like my heart and soul, were so very tired and sore. I hadn't even told Nana Meggie yet. I saw no point in waking her up to give her the terrible news that Mum had passed away. It could wait until she woke up.

Downstairs, in the kitchen, Tobey was making me the cup of herbal tea he'd insisted I needed. I was too weary to argue. My brother was safe and back home, but look at what it had cost.

He had been kidnapped and traumatized.

My mum had been shot and was gone.

And the man responsible for it all was downstairs making me a cup of tea.

He'd been in the kitchen for over ten minutes when I made my quiet way down to find out what was taking so long. As I walked towards the kitchen, I could hear Tobey talking on his mobile. Something in his tone made me halt outside the kitchen door, moving to one side so he wouldn't see me.

'Of course she did,' Tobey snapped. 'Respect where it's due – kidnapping my daughter to force me to plead guilty to Dan's murder was a stroke of genius. And, once I was in prison, no doubt it wouldn't have been long before I met with a fatal accident . . . Of course . . . Did she now? That's for definite? Dowd has disappeared . . . ? Well, Eva didn't hang about, did she? My guess is various parts of his body are littering the Albion Channel. That's one wrinkle ironed out at least . . . No, don't be stupid. This works in your favour. You can take over with no opposition . . .'

At which point, I turned round and, heartsick, headed back upstairs. I made a quick detour to check on Libby and Troy. A gentle knock, then I slowly opened Libby's bedroom door, not wishing to wake her up if she were asleep. But her bed was made and unoccupied. There was no light coming from the en-suite bathroom either. Where on earth was she? She hadn't left the house, had she? What was going on?

I went to check on Troy. The moment I opened the bedroom door, the light from the landing spilled into the room, illuminating the bed. There, on top of the duvet and both fully dressed, lay Troy and Libby, holding each other as they slept. Libby had probably heard Troy crying in his room and had gone to comfort him. Once again, tears pricked at my eyes as I watched them.

My brother, Troy. There was nothing I wouldn't do to keep him safe. Nothing.

Should I wake them up so Libby could return to her own room? After a moment's deliberation, I decided against it. They had both been to hell and back. It would take a long time before either of them felt truly secure, and ironically one of the few spaces and places they would feel safe was with each other.

I closed Troy's bedroom door behind me and headed back to my own room.

Twenty minutes later and Tobey was still downstairs. Mastering the use of the electric kettle was obviously proving to be a challenge. Tobias Durbridge . . . the driver of all the misery that had smashed into my family over the last few days. Yes, Libby's mum and Jon were the ones who had arranged for Libby to be kidnapped in the first place, but, if it hadn't been for Misty and Libby, Troy never would've been taken. Jon had thought he was on to a nice little earner, courtesy of Tobey. Eva had seen Troy and Libby's abduction as a chance to finally get rid of Tobey and to run the Outfit herself. I'd lost my mum, one of my best friends, and nearly lost my brother.

All thanks to Tobey.

After what he had put us through, I didn't regret Jon's demise. Not for a single second. Jon had had regrets about what he was doing to me, but not enough to stop.

As far as he was concerned, friendship was sweet, but money was sweeter.

And then there was Tobey.

When should I let him know that I knew what he'd said to Jarvis about Eva? When should I let him know that I could read lips? It had seemed like a useful skill for me to learn as I was teaching my brother the bastardized version of Albion sign language Sonny had taught me many moons ago. Three terms of once-a-week evening classes at a literary institute near to chambers had given me an excellent grounding that had come in very useful over the years. Through the course of my job, I also knew what declaring someone 'sunset' meant. Eva would never see another dawn – and Tobey had ordered that. As a barrister, a judicial officer, I had a duty to report what I had discovered. But I knew that Tobey had done it so that Eva couldn't come after any of us again. That was my dilemma. Tell the police or stay silent forever. After wrestling with my conscience for hours, I'd decided to keep my mouth shut. What kind of hypocrite did that make me? The biggest kind. When it came to protecting my own, I was no better than the man currently in my kitchen.

Thoughts like scalpels sliced away at everything I thought I knew about myself till there was little left. The coming of the dawn brought with it bitter self-awareness. I was a fake. What use were my so-called ideals when they were so easily discarded?

'Callie, here's your tea. I'm sorry it took so long. I got embroiled in a phone call while I was downstairs.'

Painting on a smile, I turned. 'Thanks, Tobey.'

'It's the least I could do.'

The smile fell off my face as I watched Tobey straighten up after putting the tea on my bedside table. His eyes narrowed as he caught sight of my expression. I always was rubbish at dissembling.

'Callie, what is it?' he asked.

I sighed. 'Is it true what was said? Were you the one behind Dan's whole organization? Were you the head of the Outfit?'

Tobey's expression tightened. Silence reigned between us. Just when I was about to give up on ever receiving an answer,

Tobey spoke. 'Do you want to know why I entered politics in the first place, Callie? To do some good. It was as simple and as complex as that. I know it sounds ridiculous in these cynical, jaded times, but it's the truth.'

'So that's a yes then?'

'That's a yes,' Tobey admitted. 'I was behind it, but not any more.'

'So who runs it now?'

'Jarvis, I suppose,' said Tobey with a shrug.

'Not Eva?' I asked.

'No, not her.'

'What happened to you?' I asked. 'Why did you get involved in that world in the first place?'

Tobey sat down on my double bed. 'When I became Mayor of Meadowview, I learned real fast that acquiring political power costs money, and keeping it costs even more. Dan and his entire operation were just a means to an end. I promised myself that, once I got into a position where I could make a real difference, I'd drop all the . . . bullshit activities that might've got me there in the first place.'

Was he for real? 'And you seriously thought it would be that simple?'

'I figured with the right combination of carrot, stick and a power base behind me, yes, I could make it work.'

The same tactics he'd tried on me, I realized. 'You pull that stunt a lot, don't you? How's it working out for you?'

A hint of a bitter smile tugged at the corners of Tobey's mouth. 'Like shit actually. I'm reassessing its effectiveness,' he said dryly.

'Do you have to be dropped on your head to realize it doesn't work?'

'No. Using the same strategy on you is one of the biggest regrets of my life,' said Tobey softly.

And there it was again, that sad, hungry look, like a child with no money gazing longingly into a sweetshop window. My face began to burn.

Get it together, Callie Rose. You have work to do.

'I want to thank you for everything you did to bring Troy home safely. I'm grateful—'

'Don't thank me,' Tobey interjected. 'That's my daughter and your brother. I would give my life for either of them – and for you.'

'Tobey, don't—'

'Don't what? Speak the truth?'

'Tobey, you're out from under now. If the police keep knocking on your door, you now know who really did kill Dan. I don't doubt for a second that Mum was right about that. I have it on good authority that the murder charge against you will be dropped, so you don't need me any more.'

Tobey opened his mouth to say something, only to close it again without uttering a word. We faced each other, a world of regrets rendering us both silent.

'I guess I should be going then,' Tobey said, sighing. 'Thank you for letting Libby stay here for a few days.'

'That was Nana Meggie's idea,' I told him. 'I just agreed with it, that's all.'

'Well, I'm grateful. I hope you don't mind if I come to see her as often as I can. When I have a room in my apartment and also in my official premises redecorated and reorganized for her to use, I'm hoping she'll come and live with me.'

'Like I already said, Libby can stay here just as long as she likes. I think both she and Troy will need professional help to come to terms with what happened and to try and put all this behind them.'

Tobey nodded his agreement. 'I was thinking the same thing. Maybe staying with Troy for a while would do them both some good?'

'I think so.' But I had another reason for latching onto Tobey's suggestion. Once Libby went to live with Tobey permanently, there'd be no reason for him and me to meet again. Tobey travelled in higher circles than I did. Is this what I wanted, to only see him on a TV screen?

Mum's words rang in my ears.

Save him.

I couldn't do that from a distance.

Mum . . . Oh, Mum . . .

Tears pricked at my eyes all over again.

'And you? Will you be OK, Callie? How're you feeling?'

'D'you want me to be honest?'

'Always.'

'Lonely,' I admitted. 'I feel like I've lost my best friend.'

'I'm so sorry about your mum, more than words can say. She was . . . one of a kind.'

A smile flickered across my face, but didn't settle. 'I'm sure Mum would thank you for that, but I wasn't talking about her. I was talking about you. It feels like you and I have finally run out of road.'

Tobey nodded slowly. So he was feeling it too. He said

with a sad smile, 'Maybe I'm just destined to go through this life alone.'

'So we both get to be lonely apart? Sounds like hell.'

Silence.

'Is it true that your career is in jeopardy because of me?' Tobey asked unexpectedly.

I stared. 'Where did you hear that?'

'Jade, my PA, told me of a rumour that you'd ruined your career and any chance of becoming a circuit judge because you chose to defend me. Is that true?'

I shrugged. 'You needed my help.'

Tobey sighed, briefly closing his eyes. 'If the case against me is dropped, will that make a difference?'

I doubted it. I'd pinned my colours to Tobey's mast. There were those in the judiciary who'd never forget or forgive that. 'Who knows? Maybe.'

'I see.' Tobey wasn't fooled for a second. 'Your mum . . . she said something to you about me just before . . . I thought I heard my name.' His measured tone couldn't disguise the unease behind the words. 'Would you mind telling me what she said?'

I considered. One of Mum's favourite sayings played in my head – a wise woman tells some of what she knows, not all of what she knows. 'Mum said, "He needs you." But she was mistaken. You don't need me or anyone.'

Pause.

'Your mum was right,' said Tobey quietly.

This halting conversation between us was pure torture.

'Tobey, if I ask you a question, will you give me an honest yes-or-no answer?'

Tobey ran his fingers through his hair and waited in silence for me to continue.

'Do you love me?'

'Yes.' His reply was immediate. 'Always have, always will.'

Did he even know what the word meant?

I took a step towards him.

'Do you still want to marry me?'

His eyes narrowed in confusion. 'Yes.'

Because I had notable credentials? An acceptable CV? Because the judgemental, unforgiving bitch had a slightly soiled but mainly impressive pedigree? Because politically I'd look good on his arm? Or because I had a place in his heart?

Another step.

'Tell me the truth, Tobey. Are you in any way still involved in the running of Dan's organization?'

Pause. I held my breath, waiting for his answer.

'Tangentially.'

Breathe in, breathe out. Start as you mean to go on, Callie.

'Yes or no, Tobey?' I raised my foot, ready to step backwards. Tobey didn't miss the movement.

Pause. Then he replied. 'Yes.'

The truth. At last.

'Would you give up that world if I asked you to?'

'Yes.' Said with no hesitation this time.

A lie or the truth?

Another step forward. I now stood directly before him.

'Would you give up your political career if I asked you to?'

No answer. I was strangely relieved that he hadn't answered immediately. It made his previous answers slightly more plausible. Slightly.

'Tobey, do you still think you can do some good in the world of politics?'

'I know I can,' he said eagerly. 'And, with you at my side, we'd be unstoppable.'

I reached out and took Tobey's hands in mine.

'Would you give up that world if I asked you to choose between it and me?'

'Which world?' Pause. 'You know what? It doesn't matter. I'd give it all up for you. The answer's yes.'

I tilted my head as I looked into Tobey's intense brown eyes, trying to work out if he truly meant it.

'I want you to give up any and every part you play in Dan's world,' I told him. 'I don't want to spend my time with you worrying about some gangland rival putting a bullet in the back of your head. I can't live like that. I won't.'

'I promise,' Tobey said, almost before the last word had left my mouth. 'It's done.'

The truth or a lie?

'Ask me then.'

'Ask you what?' Tobey frowned.

'Ask me to marry you,' I said.

Tobey looked stunned, but only for a moment. 'Callie, this is just your grief talking. What kind of man would I be if I took advantage of you when you're feeling so hurt and lost?'

'You're not taking advantage, Tobey. I know what I'm doing. So, if you still want me, ask me to marry you.'

'Callie, I—'

'Offer going once.'

'Damn it, Callie—'

'Going twice,' I warned.

Tobey took a deep breath. 'Callie Rose, I love you with my whole heart and I promise there won't be a single day when you doubt it – or me. I'll never give you reason to regret taking a chance on me. Callie Rose Hadley, will you marry me?'

'Yes, Tobias Durbridge. Yes, I'll marry you, but on one condition.'

'Anything.'

'You must promise to always be honest with me; when I ask you a question, I need to know you'll respect me enough to give me a truthful answer, no matter how painful. Is it a deal?'

Tobey didn't reply. Instead, he pulled me into his arms and kissed me, his lips hard and soft on mine.

'Here's to honesty,' I said, smiling, when our kiss finally ended.

Tobey swept me off my feet and spun me round twice before letting my feet touch the ground again, laughing all the while. The smile he directed at me was pure happiness. He thought he'd won. Endgame and checkmate. I was going to prove him wrong.

'I love you so much, Callie. You and me, babe, against the world.' He replayed our old motto like it was the only thing required to roll back the years.

I cupped his cheek, stroking the soft, scratchy stubble beneath my fingers, absorbing who and what he truly was through each of my senses – the taste of him still on my tongue, the faint aroma of soap and aftershave mixed with perspiration, his ruffled hair where his fingers had swept through it, the honeyed sound of his words in my ears.

Tobias Durbridge, I'm looking at you and, though it took too long, I finally see you.

'You and me, Tobey,' I agreed. 'The two of us, side by side, against the world.'

THREE MONTHS LATER

sixty-seven. Tobey

Hallelujah! I still couldn't believe it. After all these years, Callie and I were finally together. Officially. Openly. Obviously. Together. After Jon's revelation about me running Dan's organization, I was so sure I'd lost her for good. Callie's moral compass pointing to true north was as predictable, as inevitable as the daily sunrise.

Yet she wanted to be with me. I'd asked her to marry me – albeit at her instigation – and she said yes! What we'd both lived through had left us bruised and bloodied, but unbowed. I remember our wedding like it was yesterday. As I watched Callie Rose slowly walk down the aisle towards me, it felt as if everything I'd ever dreamed of was finally within my grasp. I would've gladly lived through that horrific Halloween night again if it led to this outcome. I wouldn't change a thing.

Except for what happened to Sephy.

How I wished, with everything within me, that Sephy hadn't died. If I could, I would have taken her place in a heartbeat. Sephy might not have liked me very much – or at all – but that didn't mean I couldn't still admire her. Her strength, her forthright nature, that way she had of setting you at ease or putting you on your arse. I always knew where

I stood with her. And, more than anything else, what endeared her to me the most was that she was Callie's mum. It was as simple and as complicated as that. I knew all about Sephy's past. Without her and her bravery, there would be no Callie Rose. And my life would just be an eternal bleak wilderness.

Even when Callie first said yes to marrying me, I still didn't quite believe that it would happen. I couldn't shake the feeling that I was taking advantage of her at her most vulnerable. I'd taken it slow, giving her a chance to back out and change her mind – even though I knew my heart would wither if she did. I was even prepared to wait a year – or however long it might take. I couldn't, *wouldn't* marry Callie unless she was one hundred per cent down with the idea. I loved her too much to do that to her, to both of us. What if we got married and Callie slowly awoke to the fact that she didn't love me the way I loved her? The thought of her eyeing me with contempt for rushing her into sharing a life with me turned my blood to icy slush for weeks. But Callie had very patiently reassured me, over and over, that being married to me was what she wanted most in the world. The clincher had been when she told me that her mum's last words in full were, 'He needs you. Save him.'

'Tobey, believe me. Mum would've approved,' Callie told me.

After that, my last remaining doubts were swept away.

To think that only a few months ago my life was a shitshow. I'd had a murder charge hanging over my head, threatening to decapitate me. I was in love with my lawyer who I thought despised me. My daughter, with whom I'd only just reconnected, had been forcibly taken from me. Now look. The court case against me had been dropped and, when the details were finally released into the public domain, my popularity rating actually rose. I had the nation's sympathy for 'triumphing in the face of adversity'. It's what Jade, my PA, called a bonus bounce 'sympathy rating'. It wouldn't last, but I was milking it for all it was worth. Corrupt and crooked ministers caught with their hands in the cookie jar had been unceremoniously sacked and my popularity rating rose. My daughter now lived with me full-time and my popularity rating rose. Callie Rose Hadley, my childhood sweetheart, was now my wife – and my popularity rating shot through the roof. There was a peculiar peace that swept over me every time I looked at Callie. Peculiar because I wasn't used to it. She only had to smile at me—

Yeah, OK, I admit it. I was helplessly, hopelessly lovestruck. Always had been, even when I denied it. I needed Callie like I needed air to breathe, but what had permanently sealed my fate was how much Callie needed me too. When her mother died, Callie had leaned on me until she could begin to stand upright again. For the first time in my life, I felt like my presence mattered to someone for more than just money's sake. Callie needed someone who would always put her first – and, with me, that's what she had.

Sometimes a nagging doubt or two whispered in my ear that I should be on my guard, that my life was too perfect. Even George Davison had kept his mouth shut so I'd never had to point the police in his direction. I was grateful for that as I was still convinced that Callie had let me listen to her mum's last voice message as some kind of test of my loyalty, to see whether or not I'd respect her mum's wishes. It'd been tempting to tip off the police anonymously about George. After all, there were still those who believed that somehow I'd been involved in Dan's death. George being arrested and charged with Dan's murder would've put a stop to the malicious gossip once and for all. But how could I? Callie was no fool. She'd know that any anonymous tip could only have come from one source.

Luckily for George, I wasn't about to disappoint Callie.

Before Libby had been kidnapped and held for ransom, my predominant, enduring trait had been cynicism. I expected the worse and that's usually what I got. Maybe because that was all I was looking for. But I didn't feel that way any more. Now I had real faith that I genuinely could make a difference, that I could make life better for most people in Albion. I had faith in all I could do and who I could be. I had faith in the new me, and in Callie, and the two of us together. I had faith that, with Callie by my side, we'd be able to move mountains. I had faith that I would love her for all eternity. I'd given her my whole heart and, if she truly trusted me with hers, then I could not only fly but *soar*.

For the first time, I had faith.

And hopefully, one day, someday, the guilt I felt at what had happened to Callie's mum would if not disappear, then at least dissipate. Because, even though Callie had never reproached me with a single look, word or action, we both knew Sephy's death was on me. Sephy had stepped in front of Jon's bullet to save me. I would never forget that. In saving my life, Sephy and her daughter now owned me eternally – heart, body and soul. It was now my lifetime mission to prove to Callie that her mum's sacrifice hadn't been wasted. Life was good – and it could only get better. Hallelujah!

The intercom button on my phone began to flash. With a sigh, I pressed it.

'Yes, Jade?'

'Sir, the Defence Secretary has arrived for your three-thirty meeting,' my personal assistant announced.

'Send her in,' I said. 'And, Jade, I'd love a cup of coffee, please.'

'Yes, sir.'

sixty-eight. Troy

It'd been snowing almost non-stop for the past three days and was now so thick it was up to my calves. A serious winter shout. Hopefully it would last a while. I loved fresh, falling snow. There was something so quiet, so calming about it. I was out in the back garden, sitting on a swing, using my heels to twist my body and the swing's chain round and round until it couldn't be tightened any more. Then I lifted my feet, closed my eyes and let the chain unravel at speed, spinning me in the process. I hadn't done this since I was a kid. Now I couldn't stop. Though the snowfall was taking a temporary break, the clouds above were a curious deep grey-white, perfectly still and waiting for just the right moment to dump more snow onto the world below. Knowing I didn't have long before either Nana Meggie or my sister called me inside, I was making the most of my solitude. It didn't last long.

'May I join you?'

Libby was standing before me and I'd never even heard her coming. Why didn't her boots crunch in the snow to warn me of her approach? I looked behind her and saw the reason. She'd walked in my footsteps so she wouldn't have to battle to make her own. I indicated the swing beside me.

Libby brushed off the snow that was centimetres thick and sat down. We looked at each other as we both rocked backwards and forward, not swinging, not twisting, just oscillating erratically.

'Are you OK? You've been really quiet since the wedding,' said Libby.

I shrugged.

'Are you still not OK with my dad and your sister getting married?'

'It's not that I'm not OK with it,' I denied, 'but why the rush?'

'Maybe Callie's pregnant?'

'That's no reason to rush into marriage. Callie knows that. Mum and her dad, Callum McGregor, were never married.' And there it was: the oh-so-familiar lump in my throat and the sting that came to my eyes whenever I thought about Mum.

Now it was Libby's turn to shrug. 'Maybe what happened to all of us three months ago made them decide not to wait for their happiness, but to grab it with both hands while they still could.'

Guess I could understand that. If nothing else, I'd learned the hard way that life was short so every opportunity should be snatched up and held tight, and those we love should be held tighter.

'Now that my dad is married to your sister, we're official!' said Libby.

'Officially what?' I asked.

'A soap opera!' she chuckled.

She had a point. My expression remained sombre. Her smile faded. 'Troy, what's wrong? Talk to me.'

Silence.

I sighed and admitted, 'My head is still all over the place. Ever since Mum died, I choke up when I think about what happened to her. And then I get so angry for the same reason. I miss her so much.'

'I understand. You should hold on to that, no matter how much it hurts, because it's coming from a good place. D'you wanna know something? And I wouldn't admit this to anyone else, but I . . . I don't miss my mum. Not even a little bit. D'you wanna hear a joke though? They say you can't miss what you've never had, but that's not true because I long for what we should've had but didn't. Nana Meggie has been more of a mother to me than my own mum ever was. Every day, I'm reminded of what Misty did to me. How money mattered more to her than her own flesh and blood. I'm glad she's gone. I'm better off without her.' Libby looked thoughtful for a moment. 'Does that make me a bitch?'

'No, it makes you honest. And human.'

'Your mum was a good person, Troy. And she's still with you as long as you remember her.'

Digging our heels into the snow, we slowly twisted back and forth.

'How d'you feel about what happened to Sonny?' asked Libby.

I shrugged. How was I supposed to feel? Five days after Mum died, Sonny was seriously injured when his car was hit by a lorry on the motorway. Apparently, the lorry driver had been texting at the time he ploughed into the back of him. As far as I knew, Sonny was still in a coma. His crash had made the news for a couple of days, with tributes being paid by the many bands and musicians he'd worked with over the years as if they'd all decided the man was never going to regain consciousness.

Sonny had been distraught when Mum died. He'd reached out to me, leaving messages via Callie, but I'd completely ignored him. What had he been thinking about before his accident? About Mum? Me? What he'd lost? What he'd got away with? Had his mind been on his driving or miles away from it? I guess I'd never know. I put it down to one of those unlucky accidents that karma sometimes dealt out like a losing hand at cards.

'Are you still convinced you were right about him?' said Libby.

I nodded.

'Have you talked to Collette about him?'

I shook my head.

'Are you going to?'

'Maybe. Maybe not.' As far as I was concerned, Sonny was currently dining at Karma Café. According to Mum, everyone got to eat at least one meal there in their lifetime.

Libby and I continued twisting back and forth on our swings. Sonny wanted to marry Mum and it didn't happen. Tobey wanted to marry Callie and it did.

They'd got married in a quiet civil ceremony with Nana Meggie, me and Libby, and Tobey's mum and sister, Jessica, as the only witnesses, apart from Tobey's bodyguards. And, all the way through the wedding service, the only thing I could think of was what Mum would've made of Tobey and Callie getting married so quickly.

Tobey was back to being PM and all was right in his

world. He was at work again and already making his mark. The guy was in the news practically every other day. Not that I paid much attention to his political doings, but a number of high-ranking officials had been arrested for fraud and corruption under his watch and he was spending vast amounts of taxpayers' money on improving the health service, properly resourcing schools, providing free school meals to all those who couldn't afford them and actively seeking to reduce Albion's carbon footprint. According to Callie, it wasn't making him popular with the traditionalists and a number of influential big businesses. Callie and Tobey thought I hadn't noticed, but over the last month our security detail had been stepped up. Libby and I were now escorted to school by two close-protection officers rather than one and, if we left the house, we always had an escort. Always. I didn't mind that. Libby did. I'd take being escorted everywhere over another dank basement any and every day of the week.

Callie had taken a year's sabbatical from her job and her permanent home was now with Meggie, Libby and me. Tobey lived in his town apartment during the week and came home at weekends – and Callie appeared OK with that. She sometimes spent weekdays with Tobey in his apartment, more and more frequently of late. But not all the time. Strange way to start married life, but she and Tobey insisted they were totally OK with it. Callie was even OK with having security actually living in our house twenty-four-seven and she usually loathed that kind of thing.

Libby and I both kicked at the snow, watching it fan upwards before us, deep in thought.

'Callie and my dad – d'you think they love each other?' asked Libby from out of nowhere.

'Would they have got married if they didn't?'

Libby gave me a studied look. My cheeks grew warm as she scrutinized me.

'What?' I frowned.

Libby shook her head. 'Nothing.'

But something was eating at her.

'What?' I asked again.

'How about the two of us doing something to help them spend more time together?' she said. 'It can't be much fun for either of them with Dad in town five days a week. He only gets to see us at weekends.'

Ah, so that's what was playing on her mind.

'Libby, if my sister is OK with it, then what's the problem?' I said.

'Couldn't we do something to help?'

'Like what?'

'I dunno.' Libby's eyes lit up. 'Maybe I could pretend to be ill so he'd come home more often—'

Ohmigod! 'Liberty, don't you dare.' I grimaced. 'I'm not mucking around. Don't even think about pulling a stunt like that.'

'But I want to help—'

'Did either of them ask you to interfere? How about we try to fix ourselves first and then maybe move on from there?' I suggested.

Libby sighed. 'Yeah, OK. I suppose so.'

I shook my head. 'Libby, I mean it. Don't get involved. Let Callie and your dad handle their own lives, OK?'

'I want Dad to be happy twenty-four-seven, not just for two days a week.' Libby's expression was so earnest, it made me uncomfortable.

'I want Callie to be happy too, but that's up to them, not us.' I said. 'Besides, I have enough troubles on my own plate without taking on theirs as well.'

'Like what?'

Like getting my head together. 'Like what to do with my life?' I sighed. 'Before we were kidnapped, I thought I knew. Exams and uni, a career, two holidays a year – I had it all worked out.'

'And now?'

'Now I can't seem to decide anything.'

'Collette says that's to be expected,' Libby reminded me.

Collette was the psychologist that Callie and Tobey had insisted Libby and I needed to see on a regular basis after we'd been rescued. Initially, I'd gone to see Collette kicking and screaming. A psychologist? I mean, please. What good would talking to a stranger do? But, after a few weeks, I had to admit that she was helping me deal with everything that had occurred, especially with what happened to Mum.

Sometimes I only had to close my eyes and I could almost feel Mum giving me one of her bear hugs. When I remembered the way I used to shrug her off . . . Oh, what I'd give just to be held once more, to see her smile at me, to hear her voice. Even though it wasn't my fault, I still partly blamed myself for Mum's death. If I hadn't allowed myself to be dragged into that van— Logically, I told myself I did all I could, fought as hard as I was able, but logic wasn't cutting it.

Something else for me to share with Collette. Knowing

that everything I said was in confidence made it easier to eventually open up and speak the truth that even Libby wasn't aware of. The truth about the fear that still lived within me, sometimes pressing so hard against my chest that I could hardly breathe. I should've fought back harder when I was bundled into the back of that van. My depression at how helpless and hopeless I'd been when alone with Libby in that basement was all I deserved – at least that's what I told myself. And yes, I wanted to rage at Libby for what her family had put us through, rage that I'd fought hard to bury while we were in the basement, but which sometimes overtook me when I was alone. I'd started boxing lessons at my local gym and bought myself a free-standing punchbag for my bedroom that I used every day – but combined they weren't enough. Some days it felt like there was something inside me just waiting to explode and then God help all those around me when it did.

That's what terrified me the most.

Only last week, Ayo had snuck up behind me and put his hands round my neck, something he'd done a hundred times before. Instinctively, I'd turned and swung at him, knocking him to the ground. It took Mr Brewster and my friend Zane to pull me off. And then I saw what I'd done . . . the blood pouring from Ayo's broken nose . . . Mrs Paxton had informed me that I was lucky not to be permanently excluded from school. Any other head and I would've been.

Flashbacks of the basement haunted me. Collette warned me it would take a while to be OK with that.

'Memories of what you went through will be with you for the rest of your life and, if you expect otherwise, you're going to be disappointed,' she said. Not what I wanted to hear, though I appreciated the honesty. 'But you will find a way to live with those memories, to manage them. And, most of all, you need to tell yourself every day that what happened to you and your mum was not your fault.'

So that's what I did each and every morning before I got out of bed. And there were some days, the odd day, when I almost believed it.

I looked up from kicking at the snow to find Libby watching me.

'D'you ever think about the two of us trapped in that basement?' I asked.

'Just all the time,' Libby said with a shrug.

'I still can't believe we were in that hellhole for less than forty-eight hours. It felt like . . . an eternity.'

'Maybe the further in time we get away from it, the more it will fade?' said Libby.

I sighed. 'D'you believe that?'

'On good days.'

'And on bad days?'

'Then I hold on to that belief even harder,' Libby replied. 'Troy, things will get better. You know that, right?'

I didn't answer. I thought of Mum: the way she smiled with her eyes, not her mouth, the terrible sentimental songs she loved to sing, her rib-crushing hugs, her raucous laugh, her bellowing shouts, her nagging when I left my clothes all over the floor, the way she sometimes smelled of the floral perfume I bought her last Crossmas, the way her voice got lower, not higher, when she was annoyed with me. So many things – some so trivial, others colossal – all of them Mum.

I could fill a whole book with the things I missed about her. But, for all the hurt I felt, the world kept turning and life went on. Mum would say that's what made life so special, something to be embraced each and every day.

'Why did you drop out of the head-student race?' Libby asked.

'It just wasn't important any more,' I replied. 'Congrats on winning unopposed.'

Libby smiled. 'Thanks. Most of the teachers now hate me though.'

I nodded with admiration. 'Especially Mr Pike!'

During her very first speech as head girl, Libby had revealed to the whole school just how Mr Pike had tried to cheat during the head-student election vote count. Mr Pike had actually stood up, spluttering and blustering, and calling Libby a barefaced liar, until Libby had called on Mrs Baxter, the Biology teacher, to back her up. You could've heard a pin drop as Mrs Baxter looked round the assembly hall and then at Mr Pike before answering.

'Liberty is telling the truth,' Mrs Baxter announced at last. 'Mr Pike tried to solicit my help in electoral fraud. He wanted the two of us to discount all votes made for Liberty or Troy Ealing and install someone else of his choosing as head student instead. I refused.'

'That's a lie!' roared Mr Pike. 'Mrs Paxton, don't believe a word Monifa says. She's lying.' He turned to Mrs Baxter, his expression – his whole body – blazing with scorn. 'But what else can you expect from a blanker?'

The gasp that went round the hall at Mr Pike's words created a vacuum almost strong enough to bring down the ceiling. Mr Pike froze when he realized what he'd said out loud, before storming out of the hall. The next day he was gone. Mrs Paxton announced in assembly that Mr Pike was no longer employed at the school. Everyone in the hall had cheered, including the teachers!

And since then Libby had been making her presence felt. One of her first acts was to put up posters all over school apologizing for some of the views she'd expressed in the past, assuring everyone that she would be a head girl working for the benefit of *all* students. I must admit I thought that was kind of brave of her. She set up a student council, with a proper paid counsellor who worked at the school twice a week, where those being bullied or those who had physical and mental issues could come and talk to someone. Libby didn't think twice about reporting all bullies to Mrs Paxton if they refused to check their attitude after she'd warned them. Nor were the teachers safe. She didn't hesitate to call any of them out for dodgy rhetoric or favouritism. And, ironically, the more she pissed off some of the teachers and students with her relentless scrutiny, the more popular she became. She was a social justice warrior, out and about and full up in people's faces and proud of it.

Me? I was the opposite. I moved round school like a ghost.

'Troy, I'm worried about you.'

'I'm OK, or I will be,' I said quietly. 'Hopefully.'

'That's what you've got to hang on to,' said Libby.

'Do you know what you wanna do when you leave school?' I asked. 'Are you still gonna be a doctor?'

'That's the plan. I was thinking I might be a psychiatrist.'

I nodded. 'I can see you doing that. You'd be a good one.'

'I think so. What about you? Are you still weighing up options?'

I shrugged.

'Troy, you can't spend the rest of your life on autopilot. You're allowed to laugh. And live. And love.'

'It's just . . . all my dreams and ambitions, they feel so small.'

'But they're yours and that makes them unique in the universe and that's what gives them their worth. Life is for living. I learned that the hard way. And, from everything you've told me about your mum, I know she'd say the same thing too.'

Startled, I looked at Libby. I'd never thought of it quite that way before. Being kidnapped had made me feel small and insignificant, but maybe Libby had a point.

We carried on kicking up snow.

sixty-nine. Callie

I sat at the kitchen table, sipping a mug of jasmine green tea, feeling strangely untethered. I'd felt this way since Mum's passing. Funerals were meant to be a time of closure, a chance to share memories and say a final goodbye. Taking place a week after her death, Mum's funeral had brought closure but no peace. Aunt Minerva had wept throughout the entire service. Nana Meggie and I had barely kept it together. And Troy had been so withdrawn. He'd barely said a word and that had been his default state ever since. The rest of Mum's family and friends had given their earnest and sincere condolences, shaking my hand or kissing my cheek until I was ready to scream. I'd got through it, but only just. Without Meggie – and Tobey, I admit it – I would've fallen apart.

One positive since Mum died was that the charge of perverting the course of justice levelled against me had been dropped, along with the murder charge against Tobey, through lack of evidence. I still believed that my ex, Gabriel Moreland, had brought the action against me, but I had no proof. Besides, it hardly mattered now. I'd dodged that particular bullet and, since I'd announced I was taking a year's sabbatical from work, Gabe could no longer get to me. Not that anyone in my law chambers expected me to return when my year was up. Their reasoning? I was the wife of the PM. Why on earth would I want to return to work? Only Sol and I knew I had nothing to return to. My decision to defend Tobey in court meant my reputation was irrevocably tainted.

That wasn't good enough for me so I was seeking new paths to forge. Being the PM's wife certainly made that easier. In fact, I was seriously considering a new career in politics and was taking a keen interest in Tobey's work – all his meetings and briefings. I was soaking in that world like a thirsty sponge, even beginning to drop the occasional hint to Tobey about working with him. So far he'd brushed all such suggestions aside, but my mind was made up. Over the next couple of years, Tobey was going to teach me everything he knew about the political world. He just didn't know it yet.

I took another sip of my tea, remembering my wedding day two weeks ago. Even though it'd been bitterly cold outside, the orangery of our home had been decorated to look as springlike as possible – the time of new beginnings. Sol had walked me down the aisle and Tobey's sister, Jessica, had been his best woman. It had been one of the few highlights in a dark winter. Tobey and I had agreed to delay our honeymoon until the summer holidays so that we could take Troy and Libby with us. They both needed to feel they belonged to our new family, which I believed with all my heart they did.

Libby was a revelation. I didn't expect to take to her as much as I did. She certainly spoke her mind. She had no trouble standing her ground when she believed she was right, and was upfront in admitting when she got things wrong. I liked that. Nor was she afraid to stand up to her father and tell him when she thought he was acting like a plank. Some of their arguments got so heated that I had to intervene to cool the temperature between them. Libby was so much like him, too much sometimes, but it was good to watch the relationship between them blossom and grow.

After Mum's funeral, Troy had filled me in on Libby's home life with Misty and, quite frankly, what he'd revealed had given me the chills. I suspected he probably only knew a fraction of what she'd had to endure with her mother. Sometimes I looked at her and grew wistful about what might have been. She might've been my daughter with Tobey, rather than Misty's, but such thoughts never lingered. I wouldn't let them. Libby was with us now and, by a twisted quirk of fate, I was her mother. Whatever else happened, she needed to be protected from fallout and cherished, and I was determined to see to that.

Especially in light of a conversation I'd overheard that had taken place in the kitchen between Troy and Libby a few days after Mum's funeral.

'Libby, let's get something straight,' said my brother. 'You and I are not family. We're not even friends. Not really. We're just two people who went through the same hell together and now we occupy the same space. I don't have a problem with that, but don't make us out to be more than we are.'

'I was only—'

'I don't wanna hear it. Stop asking me how I'm doing.' Troy began to raise his voice. 'Stop asking me if there's anything you can get me or do for me. Stop following me around like some lost puppy and, for the love of God, stop looking at me like I'm about to melt into a puddle. I'm not.

You want to do something for me? Bring my mum back. If you can't manage that, then stay the hell out of my way.'

That's when I'd entered the room to stop the argument from escalating. Troy gave me a filthy look that had practically seared the hairs off my skin before storming out. Libby hung her head, fighting back tears.

'Libby, give him time.' I raised her chin so I could look her in the eyes. 'Troy's hurting. We all are. Just be patient, OK?'

She nodded.

After Mum's funeral, Troy and Libby had taken a week's break before they both started back at school. Nana Meggie said it was best to re-establish some kind of regular routine for them so we took her advice. But, over the weeks, Troy and I had grown apart, becoming more distant, and I didn't know what to do about that.

I had hoped that my wedding a couple of weeks ago might've brightened Troy's mood, but if anything it had the opposite effect. The only thing that had spoiled an otherwise near-perfect day was that my brother had chosen not to say a single spontaneous word to me. Not one. He was hurting and, by marrying Tobey, I had hurt him more.

As if hearing the direction of my thoughts, Troy walked into the kitchen, the phone in his hand taking all his attention. I watched him for a few moments, then said, 'Hey, Troy. How's my favourite brother?'

Troy stiffened, his demeanour clouding over. He turned on his heels, ready to leave the room.

'Troy, please,' I called after him, unexpectedly on the verge of tears. 'Can we just talk? Please. It's what Mum would've wanted.'

It was low bringing Mum into it, but I'd tried everything else. From the moment Tobey and I had exchanged rings at our wedding ceremony, Troy hadn't said one word to me that hadn't been strictly necessary. I couldn't remember the last time we'd had a proper conversation. We were both grieving for Mum apart when we should've been together.

Troy spun round and launched in. 'How could you, Callie? How could you marry that man?'

'Troy, please—'

'Callie, he's no good. Everyone says so,' Troy told me. 'He only cares about himself and now he's got everything he's ever wanted – you, our house and respectability.'

'Troy, which rag did you read that in?'

'It's true, isn't it?'

'Troy, Tobey is the PM. He didn't need me to gain any of those things,' I said.

'Then why did he marry you?'

'Because he loves me.'

'And why did you marry him?'

I walked over to my brother. What I was about to say was for his ears and his alone. 'Troy, listen carefully. I married Tobey because Mum's last words to me were "save him".'

Troy stared, stunned. 'She said that?'

I nodded. 'She did.'

'Save him doesn't mean marry the bastard,' said Troy. 'If it wasn't for him, Mum . . . Mum would still be here.'

I cupped my brother's cheek. 'Mum died saving his life. Doesn't that mean she considered his life worth something?'

'I . . . I don't know. All I can see is that he's here – and she isn't. How do I deal with that, Callie?'

'The same way I do – one day at a time,' I replied.

'Which works for you because you're with him. He obviously means more to you than Mum ever did—'

Inside me, everything stilled. It was the closest I'd ever come in my life to slapping my brother. Hard. Placing my hands on his shoulders, I said quietly, 'Troy, I know you're hurting, but don't you ever, for as long as you live, say that to me again. D'you hear?'

Shamefaced, Troy nodded. 'I'm sorry, sis. I just don't understand how you can say you love that man.'

'Don't put words in my mouth. I married Tobey because I'm following Mum's instructions,' I said softly. 'To the letter.'

'Never mind saving him, what about you?' asked my brother.

'Troy, you're not hearing me. I'm. Following. Mum's. Orders.'

Troy frowned, the creases around his mouth deepening by degrees. His expression slowly cleared.

'Neither of us will *ever* forget how Mum died, or why,' I said. 'I intend to make sure that others don't forget either. That's where my head and my heart reside and that's where they'll stay until Mum's last request is fulfilled. You get me?'

'I get you. I've got your back, Callie.' Unexpectedly, Troy kissed my cheek. We both shared a smile – united in our hurt, our understanding. Our cause.

'Be careful, sis,' Troy whispered in my ear.

'Always,' I replied.

Enough said.

seventy. Libby

The whole country had endured a full week of snow, but now it was almost gone. In the back garden, the odd leftover patch of silver-white crystals reflected the moonlight, but the rest of the garden was just a wash of darkness, only one small part illuminated by the kitchen light that was still on downstairs. Dad was home for the weekend and I'd left him in the kitchen making Callie a cup of one of her assortment of herbal teas. I'd tried a couple of different ones and they were nasty. Closing my bedroom curtains, I climbed into bed.

Wasn't it strange how life worked out? A few months ago, I couldn't look at myself in the mirror without hating what I saw. Now I was OK with what shone back at me. I was definitely a work in progress, but I liked the direction in which I was travelling. My life wasn't perfect, but it was so much better than it used to be. Even Troy seemed happier these days. Less restless, more focused. And he and his sister were talking again – thank goodness. For a while there, after Callie and Dad's wedding, Troy didn't have much of anything to say to anyone. I was so glad he was coming round to the idea of the two of them being together.

Every time Dad came home, he was always so happy to see all of us – but mostly Callie. Sometimes I caught him looking at her with an amazed smile on his face like he genuinely couldn't believe his luck. And the two of them were always cuddling and kissing. Every time Troy saw them, he'd gag and say, 'Get a room, you two!' Dad just laughed and told him to get used to it, which would make Troy gag even harder.

So this was what living with a real family was like.

Look at my bedroom. It was all mine, with no lock on the door because none was required. No one ever entered without knocking and waiting for an invitation to come in first. I was loving my new home and because of that even Heathcroft High wasn't so bad. When Troy and I first returned to school, it hadn't taken long for his friends to notice the change in him. In fact, it hadn't taken long for most of our year to start whispering about him and me behind our backs. And Troy ignored it all. He'd grown good at that. None of them knew what had happened to us. It had been very discreetly hushed up. No news, no interviews, no drama. All they knew at school was that Troy and I had disappeared around the same time and then reappeared, also around the same time.

At lunchtimes, he ate alone or with me and no one else. That didn't go unnoticed either. Somehow Troy's friends got it into their heads that I was responsible for his downbeat mood. A few weeks after we'd returned to school, I was cornered. Ayo, Zane, Meshella and Femi surrounded me as I was heading to my next class, pushing me until my back was against a wall and they were all in my face.

'What's going on with Troy?' asked Ayo, getting straight to the point.

'What did you do to him?' Meshella asked, eyes narrowed.

'I don't know what you're talking about.' I tried to get past them, but Ayo wasn't having it. He pushed me back against the wall again so hard that I dropped all the books I'd been carrying, but no way was I going to bend and pick them up. For the first time since they'd surrounded me, fear darted like fireflies inside my chest. Troy had changed and they were blaming me.

And the worst thing about it was they were right.

'We've been watching the two of you whispering together at lunch,' said Femi. 'You couldn't stand each other before and now you're best mates? I don't think so.'

'You need to tell us what's going on.' By now, quite a crowd had gathered behind the initial four who were glowering at me with undisguised dislike. Troy was one of the most popular people at our school. I wasn't. It was that simple.

Without warning, there came a commotion in the crowd, then Meshella, followed by Ayo, were pulled away from me. Troy moved to stand beside me, bristling at the crowd around us.

'Someone wanna tell me what's going on?' he said, his words like icicles sharpened to a fine point.

Some of those in the crowd started to step back. Hell, if he hadn't been standing right next to me, I might've backed off too. Troy. Was. Pissed.

'Troy, we're just worried about you,' Meshella tried.

'And you thought surrounding my sister and threatening her was the right way to show that?' said Troy.

Sister?

The word rippled through our audience. Even I stared at Troy. He'd never called me that before. In fact, after he'd informed me that we weren't family or even friends, I never expected to hear such a thing from him. Tears stung as I turned back to those surrounding us.

'That's right. My sister Callie married into Libby's family, which makes Libby my sister too. Any of you have a problem with that, bring it. Now's the time.'

Troy beckoned with one hand while he made a fist with the other, and I was sure I wasn't the only one who noticed. Only the suicidal would've taken him up on that offer. He was beyond incensed now. He looked like he was ready, willing and able to hand someone their head. The crowd melted away like sugar crystals in hot coffee until it was just him and me left in the corridor. We were both going to catch hell for being late to our next lesson, but so be it. Troy bent to pick up my books. I crouched down to help.

'Thanks,' I said, my cheeks flaming.

'Don't thank me.' Troy frowned. 'You're family. That lot are just arseholes.'

He handed me my books, straightened up and walked off without another word. I stood in the hall, unable to move until my tears had stopped flowing.

Smiling at the memory, I lay down and pulled the duvet up to my neck. For the first time, I was part of a family. How much did I love that F-word!

Sunday breakfast was noisy. Music played in the background as Tobey and Callie dished up all the stuff they'd made – scrambled eggs, sausages, bacon, toast, beans, plantain, fishcakes, with a huge pot of coffee and a large carton of orange juice. We were all seated at the kitchen table, laughing and chatting. Thirstily, I drank it all in. Nana Meggie sat at the head of the table. Dad sat directly opposite me with Callie next to him and Troy at my side. Dad smiled while offering to fill my empty glass with orange juice. I couldn't help my grin as I nodded. Here I was having breakfast with my dad and my new mum and I felt like a balloon filled to bursting point. Except what filled me up was . . . joy – unfamiliar and almost overwhelming. I had a proper family, including a dad who so obviously loved me. We spoke every day even when he was away from home. I finally belonged somewhere and there was nothing I wouldn't do to hold on to what I now had. I turned to look at Troy. It only took him a few seconds before he realized what I was doing.

'What?' he said from beside me.

'What what?' I asked.

'You're staring at me,' Troy frowned.

'I'm just thinking how much I like having you as my brother.'

'OK . . . I'm not sure where that came from, but OK,' said Troy. 'I'd say the same about you, but I'd be lying. Having one sister all up in my business was bad enough. Now I've got two nagging me and trying to tell me what to do.'

'Because we care about you,' I pointed out, trying to keep my voice even. But inside? Inside I was shrieking with delight. Wasn't life funny? If anyone had told me six months ago that Troy and I would've become this close, that we'd actually have a brother-sister relationship, I would have gagged. Now I didn't want to imagine my life any other way. There existed a few seconds every morning when I woke up drowning in dread that all this was just a sweet dream and my mum was waiting for me outside my old bedroom door. Those few seconds were always excruciating. But that's all they were – a few seconds. There'd come a time when they didn't exist at all.

'Troy, d'you believe one person can make a real difference?'

'Of course. I know that's a fact.'

'D'you think you and I could do that?'

'Yes, if we really wanted to. Why?' Troy frowned.

'I've been thinking about it a lot since we left the basement,' I admitted.

'Thinking about what?'

'The reason behind everything we went through.'

'And you reckon you've figured it out?' Troy asked.

Dad, Callie and Nana Meggie had stopped chatting to listen. My cheeks began to burn, but I wasn't going to let that stop me. 'Yeah, I do.'

'Go on then. I'm listening.'

Nana Meggie smiled and gave my forearm an encouraging squeeze.

'Maybe we're here to make a positive difference, to leave this world a better place than when we entered it. Sometimes all it takes is a kind word or gesture or even a smile at the right time.'

Troy studied me. We were both remembering the basement. 'Is that what you really believe?'

I nodded vigorously. 'Otherwise, what's the point? We live, we die, but nothing ever moves forward. Nothing ever changes.'

'What was the purpose of my mum dying?' Troy asked with a hint of bitterness.

Callie reached across the table, taking his hand in hers.

'None,' I replied. 'But you're asking the wrong question. There *was* a point and purpose to her life. All the things she went through, all the lives she touched – yours, Callie's, my dad's, Callum McGregor's, Nana Meggie's – all the people she met, whether or not they agreed with her life choices. She had an effect on them all, don't you think?'

Troy considered this, then nodded. 'Yeah. For definite.' His smile was tinged with sadness, but it was still a smile.

'Troy, your mum was someone special – everyone who knew her says so. I envy you that so much. Don't you think that you get to choose your outlook? Your attitude? From what I've learned of your mum, she chose happiness and caring about others. She always looked outwards. Even when she was at her lowest, she chose to care about others before herself. That's why she'll always be remembered, and my mum won't – eventually not even by me.'

'Libby—'

'No, it's all right, Dad,' I interrupted. 'That chapter of my life is finished. I'm writing a new one now and I'm OK with that.'

'Enough serious talk,' said Nana Meggie.

We all smiled in agreement. Dad leaned towards Callie to give her yet another kiss, neither of them the least bit embarrassed. There was absolutely no shame in their game. Callie drew away slightly, her gaze strangely intent.

She sighed. 'Libby's right. Mum did choose to look outwards. It's not a bad way to live.'

'I'm enjoying what I'm looking at right now,' Dad said with a wink.

'Oh, for God's sake,' Troy muttered from beside me. For once I agreed. Mushy much?

Raising her hands, Callie traced the contours of Dad's face with her fingertips – along his eyebrows, over his closed eyelids, down his nose, across his slightly smiling mouth. Callie explored his face like she was memorizing every line, every curve. It was as though she was seeing his face for the very first time. I don't know about Troy, but I felt like a pervy voyeur. Dad opened his eyes, his smile widening.

'I love you, Callie Rose,' he said.

'I know.'

'Can you two please give it a rest?' Troy begged. 'You're putting me off my breakfast.'

'Leave them alone, Troy,' Nana Meggie rebuked with a grin. 'Wait till you fall in love!'

'Never gonna happen,' said Troy.

Dad and Callie both leaned forward on a simultaneous impulse, now kissing like they had only just discovered how to do it.

'My eyes! My eyes!' Troy complained

Nana Meggie winked at me. Inside I felt a rush of something I'd so rarely felt before. It was like bubbles rising in a shaken fizzy drink. From the first time I met her, Nana Meggie had made me feel like one of the family, like I belonged right where I was. She was so down to earth and funny and just plain lovely. No wonder Troy doted on her. She had lost so much but she still viewed the world with hope in her heart.

I looked round the table. For Shaka's sake, Dad and Callie were still locking lips!

Troy inevitably gagged.

My senses on blissful overload, I drank in the sights and sounds around me like they were nectar. Now that I knew what it was to belong to a real family, there was no way I'd ever give it up.

I smiled at Troy. He shook his head, but smiled back before tucking into another fishcake. It would take a while, but we'd be OK – both of us. All of us.

Why? Because we were friends. We were family. We had each other. And, more important than all that, we had love.

And, when you got right down to it, nothing else mattered.

THE END

Acknowledgements

Well, here it is, the final book in the Noughts & Crosses series. It has been a bittersweet experience writing this one, knowing that there will be no others. It has taken over twenty-one years to produce six novels and three novellas all set within this world, a task that has been at times frustrating and painful, but also cathartic and rewarding. When I sat down to write the first book in the series, I had no idea how my story would be received. I had a certain story arc in mind – the lives of Callum, Sephy and their daughter Callie Rose – which I naïvely thought would fit into one book. When the first book was published and Callie had only just been born, after due consideration, I reckoned the story I had in mind would take three books to tell. It was definitely going to be a trilogy. But when *Checkmate* was written, Tobey Durbridge insisted I tell his story too and so the trilogy turned into four books. Real world events inspired what I thought would be a fifth and final novel, only for five books to turn into six! With the novellas, that's a nine-book trilogy!

Writing novels is, by its nature, a solitary affair, but I didn't do this alone. So I'd like to take this opportunity to thank all those who helped me over the years to bring the story of the Hadleys, the McGregors and the Durbridges to light and life.

This includes but is not limited to Ruth Knowles, Wendy Shakespeare, Jane Tait, Francesca Dow, Annie Eaton, Sue Cook, Philippa Dickinson and all the editorial staff – past and present – who have given so generously of their time and expertise and who have accompanied me on this journey.

Huge thanks to my agent Hilary Delamere for always having my back.

And thank you to all the production staff, art designers, marketing, PR and sales staff who worked on the production and promotion of the Noughts & Crosses series, with a special shout out to Harriet Venn and Lauren Hyett.

Thank you to Fruzsina Czech and Jan Bielecki for this latest iteration of striking book jackets and to all the other book-jacket artists and designers who have worked on Noughts & Crosses over the years.

Shout out to my husband Neil and our daughter Liz for the many, many cups of peppermint tea, the hours of plot discussions, and for putting up with my absences, moods, self-doubts, dithering and impatience. Thank you for leaving me to it when I needed to be alone with my work. Love you always and forever.

Much love to my mum and sister Wendy for always giving me your honest opinions. And for turning my books face out in every bookshop you visit.

And most of all thank you to all the readers who've come on this journey with me. You are the ones who have kept Callum and Sephy alive all these years. You are the ones who have inspired and encouraged me to continue. Each and every one of you is appreciated and cherished.

Much love to you all.
Malorie xx

About the Author

Malorie Blackman has written over seventy books for children and young adults, including the Noughts & Crosses series, *Boys Don't Cry*, *Thief!*, *Cloud Busting* and a science-fiction thriller, *Chasing the Stars*. Many of her books have also been adapted for stage and television, including a BAFTA-award-winning BBC production of *Pig-Heart Boy* and a Pilot Theatre stage adaptation by Sabrina Mahfouz of *Noughts & Crosses*. There is also a major two-series BBC production of *Noughts & Crosses*.

In 2005 Malorie was honoured with the Eleanor Farjeon Award in recognition of her distinguished contribution to the world of children's books. In 2008 she received an OBE for her services to children's literature, and between 2013 and 2015 she was the Children's Laureate. More recently, Malorie co-wrote the *Doctor Who* episode 'Rosa' on BBC One.

You can find Malorie online:

www.malorieblackman.co.uk

@malorieblackman